MRS CALIBAN AND OTHER STORIES

Rachel Ingalls was born in Boston, Massachusetts and has lived in London since 1965. She has had several novels and collections of short stories published by Faber and Faber, including *Theft*, *Three of a Kind* and *Four Stories*. Her work has always been greeted with exceptional critical acclaim:

'Ingalls' uncluttered, pared-down prose shifts smoothly from the ordinary to the horrifying, from the mundane to the Gothic. Her style has an evocative simplicity that suggests far more than at first appears.'
Observer

by the same author

THEFT
THE MAN WHO WAS LEFT BEHIND
BINSTEAD'S SAFARI
THE PEARLKILLERS
FOUR STORIES
(paperback collection)
BLACK DIAMOND

Mrs Caliban
and Other Stories

———

RACHEL INGALLS

faber and faber
LONDON · BOSTON

This collection first published in 1993
by Faber and Faber Limited
3 Queen Square London WC1N 3AU

Photoset by Parker Typesetting Service, Leicester
Printed in England by Cox & Wyman Ltd, Reading, Berkshire

'Mrs Caliban' was first published in 1982 by Faber and Faber; 'I See a Long
Journey', 'On Ice' and 'Blessed Art Thou' were first published in *Three of a
Kind*, Faber and Faber, 1985; 'Friends in the Country', 'An Artist's Life', 'In
the Act' and 'The End of Tragedy' were first published in *The End of Tragedy*,
Faber and Faber, 1987.

A CIP record for this book
is available from the British Library

ISBN 0–571–16414–5

2 4 6 8 10 9 7 5 3 1

Contents

Mrs Caliban

Fred forgot three things in a row before he reached the front door on his way to work. Then he remembered that he had wanted to take the paper with him. Dorothy didn't bother to say that she hadn't finished with it yet herself. She just went back and brought it to him. He dithered for a few more minutes, patting his pockets and wondering whether he ought to take an umbrella. She told him the answers to all his questions and slipped in several more of her own: would he need the umbrella if he had the car, did he really think it felt like rain? If his car had that funny noise, couldn't he take the bus instead, and had he found the other umbrella yet? It must be at the office somewhere; it was a nice telescoping one and she suggested that someone else had walked off with it.

They had run through a similar litany many times before. It was almost as though Fred needed the set words of this ritual to keep him steady at the beginning of days which held some test for him, something he was nervous about.

'I may be back late tonight,' he said. 'Something about – I don't know yet, but I'll call from the office. OK?'

'Sure. All right.'

She stood by the door while he went out and down the front walk. He didn't look back. And, of course, he hadn't kissed her goodbye for years. This was the same way that affair of his with the publicity girl had started: staying late at the office. Maybe. Or perhaps it was genuine, but she couldn't tell anything about him any longer.

She made the beds, vacuumed, washed and dressed, and was

at the kitchen sink doing the dishes when she looked over at the radio and thought about turning it on. It was a large, dark brown old-fashioned set, the kind that looked like a 1930s Gothic cathedral.

For the past three weeks she had been hearing things on the programmes that couldn't possibly be real. The first time was during a commercial for cake-mix and the woman's voice had said in a perfectly ordinary tone (just like the rest of the ad), 'Don't worry, Dorothy, you'll have another baby all right. All you need to do is relax and stop worrying about it. It's guaranteed.' And then the voice had gone straight back into the cake-mix that couldn't fail.

She hadn't thought she was going crazy, not straight away. She believed it was just her own thoughts forcing themselves into the low-pitched sounds and their insistent rhythm. But, the next day she had heard a story on a news programme about a chicken that could play the violin – 'the Heifetz of the hen-coops', the bird had been called – and later found out through friends that that item had not been heard by other people who had evidently been tuned in to the same spot on the dial.

Well, then. It was an old radio, after all. A very old radio. Surely it was possible that the sound waves were getting mixed up, or something like that. Some kind of static or interference which made no particular irritating noise but just cut in and blended with the general tone of the programme it collided with. Dorothy did not set the sound very high, since she only wanted the noise to be in the background, to keep her from brooding but not from thinking. She had now taken to turning the sound up higher when she heard something unusual, and she honestly couldn't see where the original programme was cut or faded and the other one joined in. The voices sounded precisely similar, only the tone was somehow altered and meant specially for her.

She still didn't think she was going crazy. However, she was now apprehensive about turning the machine on. Once the talk or music began, she became happy and relaxed. Only at the

moments when she realized that one of the special announcements was in progress would she feel a thrill of expectation and
mild alarm. What she did not want to hear was anything more
about having a baby, or about her and Fred, and their marriage.
So far, that first announcement had been the only personal one.
Still, there might be others. She had not told anyone about
hearing them, least of all Fred. Of course not.

She stood with one hand on the faucet and looked across to the
radio. This was the hour when she could tune in to the foreign
stations and hear classical music without static.

She crossed to the radio and switched it on, catching a sym-
phony in the middle of an expanding ladder of big chords. She
began to hum and turned on the water at the sink. The orchestra
soared and crashed its way to a finale which was going to be really
tremendous – there were even introductory drum-rolls – and then
it all seemed to dim off and a voice, even and distinct, said:

*Ladies and gentlemen, we interrupt this programme to make the
following announcement to all citizens in the area. Early this morning,
keepers at the Jefferson Institute for Oceanographic Research were
attacked by a creature captured six months ago by Professor William
Dexter on his South American expedition. The creature, known to the
popular press by its nickname 'Aquarius the Monsterman', appears from
intensive scientific analysis to be a giant lizard-like animal capable of
living both underwater and on dry land for extended periods. It is also
highly dangerous, as this morning's tragic events all too clearly bear
witness, for two of the Institute's employees, keeper John Kelsoe and Dr
Dennis Wachter, were found dead and horribly mutilated near the
animal's empty cage. When Aquarius was first installed in the Institute,
it was hoped that he might prove an attraction for students from all over
the country, but the scientists assigned to study his habits agreed that
there was a great danger that contact with large numbers of people might
expose him to contagious diseases which, although harmless to the human
race, might be fatal to his mysteriously different physiology. And, they
added, he was possessed of incredible strength and should be considered
extremely dangerous, especially if roused to one of his furies. This
warning has now proved tragically correct, as only the loved ones of these*

*two men can know – these two who died while loyally and bravely
carrying out the rigorous duties of searchers after knowledge. We under-
line this warning to everyone in the area: this animal is violent and should
on no account be approached. If you see him, phone the police immediately. Repeat: the monsterman is dangerous.*

For a moment, Dorothy had thought that the bulletin about
Aquarius was one of her special announcements. But it couldn't
be. Her special voices never lasted long and had a soft, close,
dreamlike quality, heard in the ear as though they emanated from
the organ itself instead of outside it. This tirade had been spoken
in the usual emotionally heightened drone of the salesman-
advertiser.

If Scotty had lived, she would now be telephoning to the school
to let them know that she'd be picking him up herself in the
afternoon on account of the warning. Even though he would be a
grown boy by now; how old? He had died under an ordinary
anaesthetic given before a simple appendectomy, and afterwards
all anyone could say in explanation was 'individual reaction',
'unsuspected allergy' and 'drug sensitivity'. And, a few months
later, she lost the baby. That was the point where things began to
change with Fred. The first blow had stunned them both, but the
second had turned them away from each other. Each subtly
blamed the other while feeling resentment, fury and guilt at the
idea that a similar unjust censure was radiating from the opposite
side. Then, it became easier to sweep everything under the carpet;
they were too exhausted to do anything else. And so it went on:
silences, separateness, the despair of thinking out conversations
that they knew would be hopeless. Long before he was unfaithful, he decided on the single beds. They were both having trouble
sleeping and would wake at different times. And, after all, it
wasn't as though for the moment they were making any use of
being in the same bed. She knew it was the end when he said that,
but she didn't have the strength to do anything about it. He
couldn't have had much strength either, or they would have been
divorced by now. Sweep everything under the rug for long
enough, and you have to move right out of the house.

At ten past eleven the telephone rang and Fred told her that the car – his famous, lovingly-cared-for old car – had broken down again, that he was going to be late, and that he might be bringing someone back for supper. Just a snack, because they had to talk something over.

'Find out if he's a vegetarian or some kind of health-food freak, will you?' Dorothy said. 'I'm not serving a steak to somebody who's going to scream his magic mantra at me.'

'No, he isn't. Just anything. Beer and sandwiches.'

'Oh no, I'll give you something hot. But if you don't say right now what you want me to get in, it's going to be spaghetti Bolognese and a salad. And ice cream.'

'That sounds fine. See you,' he said, and hung up, long before she had expected him to. It left her feeling slightly upset and annoyed, first with him and then with herself.

She changed into her leotard and did her exercises in the spare bedroom. She did the regular dance exercises, not the ones you were supposed to do just to keep yourself in shape. She started without music and then brought the radio in and turned it on.

She liked being in the guest room, which had never held a guest. It was really meant for storing trunks or furniture. The one they used for guests was much larger. She had painted this one herself and put up curtains. There was already a bed, and a bathroom next door. Originally they had thought it would be a playroom for the children, which would have been convenient, since it was on the ground floor. Two or three of Scotty's toys were still in the bottom drawer of one of the dressers. Fred wouldn't go near the place. He probably thought it was still full of garden furniture and the croquet set and other things that Dorothy had moved when Mr Mendoza built the outdoor shed for them.

She was in the middle of what she thought of as a Swan Lake gesture when the music slowed down and a low voice from the radio said very faintly so that she could only just make out the words: 'It's all right, Dorothy. It's going to be all right.'

She stood up straight and found that she was covered with sweat. The music ran on as it had been before. She went into the bathroom and stripped, stood under a short burst of water from the shower, changed her clothes, washed the sweat out of the leotard and hung it over the curtain rail.

She drove in to town and bought some mushrooms and meat and cheese. In the supermarket someone took a flying run at her shopping wagon and crashed into her. It was her friend Estelle, who said, 'OK, lady, your insurance company owes my insurance company four million bucks. And you're never going to drive in this supermarket again.'

'Road hog, road hog,' Dorothy chanted, laughing. She pushed back. A girl at the check-out counter looked over at them as though they might be damaging the merchandise.

Whenever she was with Estelle, Dorothy became louder, more childish and happier than when she was with anyone else. Estelle drew forth other people's subversive instincts. The very first time they had met, they had ended up in Estelle's kitchen, drinking a whole bottle of sherry at two in the afternoon and telling each other their sad lives, which sounded so hopeless that they finally burst out laughing and couldn't stop for minutes. They had been friends ever since.

'Come on back for a cup of coffee?' Estelle asked.

'I'd love to, but it's got to be quick. Fred's bringing somebody back from the office.'

'And you're scurrying around to fulfil all your wifely obligations. My God, I don't miss that.'

'You're kidding. They're getting spaghetti and they can like it.'

They were comparing recipes for meat sauce when a figure like a huge doll came trotting down one of the aisles. It was female, dressed in a sort of drum-majorette's outfit, and carried a tray with a band that went around the back of the neck. Long curls bushed out from under a species of military hat composed of metallic-painted cardboard, red glitterdust, and side rosettes. The tray was covered with tiny squares of cheese, from the centre of each one of which a toothpick rose straight into the air.

'Ladies, can we interest you in today's special bargain?' the girl began, and launched into a rapid sales-spiel which was almost entirely free of expressive inflection. Estelle, to stop her, reached out for one of the toothpicks and after a minute pause, during which Dorothy feared she might shove the piece of cheese into the girl's mouth, popped it into her own. But the voice went on and on, apparently unconnected with the girl's drooping gaze and scarcely moving lips. Her eyes actually looked as if she had temporarily absented herself from the Earth and were seeing from the distance of another planet. She turned her face towards one and then the other of them while her voice mentioned Swiss, American and French cheeses.

'What's it like?' Dorothy whispered.

'I'll tell you when I've finished chewing,' Estelle said, pretending to have a difficult time breaking down the cheese.

The girl thrust her tray at Dorothy.

'Um, no thank you.'

'There's no obligation to buy.'

'Well, I'm afraid I've just bought the cheese I needed.'

'This one's on special offer.' It was an accusation. She offered the tray more forcefully. Dorothy took a small step backwards. The girl advanced.

'Parmesan,' Dorothy said hurriedly. 'It's the only kind that goes with what I'm fixing for supper. What's that like, Estelle?'

'Try it yourself,' the salesgirl put in.

'Bland and boring, with an over-taste of plastic, like a processed cheese.'

'This is not a processed cheese,' the girl spoke up in her clearly enunciating machine-like voice. 'This cheese is made from the finest . . .'

'OK, OK.'

Dorothy asked, 'Have you sold much of it today? I mean, more than if they just put up a sign on the cheese counter?'

'You'll have to ask the publicity co-ordinator about that. I don't have the sales figures.'

The girl did an about-face and tripped down the aisle again. Estelle said, 'You wonder what they do to them. Not a giggle, not a reaction, not a sign of life. And so young too.'

'Processed, like the cheese. I had to do it once in the Christmas rush. You know, some people would stand there and listen to you repeat the same thing five times over.'

'What were you selling?'

'Oh, some special kind of kerchief that wasn't basically any different from any other kind. All the ways you could tie it. Silly, of course. There are only two ways you can tie a scarf to make it stay on if there's a wind blowing.'

'Look, there she is again.'

Dorothy turned and saw a cheese-selling majorette bearing down on them.

'No, it's another one just like her.'

'Good day, ladies. Can we interest you in our special cheese-of-the-day offer? This cheese, blended from the finest ingredients – '

'Oh, thanks very much, but – '

'Sorry, kid. Your friend just beat you to the draw,' Estelle told her. 'I hope you don't get commission or anything.'

'Thank you anyway,' Dorothy said. The girl swung around and went in search of other customers.

Estelle said, 'If she's got any brains, she'll duck behind a corner and eat up half her little pieces of cheese, so they'll think she's a wonderful salesgirl.'

'In a place like this, they're probably X-rayed for the tooth-picks before they're allowed to go home. Have you ever seen so many tilted mirrors and hidden cameras?'

'Gives me the creeps. Really. It's a Presbyterian's dream come true – you know. God sees it all, He's watching you no matter where you are and what you're doing.'

'I bet He's really out in the kitchen getting a beer out of the icebox.'

'Will you look, can you believe it? There's another one.'

A third salesgirl came skipping towards them. This time they tried to dodge her and for the first time noticed some sign of life in the girl, as the excitement of the hunt propelled her forward after them, chin up, eyes flashing hopefully. They were nearly at the cash registers when she caught up with them. Dorothy explained before Estelle could say something smart.

On their way to the parking lot, Dorothy said, 'After all, I'm sure somebody's been drumming it into them that this is a challenge, and forcing that stuff on people is some kind of shining goal.'

'Soldiers for processed cheesedom – ugh. Coming back for coffee?'

'All right, but a quick one.'

Estelle drove in front. She went slowly because Dorothy was a careful driver who tended to become jumpy if rushed. Estelle, in contrast, was a natural speeder with superb reactions but a habit of looking for risks, especially if she thought she could teach another driver a lesson. It was only a matter of luck that she hadn't yet been in a serious accident or, at the very least, sued.

When they were sitting in Estelle's kitchen, Dorothy suddenly thought that she'd rather have tea, but was over-ruled by Estelle, who was proud of her coffee. Not only did she grind up the beans in a special machine, she bought the beans when they were still white, and roasted them herself.

They stopped talking while the machine was on. Estelle held her hand tight on the lid, which had a tiny nick at the side and if left alone would twist around and fly off. The sound was like a buzz saw, but didn't last long. Estelle poured the coffee into a paper filter and began to drip boiling water over it.

'Listen, Dorothy, let me tell you. You know Jeanie Cranston? Every once in a while they still have me over to meet some unattached creep. That's just an excuse. It's really to pump me about what I'm doing for the studio; glamorous snippets, names to drop with other people – you know. But I like to see Josh just to bat around old times.'

'Sure, I know. Josh was nice.'

' "Don't you dare come help in the kitchen," she says. "You stay there and keep what's-his-name, this creep, company." Rodge. But she'd left a plate and I forget what I wanted to ask her, but I picked up this plate and started off for the kitchen. She'd just switched on her coffee grinder – we could hear it from the table; I went through the swing door, and there was the coffee grinder screaming away empty, and there was Jeanie, spooning instant coffee into eight cups. Jesus. I mean, who's she kidding? I guess it's part of the sickness. All she ever talks about is how poor she is. They've got a yacht now. Not a big one, but, Christ, a yacht is a yacht. They charter it out when they're not using it. And the complaints about how hard it is to juggle all your taxes legally, their little place in the country, the apartment they're thinking of buying – they can rent that out, too; I should be so poor. Well. Actually, what really bothered me was Joshua.'

'Fat and defeated?'

'A-1 physical shape and thinks he should be running the country. Pontificating. Right on the edge of becoming a bore. He should have come out of the closet years ago like everybody else, and then he wouldn't have to do all that compensating.'

'It wouldn't have been an easy thing to take on, somebody like Jeanie. She works so hard, she really does. That's part of the trouble. She can't let up. And he's a bit incompetent. He's probably just going around with somebody twenty years younger and it's given him that little extra hint of . . .' She thought back to that time with Fred, '. . . of fraudulent righteousness,' she said. 'Was he praising her cooking and giving her little satisfied score-marks for doing things or saying things?'

Estelle poured the coffee and sat down at the kitchen table.

'I hadn't thought about it specially, but he was. Not for her cooking, of course. That's still TV dinner with kitchen sherry and garlic poured all over it. You really think that's a sign?'

'Oh, no, not necessarily. It just shows a general attitude. I only noticed it with Fred because he wasn't that way before. Or after. But some men are like that all the time, aren't they?'

'Josh wasn't that way before.'

'Or it could be caused by something else. He might just be unhappy. Or she might be seeing somebody else.'

'Oh, not her. Him, maybe.'

'I know you don't think she ever knew, but maybe she did

know all along. Married couples are linked to each other by such deep loyalties. You can't tell. Even when they hate each other, sometimes. I wouldn't count on either of them knowing or not knowing anything. Or how much they care.'

'It could have been something else, of course. They're up to their necks in business deals at the moment. Maybe they're doing something fishy. I just had a feeling. Maybe he's done something on his own, something just over the line, so he thinks he's been a hot-shot wheeler-dealer and that's what makes him go around looking so conceited. And furtive.'

'I doubt it, Estelle. His only importance comes through her. He wouldn't be able to pull a fast one by himself.'

'Well, at this point, I wouldn't put it past him. He's changed a lot since you knew them.'

'He must have been pontificating like crazy.'

'OK, so you think I'm exaggerating. But he was. And I was also pretty annoyed about being saddled with some dolt like that Rodge. So dim, he couldn't even size up two people like Jeanie and Josh. I don't know where they dig them up.'

'Maybe they phone one of those dating clubs.'

Estelle laughed. She told Dorothy a story she had heard at the studio about an extra who had been found dead in her apartment and the only clue anyone could think of was that she used to meet a lot of people through one of those places like Dateline. Dorothy said that she wouldn't be surprised; she had read a story in the papers the other day about a dating service that had turned out to be a big blackmail racket. Yes, Estelle said, and then there were the new religions and the horoscope experts and heaven knew what-all these days; it was getting so everything was as crooked as the real estate business. Dorothy said sure, but then it always was, wasn't it, and when she started to get really upset about everything, she just went out into her garden and planted something or pulled up weeds. Otherwise there was no end to it.

They talked about Estelle's two men, whom Dorothy referred to as friends or boyfriends, and Estelle gloatingly as lovers. They were named Charlie and Stan and they both wanted to marry

Estelle. So far, neither one knew that the other was a real lover, only perhaps a threat. But Estelle had had enough of marriage. Her work at the studios was very well paid and full of variety and interest. She had met both Charlie and Stan through her job. They were younger than she was, nor were they the only men to be interested.

Dorothy thought Estelle was looking happy and full of vitality. The glow of health, she thought. Like a lighted candle. And what was the opposite? She remembered what Estelle had looked like before and during the divorce. It had coincided with the time of Fred's unfaithfulness. There had been many afternoons when they had sat in Estelle's kitchen and just said, 'The bastards,' over and over again. Dorothy had been afraid Estelle might become an alcoholic. 'Don't have another drink,' she would say. 'Talk about it instead.'

She accepted a second cup of coffee, first trying to persuade Estelle to add some water to it. Estelle was outraged. She declared that it would kill the taste.

'Then don't fill it up. Honestly, Estelle.'

'Honestly yourself.'

'I don't know why it doesn't have any effect on you. I love it, but two cups make me feel dizzy. And like my scalp might suddenly rise up and fly away. Then there's something over here – here, is that where the liver is?'

'Dorothy, that's where the imagination is.'

They talked about Estelle's children, Sandra and Joey; and about Dorothy's plants and vegetables. Her real pride was the collection of miniature fruit trees, although she had also recently succeeded in growing apple cucumbers under glass, a feat which had delighted her at the time, and about which she was still rather pleased. They did not talk about divorce.

For a long while after her own divorce, Estelle had strongly urged Dorothy to follow suit. She had been particularly persistent, Dorothy thought, because she wanted the companionship of a similar destiny, as newly married women want all their friends to be married, too. Or women newly become mothers,

Dorothy remembered, who urge motherhood on others.

Estelle still once in a while threw out a hint about divorce, but she had really given up on Dorothy. She gave up on the day when Dorothy, worn out, had asked her to stop and explained, 'I think we're too unhappy to get a divorce.'

During those days there were times when Dorothy would lean her head against the wall and seem to herself to be no longer living because no longer a part of any world in which love was possible. And she had asked herself: was religion really the only thing that kept people together, wrongly believing bad things will happen after death? No, they all happen before. Especially divorce.

All at once she noticed the time and was so flustered that she almost forgot to take her package of meat out of Estelle's icebox when she left. They promised to meet on the fourteenth for the fashion show.

*

She was sweating when she got back. It was later than she had thought and she started mixing the sauce before anything else. She turned on the radio automatically between moves from stove to icebox to sink, and then sprinted to the bedroom to change her clothes and put some make-up on. As she ran back into the kitchen, snatching up the apron and tying it in back, a voice from the radio was saying: *Police again advise residents in the area to be on the lookout for this highly dangerous animal.*

Dorothy shook out and refolded her kitchen scarf to go over her head and keep her hair from picking up the garlic and onion smells. The radio played Chopin. She heard the front door closing, and Fred's voice.

From then on, things went quickly and she had to turn off the music to guard against any outside distraction. She kept her thoughts running – first this, then that, and at the same time such-and-such, and don't forget the pinch of thyme – and her hands moving. It was like some sort of test or race. Perhaps, like her, laboratory rats took a pride in solving the puzzles scientists set them. The pleasures of obsession. Still, how else was it possible to do anything in a short space of time? The trouble was, that you couldn't becalm your mind completely because if you weren't careful, you'd forget to turn off the stove.

She was into the living-room to greet Art Gruber, and out again with such speed that she might have been one of the mechanical weather-people in a child's snow-globe or a figure on a medieval clock, who zooms across a lower balcony as the face shows the hands on the hour. Back in the kitchen again, she had all the salad ingredients out, chopping up carrots and celery with her favourite sharp vegetable knife, had put some potato chips and nuts in bowls and just slid some cheese on crackers under the grill. Then she raced for the bathroom in the spare room.

She came back into the kitchen fast, to make sure that she caught the toasting cheese in time. And she was halfway across the checked linoleum floor of her nice safe kitchen, when the screen door opened and a gigantic six-foot-seven-inch frog-like creature shouldered its way into the house and stood stock-still in front of her, crouching slightly, and staring straight at her face.

She stopped before she knew she had stopped, and looked, without realizing that she was taking anything in. She was as surprised and shocked as if she had heard an explosion and seen her own shattered legs go flying across the floor. There was a space between him and the place where she was standing; it was like a gap in time. She saw how slowly everything was happening.

She felt that he was frowning at her, but he hadn't moved yet. Her mouth was slightly open – she could feel that – and waves of horripilation fled across her skin. A flash of heat or ice sped up her backbone and neck and over her scalp so that her hair really did seem to lift up. And her stomach hurt.

Then, swimming among all the startlingly released fragrances of her shock and terror, she caught the slight scent of burning, which warned her about the toast. That was the reason why she had been rushing in the first place. And without thinking, she darted forward, grabbed a potholder, turned the gas off, dumped the little pieces of toast on to the plate that had been set out for them, and slid the grill tray back into the stove.

The creature made a growling noise and she came to her senses. She took a step backwards. The growling increased. She took another step and bumped into the table. At the far end of the table lay the celery, carrots and tomatoes, the head of lettuce and her favourite sharp knife, which would cut through anything just like a razor.

She reached out her hand slowly; slowly she reached farther forward. She kept her eyes fixed on his. His eyes were huge and dark, seeming much larger than the eyes of a human being, and extremely deep. His head was quite like the head of a frog, but rounder, and the mouth was smaller and more centred in the face, like a human mouth. Only the nose was very flat, almost not there, and the forehead bulged up in two creases. The hands and feet were webbed, but not very far up, in fact only just noticeably, and as for the rest of the body, he was exactly like a man – a well-built large man – except that he was a dark spotted green-brown in colour and had no hair anywhere. And his ears were unusually small, set low down and rounded.

She stretched way out across the table, took her eyes off his for an instant and picked up the long stalk of celery next to the knife. The growling stopped. She took a step forward slowly, and held out the celery in front of her.

He too stepped forward and put his hand out. His fingers closed around the celery. She let go of her end. She stayed standing where she was and watched as he ate the stalk with all the leaves. Then she turned and picked up another one and handed it forward. This time he held on to her hand and touched it all over with both of his before he took the celery from her. The touch of his hands was warm and dry, but somehow more muscular than that of a human hand. Dorothy found it pleasant. He opened his mouth, and the lips, as though with some difficulty, shaped words.

'Thank you,' he said.

Dorothy managed to answer, 'You're welcome,' and registered

the fact that he had a bit of a foreign accent.

'I need help,' he said.

She thought: you need help, my God, oh my God, you need help? You need help and so do I.

'Help me,' he said. 'They will kill me. I have suffered so much already.'

She looked deeply into his eyes and thought: of course he has suffered, not being like other people, and now the police after him, and who knows what horrible experiments they did on him?

'All right,' she told him. 'But wait here first, just a minute.'

She picked up the tray of toasted cheese, nuts and potato chips, and hurried into the living-room. Art gave her a perfunctory smile, but Fred didn't even look up, just muttered, 'Thanks, Dotty,' and went on shuffling some papers they were looking at.

She ran back through the swing door and found the frogman eating up all her salad.

'Are you hungry?' she asked. 'What else do you like to eat?'

'Any vegetables,' he said. He pronounced all the syllables of 'vegetable', but she had met one or two ordinary Americans who said the word that way.

'Fruit?'

'Some fruit. Not too . . .' He waved his large hand and ended, 'that sharp taste, not that.'

'Not too acid? What about tomatoes?' She had the icebox door open and was rummaging around, putting objects in a bowl. Then she suddenly thought of the spaghetti and quickly threw some into a pot to give him before the rest of them had their dinner. While it cooked, he ate everything else, though she managed to rescue some of the salad ingredients.

She gave him spaghetti in a bowl. As she was about to spread butter on it, he growled. She got some margarine out of the icebox and used that instead. He took her wrist and leaned forward, moving his face up close to the margarine and sniffing it. Then he let go. She dropped a square of margarine into the spaghetti and swished it around until it melted. Then she sprinkled some herbs and salt on the top. He looked into the bowl, breathed in again, and seemed to be smiling. Then he picked up the bowl, held it above his face, and tipped it downwards, sucking up and chewing the spaghetti as it slipped down out of the bowl. It was a skilful performance, Dorothy thought, and rather a sensible way to eat spaghetti, but it made a lot of noise.

'I like that,' he said when he had finished.

'Was it enough?'

He nodded.

'Look,' she said, gesturing around her and towards the swing door into the living-room, 'I've got to hide you. You understand?'

'Yes, please.'

'Come with me.' She handed him the bowl of vegetables he hadn't finished yet, and hurried away to the door, the hall, and into the spare room.

'You'll have to stay here. It's all right as long as you're quiet. I'll look in late tonight if I can, but probably not till early tomorrow. We'll have to plan something. There's a bed ... um ... and bathroom?'

He seemed to know that she was wondering if he knew what they were for and how to use them.

'Yes, just like the Institute,' he said.

She showed him where all the lights were, put out some towels and sheets, and hesitated for a moment as she realized that there wasn't time to make up the bed. This too he seemed to sense, and waved it away with his hand. Then he caught both her hands in his and held them tenderly to his face. She was moved. She patted him cautiously on the back and said it was all right, and she'd see him in the morning.

*

In the morning, she really thought she might have dreamt everything. She made breakfast for Fred and herself, looked at the paper, took out the section with the crossword puzzle, and handed Fred the rest of the paper on the doorstep. She watched him drive off in a taxi, then she went from the kitchen into the little hallway and through to the guest room.

The frogman was still there, sitting on the corner of the bed, looking towards her. The sheets were made up on the bed. She took a step in. He stood up, huge.

'Are you all right?' she asked uncertainly.

'Yes.'

'You slept?' He nodded. 'Are you hungry? I'll fix you some breakfast.' She led the way back to the kitchen. Halfway there, she stopped in surprise. The frame on the hall window-ledge, where she had been growing the prize apple cucumbers, was empty.

From behind her, he said, 'Was it all right to eat the food? It was so long since I had food. Were you saving it?'

'No, that's all right,' she said. After all, it was food, and that was what food was for. 'I just hadn't expected to see it empty.'

'I ate one. That was so good. I kept eating.'

'I'm glad you liked them.'

'Very good. Excellent. I have never had this vegetable before. Are there more?'

'No, that's why I was growing them myself. But I can get you something like them. I'll buy in cucumbers when I go out shopping.'

She cooked him some more spaghetti and tried a small amount of rice with soy sauce, which he liked very much. Once again, he ate the spaghetti by holding the plate up and letting all the contents fall slowly into his open mouth.

'My name is Dorothy,' she said.

'My name is Larry.'

'On the radio they said your name was Aquarius.'

'That was what the professor named me when they caught me. But I couldn't pronounce it. Now I can, but now I'm used to being called Larry.'

'What are you called in your own language?' Dorothy asked.

'It's too different. We don't give names.'

'Isn't that confusing?'

'Everyone knows. We recognize each other.'

'Do you talk?'

'That's different, too.'

Dorothy waited. He looked placidly back at her.

'How?' she asked.

'More like music, but not like your music. Not jumping.'

She rose from the table and switched on the radio. The foreign broadcast came on. They were playing a record of Mozart.

He said, 'Is that music?'

'Yes.'

'I've never heard this kind of music. They didn't have that at the Institute.'

She started to turn it off, but he said, 'Please, let me hear,' and she left it.

'If you'll excuse me, I'll do the dishes now. Unless you'd like some more to eat.'

'No, thank you.'

She began to clear up the kitchen, while he watched her actions with great attention like a child whose eyes follow its mother wherever she goes. Because he was so different, she was not bothered by him seeing her still in her bathrobe, with her hair straggling.

He asked, 'Is the morning a time of festivity?'

'Just the opposite,' she answered, pulling the plug out of the sink.

'Is the dress you are wearing a garment of celebration?'

'It's just my bathrobe over my nightgown. What I was wearing last night was more for a party, but not formal. It was – well, which do you like better?'

'This.'

'You think it's fancier?'

'More special.'

'And my hair this way?'

'Better this way.'

'Is it because the dress and the hair are long now, and last night the dress was shorter and the hair was up?'

'I understand now,' he said. 'I like these things unrestricted. It isn't a matter of the rules of clothing. It's a question of freedom.'

'To me, it's a habit. Everybody agrees that certain clothes are worn for certain activities. Once the habit is accepted, it means something. And then, to break it means something too.'

'For me, clothes aren't necessary. I don't see a meaning.'

'For protection from the weather, for warmth and to keep the skin from too much sun, or from being cut and scratched.'

'My skin is strong,' he said. He lifted her hand from where she had been wiping the tabletop and placed the hand on his arm. He rubbed it from high up near his shoulder down to his wrist. She was shocked and pleased. Long after her hand was away from him, it seemed to remember the feel of his arm: warm, smooth and muscled.

'Yes,' she said. 'If you'll excuse me now, I generally clean up in the mornings, and then afterwards we can sit down and decide what we're going to do about you.'

'I can clean, too?'

'Well,' she laughed, 'come keep me company, that's all.'

'You could show me what to do. You see, I'm not used to this. It's so different. Before, I was only being studied. There was nothing. Now there's everything. I could do things. Couldn't I? You wouldn't prevent me?'

'Of course not. The only thing you'd better not do is go outdoors in the daytime. It would probably be all right at night.'

She rinsed the cloth, hung it up by the sink, and went through the doorway and hall, into the guest room. He followed her closing the door and shutting out the sound of the Mozart. She turned to ask him if he still wanted the radio on, and saw by the light – bright although blocked by the curtains – that when he had asked if she would prevent him from doing what he wanted to do, he might have meant something quite specific. That was another reason, which she had been too prim to mention, for wearing clothes.

He stepped forward, took off her bathrobe, letting it fall on top of the bed, and started to take off her nightgown from top to bottom, but quickly realized that it must be made to work the other way. He picked up the skirt from around her knees and lifted it over her head. He put his hand on her shoulder and pushed her gently down on the bed. He sat beside her. He said, looking at her, 'I've never seen. Men, but not someone like you.'

'A woman,' she whispered, her throat beginning to close up.

He asked, 'Are you frightened?'

'Of course.'

'I'm not. I feel good. But it's very strange.'

A lot more than strange, she thought. And then: no, it's just the same. They rolled backwards together on the bed.

'Wait. Not like that,' she said.

'Show me.'

'I'm a bit embarrassed.'

'What does that mean?'

She didn't really know. What the hell could it mean in such an encounter?

Later in the day, when they were lying side by side, she asked, 'Are you young, or are you old, or are you in between?'

'I'm between young and in-between. And you?'

'So am I, but I'm afraid I'm nearer to in-between now than to young. In the middle.'

'Is this time worse for you than it was before?'

'Not now. Now it's better.'

They made love on the living-room floor and on the dining-room sofa and sitting in the kitchen chairs, and upstairs in the bathtub. And they talked. Most of their talk consisted of asking and answering questions. She asked him, 'Where do you come from? Does everyone make love so many times in one day?'

'Is it too much?'

'No. It's just the right amount for me. It's perfect. People here are all different about it: some people like a lot, some only like a little, some change according to who they're with or what age they are or whether they're in a good mood, or even if the weather changes.'

He told her about the two men, Kelsoe and Wachter, who had mistreated him. They had taught him human speech, using an electronic gadget which gave him a shock every time he got something wrong. The teaching scheme was run by a Dr Forest, who was severe but emotionally detached. When he went away, Kelsoe and Wachter used the electric prod and other devices – the chair with the straps and the fitted eye-glasses – to tease and torture. They had also, he later told her, taken advantage of their positions of power in order to force his participation in various forms of sexual abuse, some of which she hadn't known of before. That first hesitant approach down in the guest room must have been because of what they had done to him at the Institute. She tried to explain. He said it didn't matter – he could tell that this was different. She felt incapable of making him understand how such a thing could have happened, and why the same thing done from different motives could be either good or bad, and what those ideas meant. She would have liked to say: it's the lack of love. But that too was hard to talk about. In highschool she had been asked to write essays like that: Love, Beauty, Time. Time had been the most interesting. She had written fifteen pages on that before the bell rang. But, of course, you could see Time. It was easier to write about something you could see, or of which you could see the effects.

He took showers often, several throughout the day. He liked watching television, and most of all he liked music. As for his diet, she was soon to find it no more out of the ordinary than that of the average man on a health-food kick.

That first day, she brought in her tape measure before going out to do her afternoon shopping. She measured his feet and wrote down the numbers on a piece of paper.

'I know your skin is strong, but you'll have to get some exercise, and if you go walking around here late at night, there's always a chance of picking up a nail or some broken glass. And the sidewalks can be hard.'

'It's true. Last night when I came into the kitchen, my feet were hurting very much.'

'I'll try to find you some sandals.'

'Thank you,' he said. He was always scrupulously polite. Now that she knew of the brutal methods that had been used to ram home the Institute's policy on polite manners, she found these little touches of good breeding in his speech as poignant as if they had been scars on his body.

When she left the house, she told him about the phone and the doorbell, gave him a key to his room, and warned him to keep the volume down if he wanted to listen to the radio or watch television.

She drove off to do her shopping like a young girl setting out on her first job. Not even the sarcastic attitude of the man in the shoeshop could entirely spoil the outing.

'What's this for, lady, the abominable snowman? Are you kidding?'

'For my brother-in-law,' she answered calmly. 'He has to get his shoes hand-made. And now his luggage was stolen, he's in a fix. He told us how it used to be when he was in school – how people in the shoeshops would laugh at him and make jokes. I never believed it before. I couldn't imagine people would laugh at a natural physical condition.'

'All right, all right, you're breaking my heart.'

Heart? She could picture the man with an electric prod in his hand. He called down the stairs to the storeroom. A voice answered from below, and a few moments later a boy with long greyish hair handed up a shoebox.

'Just as long as the measurements are right.'

'This is the right size.' She thought he would leave it at that, but he couldn't resist. 'Any bigger than that,' he added, 'and he'll have the wear the boxes.'

Even without the extra money for the sandals, she spent more than she had intended to. She bought extra vegetables, noodles, more rice, an extravagant pack of wild rice, and avocados, which she saw just as she was ready to head for the cash registers.

Her happiness returned, like a glow, as though she had swallowed something warm which was continuing to radiate waves of the warmth. It was a secret thing of her very own, yet she also wanted to talk about it to someone. This was the way she had felt the last time she had been pregnant. Could she say something to

Estelle? If Estelle didn't understand, if she ever dropped a hint to anyone, the police would be at the door with pistols and truncheons, or the doctors with injections of drugs, which might be even worse. They would say it was for the good of society, perhaps even for Larry's own good. And there was the evidence of the two killings to back up any such claims. On the way to the shoeshop she had turned on the radio and heard the news bulletin, which told how one of the men, the one named Kelsoe, had had his head literally torn from his body, while the other one had been 'ripped in two and gutted'.

It was better not to tell anyone, though she would have to plan out what they would do if he were seen by accident.

She was thinking of outsiders. Fred wouldn't notice anything because he never came near those rooms. In fact, he seldom came into the kitchen. He even preferred to have breakfast at the dining-room table. Years ago, they had been in the kitchen all the time, and Scotty too. That was a long while back now.

She left the highway, drove straight on, turned off into the street that ran by the plant nurseries, passed the fancy villas with their big gardens, and went around the corner. There, up in the sky, she noticed for the first time a gigantic mounded cloud, as large and elaborately moulded as a baroque opera house and lit from below and at the sides by pink and creamy hues. It sailed beyond her, improbable and romantic, following in the blue sky the course she was taking down below. It seemed to her that it must be a good omen.

*

At supper Fred was quiet, as usual. He had papers to see to, he said. And she, also as usual, retired to the kitchen.

She prepared a massive salad for Larry, took it through into the hall, and gave the prearranged knock on the door.

She sat with him for a few minutes while he ate, but soon decided that it would be better if she stayed in the kitchen. The phone might ring, or Fred might call through to her about something and, not hearing an answer, come on in and find them both.

'I'll be back later, when it's dark, and we'll take a walk.' She looked at his feet in the sandals. 'Are they comfortable?'

'All right. They're like clothes.' He turned from the television set, the old black-and-white one, which he was watching with the sound turned off. He picked a slice of avocado out of the salad, lowered it into his mouth and moved his lips. He said, 'This is the best vegetable I have had so far. It's what I like most.'

'Good, I'm glad.'

'May I have it for breakfast, please?'

'Yes, of course.'

She washed dishes and wondered how much the extra food was going to put on their weekly expenses. It probably wouldn't make any difference to Fred – prices were going up so fast anyway. At least they were in a part of the world where avocados were not exorbitantly expensive. Lucky he didn't like lobster or shrimps.

The phone rang. As she picked up the receiver, she remembered that she had meant to phone her sister-in-law about their vacation.

'Dorothy?' It was Estelle.

Oh, hi Stelle. I was going to call you. I haven't gotten around to anything today.'

Estelle reminded her about the fashion show and asked if she and Fred would like to come to a party on the following Saturday. Dorothy pushed the swing door, went through the dining-room, and put her head around the corner. Fred was sitting at the desk, his cheek propped against his fist, his weight on his left elbow. It didn't look as though he could be working very hard. She asked him about Saturday. He answered, 'No' automatically, without even turning his head.

'You sure? It might be fun.'

'Not for me. You go if you like.'

'Well, I might. I'd rather go with you.' He said nothing and didn't move. She went back to the kitchen.

'Estelle? Fred says no.'

'Why not?'

'Oh, I don't know why not. He isn't doing anything but just sitting. But he says no.'

'You come.'

'I might. Let me wait a few days. I'll tell you when I see you for the fashion show.'

'OK. See you then.'

It was true, Dorothy thought: he wasn't really working. She put the receiver back, got Larry's salad bowl from him, and told him to be ready. They would take the car. Fred never minded where she went any more, or when. At first, after Scotty and the baby when she had begun the compulsive restless walks, he had been worried about her. He had fussed. She was unprotected, he said. Anything could happen, even in the suburbs, even in a nice one like theirs. People weren't like eggs in boxes – they didn't have to stay in their own neighbourhood, they could move around. Yes, she had said, and now she wanted to do some moving around herself. She ought to get a dog at least, he had told her, for protection. All right, she had said, all right. She had bought a dog; a little, upright, friendly dog called a Jack Russell terrier. She named him Bingo and took him home. Fred exploded. 'Call that a dog?' he had shouted. 'It's smaller than a loaf of bread.' 'He's very quick,' she had explained, 'and his attention never leaves you. He's – ' 'Oh, Jesus Christ, Dot. You would go get some useless toy like that. Fat lot of good that would be if you turn the corner and bump into a gang of roughs who'd beat you up and rape you.' 'With my luck,' she had screamed, 'they'd tie me to the railings and rape the dog instead.' He had hit her, in order, he had explained later, to calm her down, and she had begun to sob and asked why he had wanted the twin beds and why they never slept together any more, even just to be together. He had said it made him feel guilty, because he just couldn't, because nothing was right any longer, but it would blow over if only they would let things alone. It might take time, but they'd get back to normal eventually, and in the meantime, if she just wouldn't put any pressure on him. Sure, she had said, it would work out.

She had taken Bingo on walks. They had walked everywhere.

She had never seen such a lively little animal. It was fun to be with him, he was so delighted by being alive. He retained his playfulness even after leaving the puppy stage. He was just becoming a full-grown dog when one day she looked up from planting some bulbs in the garden and didn't see him. He didn't come back because he had been hit by a car. Fred had found her crying in the living-room when he came home. Everything near her died, she had said. Everything; it was a wonder the grass on the front lawn didn't turn around and sink back into the earth. She cried for days, weeks. And Fred began to explain less and even to talk less. No matter how much you loved someone, there was a limit to the amount of crying you could stand hearing.

From that time onwards, he hadn't tried to stop her going out of the house alone at night, or even asked where she was going or when she would be coming back.

She put her head around the corner again and told him she thought she'd mail some letters and take the car for a drive. He just said, 'OK.' He was sitting in the same position he had been in before.

She went in to Larry, took him by the hand, led him through the hall and the kitchen, and through the door they hardly ever used, the one that connected directly to the inside of the garage. She opened the car door and stowed him in the back. He was too large to have fitted comfortably with his head down on the front seat. She put her straw bag on the seat beside her.

The evening was clear and a light breeze moved here and there. It wasn't quite dark yet. She drove down the straight, neat streets in the soft, lingering twilight. All the houses looked lovely in this light, with some lamps on but not many curtains drawn. There had been a time when she could not bear seeing lighted houses in the evening hour, because they had made her think how many of those houses represented a family, and how many of them contained children.

'I wish you could sit up and look, but it's still too light. Somebody might see you from one of the windows. It won't be long now. I'll tell you when.'

'I can smell the gardens,' he said.

She too could smell the flowers, giving out their fragrance as the light went, and the grass, which reminded her of her own childhood in school during the month of May and the early days of June, when all the windows were open and the men were out cutting the grass on the playing fields.

'I love it,' she said. 'But a friend of mine from school used to get hay fever. She couldn't get near any grass or trees or plants without coughing and sneezing – every year. I suppose by now she must be taking pills or getting injections for it.'

'For me, it's like food.'

'Me too, especially flowers.' She wondered if he would like perfume. Fred hated it. He couldn't even stand any scented soap other than Palmolive.

She drove until they reached a stretch containing relatively few houses. The air was darker now, the leaves of the trees almost black by the sides of the road and hanging down from above.

'I think it's all right now, Larry. But be ready to duck down if I tell you.' She saw his face coming up in the driving mirror. He looked ahead, and to either side. After a while, he said, 'If I had a hat, do you think I would be noticed at night?'

'It would need more than a hat. I think with make-up and sunglasses you might just get away with it. If you drove fast.'

'Could you teach me to make the car go?'

'Oh, yes. That part would be easy.'

She headed for the beach. On the highways he stayed crouched down in the seat again, until they emerged into a quiet, slightly run-down neighbourhood full of old clapboard houses and tattered palm trees. Here the buildings were closer to the sidewalks and there were few flowers. In many of the front yards there was just a square of sandy ground instead of grass. Faintly from the background, like the swish of traffic on a main road, Dorothy heard the sea. From the back seat Larry gave forth a soft moan of pleasure or pain. He had heard it, too.

'I brought some towels. We could go swimming, if you like.'

'Yes, please.'

She turned off, along a sandy road. No one was around. She branched off again on to a narrow, bumpy path and stopped the car. The sea was loud and near.

He climbed over the back seat and sat next to her. He put his arm around her. She leaned her head on his shoulder. They sat still, listening.

She thought: all during my teens, when I kept wishing so hard for this – to be out in a car on the beach with a boy – and it never happened. But now it's happened.

He said, 'You hear?'

'Yes, I've always loved the sound of the sea. I think everybody does.'

'For me, it's the sound of where I live. That's hard to explain. It's always there, like your heartbeats. Always, for our whole lives, we have music. We have wonderful music. The sea speaks to us. And it's our home that speaks. Can you understand?'

'You must be lonely.'

'More than anything. More than hunger. Even hunger sometimes goes away, but this doesn't.'

She stroked his face with her hand. She tried to imagine what his world could be like. Perhaps it was like a child floating in its mother's womb and hearing her voice all around him.

She asked, 'What was it like?'

'So many things are different. Colour is different. Everything that you see tells you something. At the Institute, they told me there are some people who are colour-blind. When you show them, they don't believe it at first. They can't believe they suffer from this thing, because they have never known any other way. That's how difficult it would be to explain the difference in the way my world looks.'

'And the sound.'

'And the way it feels. When you move, the place you live in moves too.'

'Your eyes are specially developed for seeing underwater, aren't they? I mean, I'm not sure that I'd see what you see, even if I could go down there in a diving suit.'

'Yes, they were very interested in my eyes.'

'When you escaped, did the light hurt your eyes?'

'Yes.'

'Then the idea about sunglasses was a good one after all. I'll have to get you a pair, just in case.'

'I took a hat to begin with. It cut off some of the light.'

An ordinary pair of dark glasses wouldn't work, of course. His head was much too big. She'd have to take off the earpieces and widen the central frame somehow, and then put everything back together. And would the two lenses be far enough apart, anyway? There was also the problem of where to rest the nosebridge, since the space between his eyes was flat and his eyes swelled outwards; it would hurt to have the glass lenses bumping right up against his eyes.

'If you swam out into the sea now, could you get back to your home?'

'No,' he said sadly. 'They showed me on a map where it was that they captured me, and it's far away.'

'Could you show me on a map?'

'Yes. It's called the Gulf of Mexico.'

'I see what you mean. You'd have to swim all the way down the coast and get through the Panama Canal.'

'You know it's wonderful to see another world. It's entirely unlike anything that has ever come to your thoughts. And everything in it fits. You couldn't have dreamed it up yourself, but somehow it all seems to work, and each tiny part is related. Everything except me. If I had known I was only going to stay a short while, this would have been the most exciting thing I could imagine – a marvel in my life. But to know that it's for ever, that I'll always be here where I'm not able to belong, and that I'll never be able to get back home, never . . .'

He bowed his head. She embraced him.

'I don't know how I could bear to give you up now,' she told him. 'Now that you've come, everything's all right.' She talked about her marriage and about her children. 'But I understand. If I could manage to get you to the coastline on the nearest point to your home, could you swim from there?'

'Yes,' he said, raising his head.

'Then we can get you back. We'd have to work it so that you swim down the shore while I drive the car across the Mexican border, and then once I was over, I'd pick you up.'

They talked about the idea. The actual plan seemed simple enough. It was only the timing that might be difficult. Fred's vacation was coming up and there was also the question of his sister, Suzanne, whom he didn't much care for himself, but had always pushed on to Dorothy whenever Suzanne had felt the need to see him again. Suzanne was supposed to be visiting them sometime during the next two months.

There had been a few years when they had taken separate vacations, or when he had gone on his and she stayed at home. Sometimes she went to see her parents, who were old now and occasionally irritating to be with; first one of them more than the other, then the order reversed, often nowadays both equally peevish. Could she just take the car and say she was off for a break?

Larry removed his sandals and stepped out of the car. She followed, bringing the keys and the basket holding the towels.

At first they swam together. She was amazed at the difference in his mood. It was like being in the water with a beachball, but also a powerful animal or machine. The way he looked had not convinced her of his difference, but this did: the way he moved in the water, which was his element. He came rocketing up from the deep water and picked her up in his arms, driving across the waves with her. They seemed to be going as fast as a motorboat.

After a while, Dorothy said that she wanted to get out and get dry. Larry asked her to wait while he explored.

'Be careful,' she told him. 'The coast around here has a narrow shelf under the water and then it drops right down deep. There's no gradual sloping.'

She walked up the beach, dried herself off and put on her clothes. Then she sat down and waited, and tried to think out a plan. For so many years there had been nothing. She had taken jobs to keep herself busy, but that was all they were. She had no interests, no marriage to speak of, no children. Now, at last, she had something.

What they ought to do was tell the world. There was only one word for what those terrible people at the Institute had done to him: torture. They could take it to the newspapers. Especially the part about those two men forcing him to join them in their sex games. *I Killed Defending My Manhood*. You could take it to the Supreme Court. You could plead disorient-ation. It would cause a sensation. It would be a test case. They'd have to define the nature of the term *human being*. If Larry wasn't human, he couldn't commit murder, only kill like an animal and not be punished for it. On the other hand, if he were to be considered human, he had killed in a self-protective anger brought on by pain caused through torture by two sad-ists, who had taken away his human rights and wrongfully imprisoned him in the first place just because he was of a dif-ferent race. She could imagine the headlines: *These cruel and barbaric practices are not consistent with the teachings of our religion, says frogman. Is this the spirit of American Democracy, we ask?*

But he had told her that all he wanted to do was go back home. He wouldn't want to go to the newspapers. He was right, of course. It wasn't just the crowds and the bright lights and the fast-talking media men and the people who ran for-ward to spit at you. It was also possible – as the announcer had said on the radio – that a simple disease, even a cold, could kill a creature who had never developed a resistance to it. Even worse, perhaps he might already be carrying a germ which would not declare itself to be fatal until after he returned home, so innocently bringing with him the means of destroying his whole people. Better not think about that.

She ought to try to get him away soon, but she couldn't leave just like that. She'd have to have some excuse. She'd have to wait till the vacation.

He was gone a long time, it seemed. The warm wind had blown the skies clear so that she could see the stars. She wondered what he was doing, how far out he had swum, how deep. She thought of him swimming among the wonderful colours, in surroundings which would be different from his home, but familiar – as though a man from Connecticut had been kidnapped to a foreign planet and then set down again in Norway or Japan; it wouldn't be home, yet it would be recognizable.

But down there it would be dark now, and not the lovely lighted aquarium she imagined it to be during the daylight hours, eddying with schools of tiny, delicate animals floating and dancing slowly to their own serene currents and creating the look of a living painting. That was wrong, in any case. The ocean was different from an aquarium, which was an artificial environment. The ocean was a world. And a world is not art. Dorothy thought about the living things that moved in that world: large, ruthless and hungry. Like us up here.

She was just beginning to convince herself that down at the bottom of the sea he was hurt or dying, when she saw his shape moving up out of the water. In that light and at a distance, he looked exactly like the statues of gods, except that his head was slightly larger and rounder than it should be. And he walked with a rounded, swimming motion from hip to knee, holding his large powerful shoulders and arms easily.

She handed him a towel and he dried himself off.

'Shall I start teaching you how to drive, or would you rather leave it for tomorrow? It's a little late now. I didn't know you'd be so long.'

'Tomorrow,' he said.

'Are you cold?'

'No.'

He climbed into the back seat again. Dorothy started the car. 'This would be a good place to learn,' she said. 'There doesn't seem to be anyone around and that path over there runs for a long way, just a straight stretch.'

She told him about her plan. Could he wait that long? He said yes. She asked him what it had been like in the water. He answered that it was not like his home; he had felt almost as foreign there as above the surface.

'But down there, I know how to defend myself. Down there no one attacks you for thinking. They attack if you hurt them or invade their home, or if they want to eat you.'

'And if you're different. They do that here, too.'

'But in the sea, it's not just because you're different.'

'I thought everywhere everyone had to fit in, or other people began to feel worried and threatened. And then if there are more of them than of you, they jump on you.'

'That happens here?'

'More or less. It's true that what happens first is they let you know how they think and then you've got to make them believe you think that. Something else happened. You're sad.'

'Yes. Something is going on.'

'The Institute does a lot of underwater research around here. You mean that?'

'No. I don't know. It didn't feel right.'

'It isn't where you come from.'

'Do you suppose I've changed? Maybe they did something to me in the experiments, which I didn't know about at the time, to make it so I can never go back and be at peace. They injected me a lot, you know, so I fell asleep.'

Dorothy stopped the car at the side of the road, leaned over into the back seat and put her arms around his neck. She kissed him and patted him on the back.

'Don't worry. It'll work out somehow.' She was about to turn back to the wheel, when he said, 'Could we walk?'

They were not very far from the house, but in a richer neighbourhood, in a street of large houses standing in gardens, with trees lining the sidewalks. She got out, telling him to be careful closing the door.

They walked hand in hand. At one point Larry stood still, breathing deeply. He said that there was a flower he could smell. He took off his sandals and prowled across a large grass lawn to a flowerbed. Dorothy followed, hoping that the owners of the houses would keep any dogs inside rather than outside. When she caught up with him, he had his face in some white flowers which she identified as the blossoms of a tobacco plant. They walked through the gardens for twenty minutes or so before deciding to go home.

*

During the next few days, they settled down into a routine. At night they drove out. They swam, never for such a long time as that first night, and then she gave him driving lessons. He was very quick to learn. She bought him a hat which she enlarged, sunglasses, which she altered specially for him, and some make-up, with which they experimented until he said that he thought he'd like different colours. Dorothy had made him up in a beige colour. But when he got hold of the box himself, he made himself up in three different shades: yellow-brown, red-brown and a dark brown.

'The hands,' Dorothy said.

'Gloves. Which one do you think is best?'

'The Indian colour looks the best, but it's too unusual. I think maybe the Chinese one.'

'I thought it was more Japanese. You don't like the black one?'

'It doesn't look natural. I don't know why.'

'They don't any of them look natural, but under those lights on the highway nobody looks natural.'

'Still people would notice a man with a green head. I guess I should get you a wig.'

'Good. I think I'll try a different colour every night.'

When Dorothy went out shopping, Larry generally listened to music or watched television. It was from a crime story serial on television that he got the idea of starting a car without any keys by pulling the leads out and sparking them off. The first Dorothy knew of it was when she went to his room to tell him she would be ready in ten minutes, and found that he had gone.

All the rest of that evening she waited up in the kitchen. He hadn't taken the car, but his hat was missing, and the glasses, sandals, suit, socks and gloves. She was so worried that when he finally came back she was ready to hit him out of relief and fury.

'Where have you been?' she hissed, bundling him through the hall and into his room. 'Walking around town as free as you please. I've told you, you've got to be careful.'

'I was driving.'

'The car was in all night. I checked.'

'I took a different car. Just in case I was caught and they traced me back to you. You might get into trouble, you know, for protecting a dangerous criminal. Knowledge after the event – that's it, isn't it?'

She made him sit down on the bed. He told her where he had gone and what he had seen. After he'd convinced her that no one had recognized him or followed him, he admitted that he had gotten out of the car and walked. He had walked through crowds, where many of the men were drunk and no one would want to pick a fight with someone of his size in any case. 'And I've figured out the make-up. The secret is to wear a colour that's different from most of the people who live in the area.'

'I still don't understand how you started the car.'

'I'll show you tomorrow. It was easy, but I was a little nervous at first. You know I don't like electricity.'

'Would you rather go out alone at night?' Dorothy asked. 'I mean, I'd worry, but you see so much of me during the day – would it help to make you feel you have some independence?'

Larry removed his gloves and took her hand in his. 'You understand,' he said.

'What I'd really like would be if we could be free to walk around anywhere, go out for a meal together in a restaurant, and so on.'

'I thought people were supposed to enjoy what they call "a secret vice",' he said, and made her laugh so hard that she nearly ripped the wig which she had started to put back in its box. She had sewn and cut his wig herself, making it from two she had bought, since a single one would not have been big enough.

'And am I your secret vice?' she asked.

'No, my secret vice is avocados.'

Dorothy laughed even harder. She had to bury her face in the bedclothes to hide the noise.

*

Two days after Larry began his independent nightly drives, Dorothy went to see Estelle in the afternoon.

'You look different,' Estelle said. 'You've gotten Suzanne off your back.'

Dorothy said no, Suzanne had given them four different sets of detailed instructions concerning her plans for the coming three months. Dorothy sat down. 'And I bet there'll be a new set in the mail soon. She used to call up, till I pretended the phone was out of order.'

She had great difficulty in controlling herself. Estelle would understand; but, she would also tell. She wouldn't be able to resist it. And would that be strange, when Dorothy herself was having so much trouble trying to keep herself from speaking? Better not even think about it. The thought was compelling. It was a like people who looked down from a height.

'Coffee?' Estelle asked, already pouring it out. Sandra and Joey wandered into the kitchen separately, stared glumly, had to be told to say hello, opened the icebox for food, ate standing up and shuffled out again. When they were beyond the door and out of earshot, Estelle muttered, 'They sometimes seem hardly human. I keep telling myself it's a phase. They're so crass and surly and just godawful. All they say is Yaah and Naah. At first I thought they were drugged.'

'Maybe they are.'

'No, no, that I'm sure of.'

'They've got hormones shooting through their systems a mile a minute – those are drugs. I see what you mean, though. When I was that age, I was all dimity and feminine and dreamy, reading poetry and so on.'

'Were you? I was out in a back seat with Jimmy McGraw from the other side of the tracks. Best nights of my life. After the divorce, I thought of tracking all those people down, and then I thought what's the use. The whole point about it was that it was then, not now.'

'That figures.'

'What I mean is . . . you're right, it doesn't make sense. You know what I mean.'

'It may be something to do with fitting in with the others, too.'

'Like those Irish children. It's – no, I threw it out. It was an article in a magazine: they did a sociological survey on children from several different families where the parents wanted at least one child to go into the church. And what they found was that these children were chosen quite early. You could see they were nice-looking and obedient and neat, whereas their sisters and brothers became plain and bad-tempered and sloppy-looking. What was interesting about the study was that after the children had been chosen and the time of danger had passed, the other children suddenly blossomed and stopped being plain and slovenly. I mean, they also seemed to change physically.'

'A subconscious defence. And the other ones were conforming to expectation. They'd stay that way, too.'

'But Jesus, Dorothy, I'm not trying to put my kids into the church.'

'Don't be silly. They're like any other teenagers. As a matter of fact, you're lucky they're not being brain-washed by one of those freak cults, told to break with their family and so forth. After that Jones business, anything is possible. And the teens are the dangerous age for religion. I felt that way myself.'

'You're kidding,' Estelle said. 'You? I thought you were my one reasonable friend.'

'Oh, you know. All those feelings of holiness and beauty and love. What else tries to explain them? Then you look around at most of the men and women you see, and you think that's certainly not enough, that's just routine. Let's say it was romance. Your instinct for romance is very powerful in your teens.'

'Romance, right. That's different. Romance and tragedy. Except, now I'm older, what I really go for is comedy. Even the international situation. My God, what a circus.'

'Which reminds me,' Dorothy said, 'how are Charlie and Stan? They know about each other yet?'

'Oh-ho. Sixty-four-thousand-dollar question. I think Charlie knows that there's someone, but doesn't know who it could be. He actually thought there was someone when there wasn't yet.'

'And Stan?'

'Him, he's so conceited it would never cross his mind.'

'Is he good-looking?'

'Didn't I show you the picture?'

'I didn't think it was so special.'

'He's better in the flesh, as they say.'

'But Charlie's better in bed?'

'You're not supposed to be able to guess these things so easily. Let's talk about you. Let's talk about your new lover.'

'Oh, come on. Me? What you could talk about that would help me, would be how I can get Suzanne off my neck.'

'Is she coming with her kids, or alone? Or with what's-his-name?'

'Bruce. Not this time. Just Suzanne all by herself. I almost prefer it when they all come. They're fighting with each other so hard, you don't even have to say much, just sit there and listen. And I get a kick out of seeing Fred start to get hysterical but trying to contain himself. He doesn't like them either, even Suzanne. Why he won't admit it, why he keeps shoving her on to me . . . to be fair, I thought Robin wasn't so bad last time. She's a funny-looking girl, though.'

'With the Brillo-pad head, like her mother?'

'Just the opposite. You know the Charles Addams cartoon of the thin wife with the long, stringy hair? Robin's like that, but instead of wearing a long dress that tapers down to where she disappears into the rug, she's usually wearing pants and cowboy boots. She says she wants to be a choreographer. She says she has an idea for a whole series of ballets based on the chemical combinations of molecules in action, or something like that. She drew me a picture. It looked great. Really. But she won't be coming. Just Suzanne.'

'The only way really to get rid of her is to leave the house yourself when she arrives. You know, pack everything, and the minute you see her marching up the path, you just march right out of the door with your suitcases.'

'I thought of that,' Dorothy said, and sighed.

'Fred could take her off your hands if he'd just make an effort.'

'Well I see what he means. He can't do much if he's working all day.'

'Working. That's what they all say.'

'Well, it's true.'

'It's not work like real work, like us.'

'Estelle, you're terrific. We're so exploited, we're spending our afternoons sitting around drinking coffee.'

'Another cup,' Estelle said. She managed, as usual, to over-ride Dorothy's protests.

They talked about the studio. Dorothy said that in a few months, she might ask Estelle to set up another job for her. Not now, but in five months' time or so. By that time, Larry would have gone back to his home again, and she would not dare to stay in the house, mooning around the back rooms, thinking about how everybody always left or died. Years before, when she thought she was just about to sink like a stone, it had been the jobs which had brought her back to life again. There had even been other people she had met through the work, who might also have helped, but she hadn't seen that at the time. And meanwhile, she and Fred had lost a lot of friends and stopped going out much.

As Dorothy started to leave, Estelle said, 'I'll pick you up for the show. The place will probably be packed and we'll have to fight for a parking space.'

They agreed on the time and Dorothy thanked Estelle again for the Saturday invitation, but said that since Fred wasn't coming, she'd ask for a raincheck too. She started off in the direction of home, then changed her mind and stopped to buy some avocados.

When she got home, Fred was there before her. He said, 'I may have to go out again. I've got a deal on.'

'With Art?'

'That's right,' he said, so quickly that she knew it wasn't true.

'Some time I want to talk about Suzanne and what we're going to do about the vacation.'

'OK, OK, only not now.'

'All right. Just remember that I don't want her here until after we get back.'

'All right, all right.'

'You aren't listening.'

'After we get back. Mr Mendoza left a note about the garden. Where were you? You're out driving in the car all the time. A hundred bucks a minute if the price of gas goes up any more.'

Dorothy picked up a crumpled paper from the desk. She looked at it, turned it over, and said, 'Could you make out what this means? All I can read is, "Dear Mess Jade". Usually his writing is so neat. He must have been in a hurry.'

'Well?'

'That's all. Unless this word is supposed to mean Saturday.'

'Where were you this afternoon?'

'What? Oh, at Estelle's,' Dorothy answered, still peering at the letter. 'Honestly, can't you help?' She handed the paper to him. He took it, but did not look at it. He looked at her instead.

'What?' she said.

'I called Estelle. She said you weren't there.'

'Of course I wasn't there. I'd just left.'

'It took you a long time to get home.'

'I went shopping. What is this? You can call Estelle and ask her when I arrived and when I left.'

'What did you get when you were shopping?'

'Avocados,' Dorothy said. She turned from him, strode into the kitchen, picked up the brown-paper bag and brought it to him.

'Oh, I believe you,' he said. She unrolled the top of the bag so that he could see what was inside. All at once the tight, ironic, play-acting expression went out of his face. He said, 'The whole bagful? You bought a whole bag of avocados? Jesus there must be twenty of them in there. What on earth for? We'll never get through them. They'll go bad.'

'No, they won't. I'll eat them.'

'Dorothy, that's crazy.'

Dorothy closed the top of the bag. Her voice rose. 'It isn't crazy,' she insisted. 'It's a special avocado diet. You lose several pounds all at once and just keep going.'

'They're fattening as hell.'

'Not if you don't put anything on them. And it's all a question of balance, anyway. Once you get settled in the diet, the trace elements start burning up all your fat, or something like that.'

'You could always buy gold-dust instead. In the first place, you don't need to go on a diet, and in the second place, if you did, you could go on one by just eating less than normal. A whole bag – honestly, Dot, it's crazy. It looks like the treasure of the Aztecs. A whole bag.'

'Never mind. You won't have to eat any if you don't want to.'

The phone rang. There was a tiny electric moment between them and then Fred grabbed for the phone.

'Yes,' he said, 'yes. No. About half an hour. OK.'

Dorothy wondered what would have happened if she had answered, instead. An even shorter conversation: wrong number.

'What time are you coming back?' she asked.

'Before midnight, I hope.'

'I'll want the car,' she said. 'Do you mind?'

'Couldn't you just – '

'No I need to be able to get out. Didn't the garage offer you anything?'

'It wasn't supposed to take this long.'

'Oh, Fred, it always takes this long. Everything on that museum piece has to be fixed by a fanatic. They have to scour the countryside for experts and then they have to make all the missing parts from scratch.'

He picked up the telephone receiver again and called a cab.

Dorothy held up Mr Mendoza's note in front of him.

'I don't know,' he said. 'One of the words is "tomatoes".'

'That's "tomorrow".'

'It's just about the only one I can understand.'

The taxi arrived, driven by someone who looked like an eleven-year-old girl with a beard. He had on a big leather jacket and walked up to the door very slowly, not like most of the taxicab hustlers in town. Fred answered the bell and went back down the path with the boy. He turned around to wave to Dorothy, who raised her hand in return. He hadn't done that for years.

She went back into the kitchen, where she forgot what she had intended to do next, and sat down in a chair by the kitchen table. He was asking her all those questions too, almost as if he suspected her. It might be because he himself felt guilty, or maybe she did unconsciously give out some signal that she was again a desired woman.

She made a large salad, which she tossed in the Hawaiian wooden bowl. All over the top she laid long slices of avocado. Her father's family had called them 'alligator pears', but she hadn't told Larry. She thought he might be hurt somehow. The ones she had bought were the smooth, thin-skinned type, though she had seen others that really did look like the hide of an alligator: dark green and knobbly outside, with thicker skins. Inside, the edible part was exactly the same.

She took another quick look at Mr Mendoza's note. It must mean tomatoes after all. She had forgotten that this was his day but he would be back the next week.

She carried salad and plates into Larry's room. He was listening to her foreign broadcast of classical music, but turned it off as she came in sideways with the tray.

Over the meal he said, 'I was watching TV before he came in.'

'Something nice?'

'An old movie called *Marie Antoinette*.'

'They must have put it on because of the fashion show. Some of the costumes from the film are going to be there. That's where I'm going with Estelle on Thursday.'

'That would be interesting.'

'I wish you could come too.'

'That would be even more interesting. As a matter of fact, I've also been looking at the news and current affairs, and you can't imagine what they've been saying about me. And in how many states I've been seen. The monster this, the monster that. Why should people make up such things? No one has seen me, and yet they say it and they even appear to believe it. Why?'

'That's hard to explain. Sometimes it's just to feel important. Sometimes they see something unclear and very quickly, and don't know what it is; a shadow behind a tree, or something, but they exaggerate.'

'No, they invent. I'm asking because I want to know whether this is a basic human characteristic.'

'I don't know about basic. It's pretty common, but I think it mostly depends on circumstances.'

'I know one thing. If they catch me now, they'll kill me. These people talking on the news are trying to frighten other people and trying to make them hate me. And they feel disgust. They keep talking about "alien intelligence" and "animal instincts".'

'They won't catch you. As long as you're careful.'

'They have to get close to do it. Last time, they shot me with a dart while one of them was talking to me. A little arrow filled with anaesthetic. But now if anyone tries to get close, I'll grab him and hold him in front of me. And afterwards I'll kill him, so he can't tell where I live.'

'Don't do that. Knock him out, and we'll gag him and keep him here until you can get home. Then we'll let him go.'

'It might be a good idea to have a hostage if we drive through Mexico.'

'More trouble than it's worth. We'd have to keep our eye on him all the way. I don't like the idea of hostages, anyway. It's so cowardly. It's so like what they did to you.'

'What we should really have as a hostage is a baby. Nobody would try to shoot us with darts if we held it up in front of us upside-down.'

Dorothy set down her fork and held her hands over her face.

She told him about her two children again, this time in more detail. She started to cry. He patted and hugged her, and crooned in her ear.

'I don't dislike them,' he said. 'I would like to see one. I've seen them on television. It would be interesting. Could you bring me one to look at?'

'Larry, darling,' she told him, 'they don't just hang around street corners or something. Babies belong to people. The only time they're ever left alone is if the mother is so weighed down by shopping bags that she has to park the baby nearby in its push-chair, but just for a few seconds. Those are the only cases of baby-stealing I've heard of.'

'So they are stolen? What for?'

'Lonely women. I used to think about it myself sometimes. For a few months. I'd see them outside the supermarkets and think: see how much they care for you – you'd be better off with me, I wouldn't leave you unprotected and ignored like that.'

'We could borrow one.'

'They cry. And we'd have to put it back.'

'We could just let it go and it would find its own way home.'

'Babies aren't like other small animals. They're helpless.'

'All of them? How peculiar.'

'They're very slow to develop, and almost everything they develop has to be taught. If you don't know how to teach it, or don't bother to, they never learn it.'

Dorothy cleared the table and brought in coffee.

'Where you come from, are the births one at a time, or a number all together?'

'Both. It depends. Sometimes one way, sometimes the other.'

'It's the same here. There can be two, three, four, five, but the most common is just one. The higher the number, the more unusual it is. But, I'm sure it used to be the other way around. A long time ago.'

'Do you think that you and I –'

'I was just wondering about that this afternoon. I'd be delighted if it happened.'

'Are you sure? It might put you in danger. And any child or half-child of mine would be called a monster, wouldn't it?'

'Born on American soil to an American mother – such a child could become President. It would be American. And I'm married so it would also be legitimate. After I sold the story to the dailies, it would be rich, too. It's surprising how little people mind what they're called, so long as they have enough money.'

'A mixing of the species is said to produce a sterile offspring, isn't it?'

'The only one I know about is mules. But I don't think it holds true with plants. I should look it up. With you and me, we're so alike I'm not sure if we should really be called separate species. We might be the same species at different branches on its evolutionary development.'

'At the Institute, they said I was a different species. Even Professor Dexter said it. So we might not mix.'

'That doesn't surprise me. They didn't like you and they treated you shamefully. They'd want an excuse. For centuries people like that kept saying women didn't have souls. And nearly everyone still believes it. Same thing.'

'The soul I know about. Professor Dexter was very interested in that. He said it was the reason why he chose to study science.'

'I knew a girl once,' Dorothy said, 'who was stolen by a monkey when she was a baby. Dull girl. That was her one big moment of drama, before she was old enough to appreciate it. Her mother was in the hospital in Africa with her, a newborn baby, and the window was open. Opposite the window was a big tree, and the tree was full of monkeys climbing up and down the branches. Suddenly one of the monkeys came in through the window, picked up the baby, and ran out again into the tree. It sat on a branch, rocking the baby and looking back at the women all screaming in their beds. Her mother was frantic, of course. I never learned how they managed to get her back.'

'They were frightened the monkey would take her away and bring her up like a monkey?'

'They were probably scared it would drop her. Young monkeys

automatically cling to their mother's fur. It might have slung the baby round its neck and jumped for a branch, thinking the baby would grab on tight. Anyway, they must have gotten her back somehow, because she was there to tell the story. She did tell me, too, only I'd forgotten till just now. She seemed to think it had been such an amazing event, but that presupposes a belief that she was so much better than a monkey. And who's to say? To herself, of course, but that isn't a test of anything, ever, except to your own self. It's like saying people don't have souls, when all you mean is you're not interested.'

They went swimming together and made love on the beach. Dorothy still felt like a teenager. At the time when her hope and youth and adventurousness had left her, she had believed herself cheated of those early years when nothing had happened to her, although it might have. Later still, she realized that if she had made an effort, she herself could have made things happen. But now it didn't matter. Here she was.

They dried themselves off, drove around for a while, and walked through some of their favourite gardens in bare feet. Dorothy was less nervous than the first time they had gone out, but still felt a sense of possible danger and an edginess, which she was beginning to enjoy. She skipped and danced after Larry, as with his long legs he went loping down the length of the flower-beds. She giggled with nerves.

They found a back garden where there was a goldfish pond. The house next door had a bamboo grove, in the middle of which garden chairs and couches were set out. Dorothy stretched out on the plump cushions of a sofa. Larry sat next to her at the foot. She looked up at the stars. It was a warm night.

'I don't know how they'd get all this in if it rained,' she said. 'Maybe they just grab the pillows and let the frames get wet.'

Larry asked her about the stars, which she didn't know much about. He had seen a television programme about them. They both looked up for a long time in silence. A breeze rustled in the bamboo.

He said, 'They are real, aren't they? Not just pictures?'

'Of course they're real.'

'How do you know? It's one of the things I find hard to understand; so many things are pictures. You watch pictures, but then you see the thing, and it's a picture, too.'

'Well, I can't prove they're real, but they're so far away that it would take millions of years to get to them.'

'Maybe not. Maybe it only looks like that. It could be just a reflection.'

'I don't know enough about it to explain it. You should talk to an astronomer. Doesn't the TV programme tell you?'

'Maybe they're lying.'

'Why?'

'They lie about lots of things. Remember the cornflakes.' The cornflakes, kept for Fred, who sometimes liked them for breakfast, had made Larry throw up. While Dorothy had cleaned up after him, he had taken a bit out of the box and said he preferred the box to the stuff inside it.

She laughed. They put their arms around each other. He asked, 'Do you do this with Fred?'

'Not for a long time now. Nearly two years. We used to. Then all the other business started. You know, what I told you about. And after a while, everything had changed.'

*

The next morning Larry was standing in the living-room, watching Dorothy vacuum the rug and taking an occasional turn with the nozzle, when the doorbell rang.

Dorothy switched off the machine and raised her head. Suddenly she remembered.

'Mr Mendoza. Quick, get back into your room and lock the door.'

Larry fled towards the kitchen in large, easy leaps. Dorothy waited a few seconds, then opened the door.

Mr Mendoza stood on the path, looking to the side, as though he couldn't make up his mind whether to ring again or go away. Dorothy smiled.

'Thank you for the note. I'm sorry I wasn't in. Shall we go through the list now?'

Mr Mendoza smiled back and dipped his head. He was a quiet, charming man, slow in all his movements and with a facial expression of relaxed steadiness. Dorothy had liked him from the beginning. He had come to work about a year after Bingo was run over, and it had been a help to be with someone and not to be expected either to make conversation or to respond to it. It was still like that. She knew a little about his family, but when they talked, it was usually about plants and flowers, and they still called each other by their last names, like people of her grandmother's generation. At some point, just as she had thought of suggesting that they drop the formality, she had realized that he took it as a sign of respect.

Mr Mendoza gestured towards the far corner of the garden, up against the fence. He touched the brim of his hat and said something about the dangers of insecticide. Dorothy nodded. One of the reasons why Mr Mendoza was going through a period of great popularity was that in addition to being honest, sober, hardworking and punctual, he avoided chemicals. And one of the reasons why he remained loyal to Dorothy when other people were clamouring for his expert care and probably offering him huge salaries, was that she listened to what he said, was interested in it, deferred to his judgement and asked his opinion about things she had read or heard. Nor did she forget what he told her. She was a good gardener herself now, because he had been her teacher.

They discussed vegetables and compost, Dorothy asked if he'd like to come in for a cup of coffee, but he regretted that he had to go see Mrs Henderson. She said that she understood the regret: she had once met Mrs Henderson. Mr Mendoza chuckled quietly. He raised his hand in a lazy wave as he went down the path.

She looked in on Larry, finished the vacuuming with him, and watched a television programme. He liked to have her with him to explain things. On some days when she came home from shopping, he would ask one question after another. The only programme he enjoyed as entertainment rather than information was one peopled by puppets. The puppet she liked best was the wild one with all the teeth; his favourite was the saxophone player.

One day she had come home to find him doing an imitation of something. 'What is it?' he asked her, but she couldn't understand what he was doing: punching, stalking, listening, fighting, twitching, acting all at once. He wouldn't tell her what it was supposed to be. It was the first question she had failed to explain since her collapse over the subject of industry and progress. She had started out with the introduction of agriculture, the coming of industry, the exploitation of women, the fact that it all started in the home where there was no choice, the idea that eventually robots and machines would release people to live a life of leisure and explore their own personalities; but, just before she reached that point, she forgot how to wind it up. A friend of Estelle had once mapped it out for her so that it all sounded so clear, but now she couldn't remember just how it went. Even what she could recall didn't seem to make so much sense any more. In fact, it was sort of a mess and impossible to explain. She had stopped, confused, and added, 'But what people really want is to be happy.'

She had a cup of coffee and made Larry an early lunch. As she was drying her hands on a paper towel, the phone rang. Estelle was at the other end with a breathless story of how Sandra had the car and could Dorothy bring hers instead.

'Yes, sure. See you soon,' Dorothy said, and hung up. She talked about Estelle, and said that Estelle was the one person she would like Larry to meet, but that she just couldn't take the chance.

'Better not,' he agreed, as he sliced an avocado into the salad bowl. 'We need some more of these.'

On the way to Estelle's house, she bought another large bag of avocados. The man in the grocery store said, 'Giving a party?' and she nodded. They weren't cheap either. In a little while, Larry's presence would begin to show on the food bills after all. Perhaps, if she and Larry hadn't become lovers straight away, she would have had an ally. Fred would have been the natural person to turn to for help. She might have been able to tell him about Larry. She thought about it, and decided that maybe even now it wasn't too late.

Estelle came to the door all dressed up. Dorothy said, 'Est-elle, are they going to be filming the audience?'

'It's for my ego, dear. Drive on. I'm sorry about the mix-up with the arrangements. We're going to have to go in your car all the way, I'm afraid. Sandra's getting impossible about how much she needs the car.'

'How about Stan and Charlie – think they might be there?'

'If it was sportscars, maybe. Not dresses.'

The day was beginning to warm up. It was going to be like a summer day. Estelle put on a pair of dark glasses against the glare. Dorothy hummed as she drove.

Out at the studios, the parking was crowded even though they were early, but inside the buildings there was room to move. Dorothy was looking at the other people, most of them women, who wandered in small groups from one large glass case to another. And so it was that her attention was not really fixed on any one object when suddenly something seemed to loom in front of her. Like an animal that was showier than the peacock, and raised up as if riding in state from the safety of its glass box, a dress displayed itself to her. It was tiered, arranged in lacy scallops, pleated folds, glittering swags, and appeared to be made of solid gold. Inside, presumably helping to hold it upright, stood a woman-shaped white china dummy. But the dummy was nothing; the dress was everything. There had been no face painted on the blank head, but a powdered wig had been placed on top.

Estelle said, 'No wonder they had a revolution, huh? Think of the cost of that thing. And this one's only a copy.'

'It must have kept a lot of people in work.'

'Come on. Wouldn't you rather be the one to wear it than the one to make it?'

'Oh, sure. I didn't mean that. Anyway, I read somewhere that these cost almost as much as the originals would have. They are amazing, aren't they? It changes your whole idea of what a dress should be for. It would have been like walking around in your own little silk house.'

'Nothing below the waist, that was the idea. Women were such pure creatures. From the waist down, they were just a flow of brocade. And they didn't wear underwear, either.'

'It must have been cold. Especially without central heating. They must have worn something in the winter.'

'I can't imagine living in a different time,' Estelle said. 'Not in the future, and certainly not in the past. Can you?'

'I'll tell you something even harder to imagine,' Dorothy said, thinking about Larry. 'Can you think what it would be like to live in a different world?'

'Like Bel-Air, you mean?'

'No, not this world. A different one.'

'In the future?'

'Any time. Like science fiction. Where the people look sort of like you, but not quite the same.'

Estelle laughed. 'Little green men?'

'Big green men,' Dorothy said. She caught sight of two more dresses in their glass cases: one white, like a wedding cake, the other black. She thought suddenly of the days when gentlemen and ladies assembled in such clothes to dance the minuet, and how Larry might look among such a company; large, dark-green and handsome, bowing to a woman in a layered dress and dancing with a strong, springy step.

'My God,' Estelle whispered, 'there's Charlie. And look what he's got with him. A sixteen-year-old red-head.'

'Where?'

Estelle pointed the pair out to Dorothy, and led her behind the black dress. Charlie and the girl were moving away, their backs towards the two women.

Dorothy said, 'I think they're heading for the exit.'

'The bastard.'

'How do you know? Maybe it's his daughter.'

'How many girls like that do you know who hold hands with their fathers in public and look goo-goo-eyed at them?'

'I think you're probably right.'

'I bet he's told her he's a producer. I wouldn't put it past him. I wouldn't put it past any of them.'

'But now you're free to do the same thing. Never mind. I'm sorry, Estelle. It isn't nice, is it?'

They moved on to a grey dress covered in sparkling jewels.

'Well, it's a bit of a kick in the teeth,' Estelle said. 'If only I'd played around like that when I was young.'

'And you'd have gotten impotent men in their fifties wanting to get back at their wives and doing it through you. You had all that time in highschool with the boys.'

'I bitterly resent all that wasted time. And what I resent most of all is that the ones I did get, never, never looked like the Greek statues.'

'The Greek-statue types may have been too busy going out with other boys to notice you.'

'In a way. They were usually just too busy playing football and getting drunk. They didn't bother much about any of us.'

'Look at this.' Dorothy stopped in front of an embroidered jacket. 'I thought this was going to be just the dresses.'

'No, all the costumes. I wonder if they're going to sell some of them off, like that sale last month.'

'Thinking of buying one?'

'Mmm.' Estelle moved to a case containing another white dress. This one looked as though it had been sprinkled with shimmering dots of some kind, little twinkling bits of jewels. The past months' sales of dresses out of the studio wardrobes had included evening gowns that had been designed in the thirties and forties and could still be worn nowadays, but these – even at a costume party, they would stand out.

'Estelle, you aren't serious?'

'It would be a hell of a thing to own, wouldn't it?'

'But where would you wear it? In the kitchen while you were opening the cat food?'

'Dotty, sometimes you are just so unromantic, I can't understand it. If we all only owned the things we needed! You don't
understand the nature of desire.'

'I do,' Dorothy said. 'I do now. But I wasn't talking about that. I
was talking about how you'd look sort of sitting somewhere
eating a sandwich in a dress like a box. In the first place, how
would you sit down?'

'Slowly,' Estelle said. 'Let's see what they're giving us to eat.'

They had just finished two rounds of sandwiches and a cup of
coffee, and were going back to get a few more sandwiches, when a
man in front of them who was trying to go in the opposite
direction, said, 'Hi, Estelle.'

'Oh, hi,' she answered. They passed each other. As Dorothy
reached the table, Estelle turned and looked backwards. She said,
'Let's go.'

'You don't want the sandwiches?'

'Oh, all right.' Estelle grabbed some of the sandwiches, put
them into a paper napkin, and moved down the table. 'That was
Stan,' she said.

'Oh. He looks nice.'

'And so did the woman he was with. Jesus, both of them in the
same afternoon. Isn't there anything else going on in town but
they've got to bring them here?'

When they were sitting in the car again, Dorothy turned the key
and said, 'But they still don't know about each other, do they?
And now you wouldn't have to feel guilty about that, if you ever
did. And you don't know what relationship they have with those
women.'

'Hah!'

'Anyway, they keep going out with you. And they wouldn't if
they didn't like you.'

'Maybe I'm just Tuesday or Friday, like handkerchiefs, or those
sets of underpants with the days of the week sewn on them.'

'Not really?'

'A girl I went to school with had a set.'

'How do you know?'

'She told me. As a matter of fact, she showed me. I was so impressed. She said the writing was in a different colour for each day. She'd been given them for her birthday.'

Dorothy was happy as she drove along the highway under the blue sky. She thought about Larry. She hummed again.

Estelle said, 'I feel pretty terrible.'

They had coffee at Estelle's house. Dorothy tried to comfort her, but Estelle was more interested in thinking up some plan of revenge.

'I suppose,' Dorothy said, without thinking, 'you could hire somebody out of central casting and pretend he was your latest.'

'That's an idea.'

'I was joking. And wouldn't that drive them away?'

'I don't think so. I've told you already, they want to get married. Hah! Get married to me, and go out with their fancy-pants girlfriends.'

Dorothy clicked her tongue and shook her head. She looked over the edge of her coffee cup and said that, on the other hand, Estelle had been two-timing them both from the beginning, hadn't she?

'Oh, that's different.'

'Oh, uh-huh. How's it different?'

'That's just like insurance, that's all. In case one of them quit on me. I wasn't the one who kept asking to get married. That's what makes it so horrible. They've got to have somebody to do all their domestic drudgery full-time, and substitutes when the fancy one is out with somebody better.'

'Maybe it would make you feel better to find a third one for a while.'

'Maybe it would make me feel better to have a drink. Want one?'

'No, thanks.'

'I still think your idea about phoning up central casting is a pretty good one.'

'And if you had one of those dresses, you could probably

hide him under it. Weren't they something? It would be like
wearing another personality, a dress like that.'

'I don't think I could take any more personality. Maybe I
should forget about the dress. Anyway, it would only look right
if you had the right hairdo. You'd need one of those powdered
wigs.'

'They were pretty. They didn't look as stiff as the ones in the
pictures. But I can't stand the idea of something pressing on my
head like that. I don't know how actresses and dancers can wear
wigs all the time.'

'Have a drink, Dorothy. Don't let me drink alone.'

'So there'll be two drunks instead of one.'

'Who said anything about drunk? Just a couple of – '

Dorothy stood up. 'Estelle,' she said, 'you don't need it. You
don't need it.'

Estelle sighed. She put the bottle back in the cupboard.
Dorothy picked up her car keys and purse. They walked to the
door.

'In five years, you'll laugh about it,' Dorothy said.

'Sure. But now now.'

'Just ask yourself if you want to go on seeing them or not. And
then act according to that. OK?'

'Thanks, Dotty.'

'Any time. Thanks for the show. You still want to do that
matinée?'

'I don't know. I may have to take Sandra in for an interview. I
just don't know the day yet. Call me up.'

Dorothy changed direction on the way to the main road. She
drove back to town and then went on to the museum gardens,
parked the car and walked around, looking at the trees and
flowers. There were two old women being pushed in wheel-
chairs by uniformed nurses. Me, one day, she thought. And
between now and then, nothing that can be done to avoid it,
except an earlier death. But the gardens were pleasant. The grass
in particular was luxuriantly green and well kept. She wondered
if Larry would like to come here. There was no fence, which

meant that they could get in easily, but also that other people could, too. They might run into a gang of beer-drinking rowdies with switchblades. It was probably better to stick to the beach and maybe that garden with the bamboo grove.

She drove home, to find Fred there early. He said, 'I've got to go out to a meeting.' She nodded. On the stairs he turned. 'What have you got in that bag?' he asked.

'Oh, more avocados, of course,' she said, as if joking, and went through the door into the kitchen. A few minutes later, she heard him running down the stairs. He called out a goodbye and the front door slammed. Suddenly she went back to the living-room and looked out the window. She saw him getting into a car parked at the kerb. No one else was in the car; he must have hired it.

She had an early, leisurely dinner with Larry. They ate in the kitchen and listened to some music turned down low. The programme finished while they were still eating, so Dorothy switched it off and afterwards they talked. She told him about the fashion show and about Estelle meeting Charlie and Stan.

He said, 'Is this important?'

'I don't know. It's just something that happened today, so it's part of my life to talk about.'

'Your friend Estelle thought it was very important?'

'Yes, she certainly did. She was upset. Not as much as she sounded, but quite a lot.'

'Why?' he asked, launching Dorothy into an explanation of the mating habits of human beings. She wasn't even sure that she was right about half her pronouncements. Every time Larry asked a question, she felt less sure. They seemed to be sensible questions, and she wondered why she had never thought of them herself. Then, at one point, he said, 'For us, it's easier. Only the female is wanting and jealous and so on during mating, and the one she wants is the strong one. If you aren't strong, she stops wanting you and there is no mating.'

'But would you go to a different female if you couldn't get the one you wanted?'

'Of course.'

'And would you be as happy with her as you would have been with the first one?'

'I don't know. Is it important?'

Dorothy was nonplussed. He also said, 'When we want something, it's true. We don't want something we can't have and not like the thing we get instead. The thing you want is the thing you have, isn't it?'

'No,' Dorothy said. 'Not at all. You should know that. What about prison? You were in one. And there are all kinds of prisons in the world. Everywhere.'

Larry stood up, pushed his chair in to the table, and did the strange, contorted movements again, asking 'What is it?'

'I don't know. I told you. Is it a joke?'

'I don't know either, that's why I'm asking you. I saw it on TV.'

'Oh, no wonder. Well, I'll watch with you. Maybe I can catch it on another day.' She tried to establish a time for the programme. Larry said he thought that it was an ad of some kind.

As soon as it grew dark, Dorothy drove them out in the car. They went to the beach again and swam, and talked. She told Larry about the museum park and he said that it sounded nice. Dorothy was sorry that she had brought the subject up.

'It's much too dangerous. If anything happened, we'd be too far away from the car.'

'Let's go see.'

'All right, I'll drive past. But that's all. We won't get out of the car.'

She skirted the museum grounds on one side and across the front. Shadows of palm trees hung patterned across the way in front of them as Dorothy turned the wheel again. Larry leaned out of the window, breathing in.

'At the back, the lawns slope down to the sea. It's a beautiful view. I don't know how they manage to keep the grass and gardens so healthy with the salt air.'

'Can we stop here, please?'

She pulled over to the side of the road, stopped the car, and turned off the gas. From a distance they could hear the ocean, almost seeming to echo or imitate the sound of cars on the roads nearby. There was a tiny chirping of insects and the warm air was made fresh by night gardens.

'We can walk a little,' Larry stated. He opened his door. Dorothy reached back, throwing her arm around his neck and shoulders.

'Please,' she said. 'I'm nervous about it.' He detached her arm, got out, shut the door softly, and came around to her side. 'You come, too,' he said.

She followed him on to the immense stage of grass where the silhouetted trees and bushes leaned out into the air like the shapes of boats in a harbour. Dorothy wanted to dodge from one protecting shadow to the next, but Larry pulled her along into the open, holding her by the hand and carrying his sandals in his other hand.

He made her prowl around the grounds for a full twenty minutes, asking her questions about the museum when she thought it would be safer not to talk. Once, a car turned the corner on the road and Dorothy pulled her hand away and jumped behind a large bush as the headlights arched across the road. Larry came after her, unhurried, and saying, 'The lights would not shine this way. Or is it some other reason you're hiding?'

'No, that was the reason.'

He made her take one more turn around the palm avenue, and then agreed to go back to the car. He said, 'I like this place.'

'I do too, very much. But I think we've been damn lucky not to run into anybody. Please, let's not take any more chances like this, Larry.'

'You are too frightened. It spoils your enjoyment.'

'Larry, you're all I've got,' she said.

He spread his arms out away from the car to take in the earth and sky all around, and said, 'You've got all this. And you live here. It's your home.'

Dorothy sat behind the wheel and drove silently for about five minutes. Then she tried to explain to Larry that 'all this' wasn't much good without another person to share it with. He said that people were everywhere, there were millions of them; she said that people were all different and you had to find the ones who fitted with you. He said that he didn't understand that. How were people different? 'Inside,' she said, which mystified him, and when she asked if all the people where he came from were exactly the same, he said yes. When she told him that she couldn't believe it, he made a further statement: 'We all do the same things, so we are the same. Here you all do different things.'

Dorothy thought about that. She said, 'If that were really true, men would be more different from other men than women from other women, because men's jobs are very varied, while most women do the same things. But it isn't true – women differ from each other just as much as men do. Do you think we could trust some other people to help us?'

'No,' he said quickly.

'If they were other housewives like me? Just like me?'

'No. You are right. It's perhaps more complicated than I thought at first.'

'And you don't really mean where you come from everyone is just like you.'

'Oh, yes. That part's true.'

*

Fred asked Dorothy to come to an office party the next week. That was unusual enough, because he himself never liked that kind of thing. They sat on the sidelines in someone's house, with plates balanced on their knees. People were dancing to records and everyone said how nice it was to meet again. It was a very dull party. A few days later, he wanted to take out a visiting client and his wife, and have Dorothy come along. They went to a good seafood restaurant and had a pleasant evening. It was almost like old times. As they were leaving, Dorothy noticed the Cranstons sitting down at a special large table set for about twenty people. Jeanie Cranston jumped out of her seat to say what a surprise, and they must get together more often. Dorothy said yes, of course, but she knew they wouldn't. For years now they had really only been friends through Estelle. Dorothy took a quick look at the crowd they were with: loud, overdressed, yelling at each other across the table. Joshua looked the way Estelle had described him – smug, pompous and somehow not right.

The next morning before lunch, while Larry was peeling potatoes with her, Dorothy had a telephone call from Estelle. It was a distress call. She sounded drunk, and though what she seemed to be talking about was some dangerous characters her daughter Sandra was keeping company with, Dorothy was sure that the real trouble had to do with Charlie and Stan. She said she'd drop over in the afternoon.

'Start gargling with Listerine,' she added, 'and be careful not to swallow any, because if you're drunk when I get there, I'm turning right around and going home again. I might even phone up Charlie and Stan and tell them about each other.'

Estelle screeched with laughter and hung up.

Larry helped to start off a new crop of apple cucumbers, he made the salad for lunch, and did the dusting while Dorothy vacuumed. Then he helped her to clean the silver – what there was of it – which she always forgot until she caught sight of a blackening cream jug in the corner of the top cupboard or a ladle at the side of the middle drawer.

She looked over to where he was, seated at the other end of the kitchen table in the light which, since his arrival, she had blocked by curtains because of his sensitive eyes. He concentrated on polishing spoons with a silver cloth: six teaspoons from a great-aunt. One leg was slung over the other, which would have looked strange enough, but he was also wearing a flowered apron fastened around his waist, and it contrasted stunningly with his large, muscular green body, his nobly massive head. Dorothy thought he looked, as always, wonderful. And his hands, in spite of their size and strength, were nimble and delicate in all their movements. He said that he enjoyed housework. He was good at it, and found it interesting. It was so different from anything he had known before: the hands had to be kept in constant motion, while the rest of the body remained more or less still.

They were lying in bed and watching television that afternoon, when Larry said sharply, 'Look!'

'What?'

'What is it?'

'Where?'

'On the screen.'

'Oh, it's an ad for a dance company.'

'But what is it? Look.'

'It's somebody called Merce Cunningham. You were right – it's an ad, for a dance programme coming up next week. It's a series. He has a dance company of his own.'

'What's he doing?'

'Dancing.'

'No, no, no,' Larry said, getting out of bed, standing on the floor, and doing the strange motions he had been doing for days now. Suddenly Dorothy realized that he was giving a perfect imitation of the dance.

'That's his dance,' she said.

'But what is it? What does it do?'

'I don't think it does anything. It expresses some emotion or idea, or gives an impression of an event. It makes variations with patterns. Do you like it?'

'I don't understand it,' he said, getting back into bed.

'It's too bad I can't take you to see things. You should see some classical ballet, then I could try to explain from there.'

'I've seen it,' Larry said. 'I can understand that.'

'Really? You liked it?'

'Yes, very nice. Full of music.'

'So is this.'

'Not the same.'

'No,' Dorothy said. Most of the time, if she couldn't explain something to him straight away, he didn't push it. The last time she'd been stuck was when he said he didn't understand 'radical chic'.

Later in the afternoon, she drove over to Estelle's. Just before she rang the bell, she had a feeling that no one was at home. She rang three times. No answer. She walked around to the back and peeked into the kitchen. Estelle was sitting down at one side of the booth-and-table across from the stove, and Sandra was in the middle of the room, shouting. Dorothy could hear her right through the window: ' – Stupid old . . . never . . . bitch . . . all the time . . .'

Dorothy rapped on the glass with her car keys. Sandra looked up, her face heavy, mask-like and intent. Then she disappeared. Next to Dorothy the kitchen door was flung open.

She walked in. Sandra was just going out the door that led to the dining-room. Estelle hadn't moved Dorothy sat down at the other side of the table.

'How bad is it?'

'What?' Estelle asked.

'The hangover.'

'I've got a hangover, all right. I've got a hangover from living forty-four long years.'

'How old is Sandra now, anyway? I always forget. Is she fifteen?'

'Sixteen. They're all doing it at twelve now. She's been on the pill for two years. Well, I told you.'

'But she's going through phases very fast. She'll probably get through a lot of unsuitable people before she settles down.'

'Unsuitable,' Estelle said.

'Isn't it better to have her experiment around than go all starry-eyed and get into a marriage that's going to break up in a couple of years? Then she'd be back where she is now, except maybe she'd have a child to bring up, too.'

'If she were married, at least it might prove he loved her.'

'Oh, Estelle. Do you love Stan, or Charlie?'

'She's trying to get back at me through this.'

'Maybe,' Dorothy sighed. She waited for Estelle to launch into explanation or self-justification, but she just sat slumped against the wall.

After a long while, Estelle said, 'What a mess. I'm sorry I got you out here. I'm not very good company and I don't really know what to do about this. I don't want her to get hurt, but if I give her her head, there could be other people who get hurt.'

'Who is this boy?'

'A man. Our age.'

'My God.'

'Oh, yes. You're beginning to see now.'

'I guess we're lucky it isn't Stan or Charlie. Or is it?'

'Not quite.' Estelle rubbed her hands over her face and sat up straight. 'Coffee?' she asked.

'Just a little. And if I can't help, let's change the subject. Tell me about Joey.'

'That isn't changing the subject so much. He's developed some kind of knight-errant complex about it. *My sister must be pure* type of thing. That's how I found out. They've been fighting about it for days, till last evening it all came out what the trouble was.'

After the first cup, Dorothy wanted to go, but it was just at that point that Estelle decided to tell a little more of the story about Sandra.

'Have you seen this man?' Dorothy asked.

'Oh, I don't want to talk about it.'

Estelle went on to say that she didn't know what to do, because every move she made was being misinterpreted by her daughter. She had the feeling that the girl was just waiting for her to put a foot wrong.

'This man –' Dorothy began.

'The thing is, I've always tried to bring them up to compensate for the way I was brought up.'

'Well, all mothers do that.'

'And now it's all paying off. What really kills me is this idea that a lot of it goes back to the divorce. Punishing me for it.'

After the second cup of coffee, Dorothy got away. She was less worried about Estelle than when she had heard her voice over the telephone, but wasn't very optimistic about how long she would stay sober. As long as things didn't reach a crisis during the time when she would have to be driving Larry to safety, she ought to be able to deal with everything.

Fred wasn't home yet when she arrived. She went into the kitchen, looked in on Larry briefly, and as soon as she heard the car, walked into the living-room.

'What now?' he said, taking off his jacket. He put it over the back of a chair.

'Talk. Our famous talk we were going to have. About Suzanne and the vacation, and everything.'

'I've got to go out. Can't we do all that later?'

'It's always later. One day it's going to be too late.'

He looked at her over his shoulder, but said nothing. She thought: he was going to say, 'It's already too late,' but he changed his mind.

'Well, what do you think?' he said. 'But make it quick.'

'I thought we might try the separate vacations again, and get Suzanne to come afterwards. But I'm going to need some help with her this year. I can't stand it much longer.'

'Yes. All right.'

Nothing would happen, of course. Every year she said the same thing about Suzanne.

'So shall I call up Suzanne and tell her?' Dorothy asked.

'Yes, OK.'

'Are you really listening?'

'Of course, of course, I'm just in a hurry. I've got to go out.'

Dorothy picked up the telephone and dialled Suzanne's number. Fred went upstairs. Suzanne, as Dorothy had hoped, was in the middle of preparations for dinner: in fact, she was giving a party and sounded disorganized.

'Who? Dorothy? Why don't I call you back when we can talk?'

'No, no. No need for that. It's just to say that we're going to have to make it after the twelfth.'

'But that's ages away.'

'I'm afraid it just won't work out any other way.'

'But I'll be on vacation then.'

'Well, I'm afraid we're going to be on ours before then.'

'Maybe I can come before you go.'

'No, that's just it. We've get people staying.' Dorothy thought of a name quickly. Suzanne always wanted to know all the details of everybody's life, and never forgot any of them.

'Dorothy, we'll have to talk about it. I've really got to go now.'

'That's all right. We don't have to talk about anything until after the twelfth. OK?'

'Yes, but – '

'I'll get in touch with you then. Goodbye.'

'I'll call you,' Suzanne said. 'Goodbye.'

Dorothy wrote down on the notepad by the telephone that Suzanne was not to come until after the twelfth. When Fred came running down the stairs, still tying his tie, she told him and he said. 'Yes, yes.'

'And I've written it down on the pad in case she calls. If she comes before that, I'm moving out and taking the car.'

'All right, all right,' he said.

'Where are you going in a tie?'

'I've got to rush. 'Bye.'

He was out of the house and into the rented car before she could think of what she had been meaning to say. Now she had forgotten. She went back to the telephone, underlined two words on the pad, and continued on towards the kitchen.

She and Larry had supper, and were just settling down in front of the TV set when she heard what she thought was the front door. Larry turned off the set and told her that her husband had come back. She scrambled up off the bed, although she didn't believe it. Much more likely that there was a burglar.

She opened the door to the living-room without making a sound. Exactly in her line of vision sat Fred, his head in his hands. She approached the chair silently and stood near him. He sighed. He said, 'Oh, damn.' She put her hand on his shoulder and he jumped. She patted his back.

'What's wrong?'

'What did I say?'

'When?'

'Just now.'

'Nothing. You said, 'Oh, damn'. Where were you? What happened?'

'It's so hard to explain.'

'That's all right.' She sat down beside him.

He said, 'Well, it's so stupid and miserable. I was seeing somebody. I didn't even like her, but I was bored. She was the one who started it all. I wouldn't have thought of it otherwise. And now she says she's going to make a big scene and tell you. So, that's it. I'm sorry.'

Dorothy kept her hand on his back. She said, 'Never mind. If she wants to talk to me, let her.'

'I think it's just to hurt me, but I don't want it hurting you. That's why – I mean, I'd rather not have said anything.'

I'll bet, Dorothy thought. And he probably thinks I had no idea. Still, I too would rather not have known so exactly. She sat still, moving her hand lightly over the back of his shirt and wanting to ask, 'What's she like?'

'You don't love her any more?'

'Oh, I never did. That's what's so dumb.'

'Well, don't worry. I'll be prepared if anything happens.'

He still looked pathetic. Perhaps he wanted to warn her that if the other woman told her such-and-such, not to believe it. Well, Dorothy thought, I have Larry. I can afford to be forgiving.

'Are you going out again tonight?'

'No.'

'We can play Scrabble and plan out what's going to happen with the vacations.'

They ended up playing four rounds. Dorothy brought coffee and made him some sandwiches. He said, 'This is beginning to look like a tournament,' and she answered, 'No, just "people to people", but I'm winning.'

'That makes it people to etymological mastermind.'

Dorothy wrote down the score and looked over the letters in her rack. 'We haven't played this in a long time.'

'That's because you kept winning.'

Dorothy almost said, 'Or because you were always out at

night.' There were a few moments around quarter to eleven when she thought she sensed movement from the kitchen, which would mean that Larry was sneaking out to steal a car for the night. And, there was another point when she knew for certain that her husband had decided, all in the space of an evening and without consulting her, to put their marriage back where it had been several years ago, before the single beds.

As they went upstairs, Dorothy reminded him about Suzanne and repeated that she would leave the house if Suzanne came before the twelfth.

'We could take our vacation together,' Fred said. 'Something fancy, for a change.'

'I think it might be a good idea to go ahead and do them separately. Have time to think about things and get together afterwards. You know what vacations are. They aren't really connected to the rest of life. Like honeymoons.'

'Sounds good.'

'But you don't need to go away for that.'

'Sounds better,' he said.

In the morning, Fred was hardly out the door and Dorothy back in the kitchen, when Larry appeared before her. He said, 'They're looking for me,' and pointed to the radio. Dorothy switched on the volume knob and led him to a chair.

The announcer's voice sounded excited and happy, as if advertising something. It said:

Last night, after a lull of weeks, Aquarius the Monsterman struck again. Five young lives fell victim to the bloodlust of this creature, five families now mourn. Yesterday they hadn't a care in the world, now they know the sorrow of the bereaved. And we must also ask ourselves if it is right that alien life-forms should be brought back at great public expense to lay waste the flower of our citizenry.

'They came at me with broken bottles. One of them said, "Hey man, look at the size of him. We'll do something about that, to begin with." And then they were all around me, so I had to hit as fast as I could. I'm sorry, Dorothy. It's going to make it harder for you, isn't it?'

Dorothy made a gentle, hushing gesture with her hand. She listened to the radio. The rest of the broadcast described the 'bloodlust killings' of five boys or men in the gardens of the museum, where they had been the other night. She listened to the end, and then switched it off.

'Were you hurt?'

'Where they hit me and kicked me, but they weren't able to use the bottles. Or the knives – two of them had knives – so, my skin isn't broken.'

She ran her hand along his face. He pulled away as she touched the side of his jaw. If the dark green colour hadn't masked it, there would probably be a spectacular bruise to go with the swelling, like the time Fred got into the fight on the freeway with the driver from Kansas.

'I'll get you something for it.'

'I already put a cream on it. I found it with the medicines. It said it was for contusions.'

They spent the morning quietly until Mr Mendoza arrived. This time, he came in for a cup of coffee and talked about the news, and said that the television version now was that these young men were brave and patriotic and so on, but he had seen their pictures in the morning paper and recognized them as punks and troublemakers from good neighbourhoods, who had the money and the time to hang around getting drunk and taking drugs and beating up people who were poorer than they were and who were out on their own.

'That friend of yours,' he said. 'It will be sad for a while, but it's better the way it is, you'll see.'

Dorothy didn't know what he meant. She was terrified that he might have meant Larry. Could he have seen Larry through a gap in the kitchen curtains? Mr Mendoza said goodbye and left before she could say anything or even think about it.

He might have been referring to something in the newspaper coverage which she had misunderstood. But "your friend", if it was an allusion to Larry, would have meant that the police should have been at the house hours ago. Fred had taken the paper with him again; she hadn't even seen it.

She turned on the television set in Larry's room. He was pottering around the living-room, looking at magazines and books. The screen showed police and public officials. Occasionally there was a shot of one of the doctors or scientists who worked at the Institute. There were some interviews, which had been taped very early in the morning, and panel discussions about the nature of civilized man and the aggressive instinct. Dr Forest stressed the animal's intelligence, Professor Dexter talked about the original capture and why it would be so dangerous to approach such a creature without qualified professional help. The police and officials spoke of quick action, possible hiding places, eating habits. Without actually saying so, the presenters of the programme were managing to suggest that Larry had remained in the area because of the opportunities for eating people. Not one of the men interviewed thought it might be possible that Larry remained so well hidden because he had made friends with someone. That question was never raised.

But perhaps the police had told them not to mention it. On the other hand, if the authorities believed that, surely they would find Larry more quickly by asking members of the public to snoop around all the houses near them. Now that she thought of it, of course, it was extraordinary that he should have chosen her. Most single people don't live in their own separate houses, most married people are in and out of all the rooms of their house.

While she was watching, Larry came in and sat down on the bed.

'How can they say those things? I used to think it was only the people at the Institute who were like that, but they are everywhere.'

Dorothy turned the sound down almost to nothing, and came over to where he sat.

'You don't like it that I killed these people,' he said. 'You think it's bad. But they would have killed me.'

'I know they would. I don't think it's bad at all. I'm just disappointed that if anything goes wrong with the Mexican plan, we can't use the newspapers. Before last night, we could have told the truth about the men in the Institute, how they were torturing you for their own pleasure in addition to all the horrible experiments they thought were going to prove something useful – and we would have had the defence of a victim. But now, everyone's going to think these thugs and creeps acted in an understandable way. Everyone except me and somebody like Mr Mendoza, who has a mind of his own. People will think these boys acted the way they did because they were frightened. Of course, if they had been frightened, which they weren't, it would have been the fault of the TV and the papers. They've been whipping everybody up.'

'They always do. About everything. I've been reading and I've been watching. I'll tell you something else: I understand now.'

'What?'

He stood up and did the dance they had seen on television. To Dorothy it looked exactly as it had when he had copied it before.

'Now I understand,' he said.

'Is it different?'

'Yes,' he said, 'for me.' Dorothy was about to ask some questions concerning the dance when still photographs were put on the screen behind him. She was curious to see who the people were. Larry moved back beside her on the bed.

'There are the people in the park. Do they look the same?'

'Nothing ever looks like a picture. That's what picture means.'

'But can you recognize them?'

They both looked. One picture, two. The names weren't given. Three; and then, at the fourth picture, Dorothy said, 'That looks like Estelle's son. Joey. My God, I wonder if that was what Mr Mendoza meant.'

'What?'

'If that's the same person, I know his mother. In fact, she's my best friend. You know, my friend Estelle. I'd better call her up.'

She went into the kitchen and telephoned from there. Larry stood behind in the doorway, looking at her. All she got was a busy signal. It was true, of course, that pictures never looked like the real person, and this one would have been taken a long time ago, but it had been near enough to make her think she recognized it, even without a name.

'Larry,' she said, 'I think I'd better see if I can find Estelle. I'm sorry to leave you.'

'You don't like it that I killed him. Does it make it worse that you knew that one?'

'Yes.'

'Why? To do a bad thing is the same from a stranger as from someone you know. Maybe it's worse from someone you know.'

'But you make allowances for the people you know.'

'I told you what happened. There were five of them, they tried to kill me, and they jumped on me without any warning. They were armed, and they were enjoying themselves. That Joey one, too. Aren't you going to make allowances for me as well as him?'

'I've known him since he was a baby. I've held him on my lap.'

'You've loved me more than you ever loved him, haven't you?'

Dorothy fidgeted with the telephone cord. She nodded and sighed.

'What really worries you most, Dorothy? It isn't because of what I've done – I can see that now.'

'I guess it's Estelle. From the beginning, we were just the opposite: our families, our characters, and our marriages. But we've always gotten along so well, like sisters. We've helped each other so much. Once or twice our lives were broken up so seriously that each of us was nearly ready to go under – really. So, when something hits Estelle badly, it hits me, too. You can't imagine how she complains about her children, even when they're there in the room, but I know they're really everything to her. She just adores them. I don't know how she'll recover.'

'You did,' Larry said.

'Sometimes I wonder.'

She drove out to Estelle's house, but there was no answer when she rang the doorbell, and none when she went around to the back and pounded on the door. She got the notebook out of her purse, ripped out a page, and wrote a short letter, which she folded up to look like an envelope, and pushed it through the slot in the door.

She drove in the direction of the museum. From a long way off it was obvious that there were crowds of people driving towards the place, so she changed her mind and took the turning for the coast. She stopped the car under a eucalyptus tree and sat looking out at the ocean. She felt like crying; for Estelle at the moment and Estelle in the future, and for herself in the past, when Scotty died. She tried to think of what to do, and to arrange plans for hiding Larry, comforting Estelle, getting rid of Suzanne, taking the holiday alone without hurting Fred's feelings, and getting Larry back to his home. If I do this, she thought, it should take one week, two weeks, but if I do this . . . She couldn't attach any of her thoughts together for very long. She would much rather have cried. What she did, however, was to fall asleep, with her shoulder up against the seat and her head near the window. She woke up after about twenty minutes and drove back to Estelle's house, where there was still no answer.

*

She went back home. Fred's rented car was parked outside and he was in the living-room. He was reading a newspaper.

'Seen this?' he asked, as she passed in front of him. He crinkled the paper at her to show what he meant, but kept right on reading.

'I haven't seen any of them. You took the paper with you when you left. I saw something on TV, but they didn't give any names. Was it Joey?'

'Looks like him. I'm not surprised. He was probably so spaced out, the monsterman just gave him a push and he fell over.'

'Why do you call him a monster?'

'Well, an eight-foot-tall green gorilla with web feet and bug eyes – what would you call him? A well-developed frog? Not exactly an Ivy-league type, anyway.'

'I've met plenty of Ivy-leaguers I'd call monsters. And his feet aren't webbed, or only a little. And neither are his hands. They only seem that way at first glance. And he isn't any eight-foot tall. Only about six-seven.'

'How do you know?'

'I saw it on television. Pictures taken before he escaped.'

You know some idiot of a woman is trying to get up a petition to say this monster has been inhumanly treated, and so on.'

'She's right. He was.'

'Oh, come on.'

'How would you like to be tied down and given electric-shock treatments by force, and only given any food when they'd decided you were co-operating enough in one of their horrible experiments?'

'You sound just like this Mrs what's-her-name here – Mrs Peach. You two should get together.'

'Maybe.'

'Actually, I'm not so sure I believe there ever was a monster. Might just be some poor clone or hybrid they've been working on in the labs. Gave him too big a dose of some hormone and it sent him haywire; something like that.'

They had a quiet dinner and talked about plans for the future. Fred agreed that they would take separate vacations. Dorothy realized from the start of the meal that he wanted to say something about having children, but he didn't dare. She thought: he really is hoping to go back to where we were, and thinks then everything will work itself out.

At midnight, Estelle telephoned. She sounded very calm and tired. The newspaper story had been right: it had been a picture of Joey on the screen. Dorothy wanted to go see her straight away, but Estelle said no, to wait till the afternoon of the next day. 'The man from the funeral parlour,' she explained.

Mr Mendoza came around again the next day. They worked in the garden and talked about a new variety of rose that had been bred for one of the European flower shows: it was supposed to be blue – not the pale grey or lilac blue you could buy at the nurseries, but a genuine bright royal blue like the blue of a first-prize ribbon.

'I sure would like to have a cutting,' he said.

'Is it real? I mean, would it breed true? It takes a long time to tell, doesn't it?'

'You just have to wait and see.'

They finished work too late for Mr Mendoza to come in for a sandwich, so Dorothy said that they probably wouldn't see each other for a few weeks. He would be working at other houses in the neighbourhood, and after that, she would be on her vacation. He asked her to tell him the exact date when she knew, because then he would drop by to see that everything was all right while she was away.

She ate her lunch with Larry in his room. They only turned the television on for a few minutes to watch the news. Mrs Peach, looking – with her short, permed hair, extra-strength glasses and prim but firm expression – like a caricature of an anti-vivisectionist, gave a brief speech which Dorothy thought very sensible. She raised the point that the so-called monster had been held in captivity for several months, isolated from its own species and investigated or experimented upon by scientists. The general public had never been told what sort of animal this was. She also stated that until the capture, this creature had been unknown to the scientific world. The question of Human Rights, or just rights in general, was as important in this case as though the creature had come from outer space.

Dorothy said, 'If only she had spoken up right at the beginning. It's good, but it comes a bit late.'

'It's all too late now, I can feel it. Before I only suspected. Now, I'm certain. People are too afraid now. In a way, I'm glad. If they catch me now, they won't try to tie me up or knock me out to take me back to the Institute. They'll just beat me to a pulp and say I was trying to eat them up. Even if I gave myself up, it's too late. Haven't you noticed – they keep calling me "the killer"?'

'Yes, I know.'

'It's all right. I'd prefer anything at all to going back to the Institute.'

The afternoon came. Dorothy was not prepared to find Estelle sober, but, as it turned out, Estelle did not even look as though she had been crying. What was worse, she looked like a different person. She was very quiet, sometimes sighing long sighs. She forgot where she had put things she'd just set down for a moment, and she talked in a calm monotone about the funeral arrangements and the other parents.

Of course, Dorothy thought, there were five of them. It was going to be a joint funeral. And, naturally, the press would be having a field day.

'I think Sandra's taking it very hard. You know, we haven't been on very friendly terms. She threw herself at the man I was . . . just to hurt me, but that's all over. Over for me, anyway. She's going to have to start finding out for herself now, what's right and what isn't. I can't tell you how empty the house feels, Dotty.'

'Yes, I know. That's what it was like with Scotty. His toys, his clothes. Right at first, I kept thinking I heard his voice everywhere, coming from a different room, and I'd get up and walk into the next room just – you know, thinking none of it had happened at all. And then I'd realize again.'

Estelle nodded slowly. Her face was like the outline of a box, with no expression whatsoever.

'Estelle, did the doctor give you some kind of pills or something?'

'Have you heard of a doctor who didn't try to shoot you full of drugs? I'm not sick. I'm bereaved. That means I've got to keep all my strength to get through. And if I'm full of drugs, my resistance is going to be destroyed, isn't it?'

'Yes, of course. That was one of the biggest mistakes they made with me.'

'I know. I told you.'

'One of the things that helped the most was talking to you. And then going to work. Have you been able to cry at all?'

'I've been trying not to. At least, I think that's what's going on.'

'It might help.'

'I'm afraid it wouldn't stop. Remember what happened to you. They almost had you in the loony bin. Once you're helpless, one of those bastards steps forward with a hypodermic and the curtain comes down on your life. You stay there and they give you massive doses of sedatives every day because you're easier to take care of that way. And then your brain is pretty much slugged into submission. No more chance to find your way out of your troubles, ever.'

Dorothy said she agreed. Estelle had always felt like that about doctors, by which she meant male doctors – the women, apparently, weren't so bad. But Dorothy, until her troubles, had not agreed at all. She had twice been in hospital for minor operations as well as for Scotty, and had thought everybody was so kind and nice. Despite the boredom of waiting around, she had enjoyed being taken in to the workings of a new world. She had found it easy that nothing was expected of her, no act of hers could be a mistake, a neglect, or something she should feel guilty about. It was wonderful, she had thought, that there were experts who had dedicated their time and strength to such demanding work and who could put you right when you were in real trouble – broken, cut, bruised, scrambled up inside. Only much later did the realization of her helplessness contribute to a certainty that nurses, doctors, in fact the whole idea of medicine, had made her a victim. To her it had not brought healing. It had brought death where she was sure death had been avoidable. Her own doctor was still all right and she had one weapon against him: she could just not go, and phone to say she felt fine. But hospitals – whenever she thought about them now, she felt like a sacrificial bundle on a stone slab, with the priests whispering to each other over her head.

'Drugs, ' Estelle said. 'Money and drugs, and that's the history of civilization.'

Dorothy wondered if Estelle was still referring to doctors, or if something had come out about Joey taking drugs. She didn't want to bring up the subject herself. She asked when the funeral was going to be held. Estelle gave a deep sigh.

'Listen, don't be hurt, but I really don't want anybody to come. I think I can get through it by myself – just. But anything real would make me crack up. It's going to be a performance, you know.

Television, everything. Three of those families have sold the serial rights to the papers, and you should see them. You've never seen such people.'

'Didn't you know them before?'

'Of course not.'

'But you knew the boys?'

'No. They were just a bunch of rough kids Joey used to hang around with when he was trying to act tough. God knows what they were up to. Stealing TVs and stereos and car radios, and selling them – who knows? That's the kind they were.'

'Do you think they provoked this man, or monster, whatever he is? That they ganged up on him, maybe?'

'Monster? Oh, Dorothy, I don't believe there's any such thing. Some kind of crocodile got up on its hind legs and broke out of that Institute, but you can bet the poor thing's dead by this time. Or probably crawled back to the beach and swam away.'

'What do you think it was?'

'Oh, another gang, and they're keeping quiet.'

'There are people who say they saw him.'

'I bet there are. There are people who could see Moby Dick in Times Square. It sounds to me like a big fight. They all had bottles and knives. So if there was only one man, he'd have to be one of these karate champions. I guess that's possible, too.'

Dorothy poured out a second cup of coffee for each of them. This is all my fault, she thought. I've given him shelter and now this has happened. If I'd taken him straight to a good lawyer, we could have worked out some sort of defence for killing those two keepers.

Estelle stared into her cup. She stirred the coffee with a spoon, although she hadn't put anything in.

'Charlie and Stan called me,' she said. 'That was nice.'

'Very nice. So you've forgotten about them being with those girls at the fashion show.'

'Oh, that. Unimportant.'

'Which one of them was it that Sandra made the play for?'

'That was somebody else.'

'My God, Estelle, you've got a new one?'

'Not new. Old. Before Stan and Charlie. Years. I always felt guilty about it, but I couldn't end it, and then I guess I didn't want it to stop. But it's stopped now, all right. Let's not talk about that.'

'Has Sandra changed towards you now? I mean, has it brought you closer together?'

'Nope. I don't even know if she's going to bother to turn up for the funeral. And the way I feel now, I'm not sure I really want her around much.'

The electric clock on the wall clicked as it sometimes did when the minute hand jumped forward. Dorothy said, 'Anything I can do. You know. I'll leave it up to you to call me, but if you don't after a few days, I'll call you. All right?'

'Yes, fine. Thanks, Dotty.'

'Try to keep eating the right things, and don't let them give you pills, or use any other depressants.'

'The girl means hooch. Finally she comes out with it.'

'And I mean it.'

'I'd like to get away from everything. Just everything.'

'That might not be a bad idea. You could start packing after the funeral, and I'd take care of the house for you. You think about it. Are you sure you don't want me to be with you when –'

'No. Thanks.'

Dorothy stood up. She said, 'Anytime you want to change your mind or need to talk, just pick up the phone, or come over.' She kissed Estelle on the cheek and left.

On the way home, she thought to herself that Estelle would never just drop in without warning, any more than she herself would. It hadn't been such a great offer of friendship: do feel free to call on me for help any time between four and six, or when I'm not likely to be in the bedroom with somebody, and certainly not before the twelfth.

And if I hadn't been hiding him, she thought again, it wouldn't have happened.

About ten blocks before the house, she noticed that she was driving directly behind Fred in his rented car.

He gave no sign of realizing she was there. Where they both usually turned off to the left, he kept straight ahead until turning to the right. She followed.

She followed him for just over ten minutes. He pulled up at the kerb in a street like the one they lived on themselves, got out, and rang someone's doorbell. Dorothy couldn't see who answered. She waited for a few minutes, not long, and then he came back out, got into his car, and drove on. He had been carrying something in his hand – an office file, or something like that. So, it was business, not pleasure.

She drove home a different way, and saw the rented car there before her. Fred was in a hurry again, tying his tie at the last minute.

'Where are you going?'

'Just out to some people's. I don't think I'll be too long.'

'They need you in a tie?'

'It makes a good impression.'

'Nowadays?'

'They're that kind of people.'

'Let me do that for you,' Dorothy said.

'When have I never been able to tie my own tie blindfold? I had to do it in that school play, remember?'

'Haven't you had anything to eat?'

'I'll pick something up.'

At the last minute he turned and kissed her on the cheek, quickly and as if panicked. He was out the door almost immediately.

Dorothy went back into the kitchen. She sat down at the table and tried to think. All during the drive, she had been excited. She had expected to find something or someone. But there had been nothing. The house probably belonged to Art Gruber or someone else like that, who had taken home a report by mistake. And yet, she felt let down.

Larry came and stood beside her. It was the first time he had ever come out of his room on his own during daylight, rather than waiting for her to come tell him that it was all right.

'You shouldn't have come out alone,' she said.

'I heard he was gone.'

'But I could have had the lights switched on and only the gauze curtains. Somebody outside could have see you.'

'I saw there was no light on.' He sat down in a chair opposite her. He took her hand.

Dorothy smiled. Whenever he took her hand, it made her happy. She had had an inkling of the sensation that very first time, when he had walked into the kitchen and she had handed him the celery. She kept smiling, but she thought: he's taken his own lead now – he no longer avoids risks.

'You are sad,' he said.

She nodded. She told him about Estelle. 'And the whole business about the funeral. We'll probably be able to watch it on TV. It'll be terrible.'

'I'd be very interested to see it. You talk so much about your friend Estelle.'

'But after that, it's really going to be hard for you. I don't think it's going to be safe for you to go out at night the way you've been doing. They might not expect to see you driving a car, but once they do, they'll realize. Once a thing is in the air, everyone sees it, even if it isn't there. It's an influence. Like the flying saucers: if one person has a big story about them, half a dozen do. That doesn't necessarily mean it's impossible that they've seen anything – it just means people are prepared to notice everything, once they've been alerted. Before that, they really don't see things much.'

'You must decide,' he said. Dorothy felt relieved. If he wanted to act on his own, there would be nothing she could do. And there was another matter: when he spoke about Fred now, there was a shade to his voice. It might just be that he was jealous, that he wanted to hurt Fred. He knew how easy it was to hurt people, and he certainly had reason to want to take revenge on humankind.

She said, 'I think we're going to have to go sooner than we'd planned. Very soon. I'll have to think it out. In the meantime, it would be better to stay indoors.'

'No, let's go out, please. I want to walk on the grass in the gardens and look at the flowerbeds. Please. We could go back to the place with the chairs and the stickbushes.'

'Bamboo. But it's taking such a risk.'

'I'm going to feel sick if I can't go out. I know it.'

The telephone rang. Jeanie Cranston was calling to ask Dorothy if she knew anything about Estelle, since the phone must be off the hook and the doors were locked, and the curtains drawn. What Jeanie really wanted to know was what her own reactions ought to be – would it be all right to send a letter, a telegram, flowers? Dorothy told her to put a note through the door if she wanted to, to stay away from the funeral, and wait for Estelle to get in touch.

She ate an early supper with Larry. They took a lot of extra time over their coffee. He wanted to know all about the Cranstons. The more Dorothy told him, the more he seemed fascinated. What struck him as most interesting was the fact that although Dorothy and Estelle talked about the Cranstons being 'friends', neither of them genuinely liked the couple.

'Is this usual?' he asked. After some thought, Dorothy said she figured it probably was.

She agreed to go to the bamboo grove. While they were washing up the dishes, she asked, 'When you go back, will the others think you've changed much? I mean, because you find all these things interesting: the Cranstons, and so forth. Will it make them think you've changed for the better, or just that you aren't normal any more?'

'It's different,' he said. 'They'll come near me to find out. It's like smell. What's important is that they should still know who I am. I think they will.'

'If you stayed away for a long time, they might not recognize you?'

'Or other things could happen. My abilities could leave me. How to swim, how to stay under. I'm eating different things up here. My life is different. My way of using the food is different – what's that word?'

'Metabolism. Over a long period, maybe it would make a difference.' And, she again thought, there was the possibility of picking up a human disease. She said nothing, but wondered if he had thought of that himself.

It was still light when she eased the car out on to the driveway and into the street. A lovely, warm night, full of promise and romance as she had dreamed about it in her teens and as the advertisements had promised and still promised, for her and for everyone else too.

'You are driving very slowly,' Larry whispered from the back seat.

'It's so nice out. And it's still light. Shall we go down to the beach for a while?'

'No, to the bamboo place.'

'But we're going to have to drive round till it gets dark.'

'All right, the beach.'

Dorothy drove the car to their usual place. She leaned her head back. Larry ran his hands through her hair, then got out of the car and moved into the front seat beside her.

'You know, I think if anything happens,' she said, 'so that we're separated, or if anything goes wrong –'

'What?'

'– not that it will . . . anyway, it might be a good idea to plan to meet here. You'd have the ocean right there, so you could stay hidden for a while, couldn't you?'

'Yes, sure. A long time. Months.'

'Right. And I'd show up around this time, maybe later. You'd hear the car and see the lights if you came out on to the beach.'

'I'll remember.'

They drove to the street of the bamboo grove, parked and got out. They ran across a neighbouring yard, halting in the shadow of a tree.

'Larry, I have a feeling.'

'Lots of people.'

'Lots of cars parked in the road. There must be a party some-where near. It makes it so risky.'

'Never mind. They'll be drinking.' He took her by the hand and led her forward through the sweet evening air. They walked over the warm lawns together like the college couples she had followed in her youth with her schoolgirl friend, Joan. On perfect evenings, like this one, they had trailed courting couples for yards, for blocks, from one neighbourhood to another, wondering about whether the young lovers were really lovers, what they actually did with each other, and whether they themselves would ever be strolling along like that with a man.

'Voices,' Larry said.

Dorothy heard nothing for a few moments. Then the sound of talk came to her, as elusive as a wind-carried scent from flowering trees in the spring. It seemed to be coming from all directions at once, then suddenly it was gone.

'Where do you think they are?' she whispered. Instinctively she had ducked down into a crouching walk.

'They sound like they're where we were before. That big house with the garden and the bamboos.'

'Let's go, then.'

'No, let's look.' He pulled her along by the hand. The buzz of voices became clearer, louder, and at last fixed. Soon it was loud enough and clear enough for Dorothy to distinguish whole sentences flung up out of the babble. How people whooped when they got together, and on top of that there were the explosions of laughter or contradiction that involved groups of from three to eight voices. So many rhythms chased each other and scurried through the main rise and flow of sound.

'Is it like the sea?' she whispered. 'All the changing sounds?'

'No. Not at all. But I like the thought.'

Dorothy put her head up against his collarbone and kissed him. She still held his hand.

'Let's find the bamboo place and the garden sofas,' he suggested.

'Too dangerous.'

'Just to see if we'd be hidden from sight.'

'Well – '

'You could even go out into the crowd and bring us food and drinks.'

Dorothy began to giggle. She followed, convulsed by hysterical smothered laughter, as Larry led the way. She held her other hand over her mouth.

As they approached the bamboo grove, there was less light, and less noise. Dorothy's giggles stopped suddenly. She sensed a change more subtle than a threat of danger, but just as urgent. It was the kind of feeling you might get from an unexpected alteration of temperature. She squeezed Larry's hand.

He pulled up in front of her and stood still. They listened to the distant sound of the party, the nearby rustling of the bamboo, and then a faint sound of moaning. Dorothy was afraid. Someone out there in the shadows was hurt, by they couldn't help whoever it was without betraying their own presence.

Larry stepped forward. He seemed to intend going on, whether she accompanied him or not. He dropped his hold on her hand.

She dashed after him. And all at once her eyes were used to the changed light. It wasn't really very dark at all. Certainly it was light enough to see the two people – the man almost fully dressed, the girl naked – who face to face were using the garden sofa so athletically and rhapsodically that before Dorothy realized what was happening, her first thought was they they were engaged in some kind of feverish contest or game. The girl was Estelle's daughter, Sandra.

'Let's go,' Dorothy said, pulling away.

'No,' Larry whispered, 'let's watch.'

'Please,' she said, 'it's my husband.' She turned and blundered back through the bamboo.

Yes, she thought, and I offered to tie his tie, which he still has on. He knows perfectly well how to tie his tie. He said so himself. He was in a highschool play once where he had to tie his tie in front of the audience, as though in front of a mirror: first with one end too long, then with the other one too long, and so on back and forth until finally he got it right. He used to do it at cocktail parties years ago. It looked very funny.

She hurried off across the lawns. In the darker surroundings she could just see the car when Larry caught up with her.

'Wait – don't leave me alone,' he said. His voice sounded strange. She herself was in a kind of panic. She grabbed his hand and ran. Now she was the one who was pulling. They got into the car fast, slamming the doors.

She was out on one of the main highways before she remembered what Estelle had told her: that the older married man Sandra had taken on had been Estelle's lover for years.

She sobbed a few times and stepped on the accelerator. Larry heaved himself up over the back seat.

'We're going very fast.'

'I'm sorry.' She slowed down. As soon as she saw a place to stop, she pulled over to the side.

'I'm all upset. I don't know what to do,' she said. Larry disappeared behind the seat again.

'There's a car coming up in back of us.'

'It's him,' Dorothy shouted. She saw the car in the mirror and recognized Fred, and saw too that he had Sandra with him. 'With that girl.'

'Do you think he saw me?'

'I don't know.' Dorothy stood on the pedal and drove the car screaming out into the road. Three other cars swerved to let her into the stream. People were honking at her.

'I can't let him catch me,' she explained. It was really because she didn't want to talk to him, see him, or even think about him at the moment, but as soon as she had spoken, she realized that there was another reason. 'If we stop, they'll see you.'

'I can kill them for you, and it will be all right.'

'No, no, no. It's all right. I just hope the cops aren't out checking.'

Fred's car followed. Every dodge Dorothy made was repeated. She thought: and besides how are we going to get over the border?

'I guess we'll go down by way of the coastline. Then you can swim around to the south and join me.'

All at once the rented car shot forward. They were neck and neck now. She looked unsmiling into Sandra's frightened white face. The girl was crying. Next to her, Fred was bent forward over the wheel. He looked tense and desperate. Even from where Dorothy sat, his eyes looked all taken up by the pupils. Larry was sitting straight up. Both the others must have seen him. Fred began to try to run their car off the road.

Dorothy put her foot down harder. She began to pull away. And now Sandra was fighting Fred for the wheel. Suddenly there was a loud crack. Later on, Dorothy found out that it must have been another car behind theirs, which was trying to pass Fred. Behind Dorothy and Larry the two cars hit, parted, crashed and spun, and Fred's car, with Sandra – so it was said afterwards – twisting the wheel, reared up and out over the centre strip and into the traffic coming the other way. To the wild noises of grinding and tearing metal all around her, Dorothy squealed into a skid, travelled for yards, banged the side tail and bounced to a standstill. In the mirror she caught sight of two cars bursting into flames.

'Keep going,' Larry said.

'I can't. I'm going to have to leave you here. It's dark. And we're not too far from the sea. Do you think you can make it?'

'I don't like it.'

'Neither do I, but that's all there is to it. Remember, we'll meet at the beach. Do you have your sandals with you?'

She kissed him goodbye. Tears rans down her cheeks. He put on his sandals and stepped out of the car, looking both ways. There was no need for caution. Everyone would be looking at the burning wrecks in the road.

Dorothy started the car, drove ahead for a while, looking for a place to turn off, and then realized that she would never be able to get anywhere near Fred's car. That side of the freeway was piling up in a solid mass. Cars were turning off wherever they could, to go in the other direction. If she had stopped to think, she could have kept Larry in the car and driven him back with her. She could even have kept him there at the house. Indefinitely.

Drivers around her were honking their horns at her again. She moved forward, heading for home.

The moment she opened the door the place felt like a house she had never seen before. It didn't seem to belong to her, or ever have been anyone else's home. It was strange to think that living people could ever have spent their lives in it. The look, the silence – it was so different, so unlike the house where she had moved through so many years of her life, that she thought perhaps if she had only just come in from shopping and not from the scene of the accident, she would have known in any case.

She sat down on a chair and waited. She was home a good three hours before the police telephoned.

When she went to identify the body, Estelle was there in the corridor. She looked like a sleepwalker. She said to Dorothy in a tired whisper, 'You've killed me. We kept it from you for years, so you wouldn't be hurt any more. We could have been happy if it hadn't been for you. But you destroy everything around you. Now I'm like you, too. Even my children. That's what you wanted, wasn't it?'

Dorothy shook her head. She said, 'It wasn't me,' and passed on down the hall. She remembered that at one time, she couldn't now recall just when, Estelle had told her that she, Dorothy, didn't understand the nature of desire. And now she didn't want to understand it, or anything else, either. She had stopped feeling pity and sympathy for other people. One betrayal covered another. She was no longer ready to forgive. Only the note Mr Mendoza put through the door moved her.

Suzanne came to the funeral, of course. She brought her husband and children with her. Dorothy phoned up the doctor and made him say that Suzanne and her family would have to stay in a motel, because to have to cope with in-laws at the house would give Dorothy a nervous breakdown. What was more, her doctor seemed to believe it himself. He was very practical too, and left her with a lot of pills, just enough so that it wouldn't kill her if she took them all at once.

She drove to the beach every night. He never came. She

wondered sometimes whether he had seen her begin to drive on back home and thought she had taken the opportunity to get rid of him deliberately. But he couldn't think that, surely not. He would have noticed the traffic. And yet he never came. He couldn't have been captured, or it would have been in the papers and on the news. If he had been hurt or killed, it would be the same. That must mean, then, that there was some reason why he couldn't come. Either he had been hurt in the ocean, perhaps killed, or he was out there, but waiting.

The grave was planted. Dorothy visited it regularly. It was almost her only regular visit. She never saw Estelle, or the Cranstons. Most of the time, she took the telephone off the hook. Her lawyers wrote to her about insurance and inheritance. She looked through the want ads and wrote for interviews. Mr Mendoza went away on his vacation. She ordered the tombstone, and was on nodding acquaintance with an old woman at the cemetery who kept the grave – another new one – next to hers. One day the woman opened up with the story of her husband's life and death.

'Your hubby?' she concluded, pointing to the grave as though it were something she might sell to Dorothy, if pushed. Dorothy nodded. The old woman looked at the place where the headstone would be.

'Some of these long names,' she said, 'it's hard to fit it all in. Mine was Jim. James. What was yours?'

Dorothy hesitated, confused for a moment. 'Fred,' she said, and changed her mind, feeling even more confused. 'Larry,' she added. 'His name was actually Frederick. But I called him Larry.'

'What was it – his heart?'

'Heart, lungs, head, everything. Car crash.'

'Oh, I see,' the woman said, losing interest. 'An accident.'

Dorothy went for two interviews and was told that they would let her know. She wrote a short letter to her parents and told them to stop worrying because it was beginning to make her worry too. She packed up most of Fred's clothes to send to Suzanne, and saved one or two things to give to Mr Mendoza for his cousin in Chicago who ran the shop. She listened to the radio, but there were no special messages now.

She drove in the evenings to the beach. Sometimes by moonlight, and sometimes only by starlight, she stared at the line where the water ran over the sand. He never came. She came out of the car and walked up and down the beach, hour after hour. The water ran over the sand, one wave covering another like the knitting of threads, like the begetting of revenges, betrayals, memories, regrets. And always it made a musical, murmuring sound, a language as definite as speech. But he never came.

I See a Long Journey

Flora had met James when she was going out with his younger brother, Edward. She'd been crazy about Edward, who even then had had a reputation for wildness where girls were concerned. She'd been eighteen, Edward nineteen. James was thirty-one.

She'd liked him straight away. He was easy in talking to her: relaxed and completely open, as if they'd known each other a long time. In fact, in a way she did know him already – not just through Edward, but from her older sister, Elizabeth, who had gone out with him for about two months a few years before. He had had many girlfriends and mistresses, naturally. He was agreeable and amusing, well-known everywhere and well-liked. He was also the most important of the heirs.

When he proposed to her, she thought her decision over carefully. She wasn't in love with him but she couldn't think of any reason why she should turn him down. He'd become such a good friend that she felt they were already related.

After the marriage, Edward changed along with everything else. The barriers came up all around her. Where once, on the outside, she had felt shut out of their exclusive family, now – on the inside – she was debarred from the rest of the world.

There had been a time at the beginning when she had fought. If it hadn't been for the money, she might have succeeded. Their quarrels, misunderstandings and jealousies were like those of other families. And she was like other girls who marry into a group of powerful personalities. She was tugged in different directions by all of them. They expected things of her. They criticized her. They tried to train and educate her. When she was pregnant for the first time, and when she had the child, they told her what she was doing wrong.

But that was the stage at which she found her own strength: she clung to the child and wouldn't let them near it. They had to make concessions. It was the first grandchild and a boy. She was sitting pretty. She could take her mother-in-law up on a point in conversation and make her back down.

Shortly after the birth a lot of pressure was taken off her anyway; Edward formed a liaison with a girl who sang in a nightclub. He was thinking of marrying her, he said. He wanted to introduce her to his parents – her name was Lula. His mother hit the roof about it. She described the girl as 'an unfortunate creature: some sort of half-breed, I believe'. Quarrels exploded over the breakfast table, down in the library, out in the garden. In the kitchen, of course, they were laughing.

She met Lula. Edward took them both out to lunch. Flora wasn't nervous about it: she even tried to put the other woman at her ease by saying that she too had once been an outsider to the family. But Lula wasn't going to accept anyone's sympathy. She put on a performance, talked loudly, looking around at the other people in the restaurant, pinched Edward under the table and went out of her way to throw as many dirty words as possible into every sentence. Then she stood up abruptly, declared that it had been so very, very nice but she had to run along now, tugged Edward by the hair and left.

'She isn't like that,' he said.

'You don't have to tell me. I could see. She'll be all right when we get together next time.'

'She really isn't like that.'

'I know. I told you – I recognize the camouflage. I liked her fine.'

'I think you made her feel unsure.'

'And I'm the easy one. Wait till she meets the others. She'll have her work cut out for her.'

'They gave you a rough time, I guess.'

'It's all right. That's over now.'

'It's mainly Mother.'

'It's the whole deal.'

'But things are OK between you and James?'

'Oh, yes,' she said. 'But we're in the thick of everything. If you and I had married, we could have escaped together.'

'But we didn't love each other,' he said matter-of-factly. It upset her to hear him say it. Someone should love her. Even her children – they needed her, but she was the one who did the loving.

'Besides,' he told her, 'I'm not sure that I want to escape. Even if it were possible. And I don't think it is.'

'It's always possible if you don't have children.'

He said, 'It's the price of having quarterly cheques and dividends, never having to work for it. Think of the way most people live. Working in a factory – could you stand it?'

'Maybe it wouldn't be so bad. If you were with somebody you loved.'

'Love doesn't survive much poverty. Unless you're really right down at the bottom and don't have anything else.'

Was it true? If she and her husband were lost and wandering in the desert, maybe he'd trade her for a horse or a camel, because he could always get another wife and have more children by the new one. It couldn't be true.

'I'm sure it would,' she said.

'From the pinnacle, looking down,' he told her, 'you get that romantic blur. Wouldn't it be nice in a little country cottage with only the birds and the running streams? It's the Marie Antoinette complex.'

And at another time he'd said, 'Love is a luxury for us. If I were on a desert island with the soulmate of all time, I'd still have the feeling that I'd ducked out. I guess it's what they used to call "duty".'

'There are plenty of others to take over the duties,' she told him.

'And they'd all think: *he wasn't up to it*. And they'd be right.'

It took two years for the family to wean Edward away from Lula. Then they set him up with a suitable bride, an Irish heiress named Anna-Louise, whose family was half-German on the mother's side. One of Anna-Louise's greatest assets was that she was a superb horsewoman. Flora liked her. The boys' father, the old man, thought she was wonderful. His wife realized too late that Anna-Louise was a strong character, not to be bullied. Flora was let off the hook. She didn't allow her mother-in-law to take out on her or her children any of the failures and frustrations she had with Anna-Louise. She put her foot down. And eventually her mother-in-law came to her to seek an ally, to complain and to ask for advice. Flora listened and held her peace. She was learning.

James was the one who helped her. He guided her through her mistakes; he was the first person in her life to be able to teach her that mistakes are actually the best method of learning and that it's impossible to learn without at least some of them. He warned her about things she would have to know, strangers she was going to meet. She was grateful. But she also saw that he was part of the network and that all his actions, though well-meant, were aimed at making her just like the rest of them, whether she wanted to be or not.

It always came down to the question of money. The money made the difference. They were one of the richest families on the Eastern seaboard. Flora's own parents were from nice, substantial backgrounds; they'd had their houses and companies and clubs, and belonged to the right places when it had still been worth keeping up with that sort of thing.

She'd known people who knew the cousins, who gave parties at which she would be acceptable – that was how she had met Edward. Everyone knew about them. Everyone recognized their pictures in the papers. To marry into their ranks was like marrying into royalty, and a royalty that never had to worry about its revenues.

Her marriage had also changed her own relatives irrevocably.

It was as though they had lost their thoughts and wishes; they had become hangers-on. They name-dropped with everyone, they could no longer talk about anything except the last time they'd seen James or Edward or – best of all – the old man.

They were all corrupted. One early summer afternoon Flora sat playing cards with James and Edward and her sister, Elizabeth, who had married a cousin of the family and thus, paradoxically, become less close.

Flora thought about the four of them, what they were doing with the time they had. All except for James were still in their twenties and they were like robots attached to a master-computer – they had no ideas, no lives. They were simply parts of a machine.

She wondered whether James and Elizabeth had slept together long ago, before she had become engaged to him, and thought they probably had. An exhaustion came over her: the artificial weariness enforced upon someone who has many capabilities and is consistently prevented from using any of them.

The doctors called it depression. She worked on her tennis, went swimming three times a week, and helped to organize charity fund-raising events. She made progress. Now she was an elegant young matron in magazine pictures, not the messy-haired girl who had run shrieking down the hallway from her mother-in-law's room as she held her squealing baby on one arm and then slammed and locked the door after her. She would never again stay behind a locked door, threatening to cut her throat, to go to the newspapers, to get a divorce. James had stood on the other side of the door and talked to her for five hours until she'd given in.

And now they had their own happy family together and she moved through the round of public and domestic duties as calmly and gracefully as a swan on the water. But the serenity of her face was like the visible after-effect of an illness she had survived; or like a symptom of the death that was to follow.

*

James thought they should take their holiday in a spot more remote than the ones they usually chose in the winter. He was fed up with being hounded by reporters and photographers. And she was nervous about the children all the time. The house had always received a large quantity of anonymous mail and more than the average number of unpleasant telephone cranks. Now they were being persecuted not just because of their wealth, but because it was the fashion. Every day you could read in the papers about 'copy cat' crimes – acts of violence committed in imitation of something the perpetrators had seen on television or in the headlines of the very publication you had in your hand. If there had been a hoax call about a bomb at some large public building, it was fairly certain that the family secretaries would be kept busy with their share of telephone threats in the next few days. Everyone in the house was on speaking terms with at least ten policemen. There had been many crises over the years. They counted on the police, although James's mother, and his sister Margaret's ex-husband too, said they sometimes thought that most of the information these nuts and maniacs found out about them came straight from the police themselves.

Anna-Louise's entry into the family had brought further complications, adding an interest for the Irish connections on all sides. Anna-Louise herself wasn't afraid. She wasn't in any case the sort of woman who worried, but on top of that, her children hadn't been put in danger yet, whereas Margaret's had: her daughter, Amy, was once almost spirited away by a gang of kidnappers. 'Fortunately,' Margaret told friends later, 'they got the cook's niece instead. She was standing out at the side of the back drive, and it just shows how dumb these people are: It was Sunday and she was wearing a little hat, white gloves, a pink organdie dress and Mary Janes. If they'd known anything about Amy, they'd have realized she wouldn't be caught dead in a get-up like that. As a matter of fact, at that time of day on a Sunday, she'd be in her jeans, helping MacDonald in the greenhouses.'

They had paid handsomely to get the niece back; good cooks

weren't easy to find. But they'd cooperated with the police, which they wouldn't have dared to do if Amy herself had been the victim: it would have been too big a risk, even though in that particular case it had worked and they had caught the three men and rescued the girl. Flora later began to think it would have been better for the niece not to have lived through the capture; she started to crack up afterwards and developed a bitter enmity towards Amy, who, she told everybody, ought to have been the one to be seized.

The incident had taken place when Flora was in the beginning months of her second pregnancy. It brought home to her how difficult it was to escape the family destiny: even the children were dragged into it. And though it was only one of the many frightening, uncomfortable or calamitous events from the background of her first few years of marriage, it was the one that turned her into a woman who fretted about the future and who, especially, feared for the safety of her children. James tried to soothe her. On the other hand, his friend and chauffeur, Michael, who kept telling her everything would be all right, seemed at the same time to approve of the fact that she worried. She thought he felt it was a proof that she was a good mother.

'If we go too far away,' she said to James, 'the children – '

'We have telephones and telegraphs, and an airport nearby. It isn't any worse than if we were going to California for the weekend.'

'But it's so far away.'

He asked, 'What could we do, even here, if anything happened?' The question was meant to mollify, but it scared her even more.

'The doctor says you need a rest,' he insisted. She agreed with that. It seemed odd that a woman should live in a house as large as a castle, with nothing to do all day but easy, pleasant tasks, and still need a rest. But it was true.

'Michael will be with us,' he added.

That, finally, convinced her. If Michael came along, nothing bad could happen, either at home or abroad. She was distrustful of even the smallest disruption to her life, but she wanted to go. And she would be relieved to get away from the menace of all the unknown thousands who hated her without even having met her.

You couldn't be free, ever. And if you were rich, you were actually less often free than other people. You were recognized. The spotlight was on you. Strangers sent you accusations, threats and obscene letters. And what had you done to them? Nothing. Even the nice people were falsified by the ideas they had of your life; those who didn't threaten, begged. Everyone wanted money and most of them felt no shame at demanding it outright. They were sure they deserved it, so they had to have it. It didn't matter who gave it to them.

She too had been altered, of course. She had made her compromises and settled down. Of all the people connected with the family only Michael, she felt, had kept his innocence. His loyalty was like the trust of a child. When he drove her into town to shop, when they said hello or goodbye, she thought how wonderful it would be to put her arms around him, to have him put his arms around her. She was touched and delighted by all his qualities, even at the times when she'd seen him thwarted or frustrated and noticed how he went white and red very quickly.

'All right,' she said. 'If Michael comes too.'

'Of course,' James told her. 'I wouldn't be without him. There's a good hotel we can stay at. I don't think you'll need a maid.'

'I don't want a maid. I just want to be able to phone home twice a day to check if everything's all right.'

'Everything's going to be fine. You know, sometimes kids can get sick of their parents. It won't do them any harm to miss us for a week or two.'

'Two?'

'Well, if we don't make it at least two, half the trip's going to be spent in the plane, or recovering from jet-lag.'

*

They had parties to say goodbye: the friends' party, the relatives', and one birthday party for Margaret's youngest child,
which coincided with a garden club meeting. Flora's mother-in-
law directed the gloved and hatted ladies around flowerbeds
that were to be mentioned in the yearly catalogue. Her father-in-
law put in a brief appearance at the far end of the Italian gardens,
shook hands with a few of the women and came back to the
house, where he stayed for quite a while looking with delecta-
tion at the children digging into their ice cream and cake. Flora
smiled at him across the table. She got along well with him, as
did all his daughters-in-law, though Anna-Louise was his
favourite. His own daughters had less of his benevolence,
especially Margaret, whose whole life had been, and was still,
lived in the always unsuccessful effort to gain from him the
admiration he gave so freely to others. That was one of the
family tragedies that Flora could see clearly. No one ever said
anything about it and she'd assumed from the beginning that,
having grown up with it, they'd never noticed. It was simply one
more truth that had become acceptable by being ritualized.

The birthday room was filled with shouts and shrieks. Food
was smeared, thrown and used to make decorations. One boy
had built a palace of cakes and candies on his plate. There were
children of industrialists, oil millionaires, ambassadors, bankers
and heads of state; but they looked just like any other children,
grabbing each other's paper hats while one of them was sick on
the rug.

Michael too was looking on. He was enjoying himself, but he
was there to work. He watched with a professional, noting
glance. If anything went wrong, he was there stop it. His
presence made Flora feel safe and happy. She began to look
forward to the trip.

The next evening, it was the grown-ups' turn to be sick on the
rug. Five of their guests had to stay over for the weekend. On
Monday morning Flora and James left for the airport.

At first she'd wanted to take hundreds of photographs with
her. She'd started looking through the albums and every few

pages taking one or two out; then it was every other page. Finally she had a fistful of pictures, a pile as thick as a doorstop. James chose twelve, shoved the others into a drawer and told her they had to hurry now.

The children waved and smiled, their nurse cried. 'I wish she wouldn't do that,' Flora said in the car. 'Bursting into tears all the time.'

'Just a nervous habit,' he told her. 'It doesn't seem to affect the kids. They're a pretty hard-bitten bunch.' He clasped his hand over hers, over the new ring he had given her the night before. She tried to put everything out of her mind, not to feel apprehensive about the plane flight.

They were at the airport with plenty of time to spare, so he took her arm and led her to the duty-free perfume, which didn't interest her.

'There's a bookstore,' she said.

'All right.'

They browsed through thrillers, war stories, romantic novels and books that claimed to tell people how society was being run and what the statistics about it proved.

They became separated. The first James knew of it was when he heard her laugh coming from the other side of the shop and saw her turn, looking for him. She was holding a large magazine.

'Come look,' she called. The magazine appeared to be some kind of colouring book for children. There was a whole shelf full of the things. After the paper people in the drawings were coloured and cut free, you snipped out the pictures of their clothes and pushed the tabs down over the shoulders of the dolls.

'Aren't they wonderful?' she said. 'Look. This one's called "Great Women Paper Dolls". It's got all kinds of . . . Jane Austen, Lady Murasaki, Pavlova. Look at the one of Beatrix Potter: she's got a puppy in her arms when she's in her fancy dress, but underneath it's a rabbit. And – '

'These are pretty good,' he said. He'd discovered the ones for boys: history, warfare, exploration. 'As a matter of fact, the text to these things is of a very high standard. Too high for a colouring book.'

'Paper doll books.'

'You've got to colour them before you cut them out. But anybody who could understand the information would be too old to want one. You wonder who they're aimed at.'

'At precocious children like ours, of course. They'll think they're hysterical. We can send them these. Paper dolls of Napoleon and Socrates. Look, it says here: if I don't see my favourite great woman, I may find her in the book called "Infamous Women Paper Dolls". Oh James, help me look for that one.'

'Flora,' he said, 'the children are here. We're the ones who are supposed to be going away.'

'Yes, but we can send them right now, from the airport. Aren't they funny? Look. Infamous Women – how gorgeous. Catherine di Medici, Semiramis. And in the other one – here: an extra dress for Madame de Pompadour; the only woman to get two dresses. Isn't that nice? She'd have appreciated that.'

She was winding herself up to the point where at any moment her eyes would fill with tears. He said, 'Who's that one? Looks like she got handed the castor oil instead of the free champagne.'

'Eadburga.'

'Never heard of her.'

'It says she was at her worst around 802. Please, James. We can leave some money with the cashier.'

'Anything to get you out of this place,' he told her.

After they'd installed themselves in their seats and were up in the air, he said, 'What was the difference between the great and the infamous?'

'The great were artists and heroic workers for mankind,' she said. 'The infamous were the ones in a position of power.'

The speed of her reply took him by surprise. He couldn't remember if it might have been true. Florence Nightingale, he recalled, had figured among the greats; Amelia Earhart, too. But there must also have been a ruler of some sort: Elizabeth I, maybe? Surely Queen Victoria had been in the book of good ones. And Eleanor of Aquitaine had been on a page fairly near that. He was still thinking about the question after Flora had already fallen asleep.

*

They arrived in an air-conditioned airport much like any other, were driven away in limousines with smoked-glass windows and were deposited at their hotel, where they took showers and slept. The first thing they did when they woke up was to telephone home. They didn't really look at anything until the next day.

They walked out of the marble-pillared hotel entrance arm in arm and blinked into the sun. They were still turned around in time. Already Flora was thinking about an afternoon nap. They looked to the left and to the right, and then at each other. James smiled and Flora pressed his arm. The trip had been a good idea.

They strolled slowly forward past the large, glittering shops that sold luxury goods. You could have a set of matching jade carvings packed and sent, jewellery designed for you, clothes tailored and completed in hours. James said, 'We can do all that later.' Flora stopped in front of a window display of jade fruit. She said, 'It's probably better to get it over with.'

They stood talking about it: whether they'd leave the presents till later and go enjoy themselves, or whether they ought to get rid of the duties first, so as not to have them hanging over their heads for two weeks. Michael waited a few feet to the side, watching, as usual, without seeming to.

They decided to do the difficult presents first – the ones that demanded no thought but were simply a matter of knowing what to ask for and choosing the best. They handed over credit cards and traveller's cheques for tea sets, bolts of silk material, dressing gowns, inlaid boxes, vases, bowls and bronze statuettes. By lunchtime they were worn out.

They went back to the hotel to eat. Light came into the high-ceilinged dining-room through blinds, shutters, curtains and screens. It was as if they were being shielded from an outside fire – having all the heat blocked out, while some of the light was admitted. About twenty other tables were occupied. Michael sat on his own, though if they had had their meal anywhere in town, he'd have eaten with them.

James looked around and smiled again. 'This is very pleasant,' he said. He beamed at her and added, 'I think the holiday is already doing its job. You're looking extremely well after all your shopping. Filled with a sense of achievement.'

'Yes, I'm OK now. Earlier this morning I was feeling a lot like Eadburga.'

'How's that?'

'At her worst around 8.15, or whenever it was.'

He laughed. It had taken her years to say things that made him laugh and she still didn't know what sort of remark was going to appeal to him. Sometimes he'd laugh for what seemed to be no reason at all, simply because he was in the mood.

They went up to their rooms for a rest. She closed her eyes and couldn't sleep. He got up, shuffled through the magazines and newspapers he'd already read, and said he couldn't sleep, either. They spent the afternoon making love, instead.

'Dress for dinner tonight?' she asked as she arranged her clothes in the wardrobe.

'Let's go someplace simple. I've had enough of the well-tempered cuisine. Why don't we just slouch around and walk in somewhere?'

'You wouldn't rather get the ptomaine at the end of the trip rather than straight away?'

'Well, we've got lists of doctors and hospitals a mile long. We could get a shot for it.'

'Will Michael be coming with us?'

'Of course,' he said.

'Then I guess it's safe enough.'

'In a pinch, I could probably protect you, too.'

'But you might get your suit creased.' She made a funny face at him.

'I love vacations,' he told her. 'You're definitely at your best.'

'I told you: I'm fine now.'

'They say most of the jet-lag hangover is caused by dehydration, but the big difference I've noticed this time is the change in light.'

'Well, it's nice to be away for a while. There'll be at least three new quarrels going by the time we get back, and they'll be missing us a lot.'

'We might take more time off sometime. A long trip. A year or so.'

'Oh, Jamie, all the sweat. I couldn't do it so soon again, setting up a whole new household and uprooting the children from all their friends.'

'I didn't mean I'd be working. I meant just you and me away from everybody in a lovely spot, somewhere like Tahiti. New Caledonia, maybe.'

She said again, 'Would Michael come too?'

'I don't know. I hadn't thought.'

She pulled a dress out of the hanger and decided that it wasn't too wrinkled to wear without having the hotel maid iron it.

'I guess he'd have to,' James said.

'He wouldn't mind?'

'Kelvin? He never minds anything. He'd love to.'

She'd have to think. If it had been Michael asking her to go away with him to the South Seas, she'd have gone like a shot. But the more dissatisfied she'd become with her life, the more reluctant she was to make any changes.

She said, 'Well, it's something to think over. When would you want to make a decision about it?'

'Three weeks, about then.'

'All right. We'll have to talk about the children. That's the main thing.'

She was still worrying about the children as they started towards the steps that led to the elevators. There was an entire puzzle-set of interlocking staircases carpeted in pale green and accompanied by carved white banisters that made the whole arrangement look like flights of ornamental balconies. If you wanted to, you could continue on down by the stairs. James always preferred to ride in elevators rather than walk. Exercise, in his opinion, was what sport was for; it wasn't meant to move you from one place to another. Locomotion should be carried out with the aid of machines and servants.

'Let me just call home again quick,' she suggested.

'You'll wake them all up. It's the wrong time there.'

'Are you sure? I'm so mixed up myself, I can't tell.'

'We'll phone when we get back from supper,' he said.

They had been on other trips together long ago, when the telephoning had become a genuine obsession. Now they had a routine for it: she mentioned it, he told her when, she believed him and agreed to abide by the times he designated. The whole game was a leftover from the unhappy years when she'd had no self-confidence and felt that she kept doing everything wrong.

Michael stepped into the elevator after them. He moved behind them as they walked through the lobby.

'Look,' Flora said.

The central fountain, which earlier in the day had been confined to three low jets, now sprayed chandelier-like cascades of brilliance into the three pools beneath. Tables and chairs had been set out around the display and five couples from the hotel were being served tea. As Flora and James watched, a group of children rushed for a table, climbed into the chairs and began to investigate the spoons and napkins. A uniformed nurse followed them.

James said, 'Like some tea?'

'Unless Michael doesn't – '

'Sure,' Michael said. 'I'll sit right over there.' He headed towards the sofas and armchairs near the reception desk. Wherever they were, he always knew where to find the best spots for surveillance, and probably had a good idea where everybody else might choose to be, too. He'd been trained for all that. You couldn't see from his walk or from the way his clothes fitted that he carried guns and a knife, but he did. Sometimes it seemed incredible to Flora that he had been through scenes of violence; he'd been in the marines for two years while James was finishing up college. His placid, law-abiding face gave no sign of the fact. But she thought how upsetting the experience must have been to him at first. Even killing didn't come naturally – especially killing: somebody had to teach it to you. And boys weren't really cruel or bloodthirsty unless they had a background of brutality.

Michael's background, she knew, was quite ordinary. He was a child of an undergardener and one of the parlourmaids at the house. Once she'd asked him how he'd managed to get through his military training and he'd told her that he'd been lucky: he'd been with a group of boys who'd become really good friends. And, as for violence, he'd added, 'You got to be objective, say to yourself this is completely a professional thing. Like render unto Caesar. You know?' She had nodded and said yes, but had had no idea what he'd been talking about.

They sat close to the fountain to enjoy it but not so near as to be swept by the fine spray that clouded its outpourings. James had also taken care to station himself, and her, at a reasonable distance from the children, who looked like more than a match for their wardress.

Their nearest companions were a man and woman who might have been on a business trip or celebrating an early retirement. They gave the impression of being a couple who had been married for a long time. The woman looked older than the man. She had taken two extra chairs to hold her shopping bags and as soon as the tea was poured out she began to rummage through her papers and packages. She looked up and caught Flora's eye. Flora smiled. The woman said, 'I couldn't resist. It's all so pretty and the prices are just peanuts. Aren't they, Desmond?'

The man's eyes flicked to the side. 'We're going to need an extra plane to take it all back,' he said. His head turned to the stairway and the main door, warily, as if looking for eavesdroppers.

'Not here,' his wife told him.

'Only damn part of this hotel they let you smoke a pipe is in your own room. Place must be run by the anti-tobacco league.'

'Do you good,' his wife said. She began to talk about silks and jade and porcelain. Flora guessed before the woman started to quote numbers that they were going to be several price-brackets under anything she and James would have bought. On the other hand, like most rich people, she loved hunting down bargains.

The couple, whose name was Dixon, went on to tell their opinions of the city and of the country in general. They regretted, they said, not having made provision for trips outside town to – for example – the big flower festival that had been held the week before, or just the ordinary market mornings. They were leaving the next day. Flora saw James relax as he heard them say it: there wasn't going to be any danger of involvement. He began to take an interest in the list of places and shops they recommended. Flora was halfway through her second cup of tea and could tell that James would want to leave soon, when Mrs Dixon said, 'What I regret most of all, of course, is that we never got to see the goddess.'

'Oh,' Flora said. 'At the festival?'

'At her temple.'

'A statue?'

'No, no. That girl. You know – the one they train from childhood, like the Lama in Tibet.'

'Not like that,' her husband said.

'Well, I just couldn't face standing in line for all that time in the heat. But now I really wish I'd given myself more of a push.'

'I haven't heard about the goddess,' Flora admitted. James said that he'd read about it somewhere, he thought, but only remembered vaguely. And he hadn't realized that the custom had to do with this part of the world.

'Oh, yes,' Mr Dixon told him, and launched into the history of the goddess, who was selected every few years from among thousands of candidates. The child was usually four or five years old when chosen, had to be beautiful, to possess several distinct aesthetic features such as the shape of the eyes and ears and the overall proportion of the limbs, and could have no blemish. 'Which is quite an unusual thing to be able to find,' he said. 'Then –'

'Then,' Mrs Dixon interrupted, 'they train her in all the religious stuff and they also teach her how to move – sort of like those temple dancers, you know: there's a special way of sitting down and getting up, and holding out your fingers, and so on. And it all means something. Something religious. There are very strict rules she's got to obey about everything – what she can eat and drink, all that. Oh, and she should never bleed. If she cuts herself – I forget whether she has to quit or not.'

'She just has to lie low for a few days, I think,' Mr Dixon said.

'And she can never cry – did I say that?'

'And never show fear.'

'Then at puberty –'

'She's out on her can and that's the whole ball game. They go and choose another one.'

'So people just drive out to her temple to look at her,' Flora asked, 'as if she's another tourist attraction?'

'Oh no, dear,' Mrs Dixon said. 'They consult her. They take their troubles to her and she gives them the solution. It's like an oracle. And I think you donate some small amount for the upkeep of the temple. They don't mind tourists, but it isn't a show – it's a real religious event.'

Mr Dixon said, 'She's very cultivated, so it seems. Speaks different languages and everything.'

James asked, 'What happens to her afterwards?'

'Oh, that's the joke. She used to spend the rest of her life in seclusion as the ex-goddess. But this last time, the girl took up with a young fellow, and now she's married to him and –'

' – and there's the most terrific scandal,' Mrs Dixon said happily. 'It's really turned things upside-down. I guess it's like a priest getting married to a movie star. They can't get over it.'

'Matter of fact, I wouldn't want to be in that girl's shoes.'

'Why?' Flora asked.

Mr Dixon shrugged. 'A lot of people are mad as hell. They've been led to expect one thing and now this other thing is sprung on them. They're used to thinking of their goddess as completely pure, and also truly sacred. I guess it can't look right for her to revert to being human all of a sudden, just like the rest of us. See what I mean?'

Flora nodded.

'She's broken the conventions,' James said, which didn't seem to Flora nearly such a good explanation as Mr Dixon's, but she smiled and nodded again.

*

They took a long time deciding where they wanted to eat their evening meal. In the beginning it was too much fun looking around to want to go inside; they had discovered the night life of the streets, full of people going about ordinary business that might have taken place indoors during the daytime: there were open-air barber shops, dress stalls where customers could choose their materials and be measured for clothes; shops that stocked real flowers and also stands that sold bouquets made out of feathers and silk.

'No wonder Mrs Dixon had all those piles of packages,' Flora said. 'Everything looks so nice.'

'Under this light,' James warned. 'I bet it's pretty tacky in daylight.'

Michael grunted his assent.

'Don't you think it's fun?' she asked.

'Very colourful,' he said. She wasn't disappointed in his answer. It gave her pleasure just to be walking beside him.

She would have liked to eat in one of the restaurants that were no more than just a few tables and chairs stuck out on the sidewalk. James vetoed the suggestion. They moved back to the beginning of richer neighbourhoods and he suddenly said, 'That one.'

In front of them was a building that looked like a joke: dragons and pagodas sprouting everywhere from its roof-tops. The lower floor was plate glass, which reassured the three of them – that looked modern and therefore unromantic and probably, they expected, hygienic. 'We can rough it for once,' James said. Through the downstairs windows they could see rows of crowded booths, people sitting and eating. Most of the patrons appeared to be tourists – another good sign.

They entered and were seated all on the same side of a table. Flora had hoped to be put between the two men, but the waiter had positioned Michael at James's far side. Opposite her an old man was eating noodles from a bowl. He stared determinedly downward.

They looked at the menu. As James ordered for them, a young couple came up and were shown to the remaining places; he had a short beard and wore a necklace consisting of a single wooden bead strung on a leather thong; she had a long pigtail down her back. They were both dressed in T-shirts and bluejeans and carried gigantic orange back-packs. They made a big production of taking off the packs and resting them against the outside of the booth. When the old man on the inside had finished eating and wanted to get out, they had to go through the whole routine again. Once they were settled, they stared across the table contemptuously at the fine clothes the others were wearing. They seemed to be especially incredulous over James's outfit, one which he himself would have considered a fairly ordinary linen casual suit for the tropics.

James switched from English to French and began to tell Flora about New Caledonia. It meant that Michael was excluded from the conversation, but he knew that this was one of James's favourite methods of detaching himself from company he didn't want to be associated with. It only worked in French because Flora's limited mastery of other languages wouldn't permit anything else. James had always been good at learning new languages. As a child he had even made up a language that he and Michael could use to baffle grown-up listeners. Occasionally they spoke it even now. Flora had figured out that it must be some variation of arpy-darpy talk, but it always went so fast that she could never catch anything.

The back-packers spoke English. He was American, she Australian. Their names were Joe and Irma. They spent their whole time at the table discussing the relative merits of two similar articles they had seen in different shops. Some part of the objects had been made out of snakeskin and, according to Irma, one of them was 'pretty ratty-looking'; on the other one, so Joe claimed, the so-called snake had been an obvious fake, definitely plastic.

'It's like those beads you got,' he said. 'Supposed to be ivory, and you can see the join where they poured it into the mould in two halves and then stuck them together. Why can't you tell? How can you miss seeing it? If you keep on spending money like this – '

Irma muttered, 'Well, it's my money.'

'We should be keeping some by for emergencies,' he said. She sulked for the rest of the meal. She chewed her food slowly and methodically. Flora wished the girl had picked everything up, thrown it all over her companion and told him to go to hell. He was staring around with disapproving interest at the other diners. He wasn't going to feel guilty about hurting his girl-friend; he hadn't even noticed her play for sympathy.

Flora said in French, 'Could you really go for a year without work?'

'Sure. I'd work on something else,' James said. 'We'd get a nice boat, sail around.' He added, 'The food isn't too bad here.'

'Wait till tomorrow to say it,' she told him.

*

The weather next morning looked like being the start of another wonderful day. All the days were wonderful in that climate at the right time of year. They both felt fine. Michael too said he was OK. Flora called home.

She got Margaret on the line, who said, 'We've missed you. Anna-Louise is on the warpath again.'

'What about?'

Anna-Louise's voice came in on an extension, saying, 'That isn't Margaret getting her story in first, is it? Flora?'

'Hi,' Flora said. 'How are you all?'

'The natives are restless, as usual.'

Margaret tried to chip in but was told by Anna-Louise to get off the line. There was a click.

'Children all right?' Flora asked.

'Couldn't be better.'

'Are they there?' She waved James over. They spent nearly fifteen minutes talking to the children, who said again how much they loved the paper doll books and how all their friends thought they were great and wanted some too. James began to look bored and to make motions that the conversation should stop. He leaned over Flora. 'We've got to hang up now,' he said into the mouthpiece.

They were the second couple into the breakfast room. 'Are we that early?' she asked.

He checked his watch. 'Only a little. It's surprising how many people use their holidays for sleeping.'

'I guess a lot of them have jet-lag, too. That's the trouble with beautiful places – they're all so far away.'

He spread out the maps as Michael was seated alone at a table for two several yards beyond them. Flora had them both in view, Michael and James. She felt her face beginning to smile. At that moment she couldn't imagine herself returning from the trip. The children and relatives could stay at the other end of the telephone.

James twitched the map into place. He liked planning things out and was good at it. She, on the other hand, couldn't even fold a map back up the right way. She was better at the shopping. Now that they were used to their routines, they had a better time sightseeing. In the early days James had spent even more time phoning his broker than Flora had in worrying about the babies.

She remembered the young couple at dinner the night before, and how much they had seemed to dislike each other. Of course, it was hard to tell anything about people who were quarrelling; still, they didn't seem to have acquired any of the manners and formulae and pleasing deceptions that helped to keep lovers friendly over long periods. She herself had come to believe that – if it weren't for this other glimpse of a love that would be for ever unfulfilled – she'd have been content with just those diplomatic gestures, plus a shared affection for what had become familiar. If she had been free to choose at this age, her life would have been different. Everybody was free now; and they all lived together before they got married.

James put a pencil mark on the map and started to draw a line across two streets.

Maybe, she thought, she'd been free even then. The freedom, or lack of it, was simply ceremonial. Rules and customs kept you from disorder and insecurity, but they also regulated your life to an extent that was sometimes intolerable. They protected and trapped at the same time. If it weren't for habit and codes of behaviour, she and Michael could have married and had a happy life together.

It had taken her years to find out that most of her troubles had been caused by trying to switch from one set of conventions to another. The people around her – even the ones who had at first seemed to be against her – had actually been all right.

She said, 'You know what I'd really like to do? I'd like to see that girl.'

'Hm?'

'The one the Dixons were talking about at tea. The goddess.'

'Oh.' James looked up. 'Well, maybe. But don't you think the idea is going to be a lot better than the reality? Following it up is just going to mean what they said: standing in line for hours. Do you want to spend your vacation doing that?'

'And if you don't, regretting that you never did. I would like to. Really. You don't have to come, if you don't want to.'

'Of course I'd come, if you went.'

'Could you find out about it? It's the thing I want to do most.'

'Why?'

'Why? Are there goddesses at home?'

He laughed, and said, 'Only in the museums. And in the bedroom, if you believe the nightgown ads.'

'Please.'

'OK,' he promised. 'I'll find out about it. But it seems to me, the one worth looking at is going to be the one that went AWOL and got married.'

'She didn't go AWOL. She was retired.'

'A retired goddess? No such thing. Once a god, always a god.'

'If you become impure as soon as you bleed, then you can lose the divinity. Women –'

'All right, I'll find out about it today. Right now. This very minute.'

'I'm only trying to explain it.'

'Wasted on me,' he told her.

'Don't you think it's interesting?'

'Mm.'

'What does that mean?'

'I'll see about it this afternoon.'

Over the next few days they went to the botanical gardens; to the theatre, where they saw a long, beautiful and rather dull puppet play; and to a nightclub, at which Flora developed a headache from the smoke and James said he was pretty sure the star *chanteuse* was a man. They got dressed up in their evening clothes to visit the best restaurant in town, attended a dinner given by a friend of the family who used to be with the City Bank in the old days, and made an excursion to the boat market. Half the shops there were hardly more than floating bamboo frameworks with carpets stretched across them. Bright pink orchid-like flowers decorated all the archways and thresholds, on land and on the water. The flowers looked voluptuous but unreal, and were scentless; they added to the theatrical effect – the whole market was like a view backstage. James and Flora loved it. Michael said it was too crowded and the entire place was a fire-trap.

'Well, there's a lot of water near at hand,' James said.

'You'd never make it. One push and the whole mob's going to be everybody on top of theirselves. They'd all drown together.'

'I do love it when you get on to the subject of safety, Kelvin. It always makes me feel so privileged to be alive.'

A privilege granted to many, Flora thought, as she gazed into the throng of shoving, babbling strangers. She suddenly felt that she had to sit down.

She turned to James. 'I feel – ' she began.

He saw straight away what was wrong. He put his arm around her and started to push through the crowd. Michael took the other side. She knew that if she really collapsed, Michael could pick her up and sling her over his shoulder like a sack of flour, he was so strong. He'd had to do it once when she'd fainted at a ladies' fund-raising luncheon. That had been a hot day too, lunch with wine under a blue canvas awning outdoors; but she'd been pregnant then. There was no reason now for her to faint, except the crowd and the lack of oxygen.

There wasn't any place to sit down. She tried to slump against Michael. They moved her forward.

'Here,' James said.

She sat on something that turned out to be a tea chest. They were in another part of the main arcade, in a section that sold all kinds of boxes and trunks. A man came up to James, wanting to know if he was going to buy the chest.

Back at the hotel, they laughed about it. James had had to shell out for a sandalwood casket in order to give her time to recover. When they were alone, he asked if she was really all right, or could it be that they'd been overdoing it in the afternoons? She told him not to be silly: she was fine.

'I think maybe we should cancel the trip to the goddess, though, don't you?'

'No, James. I'm completely OK.'

'Waiting out in the sun – '

'We'll see about that when we get there,' she said flatly. It was a tone she very seldom used.

'OK, it's your vacation. I guess we could always carry you in on a stretcher and say you were a pilgrim.'

He arranged everything for the trip to the temple. The day he chose was near the end of their stay, but not so close to the flight that they couldn't make another date if something went wrong. One of them might come down with a twenty-four-hour bug or there might be a freak rainstorm that would flood the roads. 'Or,' James said, 'if she scratches herself with a pin, we've had it till she heals up. They might even have to choose a new girl.'

In the meantime they went to look at something called 'the jade pavilion' – a room in an abandoned palace, where the silk walls had been screened by a lattice-work fence of carved jade flowers. The stone had been sheared and sliced and ground to such a fineness that in some places it appeared as thin as paper. The colours were vibrant and glowing – not with the freshness of real flowers nor the sparkle of faceted jewels, but with the lustre of fruits; the shine that came off the surfaces was almost wet-looking.

As they walked under the central trellis a woman behind them said, 'Think of having to dust this place.' A man's voice answered her, saying, 'Plenty of slave labour here. Nobody worries about dust.'

'Glorious,' James said afterwards. And Michael declared that, 'You had to hand it to them.' He'd been impressed by the amount of planning that must have gone into the work: the measuring and matching, the exactitude.

Flora had liked the silk walls behind, which were covered with pictures of flying birds. She said, 'I guess you're supposed to think to yourself that you're in a garden, looking out. But it's a little too ornate for me. It's like those rooms we saw in Palermo, where the whole place was gold and enamel – like being inside a jewel box. This one would have been even nicer made out of wood and then painted. Don't you think?'

'That would fade,' James said. 'You'd have to re-do it all the time. And in this climate you'd probably need to replace sections of it every few years.'

They kept calling home every day. The weather there was horrible, everyone said. Anna-Louise had a long story about friends of hers whose house had been burgled. And one of the children had a sore throat; he coughed dramatically into the receiver to show how bad it was.

'They need us,' Flora said. 'That was a cry of despair.'

'That was the standard performance,' James told her. 'There's one who hasn't inherited any bashfulness. He'd cough his heart out in front of fifty reporters every day and do retakes if he thought it hadn't been a really thorough job. No hired substitute for him. It's going to be a question of how hard we'll have to sit on him to keep him down. Worse than Teddy was at that age.'

'He sounded pretty bad.'

'You're the one we're going to worry about at the moment. One at a time. Feeling faint? Claustrophobic?'

Flora shook her head. She felt fine. They strolled around town together and sat in a public park for a while. They'd chosen a bench within the shade of a widely branched, symmetrical tree. Michael rested against the stonework of a gate some distance away. While he kept them in sight, he watched the people who passed by. James pointed out a pair of tourists coming through the entrance.

'Where?' Flora asked.

'Right by the gate. It's those two from the restaurant we went to our first night out.'

'Irma and Joe,' she said. 'So it is. And they're still arguing. Look.'

The couple had come to a stop inside the gates. Joe leaned forward and made sweeping gestures with his arms. Irma held herself in a crouching posture of defence: knees bent, shoulders hunched, chin forward. Her fists were balled up against her collar-bone. The two faced each other still encumbered by their back-packs and bearing a comical resemblance to armoured warriors or wrestlers costumed in heavy padding.

James said, 'She's just spent all her money and he's bawling her out.'

'You give it to him, Irma,' Flora said. James squeezed her hand.

They stayed on their bench and watched a large group of uniformed schoolchildren who – under the supervision of their teachers – went through what seemed to be the usual class exercises and then began to play some game neither Flora nor James could understand. Two of the children passed a book through the group while the others counted, telling off certain players to skip in a circle around the rest. They they all sang a rhyming verse and formed up in a new order.

At last he said, 'OK?' and stood up. She got to her feet. In the distance Michael too stepped forward.

They were three streets from where the hired car was parked, when Flora caught sight of a yellow bowl in a store window. She slowed down and, briefly, paused to look. James and Michael moved on a few paces. She turned back, to ask James what he thought about the bowl, and a hand closed gently over her arm just above the wrist. She looked up into a face she'd never seen before. For a moment she didn't realize anything. Then the hand tightened. At the same time, someone else grabbed her from behind. She dropped her handbag. Gasping and mewing sounds came from her throat, but she couldn't make any louder noise. She tried to kick, but that was all she could do.

Michael and James were with her almost immediately, hitting and kicking. Michael actually threw one of the gang into the air. Flora felt herself released. She fell to her knees, with her head against the glass of the window.

'Here,' James said, 'hold on to that.' He thrust her handbag into her arms and pulled her back up. She still couldn't speak.

They hurried her to the car and drove back to the hotel. Michael came up to the room with them and sat on the edge of the bed. James said he was calling in a doctor.

'I'm all right,' she jabbered, 'all right, perfectly – I'm fine. I'm just so mad. I'm so mad I could chew bricks. The nerve of those people!' She was shaking.

Michael stood up and got her a glass of water. She drank all of it and put her head down on the bed.

'That's a good idea,' James said. He and Michael left her and went into the sitting room. She could hear them talking. Michael said, 'The cops?' and James said, 'Tied up with police on vacation. Besides, what good?'

'No hope,' Michael answered. 'Anyway, weren't after money.'

'Bag.'

'No, arm. And left it. Her, not the. Alley right next. A few more seconds.'

'Jesus Christ,' James said. 'That means.'

Michael's voice said, 'Maybe not,' and Flora began to relax. She slept for a few minutes. She was on a beach in New Caledonia and Michael was sitting beside her on the sand. There was a barrel-vaulted roof of palm leaves overhead, like the canopy of a four-poster bed. She could hear the sound of the sea. And then suddenly someone stepped up in back of her and her arms were grabbed from behind.

She woke up. She almost felt the touch still, although it had been in her dream. She stared ahead at the chairs by the bed, the green-and-yellow pattern of the material they were upholstered in, the white net curtains over the windows where the light was beginning to dim away. She thought about the real event, earlier in the afternoon, and remembered again – as if it had left a mark on her body – the moment when the hand had closed over her arm. Once more she was filled with outrage and fury. *The nerve*, she thought; *the nerve*. And the terrible feeling of having been made powerless, of being held, pinioned, captured by people who had no right to touch her. That laying of the hand on her had been like the striking of a predator, and just as impersonal. When she thought about it, it seemed to her that she was picturing all the men as much bigger and stronger than they probably were, and perhaps older, too. They might have been only teenagers.

She wanted to forget about it. It was over. And James was

right: it would ruin what was left of their trip to spend it making out reports in a police station. What could the police do? These gangs of muggers hit you, disappeared around a corner and that was the end of the trail. Once in Tokyo she and James had seen a man on the opposite sidewalk robbed by two boys. His hands had suddenly gone up in the air; and there was the pistol right in broad daylight, pointing into his chest. It could happen so fast. It was the kind of street crime she had come on the holiday in order to forget.

But you had to be prepared. These things were international. And timeless. All the cruelties came back: torture, piracy, massacres. The good things didn't return so often because it took too long to develop them. And it took a whole system of convention and ritual to keep them working; wheels within wheels. She was part of it. To keep the ordered world safe, you had to budget for natural deterioration and the cost of replacement. Nothing had a very high survival rate – not even jade, hard as it was.

She thought about the pavilion of jade flowers and wondered whether it was really so beautiful. Maybe in any case it was only as good as the people who liked it believed it to be. James had loved it. Michael hadn't seemed to like it except for the evidence of the work that had been put into it. He might have disapproved of the extravagance rather than been judging the place on aesthetic grounds. She felt herself falling asleep again.

When she woke it was growing dark. She got up, took a shower and changed. The three of them ate together in the hotel dining-room, drank a great deal, had coffee and then even more to drink afterwards. They talked about law and order and decent values and Flora was tight enough to say, 'We can afford to.' They agreed not to mention the incident to anyone at home until the trip was over.

James had a hangover the next day but read through all his newspapers as usual.

Any mention of our little drama?' she asked.

'Of course not. We didn't report it. A few other muggings here, it says.'

'Maybe they're the same ones.'

'Nope. They'd have gone for the bag and left you. These are all cases of grab-and-run.'

'You mean, they wanted to kidnap me; get you to pay ransom. So, they must know all about us, who we are, what you can raise at short notice.'

'Maybe they check up on everybody staying at big hotels. Maybe they saw your rings. Or it might just be that they know a good-looking woman when they see one: probably thought they could sell you to somebody.'

'What?'

'Sure. Hey, look what else. It says here, the ex-goddess was stoned outside her house yesterday morning.'

'Yesterday morning we were pretty stoned, too. Or was that this morning?'

'A mob threw stones at her. They were some kind of religious group.'

'That's disgusting. That's even worse than trying to kidnap people.'

'She's all right, but she's in the hospital. That ought to mean she's OK. It only takes one stone to kill somebody.'

'Disgusting,' Flora muttered.

'And interesting,' James said. 'In a lot of countries it's still the traditional punishment for adultery.'

*

Their hired car drove them down the coastline. They took a picnic lunch, went for a swim and visited two shrines that, according to their guidebooks, were famous. On the next day they spent the morning trying to find material for curtains to go in a house belonging to Elizabeth's mother-in-law. Michael kept close to Flora all the time; their clothes often brushed as they walked or stood side by side.

On the day of their visit to the goddess it looked for the first time during the trip as if it might rain. James went back up to their rooms and got the umbrellas. On the ride out into the country they heard a few rumblings of thunder, but after that the skies began to clear and the day turned hot and muggy. The umbrellas sat in the car while they entered the temple precincts.

They were checked at the main gate, which looked more like the entrance to a fortress than to a religious building. Flora saw James stiffen as he caught sight of the long row of invalids sitting or lying on their sides, their relatives squatting near them on the ground. She remembered his joke about pilgrims. It wasn't so funny to see the real thing. He never liked being in places where there might be diseases. Most of their travelling had been carefully packaged and sanitized to avoid coming into contact with contagion or even the grosser aspects of simple poverty. You could have all the shots you liked, and it wouldn't help against the wrong virus. She knew that he'd be telling himself again about the number and quality of the hospitals in town.

The officials looked at their papers, spoke to the driver and interpreter, and let them in. The pilgrims stayed outside on the ground. Flora wondered how long they'd have to wait, and how important it was to pay over money before you were granted an interview; or maybe the goddess did a kind of group blessing from a distance. If she wasn't even allowed to bleed, she might not be any more eager than James to get close to the diseased masses. Even when inside the courtyard you could hear a couple of them from over the wall, coughing their lungs out. The smell of decay that hung around the place might have been coming from the same source.

They were escorted across a vast, open space, through an archway, into another courtyard, across that, and to a third. The long-robed official then led them up on to the porch of one of the side buildings, around the verandah and into an assembly hall. It felt dark and cool after the walk in the open. About seventy people waited inside, some sitting on the floor and others – mainly Western tourists – either on the built-in wood bench that ran around three of the walls, or on fold-up seats they'd brought with them. There were also low stools you could borrow or rent from the temple.

The official swept forward towards a door at the far end of the hall. Two more robed figures stood on guard by it. Flora's glance flickered lightly over the other people as she passed. There weren't many children there, except for very small babies that had had to be taken along so the mother could feed them. Most of the believers or curiosity-seekers were grown up and a good proportion of them quite old. A lot of them were also talking, the deaf ones talking loudly. Perhaps the fact that one figure was on its own, not turned to anyone else, was what made Flora notice: there, sitting almost in the middle of the dark wooden floor, was Irma, resting her spine against her back-pack. Joe wasn't with her. And she looked defeated, bedraggled, lost. Maybe she'd come not because this was a tourist attraction, but because she needed advice. She still looked to Flora like the complete guru-chaser – one of those girls who went wandering around looking for somebody to tell them the meaning of life. Yet she also looked desperate in another way, which Flora thought might not have anything to do with religion or philosophy or breaking up with a boyfriend, and might simply be financial. She was so struck by the girl's attitude that she almost forgot about the goddess.

They were rushed onward. The sentries opened the double doors for them and they went through like an awaited procession, entering and leaving three more hallways, all empty and each quieter than the last, until they reached a room like a schoolroom full of benches, and were asked to sit down. Their officials stepped forward to speak with two middle-aged priestesses who had come out of the chamber beyond – perhaps the place where the goddess was actually sitting. The idea suddenly gave Flora the creeps. It was like visiting a tomb.

She whispered to James, 'Did you see Irma out there?'

'Yes.'

'I'm glad she's split up with him, but she looks terrible. I think she must be broke.'

'Probably.'

'I'd like to give her something.'

'No.'

'Not much, just – '

It would mean so little to them, Flora thought, and so much to the girl. It would be even better to be able to tell her she'd done the right thing in leaving that boy and could choose a different man now if she wanted to, and this time find one who'd really love her.

James said, 'You've got to let people lead their own lives.'

Of course, it was assuming a lot. Irma might not have broken up with Joe at all. They might be meeting again in the evening after seeing the sights separately. Even so, it was certainly true that she had run out of money. There had to be some way of helping her out, but Flora couldn't think of one. Could she just hand over some cash and say, 'Did you drop this?' Maybe she could say, 'We were in the restaurant that night and you must have left this behind, it was lying in the corner of the seat and we've been looking for you ever since.'

'She'll fall on her feet,' James told her.

'For heaven's sake. It looks like she's fallen on her head. Can't we do something?'

'I don't think so. And I don't think we should. But if you still feel the same after we get through with this, we'll see. You'll have to figure out how to work it. And don't invite her back in the car.'

Flora stared upward, thinking. She saw for the first time that the ceiling beams were carved at regular intervals with formal designs and they were painted in colours so bright that they looked like enamelwork. She'd been right; that kind of thing was much more interesting than the jade pavilion. She thought: *I'll just put some bills into an envelope and use the story about finding it in the restaurant.* It was a shame when people ignored their good intentions because it was too difficult or too embarrassing to carry them out. She usually kept a few envelopes in her pocketbook.

The interpreter came back to their bench. 'Who is the seeker of truth?' he asked.

Flora looked blank. James said, 'What?'

'Is it you both two or three ask the goddess, or how many?'

'Just one,' James said. 'My wife.'

The man withdrew again. He spoke to the priestesses. One of them clapped her hands, the other went into the next room. The robed official spoke.

'Arise, if you please,' the interpreter told them. Michael moved from his bench to stand behind James. The three of them stepped forward until the official put up his hand against them.

The priestess came out again, leading a procession of eight women like herself. They walked two by two. In the middle of the line, after the first four and in front of the next four they'd kept a free space, in which trotted a midget-like, pink-clad figure: the goddess herself.

She was like a ceremonial doll only taken out on special occasions. Her robes reached to the floor. On her head she wore an elaborate triple-tiered crown of pearls and rubies and some sparkling greyish glass studs that were probably old diamonds. Long, wide earrings dangled from her ears and continued the framing lines of the ornamentation above, so that the still eyes seemed to float among the shimmering lights of crown, earrings, side panels and many-stranded necklaces.

All dressed up, just like a little lady, Flora thought; *what a dreadful thing to do to that child.* And yet the face that gazed out of all its glittering trappings was not exactly that of a child: enormous, dark eyes; serenely smiling mouth; the lovely bone-structure and the refinement of the features were like those of a miniature woman, not a child. Above all, the look of utter calmness and wisdom were strange to see. The girl could have been some-where between seven and eight years old, although she was about the size of an American child of five.

The procession stopped. The official beckoned to Flora. She came up to where he pointed. The child, who hadn't looked at anything particular in the room, turned to her with pleased recognition, like a mother greeting a daughter.

Flora bowed and smiled back, slightly flustered but tingling with gratification. *This is weird*, she thought. *This is ridiculous*. But as the procession wheeled around, heading back into the room it had come from and gathering her along with it, she knew she would follow wherever they went and for however long they wanted her to keep going. She was actually close to tears.

The room was not a room, only another corridor. They had to walk down several turnings until they emerged at a courtyard of fruit trees. They entered the audience chamber from the far side.

The goddess seated herself on a wooden throne raised on steps. Like the rafters in this room too, the throne was carved and painted. She sat on a cushion of some ordinary material like burlap, which made her robes appear even more luxurious by contrast. Her tiny feet in their embroidered magenta slippers rested on one of the steps.

A robed woman, who had been waiting for them in the room, came and stood behind and a little to the side of the throne like a governess or a chaperone. Flora wondered if in fact the woman was to be the one to hand out the answers.

The little girl smiled prettily and said, 'Please sit.' She indicated the hassock in front of the steps to the throne. Flora knelt. She was uncomfortable. Her skirt felt too tight and her heart was thumping heavily. She raised her glance to the child and met, from out of all the silks and jewels, a look of happy repose.

'Speak freely,' the child told her in a musical voice. 'And say what is in your heart.'

Flora swallowed. She could hear the loud sound it made in her throat. All at once tears were in her eyes. She saw the figure before her in a blur, as if it might have been a holy statue and not a human being.

She began, 'I don't know what to do. Year after year. My life is useless. I have everything, nothing to want. Kind husband, wonderful children. I feel ashamed to be ungrateful, but it never was what . . . it never seemed like mine. It's as if I'd never had my own self. But there's one thing: a man. He's the only one who isn't corrupted, the only one I can rely on. I think about him all the time. I can't stop. I can't stand the idea that we'll never be together. He's only a servant. And I don't know what to do. I love him so much.' She ended on a sob and was silent.

She waited. Nothing happened. She sniffed, wiped the back of her hand across her cheek and looked up for her answer.

'Love?' the goddess asked.

Flora nodded. 'Yes,' she mumbled. 'Yes, yes.'

'True love', the sweet voice told her, 'is poor.'

Poor? Flora was bewildered. *Pure*, she thought. *Of course.*

'It is from the sky.'

The chaperone leaned forward towards the jewelled head. 'Godly,' she hissed.

'Godly,' the child repeated, smiling into Flora's anxious face. The densely embellished right sleeve raised itself as the girl lifted her arm. The small hand made a lyrical gesture up towards the heavens and back in an arc to the ground: a movement that described beauty and love falling upon human lovers below, uniting as it touched them – bringing together, inevitably, her life and Michael's without greed or insistence.

'Yes, yes,' she stammered again. She felt stunned. She knew that she had had her answer, whatever it was. It would take her some time to figure out exactly what it meant.

The child hadn't finished. 'You must rise above,' she said thoughtfully. 'You must ascend.'

'Transcend,' the chaperone corrected.

'Ascend,' the child repeated.

Flora nodded. She sighed and said, 'Thank you.' She started to get up. The chaperone came forward and, without touching, showed her the direction in which she should go. For a moment the woman blocked any further sight of the child. She indicated that Flora should move away, not try to catch another glimpse of the goddess, not to say thank you again; the interview was over.

She walked clumsily from the chamber and staggered a few times as she followed two priestesses back to the waiting-room. She bowed farewell to everyone. She let James take her by the arm. As they were ushered out, she leaned against him.

As soon as they passed outside the main gates, he began to hurry her along.

'Why are we going so fast?' she complained.

'Because you look terrible. I want to get you back into the car. You look like you're ready to faint again.'

'You're going too fast. I can't keep up.'

'Try, Flora,' he said. 'We can carry you if we have to.'

'No.'

'Christ knows why I let you talk me into this. What did she do – say she saw the ace of spades in your palm, or something? Jesus.' He and Michael bundled her into the car and they started on the drive to town.

She fell back in the seat. She still couldn't think clearly. *I must ascend*, she thought. It might be painful, but it would be necessary. *Did she mean that I have to rise above earthly love?* Maybe what the goddess had meant was that in the end everyone died and went to heaven, so it wasn't worth getting upset over unimportant things.

And perhaps the girl had also meant exactly what she'd said about love – that it was from heaven, freely given and necessary, but that rich people never had to feel necessity; if a friendship broke down, or a marriage, or a blood relationship, they somehow always managed to buy another one. Life could be made very agreeable that way. But love was what the goddess had said it was – not pure: poor.

'Well?' James asked.

'Better,' she said.

'Thank God for that. What did the creature do to you?'

'She told me I had to rise above.'

'Rise above what?'

'Oh, everything, I guess.'

'And that's what knocked you out – the Eastern version of moral uplift?'

'I just suddenly felt sort of . . . I don't know.'

He bent towards her, kissed her near her ear and whispered, 'Pregnant.'

'No.'

'Sure? You've been close to fainting twice.'

'Yes,' she said. 'Yes, I'm sure. No. What did you think of it all, Michael?'

'Very interesting indeed,' Michael answered. 'It's another way of life.'

'What did you think of her? The goddess.'

'Cute-looking little kid, but skinny as a rail underneath all those party clothes. You wonder if they feed them enough.'

'Those hundreds of people on litters believe she can cure them.'

'Yeah, well, they're sick. Sick people believe in anything.'

'Maybe they're right. Sometimes if you have faith, it makes things true.'

James groaned slightly with impatience.

Michael said, 'It's deception. Self-deception always makes people feel good. But it wouldn't fix a broken leg, if that's what was wrong with you. It might help you get better quicker, once a doctor's done the real work – see what I mean?'

'Yes, I see,' she said. He didn't understand. But there was no reason why he should. James said that she was tired and upset. 'We'll be back soon,' he assured her. 'And let's have an early lunch. I'm hungry as hell from getting up so early.'

'Is it still morning? You didn't think much of her, either, did you?'

'I thought she looked great, really fabulous – the dress, like a walking cyclamen plant, and the whole effect very pretty but a bit bizarre: like a gnome out of a fairy-tale. What I don't like is how she's knocked the wind out of you. They aren't supposed to do that. They're supposed to give comfort and strength. That's the nature of the job.'

'She did. She gave me something to think about, anyway. All the rest was me trying to get out what I wanted to say.'

He held her hand. He didn't ask what her request had been. He probably thought he knew; he'd think she'd have wanted to know something like, 'Why can't I be happy?' Everybody wanted happiness.

The car speeded up along the stretches by the coastline. They opened the windows and got a whiff of the sea before returning to the air-conditioning. Flora breathed deeply. All beaches were the same: salt and iodine, like the summers of her childhood. New Caledonia would be like this, too.

They reached town before noon. James ordered the car to wait down a side street. The three of them got out and walked to one of the nice restaurants they had tried several times before. Flora was all right now, except that she felt bemused. She could walk without any trouble but she couldn't stop thinking about the temple and the goddess. She especially couldn't stop remembering the expression of joyful serenity on the child's face. It seemed to her that if she kept up the attempt to recapture the way it looked, she wouldn't have to let go of it.

The whole business had gone very quickly, as matters usually did when well-organized, and paid for, in advance. And now they were having a good meal in a comfortable restaurant; and only at that moment did Flora recall that she'd meant to go up to Irma on her way out and hand her some money in an envelope.

'Eat,' James said.

She shook her head.

'Just a little,' he insisted.

She picked up the china spoon and looked at it. She put it into the soup bowl. James watched patiently. When the children had been small, he was always the one who could make them eat when they didn't want to, and later, make them brush their teeth: he let you know, without saying anything, that he was prepared to wait for ever, unchanging and with arms folded, until you did the right thing. Authority. And he never bothered with modern ideas about explaining things rationally. If the children asked, 'Why do I have to?' he'd answer, 'Because I say so.'

She began slowly, then ate hungrily. Before the coffee, she went off to the ladies' room for a long time and while she was there made sure that her face and hair looked perfect. She even thought of brushing her teeth with the travelling toothbrush she carried in her purse, but she'd be back at the hotel soon – she could do it there. James smiled approvingly as she emerged.

They sauntered out into the hot, dusty street again.

'Museum?' he suggested, 'or siesta?'

'A little nap might be nice. Is that all right with you, Michael?'

'Sure, fine,' Michael said.

James stopped on the corner. 'Where was that museum, anyhow?' he asked. 'Down around that street there somewhere, isn't it?'

Michael looked up. He began to point things out in the distance. Flora kept walking around the bend as the street curved to the right. She drew back against the buildings to avoid three boys who were standing together and talking in whispers. But as soon as she was clear, two others came out of the doorway. She started to move away, but they came straight towards her. And suddenly the first three, their friends, were behind her, snatching at her arms. It was the same as the day before, but this time she screamed loudly for Michael before the hands started to grip over her eyes and mouth. She also kicked and thrashed while they dragged her along the sidewalk. Right at the beginning, except for her own outburst, all the violent pulling and shoving took place to the accompaniment of low mutters and hisses. Only when James and Michael came charging around the corner did the real noise begin.

The gang had guns. The man now left alone to hold Flora from behind was jabbing something into her backbone. She knew it was a gun because she saw two of the others pull out pistols. They went for James. The voice behind her yelled, 'Stop, or we kill the woman.' Flora kept still, in case her struggling caused the weapon to go off by mistake. But Michael had his own gun in his hand and was crouched down in the road. He shot the two who were heading towards James, the third, who was waving a pistol in the air, and there was a fourth explosion landing someplace where Flora couldn't see. The arm around her gripped so tightly that she was suffocating. The voice, sounding deranged, screamed into her ear, 'You drop the gun, or I kill her!' She knew he meant it. He'd do anything. He might even kill her without knowing what he was doing.

Michael didn't hesitate. She saw him turn towards them and the look on his face was nothing: it was like being confronted by a machine. He fired right at her. She should have known.

She didn't fall straight away. The man who had held her lay dead on the ground while she swayed above him. She knew she'd been shot, but not where. It felt as if she'd been hit by a truck. And suddenly she saw that there was blood everywhere – maybe hers, maybe other people's.

She should have known that a man formed by the conventions of the world into which she had married would already have his loyalties arranged in order of importance, and that the men and male heirs to the line would always take precedence over the outsiders who had fitted themselves into their lives. James was central; she was only decoration. As long as one man in the street was left with a gun, that was a danger to James. In Michael's eyes she had passed during less than three minutes from object to obstacle. He'd shot her to pieces, and, using her as a target, killed the gunman behind her.

James had his arms around her. He was calling out for an ambulance. There were plenty of other people on the street now. And she thought: *My God, how embarrassing: I've wet my pants.* But what she said was, 'I'm bleeding,' and passed out.

*

She woke up looking at a wall, at window-blinds, at the ceiling. Everything hurt.

It was still daylight, so perhaps she hadn't been there very long. Or maybe it was the next day. It felt like a long time. She was trussed like a swaddled baby and she was hooked up to a lot of tubes – she could see that, too. And she was terrified that parts of her body had been shattered beyond repair: that they would be crippled so badly that they'd never move again, that perhaps the doctors had amputated limbs. The fear was even worse than the pain.

Someone got up from behind all the machinery on her other side and left the room.

James came from around the back of her bed and sat in a chair next to her. He looked tired. And sad, too. That was unusual; she'd hardly ever seen him looking sad. He reached over and put his hand on her bare right arm, which lay outside the covers. She realized that she must be naked underneath; only bandages, no nightgown.

'You're going to be all right,' he told her.

She believed him. She said, 'Hurts a lot.' He smiled grimly. She asked, 'How long have I been here?'

'Twenty-four hours.'

'You haven't shaved.'

He kept squeezing her arm lightly and looking into her face. She thought she was about to go back to sleep again, but he caught her attention by saying her name.

'Would you do something for me?'

She said, 'Of course. You're always so good to me.'

He put his head down on the bed for a while and sighed. He really did love her, she thought, but she'd never believed it before.

'If you could talk to Michael,' he said. 'Just a couple of seconds. He feels so broken up about how it happened. If you could just let him know you understand.'

'I understand,' she said.

'I mean, tell him you forgive him. He hasn't said much, but he hasn't been able to eat or sleep, either. Or shave. Can I tell him to come in?'

She suddenly sensed that everything was draining away from her, never to return. She tried to hold on, but it was no use.

'Flora?'

The horror passed. She felt better. The fear had left, along with all the rest. She knew that she was going to die.

'Yes,' she said. 'Tell him to come in.'

James went away. She heard his footsteps. And Michael's; heard James saying, 'Just a couple of seconds. She's very tired,' and saw him moving away out of the room as Michael sat down in the chair. She turned her head to look at him.

He was smiling. Even with her head to the side, she could see his expression exactly: a nasty little smile. His drunken uncle had been chauffeur and pander to the old man and his cousins; and, of course, Michael would have taken over the same office for the sons. She should have known. It was that kind of family: even the employees were inheritable.

Everything was obvious now, and especially the fact that Michael's unshakable politeness and deference had been an indication of his distaste for her. He'd give up pretending, now that he knew she was dying. It was more than distaste. It must be a real hatred, because he couldn't help it any longer. He wanted to show her, even with James just outside the door.

'I want you to understand,' he said quietly.

'No need,' she answered.

'You got to understand, it's for him. Far as I'm concerned, I don't give a shit. You've just got to tell him you forgive me. Then it'll be OK.'

Everything would be all right. It was simple, if you had that much money. When they reported the attack, James would see to it that everyone thought she'd been shot by the kidnappers, not by Michael. Who would question it? Two respectable witnesses; and dead men who were known criminals. The hospital would get a new wing, the police force a large donation. It would be easy. It would have been easy even if they'd deliberately set out to murder her and hired the men to do it.

'If it was me,' Michael said, leaning forward, 'I'd be counting the minutes till you go down the tubes. ''Oh James dear, look at that, oh isn't that perfectly sweet? Can I have the car window open, if it's all right with Michael: can I have it closed, if Michael doesn't mind?'' Pain in the ass is what you are. I mean, I seen plenty: one to a hundred I used to mark them, and you rate down around ten, sweetheart. A real lemon. ''Am I doing this right, am I doing that?'' I told him, ''Jimbo, this one's a dud.'' And he just said, ''No, Kelvin, this time I'm choosing for myself.'' He wouldn't listen.'

James could do it right next time, she thought. He'd marry again, perhaps quite soon, and be just as content. He'd probably go to New Caledonia after all, maybe with another woman, or just with Michael. Someone else would bring up her children, no doubt doing it very well. They'd have the photographs of her, so everyone could remember how pretty she'd been; she had always taken a good picture. The family would be able to choose the new wife, as they'd chosen for Edward. She'd been crazy about Edward; that was how everything had started. It was enough to make you laugh. But she had to stop thinking about it. She had to ascend. All the events in the house and all the holiday travelling would still go on, only she wouldn't be able to have any part in them. She had to rise above.

'I forgive,' she said. It was becoming difficult for her to speak.

'I'll get him,' Michael told her. He stood up.

'Wait.' She started to breathe quickly.

He leaned across the bed to look at her face. He said, 'I'll get somebody.'

'Michael,' she said clearly, 'I loved you.'

He stepped back. The smile vanished. He looked revolted, infuriated.

'I loved you,' she repeated. 'With all my heart.' Her lips curved together, her eyes closed, her head moved to the side. She was gone.

Michael began to scream.

The sound brought James running into the room, and two nurses after him.

Michael caught Flora up in his arms. He shouted into her closed face. He tried to slam her against the wall. James pulled him back. 'It's all right,' he said. 'Stop.'

'Bitch,' Michael yelled at Flora. 'Take it back. Take it back, you lousy bitch.'

'Calm down,' James said. 'She forgives you.' He got his arm around both of them and tugged. Michael let go, dropping Flora's body. She fell face downward. The nurses stooped to pick her up from the floor.

James and Michael stood grappled together, their faces wet with tears and sweat. Michael stared at the wall in front of him.

'It's all right,' James told him. 'She understands. Don't worry. After people die, they understand everything.'

On Ice

Beverley moved to Munich during the late summer. She found a room with a German family, enrolled as an auditor at the university and got to know her way around the town. In the evenings she went out with her German boyfriend, Claus.

They had met the year before, on the boat coming over; they'd all – her parents, too – been travelling on a charter deal that had worked out cheaper than most air fares at the time. Claus had been going out with an older girl in the big crowd she'd been with, but he'd given her his address. And so when the family was back in America, she'd looked him up.

In the spring he'd asked her to marry him. She'd said yes. From the moment of meeting him she hadn't considered anything else: that he could leave her, or that one of them might die, or that he might have been the kind of man to seduce girls and leave them flat or to carry on two affairs at the same time. She hadn't really considered much at all. She'd simply thought she'd stop living if she couldn't be with him.

He was ten years older, already a settled man: a doctor. Because of his work she didn't see as much of him as she'd have liked to; sometimes he couldn't tell when he'd be on duty. He'd show up late. In fact, he was hardly ever on time for anything. She accepted the fact that it was the job that was to blame. Since she loved him, she didn't question it. Once he turned up two days later than he'd said he would.

Now they were together nearly all the time. They had separate addresses and they ate their meals out, but she was pretty sure that in another two months or so they'd announce their engagement officially and maybe get married in the spring, or at the beginning of the summer. She wanted to go to college, but that too would work out somehow.

He had taken his holiday so that they could spend Christmas and New Year's together. He'd booked the rooms and everything. She bought a parka and a pair of ski pants and was looking forward to the trip. She'd never been on skis.

The night before he was to pick her up, she packed her suitcase, turned out the lights in her room and took a last look across the street at the steep roofs and studio apartments opposite. A thin layer of snow lay in patterns over every ridge and line. The light was off in the glass-roofed atelier where a dark-haired young man – probably a painter or sculptor – lived on his own. She used to see him from time to time when she passed by the window, or stood there to open the inner panes and put her milk and butter next to the outer ones to keep cold. One day he had waved frantically at her. And, instinctively, she had ducked away out of sight. Afterwards she'd been furious with herself, and wanted to see him again so she could wave back, as she should have done in the first place. But he was never there. It upset her that she might have hurt his feelings – that she'd been so prim and suspicious. That was the way she was, unluckily, because that was the way her family liked people to be, especially women. That was the way she was with everyone but Claus.

He arrived early, for once. His skis were strapped to the top of the car; she'd have to hire a pair when they got to the village. The weather was good for driving and Claus was in a lighthearted mood. They kissed as the car went up and down the hills, around the corners. They couldn't wait till Christmas to give each other their presents, so they stopped and opened them in the car. They'd each chosen the same thing – a scarf. But he so clearly preferred the one he'd bought for her, even telling her he didn't think much of the other's colour scheme, that she said, 'Well, they're both the same size. We can switch.' She took off the one he'd given her and handed it to him. It was a gesture of anger. She didn't imagine he'd want to take her up on the offer.

'I suppose we might as well,' he said. He held up his scarf and smiled at it. Beverley too liked her own choice better, but she would never have said so. She would never have been so brutal to someone she was fond of. On the other hand, she realized that he didn't often dare to be honest with anyone. It was like her reaction to the painter living across from her: not being able to wave back.

They drove right over the top of the big mountain passes and pulled up near a lookout station where three tourist buses were parked. Some of the sightseers were out exploring the gravelly surface of the glacier formations left over from the Ice Age, some were gathered around the hut that sold soft drinks and sandwiches. Claus and Beverley got out and walked to the grey mass of gritty material on the far side of the road. The air seemed to be colder when they reached it, the sun to go in. It wasn't at all the way a glacier out of the past should look. It was curved like the back of a turtle; dull, dirty and – as Beverley said – reminiscent of ordinary concrete. She was disappointed. She liked old things to have an air of splendour and romance.

Claus, in contrast, was mildly interested. Facts appealed to him. He didn't care so much about looks, although he was always telling her that something she'd be wearing wasn't straight, and he'd often put out a hand to neaten her hair. He was shocked that she could get along with a safety pin instead of taking the trouble to sew back a button that had come off. She could go for weeks without mending something torn.

He couldn't understand such habits and behaviour. The slovenliness of it all horrified him. But she knew that her carelessness was one of the things about her that most attracted him. Secretly he would have liked to be more bohemian, to live in the artists' quarter, never to have to say yes–sir–no–sir to the top surgeons who came around on inspection in the mornings wearing white gloves, who shook hands with everyone from top to bottom of the building and then, according to popular belief, peeled off the gloves, flinging them away for the assistant to pick up and take to the laundry or, perhaps, destroy. She was sure he had dreams of tearing all his buttons off and going to work covered in safety pins. He hated his own respectability while prizing the public and cultural disciplines that forced people into repression. He was civilized and he was frustrated. Beverley cured the frustration while he was curing other people's illnesses.

On the other side of the pass they followed the route of the mountain stream – a swift, icy green torrent that raced along beside them. 'This is more like it,' she said.

The village they were in was down in the valley. Up on the peaks were several larger, more fashionable and more expensive winter resorts, including the famous Hotel Miramar, whose rooms were said to be like art galleries for the *art nouveau* period.

Their hotel was small and overcrowded. Their room was actually not in the main building at all but in what was obviously a private house let out to accommodate tourists and make the owners some money during the season. There were many places in the world where a family could live for the rest of the year on what the house brought in during a few weeks of skiing, or sailing, or whatever was the main attraction of the region. A lot of the Cape was like that, back home.

The hotel dining-room was in the main building and had space enough for twenty tables, some seating four people. Theirs was just for two. The food was good – a combination of German and Italian cooking, and there was a lot to eat. The crisp, clear air and the exercise made Beverley hungry all day long.

Claus took her out on a slope where they could be alone and taught her how to ski downhill. It was much easier than being on the T-bar lifts, but even so, she spent most of her time picking herself up. He hadn't taught her how to turn a corner. When she began to go so fast that she was about to crash, she'd fall down deliberately, to save herself, and then get up and start over again. She wished that she had short skis like the ones they gave children to practise on. All the children she saw could ski better than she could.

They spent Christmas Eve in the hotel. The proprietor, a wolfish-looking man with suave manners, smiled aimiably at them. He leaned over their chairs to talk to them about the weather and the state of the snow. His name was Lucas, but when speaking of him between themselves, they referred to him as Lupus, because of the way he looked.

There were three other couples in the dining-room. Christmas was a time for the family. Those who had chosen to leave their relatives went out to the bars and dance-floors in search of crowds to replace them. Beverley started to drink more and more, to think about her parents opening their presents. She also wondered how much Claus loved her and whether she was always going to be able to get along with him, not to mention his family. She'd met his mother once and couldn't stand her. But that didn't matter; she loved him. She'd never love anyone else. Tears came into her eyes.

'What are you thinking?' he asked.

'About our Christmas scarves. It isn't right.'

'I thought you didn't like mine.'

'You were the one. You didn't like mine. I'm sorry. I thought it was so nice. And I actually do like it better. But I want the one you chose for me. Don't you understand?'

He said yes, he did. And they gave back their scarves on the way out, so that instead of having what they liked and being unhappy about it, they were happy despite not liking what they had.

After Christmas the whole village filled up fast. They'd been lucky to get in quickly and rent the skis. Every pair in the place had now been claimed by someone. There were people standing in line and looking at their watches for skis to become free. The night-life too speeded up. The frozen alleyways were full of partygoers on their way to and from the taverns. There was singing in the evenings; you could hear voices calling across the snow, laughter from all the doorways as people burst from lighted interiors into the cold night air and the whiteness of the snow that retained its shine even in the dark.

The best hotel down in the village was the Adler. It also had a good restaurant, very large, and a beer cellar. A painted wooden eagle hung over the doorway and everything inside was cheerful and spotless. You could tell it was the kind of place that would have geraniums in windowboxes when the weather turned warmer. They went there twice for dinner. On the second evening, just as they were leaving, a voice called out in English, 'Bev – hey, Bev-er-ley!'

She turned around. She didn't know for a moment which face to look at. Someone was waving at her. She stepped forward. And there was Angela, a friend from school, with five other American college kids all her age. It was unexpected; until that moment it had been unthinkable to Beverley that both her lives, one on either side of the Atlantic, should suddenly join up. She felt strongly that although she had always liked her fairly well, Angela should really have stayed in America.

'Hi, Beverley.'

'Hi, Ange. What a surprise.'

Angela quickly introduced the other friends: Darell, Tom, Mimi, Liza and Rick.

Beverley had to introduce Claus.

'Sit down,' Angela said. 'Join us for a beer.' She looked at Claus invitingly. Beverley spoke to him in German, saying that they had to meet friends: didn't he remember?

'Gee,' Angela said, 'you sure can rattle it off, can't you?'

'Sort of,' she said. If you couldn't speak another language after a year in bed with a foreigner, you might as well give up. 'Where are you staying?' she asked.

'Here.'

'For how long?'

'Another week.'

'I'll be in touch,' Beverley said. 'Tonight I'm afraid we've got to meet some people.' She headed towards the door again. Claus followed. When they were outside, he asked her why she hadn't wanted to stay.

She tried to explain: about the way it was back home, the gossip, everything. To run around on European vacations with your friends and probably – like rich Angela – be fooling around with all of them, was one thing; but to be falsely registered in a hotel as the wife of a foreign man ten years older than you were, was another. Nobody at home would understand. It wasn't the way people behaved there.

'I bet it is,' he said. 'I bet they do it all the time, like everywhere else.'

'But certain things are illegal. In the state I come from it's even illegal to buy a contraceptive if it's for preventing pregnancy. You can only get them on the excuse that they're to prevent venereal disease. It's all to do with religion. It's supposed to be a country with a secular government, but all the laws about sex assume it's something bad. Unless it really is bad; if it's rape, you need two independent witnesses to prove it. I just don't know that I want to spend all our holiday drinking beer with those people, do you?'

'Of course not,' he said. 'Why are you so upset?'

She put her arm around him and said she wasn't upset. But he was right, she realized. She hated it that the others had discovered her secret, happy life.

*

The next day, after lunch, he told her that he wanted to try one of the high slopes and get a good run down the mountainside.

'I asked Lupus about the timing, but it depends on the snow. I may be a little late. You could go see your friends at the Adler, if you like.'

'I'll wait at the room for you,' she said.

'It was nearly dark when he came in. He was laughing. He stripped off his clothes, wrapped himself in a towel and went across the hall to the bathroom, where they had an enormous tub as big as a bed.

He'd fallen several times. She gathered that it had actually been very dangerous, and there wouldn't have been anybody else around if he'd been seriously injured.

'Look,' he said, picking his ski pants up off the chair. 'They're all ripped. That's my only pair, too. I'll have to ski in my suit.'

'I'll sew them,' she offered. She got out the pocket sewing kit she'd bought because it looked pretty. The only things in it she'd ever used were the safety pins, although everything was there: needles, thread, a few buttons and a thimble. She sat on the chair and sewed up the long tear in the material while he changed his clothes.

'It isn't very straight,' she said. The stitches were large, the sewing like that of a child. The mend resembled a badly healed wound. But Claus was delighted. 'As long as it holds together,' he told her, and she felt proud of herself.

At supper he said he thought that the next day he'd try the neighbouring run.

'Are you sure it's OK?' she asked. 'If it's so risky, and there isn't anybody else around? You could break a leg.'

'Doctors don't break things. It's like lawyers – they never go to law.'

'Lawyers can choose. They don't do it, because they know what it costs. Anybody can break a leg.'

'Will you mind being alone down here?'

'No, that's all right.'

'You could go up the mountain to the other hotels.'

'I could even go to the really fancy place, couldn't I? They probably don't let anyone in that isn't a guest.'

'They'd let you into everything except the hotel, I think. That's a good idea. I wouldn't mind going up there, too. You can tell me what it's like. I just want to get some real exercise first. You never know what the weather might do.'

She said all right: she'd go up to the big hotel the next day.

*

A man who worked one of the ski lifts pointed out the right road to her. She was glad of her good German, which was perfectly understood even where the populace spoke more Italian and had grown up with a local language that hadn't mixed with other European tongues since shortly after Roman times. She had heard fellow Americans asking directions in English and having a spate of the home-grown dialect loosed off at them.

She bought a chocolate bar to eat later, instead of lunch, with a cup of coffee. She'd become almost addicted to a particular kind of milk chocolate that had pieces of nougat baked into it. The bar was triangle-shaped and each wedge a triangle when broken off.

She had a quiet ride up. The cable car was large, painted a dark green. There were three other people travelling with her – a young boy who carried a pair of skates, and an old couple, very well-dressed. The woman was carefully made-up, her fur coat looked soft and bushy, her fur-trimmed boots were the kind you wore for sitting down on the observation platform rather than trudging through the snow. Her husband's coat had an astrakhan collar that matched the hat he wore. The cane he held between his knees was topped by a silver knob worked to resemble a piece of wood with knots in it. Both man and woman looked as if they belonged up at the top of the mountain, at the luxury hotel: Beverley wondered why they had gone down to the valley at all. They began to speak quickly in a language she couldn't place.

She looked out of the windows at the blazing white plains and fields, the long swoop of drifts that ran from the crests to a point where the line of the mountainside shot out into infinity. The boy started to whistle and kicked the wall near his seat.

When they arrived at the top, there was a delay. They hung where they had stopped, the doors remaining shut. The old couple stood up to look. Beverley and the boy were already on their feet.

They could see two stretchers being carried by, the bodies each covered with a white sheet and red blanket; then a third, and the person being carried was fighting to throw the covers off. As the stretcher-bearers hurried past a hand flung away the blanket and Beverley caught a glimpse of a head entirely red, the crown looking as if it had been cut by an axe, and the mouth open but not producing a sound. She shut her eyes and put her head down. She could hear the old couple murmuring to each other in their own language; they sounded strangely casual, as if the vision hadn't caused them much concern. Perhaps they hadn't seen so much; perhaps their eyesight wasn't very good any more.

When the doors finally opened, she'd forgotten about coffee and the hotel and everything. She thought she'd like to sit down and drink a beer and try to wipe away the memory of the man who'd been hurt. It might even have been a woman – you couldn't tell much from a head and face so badly injured. But she had a feeling it had been a man. And she was sure that he wasn't going to live.

She began to plod along the snow-packed lanes to the centre of the village. Just as she was thinking of going into one of the taverns ahead, she came in view of the Hotel Miramar above and beyond her, shining like a castle at the top of the hill. She stood admiring it for a few seconds, then turned into a side street.

She almost skidded on a patch of ice around the corner. Opposite her was a restaurant. She went in and sat down. The waiter was an old man with white hair and a white moustache. He didn't think it unusual that she should order just a beer, alone, in the middle of the morning. A group of men in suits were seated around a table at the back; the place was obviously for locals, not for the foreign skiers. When the waiter brought the beer, she said, 'As I came up, in the cable car, I saw a man. Has there been an accident? They were carrying people. Blood.'

'Ah, the ice wall,' he said. 'We warn everybody, but they still have to try it, to prove how good they are.'

'What is it?'

'It's a wall of ice in the middle of the toboggan run. If you haven't been braking and using your skill to turn at the corners, you go over the bank and into the wall. It's solid ice.'

'They were bleeding all over.'

'Ice is very hard. Hard as stone. Hard as steel. The speeds you can achieve going downhill – fantastic.'

'Does it happen a lot?'

'Quite often, yes. We try to discourage people from going, but you can't.'

She began to drink her beer. He told her that there was another attraction, an ice maze, which was also popular but considerably less dangerous, as the walls were only about a metre high and the gradient not too steep; people used special puffy cushions to slide through it. Children loved it. It was one of the Miramar entertainments that was open to the public.

She asked directions to the ice maze and the skating rink. When she was ready to leave, he came outside the door with her and pointed up the hillside.

It was a long way up. She was out of breath by the time she started to climb the steps. And they were slippery, too. The handrail was coated with ice. She wondered what everything would look like in the summer, how different it would be. There were lakes in the neighbouring valleys; people would probably be lolling around in deck-chairs and trying to pick up a suntan. And the famous skating rink, she suddenly remembered, could be turned into a swimming pool. If Claus ever wanted to come back to the place in warmer weather, she'd be able to join him then up on the mountainside – not that she was an expert at hiking or rock-climbing either, but at least she could go for a long walk. Not knowing how to ski meant that their time was going to be divided. She hadn't thought about that before they'd arrived.

She bought a visitor's ticket and stood by the side of the rink until she felt cold. She was too self-conscious to put on a pair of skates herself. It was all right to watch, but to get out and slide around all on your own would be futile. She couldn't see anyone who was without a friend or relative. Claus was out on the slopes alone, but skiing was different. And he was a man; that made a difference, too.

She managed to find a perfect place in the after-ski lounge, a small table next to the vast plate-glass window that overlooked the rink. She brought two cups of coffee to it, drank one, started on the first section of her chocolate bar and was about to break off another piece when she heard a voice saying, 'Well, here you are again.'

It was Angela. She sat down in the second chair. She was wearing a top-to-toe outfit made of some silvery, shiny material that looked as if it might have been designed for an astronaut. She pushed her dark glasses to the top of her head, undid the earphones of her Walkman and said it was great running into each other again.

Civilization, Beverley thought, was what stopped people from telling someone like Angela to shove her earphones up her nose and get lost. 'Been skiing?' she asked.

'Till I fell on my duff,' Angela said.

'Alone?'

'No, the whole gang's here. What about you? Got your Mr Gorgeous with you? Who is he?'

'A friend,' she said.

'Some friend. He looks – you know. All those cheekbones and everything. Really European.'

'He is European.'

'I mean, like he looks. He looks European. You know?'

'Sure,' Beverley said. 'Who-all are you with?'

'Oh, just that bunch you saw the other night.'

'Who are they?'

'Well, Liza went to school with me those last two years. Tom and Rick are in my class: economics and government studies. Then, Mimi and Darell – how can I describe them?'

'Lovers?'

'No, silly.' She gave Beverley's arm a coy little push. 'Mimi and Darell are sort of in the group, except they actually didn't quite make it. First of all they were too late, and then she started to have all these doubts. So they aren't officially registered with the organization.'

'What organization?'

'The Fountain of Light.'

'The what?'

'It's our Christian fellowship foundation. We bring the culture and hope of the free world to – '

Beverley removed the saucer covering her second cup of coffee.

Angela's expression became fixed and devout. She gabbled about 'the word', the need for real estate, 'the light' and the building of training centres; 'the fountain'; the establishing of weekly lectures in notable beauty spots, the investment of cash in long-term plans for truth, light, love and a whole lot else, including medical research. Very few people outside the movement knew, she said, that vitamin intake was directly related to disorders of the personality. But some day there would be 'detoxification clinics' all over the world, where people could go to profit from the word.

'To read?'

'To resolve their vitamin imbalance, Bev. To reach God. We'd like to start up an education programme right here.'

Beverley stopped listening and drank. For Angela to have turned out to be a run-of-the-mill brainless co-ed was bad enough. For her to be part of a maverick cult bringing fountains of light anywhere was worse, though possibly slightly more interesting. She said, 'I don't know how much luck you'll have trying to give away culture and hope around here. I think they're all Catholic going back centuries.'

'But we all believe in God,' Angela said.

'Uh-huh. Did you see the accident? On the toboggan run?'

'I heard about it. It sounded terrible.'

'From après-ski to après-vie in two seconds flat.'

'Beverley, don't joke.'

'I'm not joking. I saw them. It shook me up so much I had to go get myself a drink.'

'You saw them? What was it like?'

'Red. Red and trying to scream.'

'I don't want to hear.'

You just want to ask about it, Beverley thought. She put down her coffee cup and said, 'Have you ever seen the ice maze?'

'Of course. It's fun, if you can get into it. All the kids want to play there. It's considered a children's thing.'

'But it must be dangerous, if it's ice.'

'They have these big pillows they ride on. About the size of a rubber raft. I haven't heard it's so dangerous. Want to try it?'

'OK,' Beverley said. 'Just let me go to the ladies' room.'

The ladies' room, only one of several in the building, was as full as an airline lavatory of free gift-wrapped soaps, bottles of cream and eau-de-cologne. Beverley took one of everything.

They put on their outdoor clothes again and stepped out on to the long porch that ran the length of the lodge. Spectators sat in deck-chairs all along the railings. On the level above, indoors, there was an enclosed verandah for sunbathers, who lay basking behind glass walls and windows that let through the ultra-violet rays. There had been one year when the visitors had read magazine articles claiming that the ultra-violet was just the part of sunlight that caused skin cancers; and the numbers of sunbathers dropped dramatically. But the next year everyone had forgotten the scare. They wanted to be tanned again.

Beverley followed Angela. As she walked, she thought about how strange it was to be up where all the swish hotels were and the moneyed people who went to places like that only because they wanted to have rooms with a specific look, or a certain kind of food in the dining-room and dry martinis at the bar. She passed one woman, an American, who was shouting, 'Hector, Hector,' at someone; the woman wore dark glasses and a large mink coat. On her hands she displayed an array of massive gold rings set with stones bigger than eyes. Her fingernails were painted red and in her right hand she held a plastic coca-cola cup. Why leave America, Beverley wondered, if that was what you wanted? Why had Angela left? Maybe they were people who just didn't believe the places where you took your vacation were part of the real world, especially if the native inhabitants spoke a different language.

They waited in line for two pillows and launched themselves into the ice maze, which was funnier and more exciting than Beverley had imagined, and less tiring than skiing. She sped forward through the glistening runways on her striped cushion and yelled as loudly as the children around her.

Afterwards they joined Angela's friends for sandwiches and coffee and then went out on the skating rink. When Beverley said she had to go, they begged her to stay on for tea and supper and dancing. There was a wonderful pool down inside the hotel, too. Beverley said no, she had to get back.

'But tomorrow?' Angela asked. 'Come on up tomorrow, or meet us early down at the Adler.'

'Maybe,' she said. She was sure Claus would want to be with her. She hurried as the light began to go. She was worried that he might have been waiting for a long time. But she was the first one back. When he came in, he was smiling, and in an even better mood than the day before. The slopes had been splendid, he told her: simply magnificent. Tomorrow he'd go even higher.

'Will you be all right with your friends?' he asked.

'I guess so.' She tried not to act hurt. They had a good dinner and a lot to drink, and went to bed as soon as they got back to their room.

He was up early and kissed her goodbye while she was still in bed. She set her alarm clock and went back to sleep.

For the next three days their separate daytime routines worked out well. He kept finding bigger and better ski runs up in the mountains, and she could tell him all about the hotel, the ice maze, the skating, the heated pool and the game rooms. She also told him that Angela, although she'd never mentioned it again, had confessed to being a member of some weird religious cult.

'As long as it isn't political,' he said.

'Those things never are.'

'Of course they are. What do you think?'

'Well, in this part of the world it wouldn't matter; only in the East, where they might start handing out Bibles or something.'

'What do they believe in?'

'She didn't say exactly, but the name is loony enough. I once had a terrible conversation with a couple of Seventh Day Adventists. I think that's what they were. It lasted three hours and twenty minutes. All this horrible stuff about being the elect. I couldn't get away. I didn't want to be rude. Jehovah's Witnesses, that's what it was.'

'Ridiculous. We used to get them at the door when I was in Cologne. You just tell them you're already something – Catholic, Jewish, Muslim – and say you believe in that.'

'But I don't. I didn't want to upset them, but I did finally say it didn't matter to me if I wasn't saved.'

'But you believe in God.'

'Of course,' she said. She had to say it because of the first time he'd asked her, in bed. 'Do you believe in God?' he'd whispered; and she had said yes, since she couldn't say anything else, and since what he was really asking her was: did she love him beyond anything. But later she was furious. It was as if in the throes of intercourse she had been asked, 'You do believe the sun goes around the earth, don't you?' What could you say? *Let me think about that one.* It was unfair.

He had been profoundly shocked when she'd told him that in accordance with her father's humanitarian principles, she had never been baptized. Her father had believed that people should wait until they were old enough to understand the words said over them, and could then choose whether or not they wanted to join a church.

Claus had said, 'But that's terrible. Every civilized human being – '

That was the point at which she had seen that despite his reputation in the hospitals as a rebel and a firebrand, he would always want to abide by the rules he'd grown up with, and that they included strictures of thought as well as of behaviour. When he reached up to push her hair away from her forehead, she'd pull a face and tell him, 'That makes such a bad impression,' or, 'What will the neighbours say?' She'd invented a quavery, shaking voice to quote his favourite scolding phrases back at him. But she'd kiss him afterwards.

'All this mystic nonsense that's supposed to be masquerading as a religion,' he said. 'I don't know how you can associate with them. I wouldn't want to be in the same room with people who are so stupid. Fanatics. Like being in the wards for the insane.'

'You thought they looked all right the other night.'

'Look, maybe. It's the ideas.'

'Do you think the idea of life after death is less peculiar than their plans to distribute sweetness and light?'

He talked for a long while about the ineradicable false romanticism of Americans. He said he thought it had something to do with not having lived through a wartime occupation recently, or even a war that had been fought over their territory.

She agreed with him, though she felt that since they were talking about her country, she should have been the one to criticize it. He didn't like it all that much when she had things to say against Germany; he'd tell her that her opinion was interesting but, as he'd go on to explain, somehow misinformed, if not just plain wrong: she hadn't been looking at something in the right way.

They had once had a terrible quarrel – which had gone on all night – about Germany's part in the Second World War. She had become genuinely hysterical, while he'd remained unconcerned. And after that she thought that although she couldn't live without him, she might not be able to stand being married to him. She wasn't really absolutely sure if she could stand being married to anyone: to end up like other married women who were full of recriminations, unfulfilled, nagging; and who spent their time cleaning and scrubbing and having children – all of which she'd come to eventually, of course, though at the moment the idea of such a future, such a fate, repelled her. Marriage was going to be the price of being allowed to stay with Claus.

'That hotel used to be a sanatorium,' he told her.

'I'm not surprised. I feel a lot better since I've been swimming in the pool.'

'Not that kind. For tuberculosis. A lot of famous people died there. Then they all moved to Switzerland.'

'After they died?'

'The famous people started going to Switzerland instead. And after that, people stopped getting TB so much.'

'The rich people stopped,' she said. 'They're giving a big party up there on New Year's Eve.'

'Let's stay down here. I don't want to be with a lot of other people.'

She didn't want to, either. She'd had enough of the crowds in the daytime – on the skating rink, in the ice maze, along the observation porches. She had also, temporarily, had enough of Angela's friend, Tom, who had taken her over on her second day at the ski lodge and insisted on sticking with her every minute, as if they had been a high school couple. She hadn't asked him about the religious movement, or about much else. He had kissed her in the hotel corridors between the tea-rooms and the swimming pool, and she had allowed it and kissed back even while she asked herself what she was doing in that group and why she should be letting him near her. She didn't want to have to explain about Claus. Maybe she wouldn't have to, anyway. She and Tom clung to each other against the hotel wallpaper and embraced. He knew how to kiss, all right, but in other ways seemed oddly incompetent. He was utterly lacking in the purposeful manipulations she was accustomed to from Claus. He seemed to be getting excited about her, but to be unwilling to follow through. She even wondered if he'd ever had a girl.

She also wondered why she should need this additional proof that she was desired. She knew that already. All the boys in Angela's circle approved of her. And she knew why: it was because she had been another man's woman – that was all there was to it. She was prettier than she used to be, and she was a real woman, because of Claus. But Claus had had other affairs before her. She herself had never had anyone else. It put her at a disadvantage with him.

They stayed in their hotel for New Year's Eve. Only four other couples were in the dining-room. At midnight the lights were turned out and she kissed Claus in the dark. A local band was brought in, a crowd gathered, and people began to dance. Herr Lucas danced with an old woman who might have been his mother or perhaps his wife. Beverley and Claus swayed slowly over the polished but uneven floor. She was slightly drunk and sleepy and was happy thinking about how much she loved him, how wonderful he was, even the smell of his skin, which drove her crazy; and how everything had to turn out all right in spite of his horrible mother and all the things he didn't want to talk about because he was lazy and it was easier not to think about them if he didn't have to.

Next day, Angela said suddenly, 'Are you in love with this guy?'

Beverley was just biting into a sandwich. She nodded.

'Have you really thought about what it would be like to get married to a foreigner?'

'Um.'

'Would he fit in?'

'Oh, we'd live here.'

'Here?'

'In Europe. Well, that's where he works.'

'But – gee, I couldn't stand that. I mean, it's nice but it's so different. You know.'

'That's why I like it.'

'But it isn't democratic.'

'Is America?'

'Of course. America is a democracy. Where did you go to school, Beverley?'

'For a couple of years, to the same place you did. And then, I was at one of those liberal progressive numbers where you couldn't get in if you weren't the right kind. They used to take a certain per cent of stereotype misfits and minorities to cover themselves, but it was pretty exclusive. I'm glad of it, too. I got a good education. Weren't your other schools like that? Or did you sit next to the children of roadsweepers and ditchdiggers?'

'Oh, school. I didn't mean that. I meant the country, and the government.'

'Tell me about the Fountain of Light.'

Angela said, 'It's a lifelong dedication to an ideal, Beverley. It's a force of good in the world.'

'Is it open to everybody?'

Angela began to talk about the 'Movement', as she called it. Beverley kept a straight face, but only just. From what she could gather, the Fountain of Light wasn't exactly like the Klan, but they were pretty near it. Their favourite word for people who disagreed with them was 'degenerate'.

'What does that mean?' Beverley asked.

'Psychologically evil and immoral.'

'I thought it had something to do with not living up to your ancestors.'

'No, honey – it's people that can't live up to an ideal.'

'Why can't they?'

'Because they're too degenerate.'

'I see,' Beverley said. 'That explains it.'

She asked Tom on their way to the swimming pool, 'Do you think I'm degenerate?'

He said, 'How do you mean?'

'Aren't you one of the Fountains of Light?'

'Well, yes.'

'So, do you think I'm degenerate?'

He looked very serious and said, 'Let's put it like this: I think you've fallen into evil ways.'

Beverley burst out laughing. She had to steady herself against the wall.

'It isn't funny,' he said. 'It's a tragedy.'

'What's a tragedy?'

'You and that guy you're with. What do you think you're doing?'

She took a deep breath and thought of telling him precisely.

'You must know it's wrong,' he said.

'What's wrong?'

'Well, you aren't married to him, are you?'

'No, and I'm not married to you, either.'

'That's different.'

'Oh? Why do you hold me tight and keep kissing me – do you love me? Are you planning to marry me?'

'Yes,' he said.

She was so shocked that she couldn't answer. He took her by the elbow and drew her down the hallway. He put his arm around her and began to talk about the commitment to love and the commitment to God. She felt battered. She couldn't even argue back.

They reached the doors to the changing-rooms. She said, 'Even if I were free – '

'You are free,' he told her.

'No, I'm bound to him. And I love him.'

'You don't love him. If you'd loved him, you wouldn't have let me kiss you.'

'I guess that was just because I'm so degenerate,' she said.

'We'll talk about it some more tomorrow.'

After their swim, he went to join Mimi and Darell on the ski slopes. She lay down on a mattress in the sun room and fell asleep for a few minutes. She had decided not to return to the Miramar the next day.

*

When she woke up, she heard two women talking. They were sitting right nearby on the next two mattresses and were speaking English. She opened her eyes, but she was facing the other way. She was looking at a lot of extremely old men and women in bathing suits. In the past two days the hotel had filled up with some very ancient tourists. It seemed strange that they should come just for New Year's Eve; probably it was for the healthy air more than the celebrations.

'I've told them: we've really got to improve the security,' one of the women said. 'Anybody can come up here now. Look at what happened last week.'

Something about the voice disturbed Beverley. She had the feeling she'd heard it before, but she couldn't remember where.

She turned her head and found herself looking up into a face she recognized. She said, 'Oh. Mrs Torrence,' and sat up.

The woman's head moved sharply. She was in her early eighties and she looked actually younger than Beverley seemed to recall, but it was the same woman: a friend of her grandmother, years ago, back in St Louis. Beverley remembered her from vacations there.

'Who?' Mrs Torrence said.

'Beverley. My grandmother was – '

'Oh, of course,' Mrs Torrence said. She smiled. She introduced Beverley to the other woman, a Mrs Dace, who had hair that was dyed red, although she appeared to be the same age as her companion. She smiled pleasantly at Beverley and asked if she was staying at the hotel.

'No. I'm down in one of the villages. This is out of my price range, I'm afraid.'

'Then you're all alone up here today?' Mrs Torrence said.

'I was with some friends till just a little while ago. We'll be meeting for tea as usual, and then I'll go on back down.'

'Oh, do join us for tea. We can show you the parts of the hotel you'd never see.' She turned to Mrs Dace and said, 'You remember giving little Alma the tour? This'll be just the same. Such fun to have some young faces around.'

Beverley didn't want to be impolite. She accepted the invitation. In fact, she was rather looking forward to seeing some of the private suites; they might be ones that retained the original nineteenth-century decor or, even better, have been remodelled in the more famous *art nouveau* designs. The two women would be treating her to the tea; that made a difference, too. And, in addition, she'd be able to avoid Tom.

'We can leave a message for your friends, if you like,' Mrs Torrence said.

Beverley wrote a note to say she'd run into someone from home. Mrs Dace levered herself off the mattress and took the folded paper away; she promised to find an envelope for it and leave it at the reception desk. Mrs Torrence began to tell a series of stories about St Louis in the old days when she and Beverley's grandmother were girls. Beverley was delighted. She'd been very fond of her grandmother.

After they'd changed, they took an elevator up to one of the higher floors. Mrs Dace asked to be called Minnie and Mrs Torrence said her name was Martha and she'd be angry now if Beverley used anything but her first name from that moment on. She took a gold key out of her alligator bag and fitted it into a door at the end of the hallway. Beverley would never have known that

the door led anywhere – it looked from the front like another
ordinary linen closet or a place where the hotel maids would keep
brooms and mops and maybe some extra sheets. The key, on the
other hand, could have been real gold: it was in the form of a
winged nymph naked from the waist up; her legs became the part
of the key that went into the lock.

'Here we are,' Martha said.

They stood in a hallway parallel to the one they had left. The
ceiling was higher, the mouldings more elaborate, the carpets
more opulent. Ahead of her Beverley saw gilding, parquetry,
Venetian mirrors and fresh flowers that blossomed from vases set
in scalloped niches along the walls. She looked hard at everything, hoarding details to present to Claus later on, when he was
back from the skiing and they'd be lying with their arms around
each other; she'd tell him stories as if she were a traveller who had
returned from foreign journeys; first she'd been able to bring back
part of the world that belonged to Angela, and now it would be
the places inhabited by the very rich and – so it appeared – the old.

Martha gave a commanding sign with her right arm, leading
onward. They entered an adjacent corridor and came to a bank of
windows that looked out on a view of ice-covered crags and fir
trees going down into a chasm; arched and fluted snowfields
hung in roofed masses above them.

'Wonderful,' Beverley said. She thought Claus would love it
too.

'You can only see it from this side,' Minnie told her. 'It's
reserved for us.'

'Shh.' Martha put up a warning finger. 'Beverley will think
we're bragging.'

Minnie lifted her hand to her face. She muttered, 'Oh. Of
course.'

Martha led the way into her rooms and then out again, into
Minnie's. Beverley was staggered by the apricot satin bedspreads,
the green marble sunken baths, the black and silver chairs. They
told her the names of the designers and walked her farther along
the hallways to a tea-room that looked like the main salon of an

ocean liner. Minnie and Martha waved to a few groups at other tables; the men made motions of bobbing to their feet as they bowed forward. All the people were old. There were about fifty of them in the huge room. Beverley wondered if it was like an old people's outing: if Minnie and Martha were members of some sort of exclusive club for five-star holidays. She also had for a moment a sudden sense of isolation and strangeness. If she could have thought of an excuse, she'd have asked to go back. She was almost ready to make something up, to say, 'Oh, I just remembered . . .'

'We generally come in a bunch,' Martha said. 'We're all friends here.' She smiled and added, 'Old friends.'

Tea came, with both cakes and sandwiches. Beverley began to eat voraciously. She'd worked up a hunger again from the swimming. The two old women watched as if pleased to see someone with such a hearty young appetite.

They talked about the skating and the ice maze. Martha asked Beverley how long she was staying and she answered that it would be only two more days because her friend had to get back to work. 'And you?' she said, to keep the conversation going.

'Oh, we both live here most of the year now,' Martha answered. 'I guess you could say we've retired to the mountains. Took to the hills.'

Minnie tittered and said, 'Yes, you could say that.'

'Don't you miss St Louis?' Beverley asked.

'I really try', Martha told her, 'to live in the present as much as possible. I like reading the papers and looking at TV.'

'Well, you could do that at home. You could – ' Beverley stopped. She had been about to say something that had to do with how difficult she found it to think of living in Europe for ever, not just for a while. She had been getting ready to talk about Claus and her family. Something had sidetracked her. She stared at her teacup. What was it? The feeling of isolation and uncertainty came over her again. She cleared her throat. And suddenly, she remembered: St Louis. In St Louis, ten years before, when she was just a child, she'd been to Martha Torrence's funeral.

She looked up.

'Yes, dear?' Martha said.

This time Beverley was deserted by her natural instinct to hide herself before she was certain what was going to happen. She was too surprised to cover up. 'Mrs Torrence – ' she said.

'Martha.'

'In St Louis. I went to your funeral.'

'Yes.' Martha sat smiling at her. Minnie was looking away at a corner of the room.

'Yes?' Beverley repeated. She remembered Claus saying: *A lot of famous people died there.* She breathed in. She felt her comprehension slipping. The time passed. She sat in her chair for what seemed like ten minutes, until she knew how to go on. 'Was it something to do with the insurance?' she asked.

'How smart of you, Beverley.' Martha grinned. You could see that her teeth were the best money could buy; and her cosseted complexion also, helped by face-lifts, no doubt. Beverley thought: *She probably looks a lot better than I do at the moment.*

'Not exactly a swindle,' Martha confided, 'but shall we say: a conspiracy. I was very fortunate in my doctor – a man who was five years my senior, and what he didn't know about nursing homes wasn't worth knowing. It's rather a long story. Shall I tell you?'

'Yes, please,' Beverley said. Now she was intrigued and thrilled. Claus wouldn't mind her being late, once she'd explained why. *Wait till I tell people*, she thought, *that I had a long talk with a woman who died ten years ago.*

Martha glanced at Minnie, who picked up her cup and saucer and said, 'You'll excuse me, won't you? Now that you've started in on the explanation, I'll just go say hello to Herbie.' She toddled off to a table up against a palm tree by the wall.

*

Martha said, 'A friend of mine had a terrible thing happen to her once. She was in her late sixties and her children were all in their forties. She had grandchildren and two great-grandchildren. It was a large family. And Ida, my friend, started to lose her memory and repeat things and get confused all the time. The family thought it was premature senility. You can't blame them; what can you do except take the advice of the experts? And in Ida's case the experts said she was deteriorating fast and should be in a home. And that was that. The children were devastated, but there was no choice. They had her put away and they went through the whole legal business of transferring the house and the property and the money, and dividing it up as if she'd already died. She'd been declared *non compos*, you see. And she was, of course. It was all perfectly straightforward. Except for one thing – the nursing home she was in: they automatically gave their patients antibiotics. So, suddenly, eighteen months after the trouble started, Ida was completely normal again. She'd just had some strange kind of infection. Well, maybe you can imagine: she woke up into this imprisonment, not even knowing where she was – or why – and was told that her own family had committed her and taken away everything, even her great-grandparents' silver spoons. And when the doctors came around and discharged her – it wasn't easy, you know. So much in life is a matter of trust.'

'Yes,' Beverley said, 'it's one of the most important things.' She was thinking about Claus again, and their dissatisfaction over the Christmas presents. *We each choose for ourselves*, she thought. *But does either of us trust the other to choose for both? And that's what marriage has to be. There has to be that trust on both sides.*

Martha said, 'Ida's family loved her very much. It was all a tragic mistake, or rather, a misdiagnosis. But it got me thinking: sometimes people aren't much loved by their families. I started to sound out a few of my other friends and you'd be surprised, you really would be, at how many were honestly afraid of getting pushed down the stairs or handed the wrong medicine, or just scared to death. When you're old – you've the experience, but if your eyesight starts to go, and your hearing, and you aren't so quick on your feet any more, then it's frightening to know that people who don't like you – who sometimes actually hate you – are just waiting for you to die off, the quicker the better. And you wonder how far they'd go.'

'But the medical profession is very careful about that kind of thing.'

'The medical profession can mess something up just as fast as anyone else.'

'I'm engaged to a doctor,' Beverley said.

'Then you'll know I'm right. They misplace the X-rays, they operate and leave the sponge in, sometimes a clamp too, they get the names switched around and cut open the wrong one, they bring mothers somebody else's baby to feed. Isn't that right?'

'All I meant was, if it's a matter of a person's sanity, so somebody else can get the money, then they're very careful.'

'So it seems. There are a lot of cases you don't read about because they never get to the papers. There are a lot of families who can't take it any longer. Ask a doctor in his seventies. They know. Anyway, about a dozen of us decided to do something. We formed a society. And now you've seen it.'

'You pretended to die, and got part of your money away first, and then you just came here?'

'That's right. We own this hotel and another one in Switzerland and a big place down in the Caribbean – we've got a whole island there – but the climate doesn't agree with everyone; it can be tough on arthritis sufferers. I really like it best here now. Of course, as far as the climate goes, we should really be based somewhere like Arizona, but that's too close to home for most of us. Too dangerous. We've got quite a big foreign contingent, but the majority of us are still American. There are a lot of us now, too. In ten years we've gotten up to about fifteen hundred. Quite a sizeable little club. And now you're one of us.'

'Don't worry,' Beverley laughed. 'Your secret's safe with me.'

'Of course it is. Because you'll be staying here. That's why I've been talking to you.'

'Staying? How do you mean?'

'You're going to be staying here now, with us. There's no other solution. It's what I was saying about the importance of trust, Beverley – we simply can't afford it. We've broken the law; just think of the tax situation for a start. And on top of that, we'd have the families after us. Impossible. You'll settle down soon. It can be very entertaining here, you know.'

Beverley sat back in her chair. She surveyed the people at the other tables, who, she could now see, were darting interested glances in her direction. But maybe she was imagining it. Maybe it was just because she was the one young person in the room. Or – because they all knew Martha Torrence went off the deep end like this whenever she found somebody new to talk to? Or maybe they were all in on it, and this could be some special refinement on a game they played with strangers and outsiders.

She decided to argue it through and find out how much more was to come. She said, 'Time is on my side.'

'That's true,' Martha admitted. 'In twenty years, I and all my friends will be dead – really dead. But the movement is very popular now. There are new recruits every year. And every year they're going to be just a little younger than me. Eventually, they'll be your age.'

Beverley tried to laugh, and couldn't. She wanted to get up and leave, but she knew she'd never find her way back through the corridors. And besides, she'd need the gold key. When she thought of the key, she felt sick. The picture came back to her with loathsome clarity: of the old woman's well-manicured hand clutching the winged, golden, naked girl and fitting the feet into the keyhole.

'There's nothing to worry about,' Martha said. 'We've got help from the outside. Maybe you've met some of them – the Fountain of Light movement?'

'What?'

'Of course, they're under the impression that they're fund-raising for other people. It wouldn't be right to tell them the truth. So many young people nowadays need to feel they're part of something grand and important. I don't think they'd appreciate being told that their efforts were really only keeping a large group of very self-indulgent great-grandparents in the champagne and cigars of their choice. The young are so in love with ideals. They might not see the humour of it.'

This time Beverley did laugh. That would really be something to tell Claus, and her parents, too. She lifted her cup shakily, drank, and sloshed some of the tea into the saucer.

Martha continued, 'You'll be completely taken care of. You'll be our pet. I must say, it will be a delight to have a young face to look at. And our old boys will simply adore you. You'll be idolized.'

'I'd rather be loved,' Beverley said. 'Really loved.' Tears began to roll down her cheeks. 'I'd rather', she said, coming right out with it, 'be in bed with my boyfriend.'

'I daresay. But one can overcome that. There are other things in life. You'll just have to apply yourself to them.'

Beverley put her hand up to rub it across her face. She stared back at the inquisitive old people. 'What other things?' she said bleakly.

'Well, we could start off,' Martha told her cheerfully, 'by teaching you how to play bridge. Unless you already know how. You could join the tournaments. We've got some marvellous players here.'

'I'm pretty strong. I could escape.'

'Yes. Unfortunately that's what the others have always tried. They take someone into their confidence and then – it's distressing, but if it goes that far, we have to do something about all of them.'

For the first time Beverley believed the whole story. Her room down in the village, the skiers on the slopes, even the genuine guests on the other side of the hotel seemed as far away as if they existed in a different country. The key had gone into the lock and she was separated from the rest of life. 'The three people on the toboggan run?' she said.

'I'm afraid so.'

She thought back to the swimming pool: the artificial heat and light. Minnie and Martha talking. 'And little Alma?' she asked.

'Yes, her too.'

'Who was she?'

'She was the girl before you. You see, if you hadn't said anything about remembering my funeral – well, we'd have let you go. Even if you remembered later and told people about the hotel, no one would take you seriously. But your reaction was so strong.'

'I remembered the funeral because I went with my grand-mother and I was worried about her. She died fairly soon after that. And I do remember that she cried like anything over you.'

'You mustn't be angry at me for that. My son-in-law was getting ready to have me certified for the sake of a few hundred thousand dollars. And my daughters would never have gone against him. Never.'

'Have you been happy here?'

'Blissfully happy. The peaceful nobility of the mountains – there's nothing like it. The food is delicious, the wonderful air – and we have the most fabulous doctors, of course; the hot springs and the sun rooms: I'm talking now about our own facilities on this side of the building. We only cross over, we only really come out at all, at New Year's, to see all the young people. That's the only thing we miss.'

'I'd miss it even more than you would,' Beverley cried. 'Couldn't you take my word for it that I wouldn't ever tell anybody?'

'We can't. We just can't. You've got to see that. No, dear, it's much too good a story. You could even sell it for money to the papers. I'm afraid not. You'll have to get used to it. Don't look to the others for help – they're a lot stricter about the rules than I am. You just relax now, and accept. I think you'll find it's going to be in your interest to adopt a pleasant and friendly attitude. Try to breathe in the spirit of serenity that these wonderful mountains induce.'

When she didn't come back, Claus would try to find her. He'd telephone the Miramar; he'd go down to the Adler to look up Angela and her friends. After that, he'd go to the police. Perhaps that would be the moment for an eminently respectable and distinguished-looking elderly couple to step forward and say, 'We saw her heading down the mountain just as it was getting dark. She didn't seem to know how to ski very well and she took the most difficult route.' Then the search parties would spread out over the snow, Claus among the number. But no one would really be surprised if her corpse couldn't be found. People disappeared all the time in the mountains, all year long. The mountains were like the oceans in that respect – every season was deadly.

'We aren't even in the danger zone for avalanches,' Martha said. 'Anyway, long before the unstable periods, the men get out and fire things off to loosen the snow and send it in the right direction. We're well protected in every way.' She bent forward, took Beverley's arm and stood up. 'You just come on over here,' she ordered, 'and sit down.'

Beverley rose unsteadily. She felt as dazed as if the tea they'd been drinking had been drugged. Once more tears ran over her face. She allowed herself to be steered to the small table where Minnie was talking with an old man. The man stood and bowed as they approached. Martha pushed her gently into the third chair and sat next to her.

Beverley sniffled and raised the back of her hand to her eyes. The old man held out a handkerchief to her, which – after a hesitation – she took. She thought miserably that it was no wonder the other young ones they'd held prisoner had been willing to risk escape, if not to take the risk meant year after year, for ever: never in her life to see Claus again, or to get back home, to see her family; her body and her life unused and unknown.

'Are you ready?' Martha asked. 'Good. Now try to remember: the most important thing to get straight about bridge is the bidding.'

Blessed Art Thou

Brother Anselm had come into the chapel early. He seemed to want to confess. Brother Francis had gone to the confessional and waited, but nothing had happened. When he'd come out to look, Anselm was in the covered archway, pacing to and fro; he was making vestigial, instantly repressed explanatory gestures in the air and occasionally he'd turn his head towards the square of green grass beyond the stone pillars, though he didn't appear to be taking it in.

Francis became interested. It was rare to see such signs of distress in a brother; ever since the new permissiveness, most people had become too good at dissembling. His friend, Frederick, who ran the place, had clamped down so hard on all unusual behaviour that from being a recently liberated enclosed order they had become practically suffocated by stricture. And this reaction against licence had actually forced them into a departure from tradition. Francis realized that. He would never have said so to Frederick. Their monastery was definitely a one-man show. It always had been and remained so even now, when Frederick was only the acting head. At times Francis thought of himself as the First Mate and of Brother Adrian as the Second Mate. Frederick stood indisputably at the helm.

Francis and Frederick had been through so much together that they were like old soldiers; each had sustained the other through more than one crisis of faith. They could speak their doubts and not have the words taken the wrong way. They knew their faults and still liked each other. Neither one of them was so sure that they liked Brother Adrian very much, though they certainly knew his faults, too. Brother Adrian was short, meaty, red-faced and opinionated. He was sometimes right, but, right or wrong, always at loggerheads with Frederick, who was a tall, elegant, ironic man often prone to outbursts of ferocious rudeness, bad temper and bigotry. Brother Francis was the peacemaker. He recognized the important fact that both men had faith. He knew in his heart that that would overcome all obstacles.

But there was no doubt that for the past four years life had been monotonous in the order: dull and without flavour. He had even heard young Brother William say to his friend, Elmo, that violence was not necessarily to be deprecated, as sometimes it 'cleared the air', a sentiment for which he had been reprimanded. And when the rebuke had been administered, the boy had made everyone gasp by asking, 'Is Brother Francis going to be censured for eavesdropping?' That was the last scandal they had had – two months ago. All wounded feelings had now healed. William had even admitted that he had been more or less shouting at the time. And life had returned to the uneventful rules and routines. So, it was intriguing to see Anselm displaying such uncustomary agitation.

Francis watched for a while without showing himself. He was pretty sure that Anselm wouldn't go away until he'd made some kind of decision. He began to feel more and more curious as he watched.

He was patient. He knew that Anselm was a serious young man who liked to think things over for a long time before committing himself to an opinion. His faith was divided; his approach to God was intellectual and therefore in constant danger of attack by itself. He was twenty-seven, had dark hair and dark eyes, and was nice-looking but nervy. He sometimes talked too fast. When he had the feeling that he wasn't getting through to people, or that his ideas would escape if he didn't put them into words – it was like a panic, he'd said to Francis: there was always a right moment, and you could miss it.

The order was fortunate in having so many young men. Elmo

and William were in their early twenties, James and Duncan in their thirties. Just at the time when the young ones had rushed from the open doors of other monasteries, theirs had received recruits. Frederick had said sourly that there would always be some who found relief in seeking out suffering for a while. But their young ones had stayed. They hadn't all had an easy time. Francis had felt so sorry for them that in his own recurrent crises of faith they had nearly caused him to despair. There had been one terrible, long night when he'd been roaring drunk, saying it was a crime to inflict mental torture on the young; Frederick had had to hold his head while he was sick.

*

Anselm stalked past the stone columns, the green wedges of grass showing between. 'Father,' he muttered, 'I have . . . that is to say, you aren't going to believe this, but . . .'

At last he came to a stop and sat down with his back against one of the pillars. He longed for a cigarette, but he'd given them up six years before. He shut his eyes, opened them again on the picture of stone archways, grey skies and grass, and sighed.

It had been just like this, but a wonderful day, not overcast like today: a time taken out of a milder season – springlike, marvellously full of sunshine, the sky blue as if enamelled, the air warm. And he was on the other side of the building, just like this, when he wasn't supposed to be – he'd just skipped his duties and routines and thought somebody could go ahead and report him: he didn't care. And nobody had reported him, either, which was also strange, but of course it was nothing compared to what was to come, because – he was looking out, like this, into the warm, grassy courtyard and when he'd lifted his face to the bright air there had been a loud, rapid fluttering sound, a heavy thump, and there in front of him on the expanse of green was a handsome young man, stark naked and smiling. Behind him, quivering and drawing themselves inward, were two large wings made of what appeared to be golden feathers. As Anselm watched, they pleated together and disappeared, leaving – so he was later to discover –

no bodily trace on their owner. The young man looked right at him. He was still smiling. He took a step forward and held his arms out.

Anselm knew straight away that this was the friend he'd been hoping for all his life. He had made a mistake to think that he could look deep into his own spirit and find a new and better self; the elusive other self was already inhabiting someone else. Only by loving another person did you find that part of yourself.

He moved forward, opening his own arms, falling into the waiting embrace. The young man kissed him on the cheek, on the neck, on the mouth; hugged him, stroked and patted him lightly, and started to undo his clothes. Anselm was fairly certain that there was no one around at the moment, but there might be one other person who, like him, had decided not to do what he'd been ordered to that day; so he told the young man, breathlessly, that they'd better go to his cell. He pulled him quickly across the sunny grass, into the dark stone archways and corridors, to his tiny room. He closed the door.

The young man removed the rest of Anselm's clothes and fell on the bed with him. He seemed to be shedding light from his nakedness into all parts of the room. Anselm could hardly breathe. Her knew what was happening but he couldn't quite connect it with anything else. He supposed it was really only the kind of thing he'd been warned about all his childhood: they tried to do it to you in washrooms, everyone had told him. And the Church frowned on it. Of course he'd somehow suspected it must be fun, otherwise people wouldn't be so much against it, but all the same, he wasn't prepared for this: to be touched all over, lovingly and thoroughly, in every kind of way, as he'd always – though he knew it was wicked – dreamed it would be like to make love. He was very nervous, but he was overjoyed.

He kept his head enough to ask the man's name afterwards. 'Gabriel,' his friend told him. Anselm fell asleep in his arms. When he woke, Gabriel had gone.

Anselm got up and dressed, walked back to the courtyard and looked around. He thought he could detect some indentations in the grass that might have been made by the pressure of the angel's feet as he'd taken off.

He expected Gabriel to meet him at the same hour the next day. He rushed to the place long before it was time and waited, his eyes devouring every inch of his surroundings in an excess of anticipation. But Gabriel didn't return.

Anselm waited the next day too, and was again disappointed. He began to feel desperate. He couldn't eat. He didn't think he was going to be able to live through the next day. But he still believed that Gabriel would come back.

Three different people criticized him for neglecting his duties. Although usually he was so overly diligent that he'd have been thrown into consternation by any expression of disapprobation, now he really didn't mind. Waiting for Gabriel was more important. He actually told the most persistent of his critics to shut up and mind his own business.

By the end of the week he knew that it was over. Gabriel wasn't going to come back. It had been a single visitation: not to be repeated.

He realized that he had never before known what it was to suffer. The pain of trying to accept the loss of love was too much for him. He felt himself beginning to break up, to become confused; he couldn't remember things, he couldn't keep his attention on anyone. He had to talk to somebody.

The only person he could think of was Brother Francis, who was usually understanding and kind, and got along with everyone.

He should go to Brother Francis and confess. He knew that; he was ready to do it. Not until he was outside the chapel did it strike him that it wasn't going to be that easy to begin. He worked himself into such a state that by the time he finally entered, his head was down and his arms hanging. He shuffled towards the confessional.

Francis nipped in at the other end.

Anselm stared into the darkness and sighed. He said, 'I don't know how to put it.'

'It's all right, Anselm,' Francis told him. 'Just make a beginning somewhere. Have you sinned?'

'And how.'

'I beg your pardon?'

'All over,' Anselm babbled, 'kissing and touching – it was wonderful, lovely. It was so delightful, and I know it's a sin, but it's the only truly magical thing that's ever happened to me – right out of this world. I'm not sorry about it. All I can think of is how much I want it to happen again. But every time I go there and wait for him, I know it's the end; he isn't comimg back. And I can't stand it. I just don't know what to do now. It's so lonely. It's killing me, Francis. What am I going to do?'

'Anselm, you know we're supposed to give up all – all – all that sort of thing.'

'I didn't have to give it up – I never had it. No, never before. And maybe they're right about the other kind; I don't know. But this was wonderful. The feeling of joy – and it didn't leave me afterwards. It grew. I felt transformed. I knew I should confess it, but it was like a secret he'd trusted me with. And after all, he takes precedence, doesn't he?'

Brother Francis forgot the rules. 'This is appalling,' he said.

'The only really sublime, magnificent thing that's ever happened to me. An angel – an angel from heaven, coming down to earth. But now he's gone, I feel so sad. I miss him. I can't tell you how much I – all day long, all the time, all . . .' Anselm started to cry.

Francis knew that he shouldn't say anything more without consulting someone, but he couldn't remain silent while his fellow man suffered. 'It's all right,' he said. He got up from his seat, went around to haul Anselm out into the light, and made him sit down in one of the pews. Anselm leaned forward, his head against his hands and his hands gripping the edge of the pew in front of him. Francis patted him on the back and repeated that it was all right. 'Who did you say this other young man was?' he asked.

'Gabriel.'

'I can't recall a Brother Gabriel in the order.'

'He's an angel. I told you. He came – he just landed, and folded up his wings.'

'Wings?'

'I still remember the joyfulness, but how can anything be the same again? It was amazing the way he appeared, out of nowhere. And now ordinary life isn't any good. It feels unliveable.'

'Wings?' Francis said again.

'Golden wings. The real thing.' Anselm's voice sounded choked and tearful. He slumped forward on to the floor. He seemed to have fainted. Francis pulled him up. He told him to go back to his cell and lie down, and that he'd send Duncan to him.

'I don't need a doctor,' Anselm said, but he went back to his cell obediently, lay down and fell asleep.

*

Francis was worried. He went to see Frederick. 'I think something's wrong with Anselm,' he said, and told him the story.

'Should you be telling me this?' Frederick asked.

'Consider it a confession. I don't know what to do.'

'That's simple. We find the joker and throw him out.'

'Who?'

'The gardener's boy? Damn it, you can't tell about anyone any more. He looked perfectly harmless to me. A little drip that could barely put one foot in front of the other.'

'Exactly. Definitely not the type. Not like the last one.'

'Yes, well. A heavy drinker, but marvellous with the bulbs. I suppose we'd better just wait till Anselm pulls himself together.'

'He said it was an angel. With wings. Golden wings.'

'I see. Have you asked Duncan to take a look at him?'

'He won't see Duncan.'

Anselm went back to his ordinary life. He didn't speak to anyone else about his visitation, but somehow word ran around the monastery that he had seen an angel in a vision. People began to come to his cell to ask him about it. He told them all the same thing: 'I don't want to talk about it.' But the higher powers became alarmed by this evidence of interest.

They called Anselm before them. He sat in a chair facing Frederick, Francis and Adrian.

Frederick said, 'All right, Anselm. Tell us about it.'

'It's just what I said to Francis,' Anselm mumbled. 'I don't think it should be anyone else's business. I'm trying to get used to it.'

'I'm sorry, Anselm,' Francis said. 'This is only because the others have been talking.'

'Oh, it isn't you. I don't blame you.'

'Who do you blame, then?' Brother Adrian said.

'Who do you? Why am I here?'

'Delusion.'

'You think it was an optical illusion?'

'Delusion. Delusions of grandeur. *I did it with angels.*'

'Only one.'

'Or', Frederick said, 'could it have been a man? Someone in the order, for example?'

'No.'

'These things sometimes occur, regrettable though they may be.'

'Who regrets it?'

'Who was it, Anselm?'

'I've told you. And you don't believe it. All right, never mind. May I go now?'

'Let's be more specific about what actually happened.'

'I do not propose to discuss what went on between us.'

'You don't have to. I can imagine it well enough. That wasn't what I had in mind. What I'm trying to ascertain is whether at any stage during this alleged encounter the wings got in the way.'

'I've said already: they'd disappeared.'

'Where to?'

'Inside.'

'Inside? How?'

'Well, I'm not sure. When I saw it happen, he was facing me. I guess they must be like those fold-up umbrellas you can get: you know, sort of collapsible. When you don't need them, you can – '

'Anselm, this joke has gone far enough. Come on, now. What's going on? You're feeling the need of drama and eventfulness here?'

'A lack of attention?' Adrian added. 'But you didn't join our order for that, did you?'

'I joined it because I love God. And now, at last, I've got the proof that He loves me back. He sent His angel to me and showed me. You say you can imagine, but you can't. You just can't. It was a pleasure beyond anything.'

'Oh, Christ,' Frederick muttered.

'And he was beautiful.'

'A figment of the – '

'I felt like a tree,' Anselm said wildly. 'A barren tree that's come into flower for the first time.'

'That's rather vague,' Francis said. 'What happened?'

'Well, after he took off my clothes, we sort of fell on to the bed and – '

'Please,' said Frederick. 'Spare us the details.'

'Francis asked what happened.'

'This is so sordid,' Adrian murmured.

Anselm exploded. 'How dare you?' he yelled. 'How dare you say that about any of God's creatures, much less an angel? We are not sordid. We're good. God made us and God loves us the way we are, even if we don't always do everything right.' He burst into tears. 'I can't go on,' he sobbed.

Francis made a move to rise and go to him, but Frederick held up his hand. Anselm fought for control. He began to calm down.

'I think you should have a talk with Brother Duncan,' Frederick told him.

'I'm all right now. I just got upset.'

Adrian said, 'You can claim you saw this, and you can claim you saw that, but the fact remains that nobody else saw – '

Anselm turned his head. 'You weren't chosen,' he sneered. 'I was. And', he said defiantly, 'his skin was like honey.'

'That's enough of that,' Frederick said. 'I'm ending this interview now. Anselm, if you won't agree to talk to Brother Duncan, you'll have to consider yourself confined to quarters until further notice.'

*

The incarnation was intended to be a punishment, but it also showed that they were afraid he might get out. Why would he want to do that? He lay on his bed – on the same bed where it had all taken place, and where he could remember if he shut his eyes or even lowered the lids a little – and tried to figure out why they were so worried. From their point of view, of course, he'd just been seeing things. Most closed communities were stiff with people who hadn't been able to stand the strain; even if they didn't crack, it was uncommon to find more than half of them without some kind of fissure. But they stayed, naturally. The world outside was so much worse. He himself, as they knew, had sought out the order as a refuge – a solution. And now it was where the best thing of his life had happened to him. It didn't make sense that he should want to leave, yet they were afraid. He started to feel apprehensive about their fear.

At the other end of the building from his cell, the senior brothers argued. 'You're making him a martyr,' Francis said. 'That's just what so many of the young ones want: the glory and romance of the persecuted believer.'

'He isn't all that young,' Frederick said. 'Nearly twenty-seven. That stuff's for the teenagers.'

'Haven't you noticed how the rest of them are taking his side against you?'

'Against us.'

'Except Adrian. That's a surprise. I never thought he'd agree with you on anything. I think he's just set against the poetry of it. He doesn't think other men, especially young ones, should have such fancy ideas.'

'Francis, it's the question of the morality that's so repulsive.'

'Yes, I'm not very fond of morals myself.'

'The lust, Francis. The gross flagrancy of the sexual intercourse. The immorality in any case, but in this case much more so. The perversion, for heaven's sake.'

'Perhaps.'

'Definitely.'

'I hope you and Adrian will take into account my firm conviction that it's necessary for people to be able to have their dreams. For the young, it's essential. And in a place like this, there's almost no other way to express the more flamboyant aspects of their nature. Do you understand?'

'I guess so. But it's the others I'm concerned about.'

'The others think it's too harsh to shut him away for a harmless fantasy. He didn't need to talk about it, after all.'

'Oh, talking about it was the point. You don't think all that big, lush story of kisses and touching would have been half as good without other people's reactions, do you?'

'He's always been a good boy, and conscientious. A bit serious and moody, a bit frightened of other people. But spiritually sound, Frederick. His heart's in the right place, I think.'

'It wasn't his heart he was boasting about.'

'He wasn't boasting. He was in distress.'

'Boasting. Adrian was right about that. "I was chosen," he said. And so on.'

'I just think, to be so severe – it might not be the right way to handle it.'

'One more week. Then we'll have another talk with him.'

*

Anselm let himself dream. He lowered his eyelids and remembered. He was happy, even though he didn't think it was very healthy to be cooped up the way he was. He did exercises in the cramped space, but they didn't seem to help much. He had pains in his chest. He lost interest in his theological texts. He yearned for things he'd left long ago – for instance, he'd have liked to see a really exciting movie full of car chases. It took him a long while to recover from his night's sleep. He didn't seem to wake up so quickly or so fully as usual, and the morning meal of lumpy porridge and tough old wheatmeal bread made him feel nauseated.

At last the brother who brought the food came to say that the sentence was up. The man's name was Dominic and he'd been dying of curiosity all the time he'd been coming to the cell. He had tried to sound Anselm out but had got no response, so when anyone asked him about his prisoner, he'd invent something. He made up anything he thought might be interesting, though nothing malicious; he said that one evening a bright light had seemed to be coming from under the door – brighter than could be accounted for by the ordinary lighting system available to the brothers; that kind of thing. By the time he unlocked the door and left it ajar, there was a fairly large corpus of mythological incident circulating through the monastery. He waited by the door, smiled widely and said, 'No more restrictions.'

Anselm stood up. He nodded.

Dominic said, 'Good heavens; they must really trust your sanity. I've never known them to allow anyone else in solitary to keep a razor.'

Anselm went back to the cloister, where he strolled up and down to stretch his legs. He also needed to think. He paced back and forth in front of his favourite tree, a pear tree, which had come into bud while he'd been shut indoors, and would soon be in flower. Things were no longer simple; or, if they were, then they were so simple that nobody else was going to be able to agree with him.

He went to eat lunch with the others. He sat down late. The brothers had already joined in silent prayer. When the talk began again, heads turned towards him. The bread was passed around. Brother Adrian said loudly, 'You need a haircut, Anselm. See Brother Marcus after lunch. Did you hear me?'

Anselm ignored him. He looked down the table to where the doctor sat, and said, 'Brother Duncan, if it won't be disturbing you, I'd like to talk to you after the meal.'

'Did you hear me?' Adrian bellowed.

A silence fell over the company. Anselm murmured, 'How

could anyone at this table fail to hear you, Brother Adrian? You're shouting so loudly. I'm perfectly capable of dealing with my hair, just as you must be of looking after what's left of yours.'

The roar of laughter from his companions turned Adrian red. He tried to stand up. The two brothers at his side held on to him.

Francis said, 'Argumentation is detrimental to the digestion, brothers. We all know that. Let's have some ideas and opinions on the new wines, all right?'

'They haven't settled down yet,' Brother Robert said. 'It's unfair to judge them at this stage.'

Everyone waited for Brother Robert to say more. He had a flair for the possibilities of a wine. He was a prematurely dried-up, pernickety little man, not the sort of person anyone would take to be an expert on a matter concerning the senses. He could drink huge amounts and, since the effect was to make him progressively quieter, he never seemed to be drunk – unlike Brother Adrian, who pontificated loudly and slurred very early on during the wine-tasting examinations and thought everything tasted pretty good.

'But just as a guess, Robert?' Francis asked. 'Good or bad?'

'Oh, the red is probably going to be ordinary enough. Drinkable, that's all. But the white could conceivably turn out to be something rather special for a California wine. Don't quote me. That's just off the top of my tonsure, ha-ha.'

Two of the brothers groaned. Brother William, one of the youngest, said, 'I thought the order hadn't had tonsures since Father Clement's time. I thought those were all just natural.'

'Go back to asleep,' his friend James told him.

'I wasn't asleep. I was thinking about something I wanted to ask Anselm, but now I've forgotten.'

Anselm glanced in William's direction. William twisted around in his seat and stared back. He looked baffled. He said, 'I just can't remember.'

Brother Adrian thundered down the table at Robert that the red wine this year was going to be full-bodied and rich as a ruby, not like the usual cat's piss the white wine drinkers were addicted to.

Most of the table joined in the quarrel. Since the entire monastery was divided into lovers of white wine and lovers of red, the
subject was normally a guarantee for heated debate.

Anselm didn't take part. He chewed his food slowly, watched
by the doctor from the other side of the table.

*

'Well, Anselm, what can I do for you?' Duncan asked. 'Feeling
nervous again? Depressed? Having dreams?'

'I've always had dreams, Doctor. Haven't you?'

'Of course. The thing to remember about dreams is that you
shouldn't let them run away with you.'

'I heard from somebody once that your great dream was to be a
missionary doctor, like Albert Schweitzer. Is that true?'

'That's right, yes. What good memories people have around
here. We all have our fantasies when we're young.'

'You're still not too old to do it.'

Duncan pointed to his heart. He said, 'I'm too old here.'

'So, if it was offered to you, you wouldn't accept?'

'Probably not. How did we get on to this? I was supposed to be
asking you about your health.'

'I'm not sure that what I've got is really a matter of health.'

'You look different. Were you eating all right, the past few
weeks?'

'Feel my cheek, Doctor,' Anselm said.

Duncan put out his hand and touched the side of Anselm's face.
'What's wrong?' he said. 'It doesn't feel like a temperature to me.'

'No beard,' Anselm explained. 'My beard has disappeared. It's
just gone.'

Duncan hitched his chair closer. He took Anselm's face
between his hands and turned it, first one way, then another.
'That's certainly what it looks like,' he said.

'And other things,' Anselm continued, 'have disappeared.'

'Oh?'

'And I'm getting fat. And I'd like you to take a look at my chest.'
He stood up, turned his back, unsnapped the front of his robe and

took out a towel he'd kept folded there. Then he turned around, holding the robe open so that the doctor could see: two round, exuberantly forward-pointing breasts, each about the size of a pomegranate.

Brother Duncan stood up. His mouth opened. He held out his hands as if to touch the breasts. Anselm picked up the towel and closed his robe. He sat down in the chair again.

The doctor continued to stare. At last he said, 'What the hell? Who are you?'

'I'm Anselm. You know very well. I've been in solitary confinement for a long time, so you know I couldn't have been switched. Maybe you heard something about the reason why they put me there?'

Duncan sat down. Once more he examined Anselm's face. 'I can't understand it,' he said.

'It isn't hard to understand, only hard to believe. I'm pregnant, that's all.'

'Right. Get your clothes off. All of them. This time I'm going to give you a complete examination.'

'Not on your life. I don't see why I should be subjected to any such thing without another woman present.'

'I'm a doctor.'

'Does that make you better than anyone else?'

'This is my job, Anselm.'

'But how much do you know about women?'

'I had a thorough medical education.'

'Exactly. That means: not much.'

'For Christ's sake, what do you think I'm going to do to you? I just want to look.'

'I bet. You can give me a urine test and find out that way.'

'Anselm, you don't seem to be taking this very seriously.'

'I'm taking it the only way that makes sense. I was chosen, and I accept it, and I'm glad. It's only everybody else who finds trouble in taking it. First of all they said I was crazy and seeing things. What are they going to say now?'

'Well, if it's true, how long do you think you can keep it secret?

There's going to come a time when it'll start to show.'

'It shows already, without the towel.'

'Well, everybody's got to know pretty soon, then. Unless you're planning to leave here.'

'No, I couldn't leave. Doctor, you know that's what's happened, don't you? You know it's a sacred thing. And you're bound by your oath to preserve life. You're also pledged to keep my confidence.'

'I can keep quiet. But in your condition, you'll give yourself away. Don't you think it would be better if I examined you now, and after that we could both go to Brother Frederick and have a chat?'

Anselm yawned. He said, 'I suppose so. But I'm relying on you. If they shut me up again, I won't be able to get the exercise I need. It wouldn't be healthy. If you really need to, I guess you can do an examination. But I'm warning you: try anything dirty, and I'll knock your teeth out.'

'This is what holiness has done for you, is it? Talking to me like that.'

'I've been put in a position of trust. My body is a sepulchre. It shouldn't be tampered with.'

'Relax. I'm not going to tamper. I'm going to palpate.'

'That sounds worse.'

'Anselm –'

'Oh, all right,' Anselm said. He began to pull furiously at his clothes to get them off. He found that tears were running from his eyes. He cried easily now and got irritated, and felt sleepy during the daytime. 'And my back hurts,' he said.

*

'There's no doubt about it,' Brother Duncan said. 'Anselm is expecting a child. Physically, he is now in every respect a woman.'

Anselm leaned back in Frederick's easy-chair. He had positioned the pillow so that it would give support at the small of his back. The pregnant belly loomed out in silhouette. His hair was brushed back and seemed much longer; the style made his face look like a woman's.

It took a while for Frederick, Francis and Adrian to digest the news. In the end, Frederick had to bring out the brandy. Anselm alone refused.

'Oh dear,' Brother Francis said, 'oh dear, oh dear.'

Brother Frederick looked the doctor in the eye and told him, 'It just isn't possible.'

'Who knows? Darwin wasn't wrong about everything. Eels are sexually ambivalent, and snails are both male and female at the same time; but maybe they weren't always that way. Maybe they became like that after some other way for a long time. Do you see what I mean? Maybe Anselm is only the first. He's evolved, so that – '

'No,' Anselm interrupted. 'I was chosen.'

'Perhaps mind over matter,' Francis said tentatively. 'If the desire was so strong. I'm not saying that it's psychosomatic, but . . . I don't know.'

'Yes,' Anselm said. 'I know what you mean. Love conquers all. I know that's true now. I've had the proof. In fact, I am the proof.'

Brother Adrian looked at Anselm with revulsion. He declared, 'It isn't in the realm of nature.'

'Nature covers a lot of territory. And it's changing all the time.'

'You know what I think we should do, Anselm? I think we should bring back the old practices and burn you at the stake.'

'Oh dear,' Francis said. 'Calm down, Adrian, please.'

'If it's a question of the survival of the Church?'

'But this is Anselm. We've known him for five years. He's a good boy.'

'He must have been a plant. By evil forces. Who knows what really went on? We have no idea.'

'I told you,' Anselm said.

'That's what I mean. The depths of sexual depravity.'

'It doesn't have anything to do with morality. It's all a question of love. I was given the love and it transformed me. And now that it turns out I've been given something else, that's going to be a wonderful reminder of – '

'Stop,' Frederick said. 'This is ludicrous.'

'Monstrous,' Adrian said. 'This progeny, whatever you want to call it, has got to be a monster. You're a living blasphemy, Anselm.'

'Don't say that.' Anselm took out a handkerchief and dabbed at his eyes.

'He's a medical anomaly, that's all,' Duncan said.

'This is not a miracle,' Adrian insisted. 'It's an abnormality. Brother Anselm is a freak, not a phenomenon.'

'Oh, you nasty man,' Anselm said, sniffing into his handkerchief.

'Yes, Adrian, really,' Francis said. 'Have a little compassion. In his state – after all, we don't want to upset the baby.'

'Baby? I wouldn't be surprised if it turns out to be a toad.'

'Gabriel,' Anselm whispered. He hid his face in the crook of his elbow. Francis patted his back and gripped his shoulder.

Frederick rose from his chair. He said, 'Well, Anselm, we'll just have to wait and see what you produce. In the meantime, I hope I don't have to tell you that no word of this is to leak out of this building. And while you remain here, you're to conduct yourself with modesty and decorum. That will be all for the moment. You may return to your cell. Perhaps you'd accompany him, Doctor? Him, her, whatever you want to call yourself.'

Anselm stood. 'God forgive you,' he said. He turned towards the door. Duncan took his arm. Brother Adrian shouted after them that Anselm would burn in hell for ever and ever.

Anselm let himself be led quietly to his cell. He lay down on his back and closed his eyes. He knew that he should try to think of some plan, some way of protecting himself. There were malicious and unscrupulous men around him, who despised him and who would have him at their mercy when the baby was born. He couldn't decide whether telling the outside world would help him or put him into greater danger.

He thought about the baby and smiled. He was feeling good in spite of the backaches. He fell asleep smiling.

*

Frederick went to Francis for comfort. He said, 'Francis, this thing will be the end of me. I don't know what to do. I can't tell anyone outside. On the other hand – I mean, it couldn't be. It couldn't be. You don't believe it, do you?'

'Well, the trouble is, we all know that he was a man when he arrived here.'

Frederick paced the room, smacked his hands together and pulled at his hair. He kept repeating that it wasn't possible.

'But it's happened,' Francis said.

'OK, OK. What I meant was: it isn't possible that it could be another divine birth. In which case, in which – you aren't helping, Francis.'

'In which case, it's an ordinary human birth.'

'Yes. A phantom pregnancy brought on by Anselm's over-whelming neurotic craving to become the object of his devotion: the Virgin Mary.'

'And when he gives birth?'

'It's all going to be gristle and leftover pieces of stuff.'

'Frederick, sit down for heaven's sake. You heard what Duncan said. It's going to be a child like any other child.'

'Then he was screwing somebody in my monastery, damn it all.'

'As a man or as a woman?'

'Oh, Christ,' Frederick said. 'Years clawing my way up the ladder, being polite to creeps and crazies, and playing along with the whole business: you do me a favour, I'll do you a favour. And then I got my own team and whipped it into shape. I worked like hell on this place, you know that. Not that they'd actually let me have it for my own – no, I'm only the deputy; that makes it less trouble for them. And now this happens.'

'But no matter what's caused it, it's a joyful thing.'

'Not for the man in charge, Francis. No, siree. What the hell am I going to do?'

'All these emotions – it's wearing me down. Try to relax and be happy. Don't work yourself up like this.'

'Easy for you to say. You aren't going to have to carry the can.'

'Neither are you. Nobody's going to blame you for this. Especially if you call in Duncan to explain the situation.'

'He doesn't have an explanation.'

'That's just it. What you do is what everyone else is going to do: wait and see.'

'No. We believe in God, the Virgin Birth, Christ the Redeemer, the teachings of Mother Church and the life everlasting. And that's damn well it. None of this newfangled nonsense. And don't start quoting Vatican Two at me – I'm sick to death of it.'

'But you wouldn't do anything to harm Anselm, would you?'

'How are we to know that this isn't some kind of unholy thing? That's what Adrian believes.'

'The man's a fool, you know that. He's jealous of Anselm and he's frightened of his own feelings. Forget what he believes. Let's say for the moment that we're dealing with an ordinary mother and child. It would be very wrong to do anything to harm them.'

'I wasn't thinking of harming anyone. Don't look at me like that.'

'You tell me what you were thinking about, then.'

'I don't know. There doesn't seem to be any way out. Why did this have to happen to me?'

'It didn't. It happened to Anselm.'

'But it affects us all. No man is an island.'

'And no woman, either.'

Frederick jumped up again, kicked the table, and said, 'Damn it, damn it, you can't keep them out of anything.'

*

Anselm walked back and forth for exercise. He passed his favourite tree, the flowering pear. He had stood for a quarter of an hour in front of it the night before, astonished at how its pale petals held the light so that he was able to see the whole tree blooming in the darkness.

In the daytime the tree seemed smaller than it had at night. He wondered why that should be. Maybe it had appeared large in isolation and because of being surrounded by black: a trick of the light and of the eye perceiving it. Or maybe the night showed the truth and the daytime tree was deceptively small.

He dropped all his duties and lived a life of ease. Most of the brothers felt that he had a certain amount of justification for it, though not necessarily because he had been touched by God. Everyone knew now that he had turned or been turned into a woman, and that was enough to excuse a lot. That in itself was a breach of discipline. It was breaking the rules like nobody's business.

A few people agreed with Brother Adrian and sat with him for hours at a stretch, discussing just what evil, unnatural, or evilly unnatural, or unnaturally evil cause could be behind the whole thing. But most of the young ones were on Anselm's side. And in his own wing of the building he became a focal point for afternoon meetings. He had a little club of admirers. They were zealously noted by Adrian and his followers, who reported the members to Frederick. But when Frederick suggested stamping out the coterie, Francis persuaded him that that would just make everything worse. They were to wait.

'There's a right time for everything, you know,' Frederick said. 'Remember the Bible. Sometimes it's a mistake to wait.'

'Not this time,' Francis told him. 'And that isn't what that passage is about, anyway. Calm down, Frederick.'

Anselm's friends brought him quantities of pillows, many of them silk and satin, to help support his back. He lay reclined on them like an oriental princess, smiling sweetly at the other brothers as they confided their troubles to him.

They drank coffee or tea or wine. Sometimes they'd flirt with him. Brother Elmo was especially obstreperous. You could still see the pierce-mark where he'd worn the earring in his left ear; he'd received the call, so he said, on a trip. 'A trip to where?' Brother William had asked. 'A trip to outer space, man. A trip on speed. Get in focus, Billy.'

Elmo was delighted with Anselm's transfiguration. It proved, he claimed, that he'd been right all along: anything could happen in life, and everything did, only most people were so unaware, so lacking in powers of observation, that they didn't notice. He stared possessively at Anselm and asked, 'So when are you going to let us have some fun with you, babe? It better be soon, before you get too big.'

'Don't be naughty,' Anselm said. He made a motion of hitting at Elmo with a small peacock-feather fan that had come wrapped up with one of the pillows.

'Come on, Anselm. We're your friends, aren't we? Who else are you going to play around with if it isn't your friends?'

'It's not a joke.'

'At least let us see your tits.'

Anselm fanned himself lazily.

'We'll bring you some extra food. You're eating for two now, remember.'

'I do have these terrible strong desires for certain tastes: dill pickles, cheesecake, raspberry ice cream, walnut and pecan mousse, smoked mackerel and watermelons.'

'We'll get them for you.'

'Promise?'

All the brothers nodded vehemently. Anselm undid his robe and exposed the full, cup-shaped breasts of which he was now immensely proud. There was a silence until he started to pull the robe together again.

'Wait,' Dominic said, and William begged, 'Not yet. I haven't finished looking.'

'Crazy, man,' Elmo said.

'Weird,' said Dominic.

'Cute. They look just like a girl.'

'Weird.'

'Can I touch one of them, Anselm?'

'Certainly not.'

'Why not? I just want to feel.'

'That's all meant for the baby, you know.'

'How did you work it?' William asked. 'How did you get them to grow? Did you wake up in the morning and find them like that?'

'No, it happened gradually. They got a little bigger every day.'
'Did it hurt?'
'Not hurt, exactly. Everything felt very tender and sore all over my chest. And so forth.' He snapped up the front of his robe again.

Brother James, at the back of the group, said he thought he had an explanation. 'Maybe –' he said, 'it's got something to do with radioactive fall-out from the atom bombs.'

'Or Mount St Helen's,' Dominic added.

'It was the angel,' Anselm said. 'I told them in the first place. It was Gabriel.'

*

'They're sitting around drinking wine in there,' Frederick said. 'Next thing you know, there'll be luxury and viciousness all over the place. Everybody knows about the stimulating properties of alcohol.'

'We should,' Francis said. 'We make a living out of it. They're just talking.'

'It makes me jumpy.'

'How can you stop them being interested? It's an absolutely extraordinary thing.'

'It's unnatural.'

'It's what happened to Our Blessed Lady.'

'I don't want to get into that argument. Anyway, when it happened to Mary, it wasn't a sin. It was pure. This is terrible.'

'You've been listening to Brother Adrian.'

'He talks a lot of sense sometimes, in spite of being a little over-emphatic.'

'Crass. He's a crass man, and frightened. And now he's infected you. Did you drink up all the whisky? That's right, he always has that effect on you.'

'Unnatural,' Frederick insisted.

'How can it be unnatural if it's happened?'

'It shouldn't have happened.'

'What do you call conception through the ear-hole? That's

supposed to be the way the Holy Ghost got in, isn't it?'

'We have to regard these events in a philosophic light, as representing symbolic manifestations of spiritual truths.'

'What?'

'And Brother Anselm just isn't in that league. Also, the whole thing is against the teachings of Mother Church.'

'Nonsense. A miracle is a miracle is a miracle.'

'Is that what you really think this is?'

'I don't know what it is. Truly.'

'Brother Duncan says he thinks Anselm was androg . . . an andr . . . whatever the word is.'

'Hermaphrodite?'

'And he lived all one way for years, even though the other half was there all the time, lurking under the surface, just waiting to show itself – which it finally did, all at once.'

'Complete with child?'

'No. That came later. First of all he hid it and had carnal relations with somebody in here, and when he found out he was pregnant, then he came to you.'

'Neat.'

'The whole rigmarole is having a profoundly unsettling effect on the order.'

'Especially on you.'

'On me too, of course. I don't deny it. But look at Adrian. And in the other direction – what about Marcus?'

Brother Marcus had become a regular visitor to Anselm's room. He had been so completely won over that it was now his greatest pride to be responsible for making Anselm look as attractive as possible. He delighted in finding new arrangements in which to set Anselm's luxuriant dark hair, which was growing so quickly that it was already down to his shoulders. 'Let's put it up today,' Marcus would suggest, or, 'How about side-swept for a change?' He came every morning and evening, his sausage-like fingers deft among the glossy masses of hair. He had managed to acquire a set of pins and ornaments for keeping the hair in place and twining it into piled-up shapes. And while he worked, a light of happiness

shone from his face. He had changed. He'd always looked as strong
and coarse as a picture of a Victorian butcher, but now he displayed
moods of elephantinely delicate playfulness and good humour.

'God Almighty,' Brother Adrian said under his breath as
Anselm moved up to the table with his slow, billowing gait and
his elaborately perched hair-do, 'it's like sitting down to dinner
with the Whore of Babylon.'

'You should be so lucky,' Brother Robert told him. 'What I hear
is: he doesn't sell it and he doesn't give it away for free. Admiration from afar is his line.'

'Maybe he's saving himself for another bout with the super-
natural.'

'If it's true,' Brother James said, 'no amount of repentance is
going to make up for the way you're talking about him now.'

'It isn't true,' Adrian told him. 'And it's a blasphemy even to
think it might be.'

*

Before Frederick's era, the monastery had been run by Father
Clement. He had been a rather absent-minded, scholarly person,
until Vatican Two. And then he threw over the traces with a
vengeance. As Frederick had said at the time, no one could have
suspected such an intense urge towards chaos in the man. All at
once Father Clement espoused every cause and crackpot movement that had been hitting the headlines for the past three
decades while he'd been supposed to be tilling the vineyards and
praising the Lord. He went from Flower Power to Hard Rock in
three weeks. He became interested in Scientology. And he
allowed anybody in: Hell's Angels, ballet dancers, health food
freaks and gigolos.

That was the trouble with tolerance: you could get too much of
it. Too much – and people stampeded over you. The time came
when Father Clement welcomed a set of what were to anyone's
eyes ordinary winos so far gone in the abuse of alcohol that they
were already brain-damaged. There was a scandal. The papers
got hold of it. It was deplorable; atrocious. Father Clement was

now, so everyone believed, in Hawaii, teaching Shakespeare to the Japanese. And the monastery was still awaiting a replacement, although in the meantime Brother Frederick was in command. It meant a great deal to Frederick that his interregnum should be peaceable and well-ordered. A promotion to the top was more than merely possible.

He had thought that he'd begin by weeding out the more sinister or cranky newcomers, but by the time he took over, the men were leaving so quickly they were practically tripping over each other trying to get to the door. They were like the rats leaving a sinking ship. And then, miraculously, the new influx arrived, even younger: a fresh generation of believers; however, their belief wasn't of the old quality, their education up to the same level. Some of them had had hardly any religious instruction at all. 'Beggars can't be choosers,' Brother Robert had said over his wine one evening. 'God', Frederick had answered grandly, 'does not need to beg.' Robert had given him a pitying look and shaken his head, and almost immediately been proven right: a bad flu rampaged through the order, turning the place into a geriatric ward. The old monks began to die off. Those who didn't die had to be cleaned, fed and manoeuvred on to bedpans. Frederick realized that he wasn't going to be able to kick many young men out. The solution would be to keep them there and change them into better monks. And, all in all, having had inferior material to work with, he hadn't done too badly. He was proud of his record.

Sometimes he thought about the ones his own age who had left – who had voluntarily jettisoned the calling to which they had been dedicated, reneged on their vocations. He thought of them as deserters or, at times, escapees. They thought of him, too. A lot of them regularly sent postcards and letters back from the outside. When he was feeling particularly glum and grouchy, he'd remember the messages:

> *I never knew what living was like till I left the order.*
> *What are you trying to prove?*
> *Come on in, the water's fine.*
> *Freddie, you're a jerk to stay.*

Often the more strait-laced they had been, the more fatuous their greetings were. The Classicists had gone, to become pragmatists. The Romantics stayed.

Brother Francis used to say that there was no need to keep anyone who didn't have faith. As far as the vineyards went, they could hire workers. The order was dedicated to God – there was no necessity, and should be none, to accept anyone below standard. But Robert told him, 'We just cannot afford to turn down men who come to us for our novelty-value. We have to assume that there's a genuine desire underlying the frivolous impulse.' And it was true that now you could see he'd been as acute about that as about the grapes. They'd had many vintage years for wine lately; not so many for men. They needed the numbers.

Most of Anselm's admirers were entirely untutored; they'd had no religious training in childhood. Many of them had come to their faith, as he had, under the pressure of some dramatic event or crisis. Elmo, who had served with the Oakland Fire Department, had preserved the lives of people who later tried to murder each other; and he had failed to rescue the innocent. He'd had a breakdown after a particularly ferocious tenement conflagration in which they only member of a large and quarrelsome family that he hadn't been able to save was the baby: it lay at the top of the house, its lungs scorched by smoke, while the demented relatives down below shrieked with frustration and beat him nearly to death, calling him a son of a bitch and a bastard. He had been furious, ashamed, and found that whenever he remembered the helpless baby up at the top of the fiery house, he wanted to cry. It took him six months to work out his thoughts and feelings. In the end, it came down to a simple formula: if there was nothing, he couldn't stand it; but if there was something, then in some way – even though no one knew exactly how – the baby was all right.

William's conversion had come through someone else: his young wife, who had fallen from an open stairway on a pier and hit one of the boats near their own. She had injured her spine so badly that at first the doctors thought she'd die in a few hours. It took her weeks, and during that time she was in agony. William had stayed with her right up to the end, when she suddenly received a revelation of God and said that the pain had vanished completely. She was dying then; they had a few final days together and William caught her belief as if it had been a germ in the hospital. But he didn't want to be cured of it afterwards. He was happy with the monastic life – that is, he was happy until the strange business about Anselm took over.

Dominic's was another case of hospitalization, though he had been the chief actor in the drama: he had been struck by lightning, thrown forty feet into a neighbouring field, and was in the hospital for four weeks recovering. Then he was at home for three months, just thinking about it. Twelve cows in the same field had been killed by the bolt. He had an idea that he'd been given a warning of some kind because his life wasn't the model of righteousness it was designed to be. A cow was a very big animal; twelve of them had died, yet he had been spared. That seemed to be a sign. He made preparations to try to save his soul.

James was different. He'd gone to Italy on a holiday after college. 'I was such a hick,' he said. 'I didn't know anything. Some friends asked me to the opera, and that's how it began. I stayed longer than I'd intended to. Then another friend took me to see the mosaics in Ravenna. And that's how I became a Christian. I had no idea of the way of life. That all came later. I'm probably the only example you'll ever meet of the redemptive power of art. Nature, and human nature, is so much more impressive.'

'And how about you, Anselm?' the brothers asked.

Anselm had started out in the order by keeping the books, as he had done in the world outside. He had entered just in time to take over from a Brother Timothy, who died, as everyone had expected, the next day. In view of the fact that the auditing was just about to come up, Anselm's arrival was seen as providential.

He had been trained as an accountant, had jobs in various small firms and then begun to work in large corporations, finally settling in a well-paid and interesting job at a bank. He was ready to branch out in his career and aim for the heights, when one day he saw a newsreel about surfboarding. The next morning he quit work and went down to the beach.

He had decided to become an expert. Only the experts could ride the big waves out in the islands: the ones like the one in the movie, which had shown a huge wall of green glass quivering forward, and – tracing a thin white line across the middle of it – a tiny dot: the surfer. He wanted to be good enough to go through the really dangerous waves – the ones that curled over on themselves, forming a tube, so that you could ride down the centre as if going through a tunnel; but, because your feet would be lashed to the board in case it bounced up, threw you, and came back to hit you on the head at a hundred miles an hour, you'd be in danger of losing your foot: if a sharp piece of coral caught you as you were going by, that was it – the foot would be sliced off. At least that would be better, the other surfers told him, than getting killed by your board.

He got night work in factories and as a watchman in warehouses. He finally found a job in a vast complex of storage buildings where he worked with two men who agreed with him to spell each other so that two of them could always get six hours' unbroken sleep every night. And then he found the right day, when all the waves were perfect. And the right wave – just like the one in the newsreel – which he knew would never end; he'd be able to ride it for ever all around the world from ocean to ocean.

And then all at once, unexpectedly, he was in the water. Something had slammed him hard on his head, shoulders and back and he was under the surface, not knowing which way was up. He must have taken a breath instinctively and saved his life that way. But soon he started to thrash around in terror. He needed air. He fought wildly – luckily without success, since the water itself buoyed him to the surface against his efforts. He was saved. And from those moments of remembered fear, his wish for a faith was born. Looking back, he figured out that – unlikely as it seemed – he must have been struck by some kind of fish jumping from the sea; a board or any other hard object would have broken every bone in his body. But the agent of the accident was a minor question. The truly puzzling mystery was his survival.

He simply couldn't understand how he had escaped death if something else hadn't been helping him. What could it have been? What was more powerful than a great force of nature like the sea?

'That was how it started,' he said. 'I tried to think it out. But now I know thought is useless when it comes to the important things.'

*

The front of Anselm's robe was studded and stuck with the trinkets and tokens he'd been given by other monks. Some of the gifts looked like votary offerings. He never asked where they came from. For years the cells and cloisters of the monastery had been bare of ornament; now from nowhere shiny buttons and pins appeared, so that they could be presented to Anselm.

'The creature is positively bedizened,' Brother Adrian snarled. 'Decorated like a Christmas tree.' He got drunk for two days and couldn't be roused.

'You see', Frederick told Francis, 'the effect it's having.'

'Just on Adrian. He was nearly this bad over the legal rights on the new vineyard eight years ago. Remember? That's the way he is. He wouldn't be tolerated for a minute in the outside world.'

'Don't kid yourself – he'd be one of the ones running it. And in his clearer moments, he's actually extremely capable.'

'But not likeable. Even talent has its limits.'

Francis heaved an enormous sigh. He threw up his hands to heaven and for a few second scrabbled at the air before sighing again and returning to normal. 'I got three postcards today,' he said. 'Brother Aloysius has become a Buddhist. He says he doesn't hold anything against us.'

'That's nice of him.'

'Ungrateful old swine. I hope they have as much trouble with him as we did.'

They turned to the right by the chapel and saw Anselm in the distance.

'What do you think?' Francis said.

'Oh, it's a mess. Just the kind of slipshod entanglement a boy like Anselm would be apt to get himself into.'

'Not a miracle?'

'Are there such things?'

'You know very well there are. But maybe you have to wait for somebody else to tell you that's what they are.'

'Your nasty moments are always so refreshing, Francis. One doesn't expect them.'

'I put it badly. What I meant was that it's like seeing a new movie or a new play. Some people say it's all right, one or two that it's wonderful, and a lot say it's worthless. Or the other way around. In time, everyone knows what to think. When something is completely new, it's got to be fitted into its place. It has to be assimilated. And every age has its miracles.'

*

Anselm looked through the papers. He came across a story about a Chinese boy who could read through his ears instead of his eyes; they'd blindfold him, hold a book up to his right ear, and let him read it. (The left ear appeared to be illiterate.)

He turned to a page near the back. A column next to the gardening news reported the uncanny ability of a five-year-old girl to turn tennis balls inside-out by the power of thought. And in the same issue there was a short item that told of a man who had died from just drinking water. He'd drunk thirty-five pints. According to friends of his, he'd said that he was 'trying to clean out his system'.

He started to order books from the public library. He got them through Brother Duncan, whose attitude towards him was becoming irritatingly proprietorial. The books were all about babies and the habits that could be discerned in them as soon as they were born. The romping movements, Anselm read, were for exercise; the grabbing and clinging instinct apparently went way back to the time when the human young would have to be able to get a grip on the mother's fur.

'Fur?' Elmo said. 'Have you been holding out on us? We thought you only had the usual accessories.'

'Shh,' Anselm told him. He continued to read from the book. The brothers were fascinated. Everyone wanted to help bring up the baby.

Eventually they talked about what sort of a child it would be, why it had been 'sent', and how they should educate it. Or perhaps it would be enough just to love it.

Other monks, at the far side of the cloister, also talked. Two of them on the way to Matins hurried across the courtyard together. One said, 'She came among us in a disguised form. That's why we didn't recognize her.' The other said, 'No, it's just the reverse. He's in a disguised form now.' It was like a quarrel about whether a dog was white with black spots or black with white spots. And, in any case, they weren't supposed to be discussing it.

*

Deep in thought, Anselm strolled along the pillared porches. In the distance he could see William standing still and looking intently, forlornly, at him.

Anselm moved closer. William began to edge nearer. He was in love with Anselm. He had picked a blossoming branch as an emblem of his love and wanted to offer it, but didn't quite dare.

Anselm rocked gracefully towards him, the swell of his skirt bearing him forward as if by sail or by balloon. He reached the spot where William stood transfixed by the sight of him. Anselm gave him a soft glance; the long lashes over his dark eyes were longer than ever. 'Hello, William,' he said.

'I wanted to give you this,' William told him. He held out the branch.

Anselm recognized the flowers as part of his favourite tree. He blinked languidly.

'For the baby,' William whispered.

Anselm took the branch. 'Thank you, William,' he said. 'How sweet of you.'

William dropped to his knees. He caught the edge of Anselm's robe in his hands and buried his face in it.

Anselm bent down slowly, touched William's head as if in blessing, and passed on.

William remained on his knees and began to pray.

*

'You've seen how Brother William is taking it?' Adrian demanded.

'A simple heart,' Frederick said.

'Rife for corruption.'

'Ripe.'

'This place could become a hotbed of debauchery overnight.'

'Really, Adrian, I think that's overstating the case.'

'All I want to know is what you're going to do about it.'

'You leave that to me.'

'No, Frederick. We've all waited long enough. If I don't see some action, I'm reporting it.'

'Be careful, Adrian. If you go too far, you'll be confined to quarters. I don't want any heroics out of you.'

'Me?' Brother Adrian cried. His tone was one of wounded innocence, his face nearly purple. Frederick knew that this mood of his was even harder to deal with than his rages.

*

Anselm waited for Francis outside the chapel until an older monk, Brother Theodore, had left. Then he came forward.

'Francis, may I ask you a question?'

'Certainly.' He hadn't heard Anselm's approach and was startled by the way he looked – so obviously pregnant, so like a young woman of the ancient world as it was pictured by the great Renaissance painters; and so pretty.

'This isn't a confession,' Anselm said.

'That's all right. Sit down.'

They sat in the pews, Anselm sliding in sideways and near a corner, to rest his back. 'What I want to know,' he said, 'is if you think that after the birth I should continue to lead a single life.'

'I hadn't thought that far, as a matter of fact.'

'Because there's somebody who loves me. And I feel that we'd be very well matched and everything. And a child needs a father.'

'Yes,' Francis said. 'But supposing – I mean, perhaps it would end up having two of them. It might be possible that after the birth, you'd go back to the way you were.'

'It might. Anything could happen. In that case, I'd have to find a mother for my child instead, wouldn't I?'

'Not necessarily. You could raise it alone. After the first few weeks, it's the father that's important: a figure of authority. A loving authority.'

'That doesn't matter. Authority is what you are or where you stand, not whether you're male or female. It's politically determined.'

'Authorities are male.'

'Only because things are organized like that.'

'But if you're trying to come to a decision, that makes a difference, doesn't it?'

'I guess. And I've become so fond of this person.'

'Brother William?'

'Sweet William. Before the Annunciation, I used to think he was a bit of an oaf. Now he seems so nice – true-hearted and full of life.'

'If you reverted to your former state, you might return to your first opinion of him. It might go with the alteration. So maybe you'd better wait.'

Anselm ran a hand through his hair, rumpling the sleekly regimented locks. 'I'd thought all the problems were solved,' he said, 'everything taken care of.'

'It's causing a lot of complications around you, you know.'

'Oh, that. That's just people's attitudes.'

'I worry about it.'

'Good. You can worry about it for me. I'm not going to.'

'Anselm, I do worry. Not everyone is kind. And it isn't every-one who can take the detached view.'

'Well, do you have an answer?'

'You haven't been to Mass in a very great while.'

'No.'

'It's for your sake, not mine or ours.'

'Don't let it bother you, Francis. I'm in God's hands.'

'We're all in God's hands. I just thought – well, I don't know. Your prayers are important, too. It isn't enough just to exist and not take part.'

'But every minute I live is given to God. He sent his angel. He – '

'The Mass, Anselm.'

'For me, that's secondhand now.'

'That's a very arrogant and wrong-headed thing to say.'

'Why? It's true.'

'Oh dear,' Brother Francis said.

*

'I don't want any X-rays.'

Brother Duncan said, 'It isn't an X-ray. It's a scan for finding out if the baby's going to be a girl or a boy.'

'Scan – what does that mean?'

'It's – '

'You can hear the heartbeat. Isn't that all right? And you can feel it kicking now. We'll find out what sex it is when it's born.'

'It would be nice to know now.'

'Nice for who?'

'Aren't you curious?'

'Doctor, I want you to promise me something. This child has got to be born alive and well, whether it's normal or not.'

'Who says it isn't going to be normal?'

'I want you to promise. The decision is not yours. Do you understand?'

'I've taken the Hippocratic oath, Anselm.'

'And we all know how much that's worth.'

'Who's been filling your mind with these fears?'

'They come naturally. It's an anxious time. Look at all my badges and buttons. I'm superstitious about everything now.

I've got to be able to trust you. I know you don't believe what happened, but I've got to have your help.'

'I definitely believe you changed sex. There's no doubt about that.'

'I'm asking you as a doctor, and also as a Christian. The temptation is going to be great. They're leaning on you, aren't they?'

'There's a certain amount of pressure, of course. That's my problem. I can handle it.'

'Since I've been pregnant, I've begun to understand a lot of things about doctors and women – telling them what to do, regulating them, applying a system. I used to think there were so many more male doctors than female ones just because it's such a highly paid job, but now I'm not sure. Now I'm coming to believe it's all to do with power – that men look at all other creatures as things on which to practise their power, that they think freedom means being able to carry out that practice; and they don't like it if anyone is really free just to be the way they are.'

'Anselm, you're going to find that you're increasingly prey to all kinds of fears, but – believe me, they have no foundation. I'm a doctor; I know.'

'You may be a doctor, Duncan, but compared to me, you're an ignoramus.'

'Thanks a bunch.'

'My knowledge comes directly from God.'

'So you've said.'

'Where do you think this child came from?'

'I'm not asking that question. I'm interested in facts as they are.'

'But they're so changeable. Facts can change in an instant. That's what happened to me. It's like peacetime and wartime, like happiness and sorrow. You never know when the change is going to come.'

'But not like male and female.'

'How do you know?'

Do you think you're the only person this so-called visitation ever happened to? Except the first instance, I mean.'

'I've wondered about that, too. All I can say is that if there were others, they kept quiet about it. Or it was hushed up. Or no one believed it. That would be the most likely explanation. Not many people here believe me, either.'

'You don't think you're the only one?'

'I do. But that may only be because everything that happens to people seems to be special to them. It seems unique.'

'I've never heard or read of anything like it. The occasional hysterical woman, yes – nothing like this.'

'That's the trouble. Right from the start it was medically exciting. You still think it's the prize-winning case-history. But they're giving you orders above me, aren't they?'

'Nobody wants anything but your own good, Anselm.'

'And if they didn't, what could I do about it? It's giving me the creeps. Look at the way I am. How could I defend myself? They're all running themselves in circles about scandal and reputation and theology. This matters more. If you're any kind of a doctor, there must have been a time when you thought so too.'

'I wanted to become a doctor,' Duncan said, 'because I wanted to know about the human soul, life and death, where people went to when they died, why they were the way they were. I studied in the laboratories, in mortuaries. I had parts of people on the table in front of me like pieces of a Sunday chicken. We had all kinds of things – insides – to look at. When I was a student, I had a collection of innards in jars. A whole shelf full. I even had a foetus in a bottle. I studied it. I also used to wonder about it a lot – whether it was a miscarriage, or whether the mother wanted to get rid of it; a lot of them do, you know. A lot of them wouldn't give you two cents for the Hippocratic oath. It seemed to me at that time, even more important than the question of where we went was the question of where we came from. The embryo I owned was a person. They were all, all the pieces in jars . . . Then I got to thinking about how the whole of that side of life was entrusted to women. And that was where my understanding broke down. They're so patently unworthy. Strange as your case is, Anselm, the one thing about it that makes sense to me is that, if it's true, it should have been a man who was chosen this time. If that's what happened.'

'That's what happened. But that isn't the part I think is important. I'm the same. I'm the same person now that I was then. I've got a different body, that's all. Do you think we're what our bodies are?'

'We live inside them. We inhabit them. We're influenced by them, very. The state of a person's health can change his personality.'

'It can't change him into something he had no capacity for from the beginning. Or can it?'

'You think you were a woman all along?'

'I think I was chosen, and because the female body is the one made for carrying and feeding children, I was given that. Do you think I'm going to change back afterwards?'

'What?'

'As soon as I stop breast-feeding, do you think I'll go back to being a man?'

'Oh my God, Anselm.'

'It's like a joke, isn't it?'

'It simply never occurred to me.'

'I hadn't thought that far myself. I was just happy. But now I'm beginning to get a little anxious. I don't want anything to go wrong.'

'Nothing will go wrong. Relax. You're very healthy.'

Anselm stood up. It took him several movements now. He felt as ungainly as a camel getting to its feet.

He went for a walk in the courtyard and then down past the potato gardens. He stopped a few times to think. He leaned against one of the stone walls in the garden and partly closed his eyes. He remembered the way it had been at the beginning: Gabriel alighting on the green square of grass. Once again, like warmth from a flame or a breath from the air, the remembered touch ran tickling over his skin.

He knew that the central event was all right and assured. His worries were all about the peripheral effects. Whether man or woman, he was living in the world as it was at a particular time. And in most parts of the country, despite the revolution in morals, changed attitudes towards sexual freedom, the high incidence of divorce and the promulgation of certain doctrines by the women's movements – still, in general, illegitimacy was disapproved of. Because he was single, things were going to be made difficult for him. And if he remained single, they'd be made difficult for the child too. There were hundreds of ways in which a child could be hurt, shocked, shamed or cruelly teased by other children at school. Schools were full of quarrels and fights and name-calling.

On his way back to his cell he went near the chapel, where the brothers were singing Compline. The baby began to move boisterously. Whenever there was music, it kicked hard. Anselm thought may be it picked up the vibrations and was trying to dance.

He passed by, going to the right and down the hallway that led to his corridor. A burst of laughter came from behind one of the closed doors; shouted opinions followed. There seemed to be at least three, perhaps four voices. Anselm heard himself named and turned back.

'What I think –' one of the voices said.

Another one interrupted: 'She's asking for it.'

'Miracle, my arse.' The voice could have been the first man again, or a different one. Through the closed door it was hard to tell. One of them said something in a low murmur that Anselm didn't catch. The others cackled like witches. He could guess, from the remark that had gone before, what kind of comment it had been. After that, there was a loud crash and a despairing cry: 'Jesus fucking Christ, you've done it again.'

'Not so loud.'

'Second one you've broken.'

'Shut up.'

'Let's have some more blood of the lamb, Brother Eustace.'

'Let's go pay Sister Anselm a call.'

'One more drink.'

'I don't want to get mixed up in anything like that. He's got a lot of friends now.'

'I wouldn't give a plug nickel for his friends. My friends are bigger than anybody's friends.'

'I don't give a damn. I don't give . . . I don't give a whatever, not about anything.'

'It might be true.'

'Oh, come on.'

'I'm not saying it is, but you just tell me how you can explain it.'

'It's a rip-off, of course.'

'What kind of a rip-off can do that?'

'What I think is, we shouldn't take it for granted.'

'Take what for granted? What are you talking about now?'

'Anything, anything. You should never take nothing for granted. Eyesight, now – a wonderful thing, a marvel. It can be lost in a second. That's true, you know. I have a brother-in-law; but never mind. What I'm saying is, you shouldn't count on it. Course, in the end we lose everything: sight, hearing, so on.'

'Jesus, don't get so gloomy. You're spoiling the fun. How could we lose everything?'

'Getting old.'

'That isn't so bad. I know a lot of pretty old people. Well, not a lot. Some.'

'And then we die.'

A different voice said, 'But we live again in Christ.'

'Well,' the first man answered, 'it's a nice thought.'

Anselm felt dizzy. He made his way to his room, lay down on the bed and closed his eyes. He thought he'd like to pray lying down, since it was so uncomfortable getting on to his knees and having to bend forward.

He put his hands together. 'Holy Mary,' he began, and stopped. He couldn't think of anything more to say.

Surely, he thought, William would understand. If he remained the way he was, a woman, they could stay together as a family. And if he changed back, they could split up, or even keep on going like that, too.

He didn't join the others for supper. Dominic brought him a bowl of soup, some bread and butter and an apple.

'Aren't you feeling well, Anselm?' he asked.

'Sure. I'm all right. Just tired.'

'You take care of yourself. We've all got bets riding on you.'

'What's the verdict?'

'Oh, everybody thinks it's going to be a boy. If it's a girl, about three people are going to clean up. They'd be millionaires. Everybody else would be out in the cold. You want a boy too, of course, don't you?'

'Naturally. That's the way it's supposed to be.' He drank his soup and felt better. Brother Ignatius and Brother Sebastian in the kitchen were working overtime now, making sure that nothing sat too heavily on his stomach.

He started to feel still better late in the night when he thought about the birth. He was afraid of the pain but he was certain that the event was going to be of such cataclysmic importance and excitement that the pain would have to become secondary. And it would all be worth it, anyway. Now that he could feel the baby pushing and bumping, he was beginning to know it. It kept him company. He talked to it. He told it stories – things he made up, as well as the more traditional fairytales he remembered from his own childhood.

Once upon a time, he said to himself, *there were three bears: a mamma bear, a pappa bear and a baby bear*. There was a king who had three daughters, a woodcutter with three sons. *Once upon a time there were three little pigs and they all lived in the forest, where there was a big, bad wolf*. Everything went in threes and everything was told as if it had happened only that week, or it could just as easily have been centuries ago. *Once upon a time*, he thought, *there was the Father, the Son and the Holy Ghost*.

*

'Brother Adrian', Francis said, 'is in trouble. I think he's going out of his mind, Frederick.'

'No more than usual. And he's always got emotional troubles.

You know Adrian – that's the way he is. He runs on it: it's like a fuel. Francis, I want to ask you to help me with something.'

'I don't know how much good advice I've got left for today.'

'I don't need advice. What I'm going to need is your vote. I want to get William transferred.'

'That would be hard on Anselm, just as his time is drawing so near.'

'Francis, they're planning to get married.'

'Not yet. I think they're going to wait till after the birth. To find out if Anselm reverts.'

'Judas Priest, there's no end to the ramifications. This whole thing has degenerated into a farce. It's preposterous.'

'It's a mystery, Frederick. That's what it was from the beginning, and that's never changed. The rest is what we make out of it.'

'No.'

'We interpret and we explain. But the central fact is the only truth, and it's inexplicable.'

'It was a sign and I failed to act on it. I didn't even see it till the business about William. Francis, I've missed the boat – I should have gone to a higher authority right at the beginning, and I didn't. Now it's too late. I didn't recognize this as the great trial of my life – of all our lives. No, I don't believe it's a miracle, damn it. But I do believe it's here to test us. And I've been found wanting.'

'Don't be silly.'

'In my own eyes, first of all. But what are the others going to say?'

'They wouldn't have acted any differently.'

'Who knows? You never know these things till they happen. You say to yourself, "If. If." But that's no guide. Brother William has got to go.'

'If we sent Brother Adrian away instead –'

'He's only an outside irritation. Brother William is about to become intimately involved.'

'Do you dislike Anselm?'

'Of course not. I resent the confusion he's caused, that's all. He causes it, I have to deal with it. If you can't help me with William, it's Anselm who'll have to go. Either way, they've got to be kept apart.'

'I just don't see why.'

Frederick settled himself deeply into his chair. There were three ways he could appeal to Francis's fears, hopes and sense of right. He prepared to use them all in the order of their power to tempt and persuade. He said, 'Very well. We'll go through it again till you do.'

*

'That's right,' Brother James told Anselm. 'He wasn't at supper and he wasn't at breakfast. They drove him away in the early evening.'

Elmo and Dominic corroborated the story. Elmo said he'd heard from Brother Anthony that the car had left from the kitchen entrance. Brother Ignatius had seen it.

Anselm held tightly to the crumpled paper he'd been handed by Marcus when he'd come to do his hair that morning. The note was from William, who said that he was being moved to another place, that he would remain true and never forget him, that Anselm and the baby would be in his thoughts and prayers, and that William loved him.

'It was Adrian,' Elmo declared.

Anselm said, 'It was Frederick.'

'Brother Adrian's been bucking all month to get at least one of us out. But don't worry. You've still got friends.'

'Adrian wouldn't have the authority. Somebody had to take the responsibility for this. The only one it could have been is the man at the top.'

'It's incredible how everything always ends up political,' Dominic said.

'It's because the structure is political,' Elmo told him. 'Anything extra you put in it is going to assume that shape.'

'He won't see me,' Anselm said. 'I've asked for an appointment and he won't give me one. I can only talk to Francis.'

'Are you coming to eat?' James asked.

'I'm banned. I'm lucky I haven't been confined to my room.'

'We'll do something about it,' James said. 'This is beyond the limit.'

Anselm nodded feebly. He held the letter to his heart and turned his head away.

*

When he woke, Brother Sebastian was bringing in a cup of soup and some crackers. 'They're having a big fight,' he whispered. As soon as he'd put down the tray, he started to hop with impatience, gesturing towards the door. 'Brother Eustace and Adrian against the others. When I left, they were all screaming like monkeys. I'll be back later, Anselm. I want to see what happens.'

Anselm waved his hand graciously. He started on the soup and flipped through a new magazine that had arrived in the morning mail. On the cover was a picture of a really darling baby, just the kind he wanted.

*

In the dining-room no single voice could be heard above the total uproar. All the brothers were yelling and pelting each other with food. A few of them were throwing bowls and bottles, too. Francis was socked hard in the side of the head while trying to make peace between one man holding a broken glass and another one brandishing a knife. He lost his hearing for a moment and had to sit down. He put his hands over his ears and let the tumult rage around him. Frederick, who had played right half-back at the seminary, fought his way to the door. He punched and jabbed a great many brothers on his way out and left the room feeling satisfied and invigorated.

*

Anselm read through the letters to the editor in his magazine. He liked finding out about how new mothers felt and what problems they had to contend with.

The first letter was from a woman who wanted to know how she could overcome her fear that friends who came to the house were going to pass on their microbes and bacteria to her baby. The editor advised her to relax and stop worrying. Anselm thought she had a point: these things were, after all, invisible. The second writer asked why sanitary towels weren't state-subsidized, as she was finding them increasingly expensive and it wasn't her fault that she had to have them – all women of child-bearing age needed them; they couldn't help it. The editor said that as a matter of fact, in poorer countries where people weren't so well-nourished, the women didn't wear any special clothing against menstruation and only ever saw a couple of drops of blood in a month; so, if you were healthy enough to menstruate heavily, that probably meant you were rich enough to afford the kotex and tampax.

The third, and last, letter was from a woman who claimed that according to her experience, unmarried mothers in the hospital she'd been in were treated with a coldness, hostility and neglect that could be dangerous for the child and certainly contributed to the mother's sense of loneliness and inferiority. Many of the nurses, she said, came from strongly religious backgrounds, and she thought it was a shame that people who were supposed to believe in peace and love-thy-neighbour should be so unfeeling, snobbish and narrow-minded.

Of course, Anselm thought, it would be true. No matter what the woman herself thought, the doctors and nurses would regard the pregnancy as an unfortunate, unplanned and unwanted accident, maybe even thinking they would be doing the mother a favour to let the child die.

He slapped the pages of the magazine together and threw it aside. He had always imagined that women enjoyed a special kind of freedom because nothing was ever going to be expected of them, but now he saw that they were just as trapped as men. He had to find a husband, and as soon as possible. It didn't matter now whether it was someone he was genuinely fond of, like William, or a man he didn't care about at all. Anybody would do, and for the baby's sake any deception would be justified. He shouldn't have second thoughts about explaining anything, or mentioning possible future transformations. Whatever the nurses were like in the hospital Duncan had chosen, he was certain their prejudices would be the same as those of other nurses. And even before he got that far, there was his life in the monastery to consider. Brother Adrian had forced Frederick to remove William: there was no telling what might happen next.

Well, he thought, he was going to have to start being like other people – to set things up and make them come true, to hustle and manipulate. He'd have to try to get rid of his enemies. If he were alone, he wouldn't care; but for the baby's sake, he had to.

Frederick could hurt him officially. But Adrian was more dangerous: violent and unpredictable. And he made Frederick nervous enough to feel compelled to act.

Anselm got up and went for a walk through the cloisters. He heard a commotion coming from the dining-room. The monks sounded like howling spectators at a football game. He kept going, down corridors and across courtyards.

He came to his favourite tree. It was a different shape because it was in leaf now. It seemed also to look older. First it was in bud, then all blossom, then covered in leaves, then came the fruit. And next year, all over again; like the stages of a woman's life.

Soon after lunch Brother Adrian went berserk and had to be taken away in a straitjacket. Before the jacket, they had used a rope.

Anselm had seen him rushing from the direction of the dining-room and coming towards him very fast, oblivious to everything around him until all at once he realized that Anselm was only a few yards away. He stopped dead, his pudgy, engorged face stiff with angers and grievances he'd been recalling.

Anselm sauntered negligently towards him, smiling kindly. Brother Adrian didn't know what to do. He looked wary, then embarrassed, and then almost afraid.

Anselm came right up close, looking into Adrian's face, and with one of his pretty, long-lashed dark eyes, winked.

The reaction was beyond anything he'd have considered possible: Adrian shrieked obscenities and fell writhing to his knees. He tried to pull at Anselm's robe, but Anselm swished decorously away. Adrian crawled after him, screaming that he was going to tear off the garment and show the stinking sin beneath; he scrabbled along the stone floor, he gibbered and finally laughed with fury. But Anselm walked ahead, whisking his skirts to the side in order to avoid the clawing hands. And when he came to the next turning, he scooted around the corner as fast as he could, and went back to his room.

*

'Did you provoke him, Anselm?' Francis asked. They were standing outside Frederick's office.

Anselm looked tranquil and he was smiling. 'Brother Adrian provokes himself,' he answered. 'That's his misfortune. It appears to be an exaggerated sense of aggression against others, but actually the main conflict is within.'

'He cracked completely.'

'It may mean that when he comes out, he'll have solved the original trouble.'

'He might not ever come out of it.'

Anselm would have liked to say: *It was him or me.* He asked, 'Do you think he was a bad man?'

'Was?'

'We're not sure what he is now. He's just collapsed.'

'Not bad, no.'

'And me? Do you think I'm bad, or morally reprehensible, or something like that?'

'Of course not. But I do think it's bad that you haven't been to confession or to Mass, or anything, in so long.'

'I've told you: there's no need. I'm in the care of a higher power.'

'It's been months.'

'Since the Annunciation, yes.'

'Was it a higher power that struck down Brother Adrian?'

Anselm laughed. 'I love these verbal tennis games,' he said. 'They're just like theology. This is the way they decide how many angels can dance on the head of a pin, and get the exact number, too. Disquisitions and inquisitions. Nobody's interested in the truth. Look at me, Francis. This is the truth.'

'Anselm, I think you're going about things the wrong way.'

'If you were in my place, would you be scared?'

'I don't know what I'd be.'

'You were always the understanding one. You have a sense of humanity. But against Frederick's ambitions and neuroses, you're impotent.'

'I wish you wouldn't talk like this.'

'Francis, who was there to speak up for me against Adrian? I needed protection against him. Did you or Frederick give me that? No. You stand there and ask me if I provoked him.'

Thudding and scraping sounds came from beyond the door. It sounded as if Frederick had begun to move the furniture.

'Don't feel bad about it,' Anselm added. 'I still like you, Francis. I just don't like the situation.'

The door opened suddenly. Frederick glared out at them. 'All right, Anselm,' he snapped. 'Come on in.'

'Should I – ?' Francis offered.

'You go back to the chapel.' Frederick held the door for Anselm and then swung it away fast so that it slammed. He hurled himself solidly into the best chair. 'Sit down,' he ordered.

Anselm settled himself gingerly on the side of the sofa, with plenty of pillows behind him.

'Anselm, you do realize we can't keep you here?'

'Oh? Isn't the mother of God good enough for your order?'

'It's a question of morality.'

'It always is.'

'Men and women under the same roof. Besides, there's no proof that there was divine intervention.'

'You could say that every woman is the mother of God.'

'You could. I wouldn't. And in your case it isn't even proven how far the womanhood extends.'

'Was the divine aspect proven the first time? I thought they just took her word for it. She told her old husband and he believed it, or said he did.'

'There's a certain amount of feeling in the community that your story is put at a great disadvantage by the absence of, ah, a halo.'

Anselm glanced up, looking at a reproduction of the madonna and child which hadn't been on display the last time he'd been in the room, or at any other time he could remember. It was undoubtedly the cause of the noise he and Francis had heard from outside: it must have taken a long time to get it out from where it had been hidden. The heads of mother and child were each encircled by a band of light like the orbit of a moon around a planet.

'The halo', Anselm said, 'is a symbolic representation of an inner warmth or glow. Fire around the head is supposed to indicate enlightenment of the mind. It isn't peculiar to the Christian tradition.'

'Nevertheless, it is strongly felt that the presence of a halo would be a desirable adjunct to anyone entertaining aspirations to a holy state. It would add authenticity to your claims. Such as they are.'

He had never believed it. Frederick wouldn't countenance anything that wasn't in the books.

'If you doubt me all along the line,' Anselm said, 'what do you think the explanation is?'

'I wouldn't presume to advance a theory as to that. All I know is that the Church is against it.'

'How do you know that?'

For a moment Anselm thought that Frederick would actually break loose and say: *Because the Church is against women.* It seemed to be what he thought; but instead he answered, 'Because it doesn't make sense.'

'What does?'

'It doesn't fit in with scriptural, social, or indeed biological precedence.'

'You think it should have happened to you?'

'Heaven forbid. You don't even seem to understand that in other people's eyes this is a hideous and freakish thing to have occurred.'

'I know that. Oh, yes. Or funny. But not for all of them. A few have been good about it. I expect it's those few that scare you.'

'Scared? The Church has weathered a great many storms over the past centuries.'

'And caused some.'

'It isn't scared.'

'I give up,' Anselm said. 'You won't even think about it, will you? You just push it away. All right – you don't want me here; where do I go? I'll have to live on something, and I won't be able to work when the baby comes.'

'Brother Duncan has given me the name of a reputable nursing home.'

'The arrangement was that I was to go into a place where they'd have all the latest equipment. Either that, or stay here and have an old-fashioned home delivery. Duncan didn't want to risk that.'

'Well, the arrangements have been changed. Brother Duncan now agrees with us that the discretion of the private clinic outweighs the conviviality of a public ward. The medical attention will be in all respects identical.'

Anselm clasped his hands lightly over his bulging front. He knew now what they were going to do to him. First it was William, and then the business with Adrian must have given them a better idea: to put Anselm in a home for the insane. He was sure that that was what they had in mind.

'All right,' he said. He fished around awkwardly for support and lumbered to his feet. Frederick made no move to help. *I hope your nose rots away*, Anselm thought, *and your fingers drop off one by one. I hope you die in pain. I hope it feels like your death lasts longer than your life ever did.*

'Goodbye, Frederick,' he said. 'I hope you think about me sometimes.'

'Of course, Anselm. I don't reproach you.'

'I hope you think about what you've done.'

'I have the welfare of the order at heart, you know that.'

'Horseshit.'

'If that's the way you're going to behave, perhaps you'd better leave now.'

'I'm trying to.' Anselm reached for the doorknob and opened the door. He said, 'And now you can go wash your hands.'

*

He pounded on Duncan's door with his fist and opened it himself. The doctor was sitting at his desk, papers in one hand and a ballpoint pen in the other. Anselm closed the door behind him.

'Are those my committal documents?'

'How's that?'

'Don't smile at me, Judas. The whole damn gang of you.'

'Anselm, we're doing our best for you.'

'Going to put me in the loony bin, and my baby too.'

'The child will have the best care imaginable.'

'The best care imaginable is me.'

'An unmarried mother cannot be said to be a person of high moral standards.'

'Then I think you'd better marry me.'

'I thought you didn't like me. Or, so you said.'

'There isn't any choice. You're the last one on the list. William was the one I wanted. And after that, Francis is at least a good man. But he doesn't have any strength left. You're the only one around who can protect me.'

'I see. And why should I?'

'What did he give you, Duncan?'

'I don't know what you mean.'

'Oh yes, you do.'

'It doesn't matter.'

'Then it won't make any difference if you tell me. What was the bribe?'

'They promised me I could go to Africa. Have my own hospital. A crew of novices working under me – everything. All my dreams.'

'That's a lot more than it's worth, unless my story's true. And if it is, then there isn't any price high enough, is there? Do you think they'll keep their word?'

'Now that I think about it, no.'

'Of course not. They've strung you along for so many years now, they know they can do it for ever. All the part of you that could have been your life has become your fantasy world. And your real life has become theirs. It's been going on for years, till you don't have a life of your own any more. You do what they tell you.'

Duncan dropped the pen and papers. 'Go away,' he said.

'And they're telling you: *Get rid of Anselm.* You know what that means. If you have to kill me, they won't care. How much does being a doctor mean to you?'

'It's the way I came to God.'

'And when did you stop believing?'

'Right at the beginning,' Duncan said. 'During the long cold spell when all the old men stayed in their beds.' He looked away and sighed. 'That was before your time. I realized they'd be better in a nursing home, but I also saw how they were degenerating from day to day; how the decay of the body was becoming the decay of the mind. It was a natural progression. And the next stage was for both to come to a stop.'

'Why did you stay?'

'Because it broke me. I used to think I was too good to stay outside. I found out I wasn't good enough to go back. I didn't think it was worthwhile trying to save anybody from anything.'

'Are you going to marry me?'

Duncan's gaze ranged over the shelves where his medical reference books stood, and the filing boxes that held all the case histories of the monastery for the past twelve years. He looked at his framed certificates hanging on the wall, at the small crucifix propped against the one-volume Webster's dictionary; and at Anselm.

'All right,' he said. 'Get ready to leave tonight. I'll come to your door at eleven.'

*

They drove all night, Duncan behind the wheel. Anselm fell asleep and woke to hear the doctor talking to himself.

'Silly', Duncan muttered, 'to worry about them being able to stop me getting to Africa. I see the light now. The case of my career. Lucky I've taken a lot of notes.'

They were driving along a straight desert road at a speed of nearly ninety miles an hour.

'Slow down,' Anselm ordered. When Duncan didn't seem to hear, he shouted, 'Slow down, I said. 'We're going too fast.'

The doctor eased his foot from the pedal. 'I was thinking about something else,' he said.

'Think about the road.'

Anselm went back to sleep and woke once more to find that they were driving very fast again. It kept happening all through the night. Towards morning he was exhausted and beginning to feel cramping pains. They came to a place in the road where he could see slopes of green meadows ahead and a stream beyond.

'Stop the car,' he said.

'We've got to get as far away as possible.'

'I've got to go to the bathroom. Now.'

Duncan pulled over to the side.

They were in the middle of an empty landscape. It was just before daybreak; everything lay quiet in the grey light.

Anselm got out. He nearly fell. The pains were growing worse. He staggered across the field towards the stream. He was frightened. He thought he might be dying or that the baby could have been hurt, or that he had started to bleed. And he remembered how Duncan had said that as a student he used to have a foetus in a bottle and had studied it.

It would be better, he thought, to drown himself in the river straight away.

'Come back,' Duncan called after him, but Anselm struggled forward against the surging pain that threw him from side to side.

He was coming to the bank of the stream just as Duncan caught up with him and grabbed him by the elbow. Anselm beat back with his free hand, screaming.

'It's all right, Anselm – I'm a doctor,' Duncan shouted at him.
'Let me go – '

'Cut it out. Stop that, or I'll give you an injection.'

'Bastard!' Anselm shrieked. He kicked and twisted. The doctor let go, dropped to the ground and took a tight grip on Anselm's knees. Anselm fought. He dragged himself forward with the doctor hanging on. The dawn began to break around them. He tried with all his strength to gain the bank. He screamed for help until at last, impelled on the tide of his urgency, he reached the water's edge.

The sky opened. Brightness rained down on him. And he was carried along quickly, borne up and up and forward in the sweeping rush of the power he'd been searching for all his life: the wave that goes on for ever.

Friends in the Country

It took them an hour to leave the house. Jim kept asking Lisa where things were and why she hadn't bought such and such; if she'd intended to buy that thing there, then she should have warned him beforehand. 'Otherwise,' he told her, 'we duplicate everything and it's a waste of money. Look, now we've got two flashlights.'

She let the shopping bag drop down on the floor with a crash. 'Right. That's one for you and one for me,' she said. 'And then we won't have to argue about it when we split up.'

His face went set in an expression she recognized. He'd skipped two intermediate phases and jumped to the stage where, instead of being hurt, he started to enjoy the battle and would go for more provocation, hoping that they'd begin to get personal. 'In that case,' he said, 'I hosie the blue one.'

She laughed. She leaned against the wall, laughing, until he had to join in. He said, 'We can keep the black one in the car, I guess. It might come in useful.'

'You think we should phone them?'

He shook his head. He didn't know anything about this Elaine – she was Nancy's friend – but he was pretty sure her cousin wouldn't want to begin eating before eight on a Friday night, especially not if she lived out of town. 'And they shouldn't, anyway,' he added. 'Eight thirty would be the right time.'

'But some people do. If you're working nine to five, and if you – '

'Then they ought to know better.'

There were further delays as he wondered whether to take a bottle of wine, and then how good it had to be if he did. Lisa heard him rooting around in the kitchen as she stared closely into the bathroom mirror. She smeared a thin film of Vaseline on the tips of her eyelashes, put her glasses on, took them off and leaned forward. Her nose touched the glass. Jim began to yell for her to hurry up. Her grandfather used to do the same thing: she could remember him shouting up the stairs for her grandmother; and then if there was still no result, he'd go out and sit in the car and honk the horn. Jim hadn't learned that extra step yet, but he might think of it at any minute. They'd been living together for only a few months. She was still a little worried that one day he might get into the car and drive off without her.

They were out of the house, in the car, and halfway down the street when she remembered that she'd left the bathroom light on. She didn't say anything about it. They moved on towards the intersection. Jim was feeling good, now that they'd started: the passable bottle of wine being shaken around in the back seat, the new flashlight in the glove compartment. He looked to the left and into the mirror.

She tried not to breathe. She always hated the moment of decision – when you had to hurl your car and yourself out into the unending torrent of the beltway. Jim loved it. They dashed into the stream.

The rush hour was already beginning, although the sky was still light. Pink clouds had begun to streak the fading blue of the air. When they got off the freeway and on to the turnpike, the street lamps had been switched on. They drove down a country road flanked by frame houses.

'What did that map say?' he asked.

'Left by the church, right at the school playing field.'

They were supposed to go through three small towns before they came to the driveway of the house but – backtracking from the map – they got lost somewhere around the second one and approached the place from behind. At any rate, that was what they thought.

They sat in the car with the light on and pored over the map. Outside it didn't seem to be much darker, because a fog had begun to mist over the landscape. He blamed her for misdirecting him, while she repeated that it wasn't her fault: not if he'd worked it out so carefully beforehand; she couldn't see all those itsy-bitsy names in the dark, and anyway she'd said for him to go exactly the way he'd instructed her.

'Well,' he said, 'this should do it. Can you remember left – right – left?'

'Sure,' she answered. And so could he; that was just the kind of thing he'd told her back at the house.

He started the car again and turned out the light. They both said, 'Oh,' and, 'Look,' at the same time. While they'd been going over the map, the fog had thickened to a soupy, grey-blue atmosphere that filled the sky and almost obscured the trees at the side of the road. Jim drove slowly. When the road branched, he said, 'Which way?'

'Left – right – left.'

They passed three other cars, all coming from the opposite direction. As the third one went by them, he said, 'At least it doesn't lead to nowhere.'

'Unless it's to somewhere else.'

'Meaning what?'

'I don't know,' she said. 'It just came to me.'

'Wonderful. You should be working for the government. Which way now?'

'To the right.'

'And there's a street sign up ahead. At last.'

When they got near enough to the sign to make out what it said, they saw that it didn't have any writing on it at all. It was white, with a red triangle painted on it, and inside the triangle was a large, black shape.

'That's great,' she said. 'What's it supposed to mean – black hole ahead?'

'Look, there's another one. The whole damn road's full of them. What's the black thing? Come on, you can see that.'

Lisa opened her window. The signs were as closely spaced as trees or ornamental bushes planted along a street to enhance its beauty and give shade during the summer.

She leaned her head out and looked at the black object inside the red triangle.

'It's like a kind of frog,' she said, pulled her head back in and shut the window. She'd just realized that she hadn't brought her glasses with her; not that it really mattered for a single dinner party, but she always liked to have them with her in case she had to change her eye make-up under a bad light, or something like that.

'I remember now,' he told her. 'It's OK. I've just never seen it before. It's one of those special signs for the country.'

'What?'

'They signpost all the roads they've got to cross to get to their breeding grounds or spawning places, or something. People run over so many of them when it's the season. They're dying out.'

'Frogs?'

'No, not frogs. Toads.'

'I hope it isn't their breeding season now. That's all we need.'

'Which way at the crossroads?'

'Left.'

In fifteen minutes they came to a white-painted wooden arrow set low in the ground. It said 'Harper' and led them on to a narrow track. The headlights threw up shadowy patterns of tree branches. Leaves brushed and slapped against the sides of the car.

'This better be it,' he said.

'Otherwise we break open the wine and get plastered.'

They lurched along the last curve of the drive and out into a wide, gravelled space, beyond which stood a building that looked like a medievalized Victorian castle. Lisa giggled. She said, 'So this is where your friends live.'

Jim reached into the back seat for the wine and said he hoped so, because otherwise it was going to be a long ride to anywhere else.

*

The door was opened by someone they couldn't see. Jim stepped forward into darkness and tripped. Lisa rushed after him. There was a long creak and the heavy door groaned, then slammed behind them.

'Are you all right?' she asked. She fell on top of him.

'Look out,' he said. 'The wine.' It took a while for them to untangle themselves. They rose to their feet like survivors of a shipwreck who suddenly find themselves in the shallows.

They could see. They could see that the hallway they stood in was weakly lit by a few candles, burning high up on two separate stands that resembled iron hat racks; each one expanded into a trident formation at the top. The candles were spitted on the points.

Lisa turned to Jim, and saw that a man was standing in back of him. She gave a squeak of surprise, nearly blundering against a second man, who was stationed behind her. Both men were tall, dressed in some kind of formal evening wear that included tails; the rest of the outfit looked as if it might have been found in an ancient theatrical wardrobe trunk. 'Your coat, sir,' the one next to Jim said. He held out his arms.

By the time their coats had been removed and the bottle plucked from Jim's hands, they were ready for anything.

One of the men led them down a corridor. Like the hallway, it was dark. The floor sounded as if it might be tile. The air was cold and smelled unpleasant. Lisa reached for Jim's hand.

The tall man in the lead threw open a double door. Light came rushing out in a flow of brilliance. In front of them lay a bright, inviting room: glass-topped tables, gilded mirrors, chrome and leather armchairs in black and white, semi-circular couches. There were eight other people in the room. They'd been laughing when the door had opened on them. Now they were turned towards Jim and Lisa as if the room had become a stage set and they were the cast of a play.

'Your guests, madam,' the first butler said. He snapped the doors shut behind him.

A woman who had been standing by the mantelpiece came

forward. She had on a long, blackish velvet gown and what at first appeared to be a head-dress, but which – seen closer – was actually her own dark hair piled up high; lines of pearls were strung out and perched in wavy configurations along the ridges and peaks of the structure.

Jim let go of Lisa's hand. She could feel how embarrassed he was. He'd be fighting the urge to jam his hands into his pockets.

'Um,' he began, 'Elaine – '

'We thought you'd never get here,' the woman said. 'I'm Isabelle.'

She took his hand lightly in hers and let it go again almost immediately. Then she repeated the action as Jim made the introductions. Lisa realized that although the woman was certainly middle-aged and not particularly slim, she was beautiful. But something was wrong with the impression she gave. She had enough natural magnificence to carry her opera-diva get-up without appearing ridiculous; and yet she seemed out of date. And the touch of her hand had been odd.

Isabelle introduced them around the room. Dora and Steve, the couple nearest to them, were grey-haired. Steve wore a grey flannel suit that might once have been office regulation but at the moment looked fairly shapeless. Dora sported a baggy tweed jacket and skirt. Both husband and wife were pudgily plump, and they wore glasses: his, an old-fashioned pair of horn-rims; hers, an extraordinary bat-wing design in neon blue, with rhinestones scintillating at the tips. It came out in subsequent conversation that the two were schoolteachers and that they were interested in the occult.

Isabelle gave no hint as to the marital status of the next four people introduced: who was paired with whom, and in what way. There were two women and two men. The women were both young: Carrol, a plain girl with long, straight orange hair and a knobbly, pale face; Jeanette, pretty and brunette, who had shiny brown eyes and a good figure. She was an airline stewardess.

'And Dr Benjamin,' Isabelle said.

The doctor bowed and said, 'Oh, how do you do.' He was a small, stooped man, just beginning to go white at the temples. He reminded Lisa a little of the father of a girl she'd been to school with.

'And Neill. You probably recognize him.' The young man Isabelle indicated gave Jim and Lisa each an effortless, charming smile, just specially for them. He said, 'A lot of people don't watch TV.'

'I'm afraid we don't,' Jim said. 'We get home tired, and then we eat.' And then they jumped into bed, or else they did that before eating, or sometimes before and after too, but they hadn't watched much television for months.

'Are you in plays and things?' Lisa asked.

'I'm in a mega-soap called *Beyond Love*. The cast calls it *Beyond Hope*, or sometimes *Beyond Belief*. It really is.'

'What's it about?'

'The short version, or the twenty-three episode breakdown?'

'We all adore it,' Isabelle said. 'We miss it dreadfully now that the electricity's going haywire again. We were hoping to watch it over the weekend.'

'Just as well you can't,' Neill said.

'Not another shooting? They aren't writing you out of the script, are they?'

'I think this is the one where I lose an arm. My illegitimate father whips me from the house, not knowing that – you did say the short version, didn't you?'

Isabelle said she didn't believe any of it and he'd better behave. 'And finally,' she told Lisa and Jim, as she swayed ahead of them over the satiny rug, 'my husband, Broderick.' She left her hand open, her arm leading them to look at the man: swarthy, barrel-chested, bald and smiling. He looked like a man of power, an executive of some kind, who relaxed while others did the work he'd set up for them. He was leaning against the mantelpiece. The introductions had brought Jim and Lisa full circle in the room.

'A quick drink,' Isabelle suggested, pouncing gracefully upon two full glasses next to a silver tray. She handed them over, saying, 'Our very own mixture, guaranteed harmless, but it does have some alcohol in it. If you'd rather have fruit juice – '

Lisa was already sipping at her drink. The glass was like an oversized Martini glass but the cocktail wasn't strong, or didn't seem to be. It tasted rather delicate: herblike, yet pleasant. 'This is fine,' she said.

'Sure,' Jim added. She knew he wouldn't like it but would be agreeing in order to be polite.

'Now, we're going to move to the dining-room soon, so if any of you ladies need a sweater or a shawl, there's a pile over there. Or bring your own from your rooms.' She said to Jim, 'It's such a nuisance – we have to keep most of the rooms a little under-heated. Something to do with the boiler.'

'Not the boiler,' Broderick said.

'Well, pipes, or whatever it is. Poor Broderick – he's suffered miseries over it.'

'On the contrary. I just kicked out those two jokers who were trying to fleece us for their so-called work, and that's why we're up the creek now. Can't get anybody else for another three weeks. Maybe it'll get better tomorrow. It ought to be a lot warmer at this time of year.'

'It wasn't bad in town,' Jim said. 'I guess you must be in a kind of hollow. We hit a lot of fog. That's why we were late.'

'Yes, it's notorious around here,' Isabelle said. 'The locals call it Foggy Valley.'

One of the mournful butlers opened the double doors again and announced that dinner was served. Jim and Lisa tilted their glasses back. On the way out with the others, Lisa lifted a shawl from a chair near the doorway. All the other women had picked up something before her.

*

Carrol sat on Jim's right, Jeanette at the left. He preferred Jeanette, who was cheerful, healthy-looking and pretty, but somehow he was drawn into talk with Carrol.

The room was intensely, clammily, cold. He started to drink a lot of wine in order to warm himself up. Lisa, across from him, was drinking too – much more than usual.

Carrol kept passing one of her pale, bony hands over her face, as if trying to push away cobwebs. She said that she'd felt very restless and nervous ever since giving up smoking. 'I tried walking,' she said. 'They tell you to do that, but then I'd get back into the house and I'd want to start eating or smoking. So, I knit. But you can't take it everywhere. It sort of breaks up the conversation. And I'm not very good at it, even after all this time. I have to concentrate on the counting.' She blinked several times, as if about to cry.

From his other side Jeanette said, 'I guess we're all looking for different things. Except – I bet really they're not so different in the long run. In my case it was the planes. I'd get on and begin the routine, get everything working right, count the meals, look at the chart, see the passengers going in, and suddenly I'd just know: this one is going to crash.'

'What did you do?' Jim asked.

'I got off. They were very nice about it when I explained. They didn't fire me. But they said I had to take therapy.'

'And?'

'And I did. It was fine. It was a six-week course and it really made me feel a lot better. So, I went back to work again and everything was OK for another year. I thought I had it licked. And then it started up again, just like before. That's where I am now.'

'What are you doing for it this time?'

'I'm here,' Jeanette said.

Jim took another sip of the thick, brownish-red wine. It tasted dusty and bitter, although it seemed to be fairly potent, too. The bouquet reminded him of some plant or flower he couldn't place. He took another swallow. His feet were beginning to feel cold. 'You mean, here to relax?' he said.

'I'm here to consult Isabelle and Broderick.'

'Oh. And is that helping?'

'Of course. They're wonderful.'

'They've helped me too,' Carrol said. 'No end.'

The two cadaverous butlers managed the refilling of the wine glasses and the serving of the meal, the main course of which was a stew that they ladled out of an enormous green casserole.

Lisa looked longingly at the food as it started to be passed around. She wished that she'd taken two shawls with her instead of one. It wasn't just the cold, either, or the general darkness of the room; there was a distinctly disagreeable, dank smell emanating from the corners, from the floor under the lovely old rug. Perhaps there was some reason, connected with the low temperature, for the odour: mould, or that kind of thing. She'd suspected at first that it might be coming from the wine, which she'd nearly choked on: it was like taking a mouthful of plasma. Neill had asked for, and been given, two more cocktails. She was thinking that she should have done that herself, when he handed both glasses straight to her without asking if she wanted them.

She'd been seated between him and Dr Benjamin. She turned her attention to the doctor first. 'Are you a medical doctor?' she asked.

He said no and told her what he was, which she didn't understand. 'Algae,' he explained. 'Pond life, biology.' Then he made an encompassing gesture with his right hand and arm, adding, 'But it's all connected, you know. The animal kingdom, the vegetable kingdom, fish, flowers, rocks, trees. Fascinating. We're only part of it.'

'Oh,' she said with delight, 'yes.' She'd caught his enthusiasm and all of a sudden she was drunk. She said to Neill, 'I think I got a better deal on the cocktails. It's just hit me. What's in them?'

'I should have warned you – they're pretty strong. The ingredients are a closely guarded secret, but the rumour is that they're dill, parsley and vodka, with a squeeze of lemon and a touch of aniseed. But mostly vodka.'

'Nice. Better than the wine.'

'The wine is an acquired taste. You'll get to love it.'

One of the butlers put a heaped plate of the stew in front of her. A rich, spicy aroma steamed up into her face. She looked towards Isabelle, who had lifted her fork, and dug in.

The food was nearly as strange as the wine. The meat had a tang like game. 'What is it?' she asked, after she'd chewed the first mouthful.

'Chicken livers, I think,' the doctor said. 'Delicious.'

Lisa continued to eat. Surely they didn't make chickens that big. And anyway, the pieces of meat were so chewy and tough, you could almost imagine they were parts of a bat.

'I've never tasted any chicken livers like this,' she said.

'Oh, it's all health food,' Dr Benjamin assured her. 'The flavours are much stronger and more natural. Our jaded palates aren't used to them.'

'Except the wine,' Neill said. 'It isn't one of those health wines.'

'Quite superb,' the doctor agreed, raising his glass. The two men smiled at each other across Lisa. She bit down on another piece of her meal and hit a horny substance that resisted. It was too slippery to get back on to her fork again. She chewed rapidly, then gave up, reached in, quickly took it out of her mouth and put it on the side of her plate. It was a large, rubbery black triangle of cartilage. Her glance darted to the side. The doctor had noticed.

'Wonderful stuff,' he pronounced. 'Terrific for the spleen.'

'If you can get it that far,' she said.

'It's good for the teeth and gums to have to chew.'

'That's true,' Neill said. 'I've got caps. Anything happens to them, it's my salary in danger. But I've never hit a bone in this house. You can relax.' He began to talk about the degree to which a television actor was dependent on his face, how you began to look at yourself completely dispassionately, as if seeing a mask from the outside. And then you stuck the emotions on afterwards. To do it the other way – beginning with the emotion and building towards the outward expression – was so exhausting that you could kill yourself like that, or go crazy. 'You can go crazy in any case. I started to flip about three years ago. That's why I'm here.'

'I thought actors were supposed to like pretending and showing off.'

'It was the series. Auto-suggestion. I got to the point where I'd think the things they were making up in the story were actually happening to me. Those characters in the soaps – they really go through it, you know. I was like living that crap. It broke up my life. Broke up my marriage.'

'You got divorced?' she asked. 'Separated?'

'It started with a coldness. Then there was an estrangement.'

He stopped speaking. The mention of cold had made her conscious once more of the chilling damp. It seemed to be pulling the room down into ever darker and deeper layers of rawness.

'Then,' he said, 'she took the children and left, and got the divorce.'

'That's awful,' Lisa said. She looked at him with sympathy, but he smiled back, saying, 'It turned out to be all for the best. It's how I found this place. I'd never have known how far gone I was. I wouldn't have tried to get help. Maybe an analyst, maybe not. But now I'm fine.'

'How?'

'Broderick and Isabelle.'

'Are they doctors?'

'He's a healer. She's a medium. They don't advertise it or anything. They aren't in it for the money, like the fakes.'

Just for the power, Lisa thought. She was surprised that a couple who looked as capable as Broderick and Isabelle should be mixed up in the occult. That, she thought, was for people like Dora and Steve.

'I take it you're not a believer,' he said.

'Oh, I believe in faith-healing. That's half of medicine. Well, not half. Forty-five per cent.'

'You'll come to see the rest, too,' Dr Benjamin told her complacently. She felt angry suddenly. She didn't know what she was doing at this stupid dinner, with these weird people, in a freezing room and eating such revolting food. Even the liquor was peculiar. She tried to catch Jim's eye, but he was stuck with Carrol.

The dessert arrived: a minty sherbet that hadn't set right. The constituents were already separating, and the areas not beginning to melt were oozing and slimy. Lisa took one bite and left the rest. The after-taste was peppery. Jim finally looked at her from across the table. He gave her a defeated smile. She almost made a face back.

'Coffee in the living-room?' Isabelle asked the table. She stood up. Everyone followed. Lisa went straight to Jim. She whispered that she hoped they'd be cutting the evening short, right after the coffee. He nodded and whispered back, 'You bet.'

'They're some kind of psychic health freaks,' she said.

'They cure people of psychosomatic things. Fears and stuff.'

'I've got a fear of horrible food.'

'Jesus, yes. Even the rolls and butter.'

'I didn't see them.'

'It was sort of like trying to eat my jacket.'

They wanted to stay together but Broderick moved them to chairs where they'd be near the people they hadn't sat with at dinner. Lisa was expected to talk to Dora; the heat of the room felt so good that she didn't mind. She attempted to look interested, while Dora spoke about the difficulty of finding a really good nursery. For several minutes Lisa thought they were talking about children.

She was handed a cup of coffee and lifted it to her lips. It was black, scalding, acrid, and didn't taste like coffee. It was like trying to drink a cup of boiling urine. She set it back on its saucer and looked across the room. Isabelle's neat hands were still busied with the silver pot and the cups. Carrol was actually drinking the stuff; so were Neill and Jeanette and Dr Benjamin. Dora's husband, Steve, was positively slurping his with enjoyment.

She watched Jim take his first swallow. His nostrils flared, his eyes screwed tight for a moment.

'And that's the most important thing, isn't it?' Dora said.

'What?'

'The soil.'

'Of course. Basic,' Lisa said. She knew nothing about gardening. When her sister had been out in the back yard helping their mother to do the weeding, she'd stayed indoors to draw and cut up pieces of coloured paper. She said, 'Do you teach botany at your school?'

'Biology.'

'Like the doctor.'

'He's a specialist. Most of his work is done through the microscope.'

'I guess a lot of his job must be finding out how to get rid of all the chemical pollution around.'

'It's a crime,' Dora said. 'Is that your field?'

'I work for a museum,' Lisa told her. 'I help to plan the exhibition catalogues and everything.'

'How interesting.'

It wasn't actually very interesting so far, because she was right at the bottom, just picking up after the other people who did the real work. But some day it was going to be fine: she'd travel, and do her own designs, and be in charge. The only trouble would be trying to fit everything in so that it worked out with Jim.

She could see that Dora was about to go back to biology when Jim stood up at the far end of the room. Lisa said, 'Excuse me just a minute.' She got up and joined him.

He was talking to Isabelle, who had made him sit down again, beside her on the couch; she was saying, 'But you can't.' She looked up at Lisa. 'You can't possibly just run off. You're staying for the weekend.'

Lisa sat next to Jim. She said, 'Just for dinner, I thought?' She took him by the arm and dug her fingers in.

'It's very nice of you,' he said, 'but we must have gotten the signals wrong. We don't even have a toothbrush between us.'

'Oh, we can lend you everything.'

'And Aunt Alice tomorrow,' Lisa said, 'and Mrs Havelock at

church on Sunday.' She'd used the same made-up names for the past year: ever since the evening when she'd flung a string of them at Jim and he'd repeated them, getting every one wrong. Now they had a private pantheon: Aunt Alice, Mrs Havelock, Cousin George, the builders, the plumber, the twins, Grandmother and Uncle Bob, Norma and Freddie, and the Atkinsons.

'I'm afraid it's too late in any case,' Isabelle said. 'The fog here gets very bad at night around this time of the year. I don't think you'd be able to see your hand in front of your face.'

'It's true,' Jeanette said. 'I took a look before we sat down. It's really socked in out there.'

'If it's anything urgent,' Isabelle suggested, 'why don't you phone, and stay over, and then you can leave in the morning. All right? We'd rather have you stay on, though. And we were counting on the numbers for tomorrow night.'

Jim turned to look at Lisa. If the fog was worse than when they'd arrived, there was probably nothing they could do. He said, 'I guess – '

'If we start off early in the morning,' Lisa said. 'It's nice of you to ask us.'

'I'll show you the way right now,' Isabelle told them.

*

Lisa stared at the huge bed. It was the biggest one she'd ever seen and it was covered in a spread that looked like a tapestry. The room too was large; it seemed about the size of a double basketball court. Everything in it was gloomy. All the colours were dark and muddy. The main lighting came from above: a tiny triple-bulbed lamp pronged into the ceiling above the bed and worked from a switch by the door. There was also a little lamp on a table at the far side of the room.

'This old place,' Isabelle said. 'I'm afraid the bathrooms are down the hall. Do bear with us. We try to make up in hospitality. Broderick simply loves it here – his family's been in the district just forever. But I must say, I can never wait for the holidays. Then we go abroad to Italy. When the children come back from school.'

'How many children do you have?' Lisa asked.

'Three boys. I don't know why I keep calling them children. They're already taller than their father – hulking great brutes.'

Isabelle led them down the corridor to a bathroom that was nearly as big as the bedroom. There was a giant tub on claw feet, a toilet with a chain, and a shower partly hidden by a stained plastic curtain. The place was tiled halfway up to the high ceiling. In the corner opposite the toilet the tiles were breaking apart or disintegrating as if the cement had begun to crumble away.

Isabelle said, 'I'll just go see about getting you some towels. We'll meet downstairs. All right?' She left them standing side by side in front of the bathtub.

Lisa whispered, 'Some friends you've got.'

'It's pretty weird.'

'It's unbelievable. What was that stuff we were eating?'

'Jesus, I don't know. I kept trying to guess. I got something on my fork I thought was an ear, and then a hard piece that looked like part of a kneecap. It all tasted like . . . I don't know what.'

'They're crazy, aren't they?'

'I doubt it. Pretentious, maybe. Dora and Steve are the crazy types: dull and normal on the surface, but really looking for leaders to show them their occult destiny.'

'She's got a thing about soil. God, I wish we didn't have to stay over.'

'At least it's warm up here,' he said. 'And they're right – it's like pea soup outside.'

'First thing in the morning, we leave. Right?'

'Definitely. I get the strangest feeling when I'm talking to Broderick, you know. And Isabelle, too.'

'I know what you mean.'

'I mean really. As if there's something wrong. As if they're the wrong people, or there's been a mistake.'

'I've just thought of something. Wouldn't it be funny if you didn't know them at all?'

'Well, I don't. They're friends of Elaine's parents. Or of her mother's cousin. Something like that.'

'I mean, maybe we took the wrong road. Are you sure they're the right people? That sign we passed: the one that had a name on it – that isn't their name, is it? Or the name of Elaine's friends, either.'

'Well . . . I don't know what we could do about it now, anyway.'

'It really would be funny, wouldn't it?'

'And embarrassing. It would be just about the most embarrassing thing I can imagine.'

'Oh, not that bad. Not after that fabulous meal they just gave us. And the coffee; how do you suppose they cooked that up?'

'Maybe they had those two butlers out in the pantry just spitting into a trough for a couple of days.'

Lisa pulled the shower curtain to one side. 'Look at this,' she said, holding it wide to inspect the stains, which were brown and might almost have been taken for bloodstains. 'The whole house.' She pulled it farther. As she drew it away, she could see the corner of the shower. A mass of dead brown leaves lay heaped on the tiles. 'See that?' she asked.

'Smells bad, too,' Jim said.

They both stared down. Lisa leaned forward. Suddenly the leaves began to move, the clump started to split into segments.

Her voice was driven, growling, deep into her throat. She clapped her hands to her head and danced backward over the floor, hitting the opposite wall. Then she was out of the door and down the hallway. Jim dashed after her. He'd just caught up with her when they bumped into Isabelle.

Isabelle said, 'Good heavens. What's happened?'

'Toads,' Lisa groaned. 'A whole gang of them. Hundreds.'

'Oh dear, not again.'

'Again?'

'At this time of year. But there's nothing to worry about. They're harmless.'

'They carry viruses,' Lisa babbled. 'Subcutaneous viruses that cause warts and cancers.'

'Old wives' tales,' Isabelle laughed. 'You just sit down and relax, and I'll deal with it.' She continued along the corridor and down the stairs.

Jim put his arm around Lisa. She was shivering. She said, 'I can't stay here. Jesus. Right in the house. Thousands of them. Please, Jim, let's just get into the car and go. If we're fogged in, we can stop and go to sleep in the back seat.'

'We can't now,' he said.

'Please. I'm grossing out.'

'Just one night,' he told her. 'I'll be with you. It isn't as if they're in the bed.'

'Oh, God. Don't.' She started to cry. He hugged and kissed her. He felt badly for not having been able to resist the temptation to frighten her. It was so much fun to get the reaction.

'Come on,' he said. 'I'll try to find you a drink.'

'Oh boy,' she sniffed. 'Some more of that wonderful coffee.'

'They've got to have a real bottle of something, somewhere. If everything else fails, I'll ask for the one we brought with us.'

He led her back to the brightly lit living room. Broderick stepped forward with a glass in his hand. 'Say you forgive us, please,' he begged. 'And take just one sip of this.'

Lisa accepted the glass. She raised it to her lips. She wanted to get out of the house and go home, and never remember the place again. She let a very small amount of the liquid slide into her mouth. It was delicious. She took a big gulp.

'Nice?' Broderick said.

'Terrific.'

'Great. We'll get you another.' He pulled her over to the couch where Neill was sitting. Neill began to talk about making a TV film in Italy one summer a few years ago: Broderick and Isabelle had been there at the time. And Broderick talked about a statisticians' conference he'd been attending.

Everyone began to drink a great deal. Lisa felt wonderful. She heard Jim and Carrol and Jeanette laughing together across the room and saw Dora and Steve sitting on either side of Isabelle, the doctor standing behind them. She had another one of the drinks, which Broderick told her were coffee liqueur plus several other things. She laughed with pleasure as she drank. She wanted to hear more about Italy and the museums and churches she'd only ever seen pictured in books. It would be so nice, she said, to go there and see the real thing in the real country.

But why didn't she? Broderick thought she certainly should: go to Italy as soon as possible; come with them that summer and stay at the villa. 'Oh, wouldn't that be nice,' she told him; 'wouldn't it be just like a dream? But Jim's job. And mine, too . . .'

There was a break. She came back, as if out of a cloud, to find herself in a different, smaller room, and lying on a couch with Neill. She knew she was pretty drunk and she had no idea if they'd made love or not. She didn't think so. They both still had all their clothes on. Her head was heavy and hurting.

As she moved, he kissed her. She sat up. He reached towards her. She could see under his shirt a red patch composed of flaking sores. It looked as though the skin had been eaten away. 'What's wrong with your chest?' she said.

'Make-up allergy. Badge of the trade. Come on back.'

'I think I'd better be going. I'm pretty plastered.'

'So's everybody.'

'But I'd better go.' She got up. He let her find her way out alone. She stumbled through hallways in near darkness, thinking that any minute she'd fall over or be sick. She came to the staircase and pulled herself up, leaning on the rail.

The bedroom was empty and autumnally moist. There was a smell, all around, of rotting leaves. A pair of pyjamas and a nightgown had been draped over the foot of the bed. The sheet was turned down. She got undressed and climbed in.

The light was still on. She was thinking about having to get up again to turn it out, when Jim lumbered in. He threw himself on top of the bed, saying, 'Christ, what a night. Where did you get to? I looked everywhere.'

'I don't know,' she said. 'I feel terrible.' She closed her eyes. When she opened them again, he was already sleeping. The light was still on. She turned her head and fell asleep herself.

When she woke again, the room was in darkness and stiflingly hot. The odour in the air had changed to one of burning. 'Jim?' she said. She started to throw the covers back. He wasn't anywhere near. She felt around in the dark. It was so pitch-black that it was like being trapped in a hole under the ground. What she needed was a flashlight; they'd brought one with them – the black one – but it was still in the car. 'Jim?' she said again. She sat up and clasped her knees. She was about to peel off the borrowed nightgown she was wearing, when he touched her hands.

'I can't sleep,' she said. 'It's so hot.'

His hands moved from her fingers down to her shins, to the hem of the nightdress and underneath it, up the inside of her legs, and rested on her thighs. She held his arms above the elbows. He sighed.

She said, 'Let me get out of this thing,' and was reaching down and back for the nightgown hem when a second pair of hands slid gently up to the nape of her neck, and a third pair came forward and down over her breasts. Close to her right ear a fourth person laughed. She yelped. Her arms jerked up convulsively.

They were all on top of her at once. She whirled and writhed in the sheets and yelled as hard as she could for Jim, but they had their hands everywhere on her and suddenly she was lifted, thrown down again, and one of them – or maybe more than one – sat on her head. She couldn't do anything then; the first one had never let go of her legs.

She couldn't breathe. Two of them began to laugh again. She heard the nightdress being ripped up, and then, from a distance, the doorknob turning. Shapes bounded away from her across the bed. Light was in her eyes from the hall. And Jim was standing in the doorway. He switched on the ceiling lights.

She fell out of the bed, on to the rug, where she knelt, shuddering and holding her sides. She whined about the men: how many of them there were and what they'd been trying to do to her. The words weren't coming out right.

'What's wrong?' Jim demanded. He put down a glass he'd been carrying.

'Where were you?' she croaked.

'I went to get some water. What's wrong?'

'Men in here – four, six maybe, a whole crowd of them.'

'When?'

'Just before you came in.'

'They left before that?'

'The light scared them.'

'Are you OK?'

'I guess so,' she said.

He made her drink half the glass he'd brought back. 'Which way did they go?' he asked.

'They're still here. Unless they ran past you when you opened the door.'

'No,' he said. He looked around. 'There isn't anyone,' he told her. 'Look. Nobody here. Just us.'

'They're under the bed.'

'Come on.'

'Take a look,' she ordered. Her teeth started to chatter. She wrapped herself in the torn pieces of the nightgown.

He got down on his knees and peered sideways under the bed. 'Nothing,' he said.

She joined him and took a long look herself.

'See? Nobody,' he said. 'Nothing. Not very clean, but no other people.'

'They were here.'

'Look at your nightgown,' he told her. 'How much did you have to drink, anyway?'

'Not enough for all that.'

'We could both use some sleep.'

'I'm not staying in this room unless the light's on. I mean it. If you want the light out, I'm sleeping in the hall: I'm running out of the house. I won't stay here.'

'Take it easy. You want the light on, we'll keep it on.'

'And the door locked.'

'I thought they were still in here.'

'The door,' she shouted.

He went to the door, which had a key-hole but no key. He

pretended to be twisting something near the right place, and returned to the bed. He got in under the covers and put his arms around her.

'I can't wait to get home,' she said. 'Tomorrow. As early as possible.'

'Um. But we might stay just a little.'

'No.'

'Broderick was telling me about this business deal he's got lined up. It sounds really good. We could travel, everything.'

'Jim, we don't even know them. And this whole house is completely crazy. And all this occult crap, and – Jesus, nearly getting raped the minute you walk down the hall.'

'I think we all had a lot to drink.'

'Not that much.'

'I didn't mean you. If there was anybody, maybe they thought this was the wrong room. Maybe it's part of that occult stuff they were talking about at dinner.'

'Oh?'

'That would explain it, wouldn't it?'

'If you call that an explanation.'

'There are even people who spend every weekend that way.'

'Sure.'

'They do.'

'Not in this part of the world.'

*

Broderick sat at the head of the breakfast table. He'd finished eating, but drank coffee as he read the papers. He was still in his pyjamas and dressing gown. At the other end of the table Isabelle poured tea. She wore a floor-length housecoat that had a stand-up collar. Her hair was pulled high in a coiled knot.

They were in a different room from the one in which the last night's dinner had been laid. The windows looked directly on to a garden, although nothing was discernible of it other than the shadow of a branch next to the panes. Everything else was white with fog.

'Tea or coffee,' Isabelle said, 'or anything you like. Just tell Baldwin or Ronald if you don't see what you want on the sideboard.'

The other young members of the party weren't yet down. Dr Benjamin was seated on Isabelle's left. He dipped pieces of bread into an egg cup. Dora and Steve sat side by side; he was eating off her plate, she was buttering a piece of toast. 'I just love marmalade,' she said.

'Is it always like this?' Lisa asked, looking towards the windows.

'It's a little worse than usual today,' Broderick said, 'but it should break up by lunchtime. We'll just have to keep you occupied till then. Do you swim? We've got a marvellous swimming pool. Really. Art Nouveau tiles all over. This place used to belong to – who was it? A real dinosaur. But the pool is great. And it's got three different temperatures.'

'I don't have a bathing suit,' Lisa said.

'We've got lots of extra suits.'

Lisa and Jim each ate an enormous breakfast. She looked at him swiftly as they rushed to the sideboard for third helpings. They almost started to laugh. The food was entirely normal, and the coffee too.

The morning passed pleasantly. Broderick showed them over most of the house. Some of the rooms were light and modern, others old-looking and apparently mouldering. 'We used to rent parts of it out,' he told them. 'For a long time that whole side over there was used as a retreat by a religious organization that Isabelle's Aunt Theda was involved with. If we sold it, I guess somebody'd turn the place into a school. They all want me to sell. But I couldn't bear it. My parents bought this house when I was seven. I remember moving in.'

There was a billiards room, a game room with ping-pong tables in it, a library. The pool was indeed magnificent. Jim and Lisa put on the suits they were offered. Broderick and Jeanette joined them. Neill sat in a canvas chair where it was dry; he said the chlorine made his skin allergy itch. And Carrol, who had sat down next to him, pulled out her knitting and shook her head. She was waiting, she said, for her consultation with Broderick.

Broderick swam for about ten minutes, got out of the pool and went up to Carrol. 'Right,' he said. She packed up the knitting without a word and left with him. Neill challenged the rest of them to a ping-pong match.

It was surprising, Lisa thought, how much she was enjoying herself. But after the ping-pong they passed through a hallway that had a window, and she rushed forward to look out. The world was still white, but it was as bright as electric light. The sun was going to burn off the fog quickly.

'We can start soon,' she said to Jim.

'Well, not right away. We could stay for lunch.'

'As soon as possible.'

'It wouldn't be very polite.'

'What happened last night wasn't very polite, either.'

'Let's not start on that again.'

'OK. Let's just get out fast.'

'This thing Broderick talked about – it sounds really good. It could make a big difference to us.'

'Jim, for God's sake,' she said.

'Just cool it, Lisa. There's no hurry.' He pushed forward ahead of her and turned to the right. She leaned back against a green stone statue that held a bowl meant for flowers. She wondered if she had the strength of will to get into the car herself and just drive away on her own.

He had the keys. It was his car. And he was the invited guest, even if this wasn't the right house. All the embarrassment would be his to deal with after she'd gone. She couldn't really do that to him.

Jeanette met her at a turn in the corridor. 'Are you staying for the session?' she asked.

'I don't think so. We'll be leaving pretty soon. We've got to get back to town.'

'That's too bad. The sessions really help.'

'In what way?'

'Well . . . just talking. Broderick says that fear – fear itself is a disease. Do you believe that?'

'To a certain extent. Sure.'

'It helps to talk about it.'

'It helps if the thing you're afraid of goes away. If you can make that happen by talking, I guess that's good.'

'Of course you can. Because it's in the mind.'

'The things I'm afraid of,' Lisa said, 'are definitely not in the mind. They're in the world.'

'But if they haven't happened yet – '

'A little anticipation keeps us all alive. Right?'

'It keeps us frightened.'

'Frightened people are careful. And careful people live longer.'

'Sometimes it isn't worth it,' Jeanette said.

They reached the breakfast room. Steve and Dora were still at the table. Sunlight streamed in through the windows.

*

She ran upstairs, got her purse and raced down again. She felt wonderful: the sun was out and at last they could leave.

Broderick met her at the foot of the stairs. 'Where to, and so fast?' he said. He smiled jovially but his eyes gloated at her.

'We've really got to get back now,' she said.

'But Jim said you were staying through lunch.'

'I'm afraid not.'

'It's all fixed. He said he'd phone whoever it was you had to meet.'

'It isn't that simple. Where is he?'

'Out in the garden somewhere, I think. Want me to help you look?'

'No, thanks,' she said. 'It's all right.'

She stepped out the side door on to a brick terrace. Stairs led down to a garden of white-flowering bushes. Beyond them stood a statue of a woman, one signalling arm raised out of her marble drapery. Neill was sitting on a bench at her side.

Lisa asked, 'Have you seen Jim?'

'No.'

'Who's this?'

'One of those goddesses. Artemis, maybe. Bow and arrow – is that right? I didn't pay much attention in school. Most of the time I was bored stiff. Couldn't wait to get out and see the world.'

'I loved it,' she said.

'Sit down.'

'I just came out to find Jim. We're leaving.'

'I thought you were staying till Monday. I hoped you were. Don't go.'

'We really have to,' she told him, walking away.

He got up and fell into step beside her. He said, 'Tonight and tomorrow are the best times. People come from all around. It's when we hold the séances.'

'Oh, God,' she said. In the distance Jim was walking towards them. He raised a hand. 'There he is. I'll just have a couple of words with him.' She hurried ahead.

*

'We're staying,' he said.

'Jim, I can't stand another minute in this place.'

'Every time I turn around, you look like you're having a great time with that Farley Granger clone.'

'Last night I was nearly raped by four men while you were getting a drink of water.'

'Last night you were completely pie-eyed and suffering from massive wish-fulfilment.'

'Oh Jesus, how can you be so stupid? How – '

'We're leaving right after dinner, but if it's too late, then we'll go in the morning. Whatever happens, we're definitely staying till the late evening, because Henry Kissinger's invited.'

'Who?'

'Ex-Secretary of State, Kissinger, a name you may have seen in the papers?'

'What are you talking about?'

'He's coming here for dinner tonight.'

'Why?'

'Christ. Because he was asked, of course.'

'Well. Well, so what?'

'Look, Lisa: I see nothing wrong about name-dropping, and if I get a chance to sit at the same table with a name like Kissinger, a part of American history, I'm sure as hell not going to miss it. Are you? Isabelle says he tells wonderful stories. Come on, Lisa, are you with me or what?'

'Give me the keys,' she said.

'Keys?'

'I'll drive back, and you can get a ride with Henry Kissinger or somebody else.'

'Of course not. It would be unforgivably rude.'

'I don't believe he's coming.'

'He is.'

'I'll make a scene.'

'Hah.'

'I'll say I recognize him from photographs as the Nazi commandant of a concentration camp. I'll – '

'Lisa,' he said, 'you just shut up and be nice. It's been a little strange, but you're going to have to take it. I've got an important deal on with Broderick and if you mess things up, believe me you're going to be sorry, because I won't stand for it.'

He'd never spoken to her like that. She felt her whole body, and especially her face, go rigid with fury and desperation. She wheeled around and ran off across the lawn.

She reached the front drive and slowed down. It wasn't yet noon, the sun was bright; she could walk through all the country roads until afternoon, and by that time she'd hit the highway and find help. She'd phone the police or the Automobile Association, or a friend from town, to come get her.

She settled into a regular stride. It wasn't going to be easy in her party shoes, though they weren't too high and so far felt comfortable. Her lips moved but she wasn't actually muttering. She was thinking about all the times he'd been in the wrong and unfair to her – how this was really the limit and it would serve him right.

She ploughed through a muddy field of deep grass and came out on to the driveway. It took her a lot longer than she'd expected to reach the road. Everything looked different in the daytime. In fact, it all looked beautiful. If the house hadn't been such a perfect replica of Haunted House Gothic, the setting could equally well have accommodated a fairytale palace. Everywhere she looked there was a superabundance of blossoming hedges, gnarled trees, mossy banks and starry flowers. She began to feel stronger as she went on, despite the shoes: a long walk over stony and uneven ground wasn't going to do them any good – she could tell that already. They'd be ruined afterwards for anything but rainy days.

She hummed a little. She reached the road and stopped, looking from left to right and rubbing her hands. She realized suddenly that she'd been scratching at her hands for a long while, trying to get rid of an itch in the folds between her fingers. She'd made all the itchy spaces bright pink. Red spots like the beginnings of a rash had come up between two of the fingers on her left hand. Nerves, she thought; or possibly a reaction to the peculiar food from the night before.

She turned to the left. For five minutes she walked without seeing a car or a person. Then ahead, coming towards her from around the next corner, she saw two men: rough-looking, bearded and wearing dungarees. She felt apprehensive straight away. She wanted to turn around and go back. Should she look at them, or past them; say hello, or what? What could she do to make them walk on and not take any notice of her?

One was short, the other tall. They didn't look right at her as they went by, but they were fooling. Almost as soon as she'd passed they were back again, one on each side of her, walking in her direction and near enough, if they wanted to, to grab her arms.

'Looking for something, girlie?' the short one said.

'No thanks, I'm fine,' she answered in a small, tight, terrified voice that made her even more frightened.

'Well, we'll just walk along with you a-ways,' the big one

said. 'Keep you from getting lonely. Just in case something was to happen to a nice little girl like you.'

She looked up quickly. They were both grinning. Would they just terrorize her, or did they mean to act? Maybe they'd kill her afterwards, so she couldn't identify them. Maybe they meant to kill her anyway, just for fun. She'd never be able to run fast enough. It was probably better to give in as soon as possible and die quickly. If she were strong, at least she'd be able to hurt them back somehow.

The little one was beginning to jostle her. They were ready to start; pretty soon his friend would be doing it too. She stepped back and to the side, saying, 'Well, if nobody's going to leave me alone today, I might as well go back to my friends. They were right behind me.' She began to walk back, in the direction of the house.

They turned and came with her.

'Now isn't that a shame?' the tall one said. 'She doesn't like our company.'

'That really hurts my feelings,' the short one told him.

She was itchy and sore all over now. It was difficult to keep walking.

'You think she meant to be mean like that?' the small one asked. 'You think she's one of those stuck-up bitches that takes it out on you?'

'I think maybe that's just what she is,' the big one said. 'I met plenty like her. I know her type.'

Her pulse was drumming in her throat and the hairs rising on her arms. Surely it wouldn't happen. It couldn't happen, because she was having such a hard time simply continuing to breathe that long before they started to drag her across the road, she'd have a heart attack. She hoped she'd have one – that everything would just stop all of a sudden and be no more.

She took her eyes from the surface of the road and looked towards the turning. In front of her, emerging from a thicket of bushes to the left, were two people who waved. 'There they are,' she called out, and sprinted ahead. She could run after all. But she stopped when she was a few yards away. It hadn't occurred to her that she might really know the couple. Now she recognized them: it was Dora and Steve.

'Friends of yours?' Steve said.

'I never saw them before.' She turned and looked back. The two men were gone.

'I didn't think they looked very trustworthy,' Dora said. 'This is a lonely road. You'd better come on back with us.'

'So, you're a friend of nature, too?' Steve asked. He had a notebook and ballpoint pen in his hand, field-glasses hanging from a strap around his neck. 'This is wonderful country for it. Best in the world. That's the other reason we keep coming here.'

'I can't stay,' Lisa told him. 'We were only coming for supper last night, that's all. I've got to get back. For private reasons. And now Jim won't even let me go by myself. But that's silly. It isn't fair. I was trying to walk it.'

'In those shoes?' Dora said. 'Oh, dear.'

'You have a car here, don't you? Could you drive me? Just to a bus stop or a train station?' She scratched violently at her hands.

'You've got that chlorine reaction, too,' Dora said. 'I've got an ointment I can lend you.'

'I just want to get home,' Lisa wailed.

'But you wouldn't want to miss the party. You know who's going to be here tonight, don't you?'

'This is important. It's a family matter. Couldn't you?'

'All right,' Steve said. 'Of course. Right after lunch. Just let us finish the notes first, otherwise we'll have to start all over again. That's soon enough, isn't it – say, just before three? I'd make it earlier, but this is a working weekend as well as pleasure. We're compiling a book – did I tell you?'

'Oh?'

'Toads.'

'Dear little things,' Dora said. 'And fascinating.'

'You could stay indoors and do all the research you need,' Lisa said. 'They're in the house, too.'

'What do you mean?'

'In the upstairs bathroom, in the shower. There was a whole nest, a big pile of them. Last night.'

'Don't tell me they got out?' Steve said.

'It must be another batch,' Dora told him. 'Ours were fine this morning. I guess you're lucky they didn't nip your toes when you were stepping in there. They're carnivorous, you know.' She laughed in hearty barks that ended in a whoop of amusement.

Lisa said, 'Thanks for telling me.'

They came in sight of the house. Dora said she'd go get that tube of medicine, and added that she couldn't believe Lisa was really going to run off and miss the opportunity of meeting Henry Kissinger. They walked around the terrace to the far side, passing as they went a line of large, brand-new and expensive cars parked against the balustrade. Steve said the cars belonged to patients.

'You'd be surprised,' he told Lisa, 'how many people consult Broderick and Isabelle. In all walks of life, too: movie stars, politicians, big businessmen – you name it.'

'Kissinger?'

'I think he's just an ordinary guest.'

'Norman Mailer was here last weekend,' Dora said. 'He talked for hours about glands.'

'Hormones,' her husband corrected.

'And Henry Fonda before that.'

'He's dead,' Lisa said.

'Well, maybe it was the other one.'

'Which other one? The son?'

'Gary Cooper. Or was it John Wayne?'

'I think we're getting all these names a little mixed up,' Steve explained. He winked at Lisa.

'Anyway,' Dora said, 'he was very nice.'

*

They had a cold lunch of food that once again, like the breakfast, was good: salads with chicken, ham and beef; fruit and ice cream afterwards. The coffee looked all right too, but Lisa didn't want to try it.

Jim wouldn't look at her. She heard a long account from Dr Benjamin about tree frogs in Africa. He examined her hands and told her there was nothing to worry about: all the redness was simply a result of friction. As she listened, she could see Carrol, only four seats away, scratching and rubbing herself, touching her face all the time.

She said to the doctor, 'Steve and Dora are giving me a ride back to town at three, but I'm in kind of a hurry. I'd like to get away sooner than that. Did you come by car?'

'I came with them,' he told her. 'And I think Broderick picked the two girls up on his way out from town. Why don't you ask him? I'm sure he'd run you in.'

'I'd hate to bother him,' she said. 'We'll see.'

She went upstairs to wait till three. She paced all around the bed, looking carefully at the dark edging of the heavy, brocaded spread. She sat down on top of it, inspected the material and then slowly prepared to curl up. She lowered her head, but she kept her shoes on. She slept for a few minutes, waking up in a rush as soon as she heard someone walking down the hall.

Jim opened the door, shut it behind him and came over to her. He said, 'What's wrong with you?'

'I want to go home. Please, Jim. Remember the food last night?'

'It was fine just now.'

'And the cold, and the smell. Those animals in the shower. And I mean it about what happened when you left. You don't believe me, but you don't believe anything from me any more.'

'I'm not staying here for an accusation session.'

'Just let me have the car keys, for God's sake. What difference is it going to make to you?'

'If you walk out of here, if you're rude, if you make a scene – it makes me look bad.'

'No, it doesn't. I act on my own.'

'You're here with me.'

'I tried to leave. I was going to walk. Look at my shoes. Two guys on the road tried to grab me.'

'Uh-huh. Guys trying to grab you every time you turn around.'

'Just let me get out, Jim. Please.'

'We're leaving Monday morning.'

'Monday? This is only Saturday.'

'We've been invited for the weekend.'

'Well, if this is even the right house, it was only supposed to be supper on Friday. I don't have a change of underpants or anything. Neither do you.'

'Isabelle says she can let you have whatever you like.'

'What I'd like is to get back to town.'

They argued back and forth in a normal tone at first, then in whispers, and nearly shouting. He wanted to know how she could be so parochial as to leave just when Henry Kissinger was about to arrive: wasn't she interested in world politics, in history?

She said, 'You don't believe he's really coming here, do you? To eat mud soup and old tyres? Him and Norman Mailer and John Wayne and all the rest of them? They just want to get us to stay here, that's all.'

'Why?'

'I don't know. They just do.'

'You mean, they're telling us lies?'

'Of course they are.'

'But why would they do that?'

'Because they want us to stay.'

'It doesn't make sense.'

'Does any of it? Look at me.' She held out her hands. The skin was patched with pink lumps. 'Look at my hands,' she told him.

'What have you done to them?'

'I haven't done anything. They're itching because of something in this house.'

'Oh, Lisa. I don't know what's gotten into you. Try to calm down.'

She stood up. 'Right,' she said. 'Steve and Dora can give me a ride. And now I know how much I'd be able to count on you.' She snatched up her purse and looked at her wristwatch. It said four thirty. 'God, I'm late. Oh, God.'

'That settles it.'

'Yes. I'll see if they'll still do it. And if they won't, you'll have to.'

'Nope.'

'And if you don't, we're through.'

'That's up to you. You're going to feel pretty foolish when you look back and see how unreasonable you're being.'

'And I'm calling the police.'

He stood up and threw her back on to the bed. 'Everything you want,' he hissed at her. 'Always for you and never for the both of us, never for me. Who's going to have to build up a career and pay off the mortgage and all the rest of it, hm? You won't cook for my friends, you won't do this or that –'

'And what about you?' she screeched. 'Leave me there with a list of all the errands I've got to run for you: I've got a job too, you know. You're a grown man. You can wash your own goddamn socks once in a while.'

'You aren't going to give me that Women's Lib stuff, are you?'

'Just this once – just get me out of here and I'll do anything. You can come straight back, if you like. Please.'

'Don't cry like that. Somebody could hear you.'

'Please.'

'All right,' he said.

She sprang towards the door. He followed slowly. They went down the stairs together, Lisa running ahead.

Isabelle was standing at the foot of the staircase. She was dressed in another long, dark robe and her hair was even more elaborately arranged than on the night before. This time the string of pearls that twined through the pile of stacked braids included a single jewel; it hung from the centre parting on to her forehead. It looked like a ruby, surrounded by tiny pearls. 'And where are you two off to?' she asked.

Lisa said, 'I'm sorry, Isabelle – I really am. It's been so lovely here, but we left town thinking it was just for supper last night. I had three people I was supposed to see today, and now I've got to go – I've really got to. The others are going to be furious. I'll have to patch that up somehow, but my mother – ' her voice quivered. 'My mother's operation comes first. I've just got to get back. We should have said straight away. Jim – ' she turned to him; he could do some worrying for a change, after putting her through all this: 'Jim thought you'd be upset if we refused your hospitality. I was sure you'd understand. He can stay, of course. But my mother can't wait, I'm afraid. Not even for Mr Kissinger.'

'That's another disappointment. He just called. He can't make it tonight. Maybe tomorrow, he said. Such a shame. We look forward to his visits so much.'

'Tomorrow?' Jim repeated. He sounded hopeful.

'Not for me,' Lisa insisted.

Broderick had appeared at the end of the corridor, the other guests grouped behind him. He began to lead them all down the carpet towards the staircase and the light. 'What's this?' he said.

'Lisa wants to leave us,' Isabelle told him.

'I don't want to. I've got to, that's all. My mother's having a serious operation.'

'When?' Broderick asked.

'On Friday afternoon they told me it was going to be tonight, possibly tomorrow morning. I've got to get back.'

'I can drive you,' Broderick offered.

'Thanks, but Jim's going to.'

'I know the roads around here. And I'm used to the fog. Have you seen what it's like?'

'We waited for you,' Steve complained. Dora, beside him, asked, 'Where were you? You said three.'

'I couldn't find you,' Lisa said. She suddenly didn't believe that they had waited, or that Henry Kissinger had ever been on the guest list, or that she was going to be allowed out of the house, which was definitely the wrong house. She put her hand on Jim's arm. Her fingers, her whole arm, trembled.

'Why don't you phone the hospital?' Isabelle suggested. She

picked up the receiver from the telephone on the table next to her.

They were going to try to fake her out, Lisa thought. But she could phone a taxi, or even the police, if she wanted to. Or – a better idea – a friend: Broderick was undoubtedly on good terms with all the lawyers, doctors and policemen in the neighbourhood, as well as any local politicians who lived nearby. 'That's a good idea,' she said. She let go of Jim's arm and came down the last few stairs.

Isabelle put her ear to the receiver. She said, 'Well, wouldn't you know it? It does this sometimes in a thick fog. It's gone completely dead.'

Me, too, Lisa thought. She turned to Jim and said, 'I mean it. Now.'

He spread his hands towards Isabelle. 'I'm really sorry,' he said.

'Another time,' she told him. She shook his hand and smiled. She shook Lisa's hand too, holding the friendly look and the smile.

Broderick called after them, 'Come on back if the fog catches up with you. They can be dangerous. People can actually choke to death in them.'

*

All the air outdoors was smoky. They got into the car. Lisa said nothing, although she felt safe already. If they had to, she wouldn't mind sleeping in the back seat. At least they'd be away from the house. Jim turned the key. He drove the car across the gravel. Lisa waved at the dimly lighted doorway.

They moved down the drive, along the woodland road and out on to the highway, where almost immediately they hit the real fog. Jim went very slowly. The fog came towards them in long strips like white veiling that kept tearing in pieces or bunching up around them.

'What was all that about your mother?' he said.

'I had to think of something they couldn't explain away. It would have looked bad if they hadn't been sympathetic.'

'Isabelle was very nice about it.'

'She was mad as hell.'

'She was not. She was kind and understanding.'

'And she has Kissinger for dinner just all the time – oh, yes. And what a surprise: the phone doesn't work.'

'What are you getting at?'

'Those weirdo people holding occult meetings together.'

'They're wonderful people. They're studying phenomena that can't be explained yet by any of the scientific principles we know of so far. How do you think anyone ever gets to know things, anyway? There's always a time when it sounds crazy and crackpot – when it's all being tried out experimentally. As soon as a thing's accepted, then it's considered normal.'

'You think that house is normal?'

'Well, the heating's kind of erratic and the pipes don't work so well, and what do you expect? It's a big old place down in the country. It'd cost a fortune to fix it up.'

'It wouldn't cost a fortune to give us tuna salad to eat, instead of whatever that horrible stuff was. It wouldn't – '

'Wait,' he said. All the windows had suddenly gone stark white. The effect was blinding until he turned off the lights. He slowed the car to a crawl. 'If it gets any worse, you'll have to walk in front, to show me where the edge of the road is.'

'No. We can just stop here and sleep in the car. Pull off the road.'

'You heard what Broderick said about the fog.'

'I don't believe it.'

'Well, I do.'

'I'm not going back there, Jim,' she said.

'Jesus Christ,' he shouted, 'what's wrong with you?' He stopped the car and switched off the ignition. 'I think you're crazy,' he said. 'I really do. Just like your whole damn family.'

'OK. You can think what you like, as long as we never have to go back to that place.'

'This is the end of us, you know. I can't go on with you after this.'

'If we just get home, we'll be all right.'

'You screwed up everything with them. I don't know how anybody could have behaved the way you did. Completely hysterical, and lying your head off. It was obvious.'

'But does that mean I've got to die for it?'

'Die? Nobody's going to die.'

'And why do we have to split up? Why do they mean more to you than I do? You didn't even know them before yesterday.'

'I guess maybe I didn't know you very well, either.'

'Oh, shove that.'

'Uh-huh. Nice.'

'You know me. And you know how I feel about you.'

'Maybe not.' He opened his window a crack. They could see the white fog creep in like smoke. He tried the lights again. This time the glare wasn't thrown back, but the lights didn't seem to penetrate more than a few feet into the shifting areas of blankness.

She said, 'When you got up for that drink of water last night, where did you go?'

'Down the hall to the bathroom.'

'You were with somebody else, weren't you?'

'No,' he said. 'But it's a good idea.'

The whiteness became all-enveloping. The temperature began to drop inside the car. The sound of rain seemed to be coming from somewhere, though they couldn't see any.

'I don't understand,' she said, 'how you could have let us get into all that.'

'It was too foggy to drive back. It was like this.'

'And this morning, when I asked you for the keys?'

'This morning you were already crazy; people grabbing you left and right. If this doesn't clear soon –'

'We sit it out.'

'I suppose so.' He was about to cut the lights, when something dark thudded against the windshield and was gone again.

'A bat,' Lisa called out.

'No. It didn't look . . . I think it was rounder. Maybe a bird. I guess the light attracted it.'

There was another sound as two more of the things struck Lisa's side window. She undid her safety belt and moved nearer to Jim.

He was watching the glass in front of him. Several more of the dark shapes hit. They sounded like rubber balls being thrown against the car, all over the metal parts suddenly: on the roof, too. He leaned forward. 'Frogs,' he said. They were everywhere, bouncing up and down, lying still, or slithering across the glass.

'Not frogs,' Lisa moaned. 'Toads.'

'Jesus, will you look at them – there must be hundreds.'

'Thousands,' she said. 'Oh, my God.'

He turned off the lights. It didn't have any effect. The toads continued to bombard the car.

'Maybe if we start moving again,' he said.

'We can't. They're jamming themselves into the exhaust. Can't you hear them?'

'I could really step on it and blow the muffler off.' He switched the engine on again, turned the lights high.

Now the toads were all over. They blocked the view from the windows. They were also a great deal bigger than before. When one of them landed, it sounded like a soccer ball.

He started to drive. The exhaust pipe roared, the car inched forward. He tried to use the windshield wipers, but the toads hung on until the blades stuck in one position. There were swarms of the animals, uncountable. Clusters of them lay squashed or flattened on the windows. And the big ones crashed down on top of them. A dark liquid began to run over the panes.

'Could they break the glass?' she asked.

'I don't know. It's safety glass. They might be able to bang into it hard enough, if they all jumped together.'

'They're carnivorous,' she said.

An Artist's Life

Axel and Eino met only because one morning Axel turned his head; he'd heard the cry of a bird – a sea-bird of some kind. The wind whipped into his face and he pulled down his hat. At that moment he saw ahead of him on the bridge a young man, walking towards him, who made a similar gesture and then put up his other hand to adjust a scarf around his throat.

The next day at about the same time Axel caught sight of the man at a different spot, this time beyond the bridge; he was hurrying forward, his head down so that it was impossible to see his face, but Axel recognized the clothes he was wearing, which were copied from the Bohemian Paris of earlier decades.

Axel, whose family was more than three-quarters Swedish and had money and houses and land, wore French and English clothes of good quality and cut. He might have been mistaken for a Parisian. He was tall, grey-eyed and brown-haired. He had the languid demeanour – in fashion at the time – supposed to denote good breeding; among those who adopted it, at any rate, the attitude was a sign that they thought so.

Eino was of a different stamp: very blond, round-headed and burly. He walked quickly, with a jerky, bobbing gait. He held the upper part of his body – shoulders, back and arms – like a man who was strong. On the first day Axel saw his face, Eino looked ready to kill someone. He must have been cold as he turned against the wind.

On the third day, Axel saw him after crossing the bridge. Eino was searching the gutter for something. Once more he had his head down and Axel noticed the clothes.

He didn't see Eino for a while after that and when he did, he heard him first: he heard a voice saying in Finnish, 'Do they think we're idiots?' and he stopped.

He looked around. The man who had made the remark was standing with his back towards Axel; he had his hands in his pockets and was shifting quickly from one foot to the other. He was examining the objects in a shop window. The awning above protected him from the light drizzle that had begun to fall. Axel had his umbrella.

He knew that he'd seen the stranger before, although he hadn't thought the man would be a fellow countryman. He walked up to the shop window and stood beside Eino, to look at a large, pink ostrich feather and a set of stands stacked with jars of cosmetic cream. Ribbons had been made to cascade from top to bottom of the display, so that the separate groupings seemed like bouquets of flowers. Several coloured sketches of young women illustrated the beneficial properties of the ointment.

'Who do they think they're fooling?' Eino muttered. 'If the woman's good-looking, she doesn't need anything.'

'And if she isn't,' Axel said, 'it wouldn't help her.'

'Exactly. Women like that must be weak in the head.'

'They have hope. They might start to look better because they're in a good mood.'

'But the stuff is worthless.'

'Of course.'

'Half the damn things you see in shop windows are worthless.'

'But – they sell.'

'Because people are fools.'

'The ones who buy, perhaps. What about the ones who sell?'

Eino laughed. 'Swindlers. All of them.'

'It can't be that bad.'

'It's worse.'

Axel moved away. He was far down the street and thinking of other things when he was pulled from behind. He whirled around, to find himself staring at Eino, who said, 'You were speaking Finnish. I didn't realize. Talk to me. Talk to me in Finnish.'

Axel repositioned his umbrella. The man looked desperate as well as poor, but was about his own age, which – at his age – seemed to make him all right. 'We'll go to a café,' he suggested.

'I don't have any money.'

'I think I've got enough to buy you a beer.'

'No,' Eino told him. 'We'll walk.'

Axel agreed. He went as far as the café on the street corner across from the park and then said, 'If it were better weather, we could sit here, but as it is, I'm finding it difficult to keep in step with a man who doesn't have an umbrella. If you won't come into the café and let me buy you a drink, I'll say goodbye.'

They went in together. Axel ordered tea and biscuits. Eino drank coffee. There were four other men in the room, all old and all reading the papers.

'I've walked by this place plenty of times,' Eino said, 'and never gone in. I've never even wondered what it was like inside.'

'There must be thousands of cafés in this part of town.'

'I love big cities. You never get to the end of them. Every street has a row of new places you've never explored.'

'The whole world is like that,' Axel said.

'Some of it. Not the part I grew up in. Not Finland. You grew up in town, didn't you?'

'Oh, nothing like this. A small university town in Sweden, a village in Finland; a few summers in St Petersburg when my grandparents were alive – that was the nearest I got, but I was still a child then. Paris was always my dream.'

'Has it lived up to what you expected of it?'

'Yes, completely,' Axel said.

At the beginning it had been even better than the expectation, except in one important respect, but he didn't know Eino well enough to talk about that: it hadn't fulfilled his hopes for the erotic, as well as the romantic, life. He'd imagined that it would be simple to meet women who were easy to ask, but so far he'd managed to find only the places where all the girls were too obviously professional, and that still made him a little nervous.

He'd had two affairs with girls down in the country and one with a scandalous young woman who'd said she was getting a divorce from her elderly husband: that one had been the most fun. It had lasted throughout the summer and ended because Axel had made a scene when he'd found out that he wasn't the only man she was seeing. She'd screamed at him that he was unsophisticated. And the next week, when he'd gone back to apologize, she'd laughed at him while the maid stood by the door, holding his coat and listening to everything. After that, he'd had a steady, once-a-week meeting with a married woman in her late thirties: Martha. She'd been in love with him. For him the meetings had been merely a convenience – he was always looking for someone else. But for her they became the centre of life and she couldn't help showing it. As she kept wanting more of him, he retreated. By the time he broke it off, he could barely stand to be near her. He didn't even care that – as he'd once feared – she might try to commit suicide.

He saw her in town on three different occasions after the break; once at a concert, when she didn't realize he was standing at the back of the room. She had the look of a woman who was dying.

She'd written letters to his mother, pleading that he be allowed to see her. That had been his fault: rather than saying outright that he didn't love her, he'd invented a story in which his parents' views played a ruling part. *A married woman*, he'd said: they'd be horrified.

Axel's mother was indeed horrified. She couldn't understand why, instead of asking his father for advice about these things, he'd implicated a decent, married woman in his philanderings; and evidently hurt her very deeply. But, Axel had answered, his father's advice had been to get married as soon as possible to a rich girl with no looks, who would bring him enough money for a comfortable life and would always do what he told her. His mother wasn't too happy about that reply. Over the next few days his father came into the argument too, and it was eventually decided that if Axel agreed to take a job working with Thorvaldsen's cousin at the bank, they'd let him go to Paris for a year, as he'd always wanted – to see if he could become a painter.

He'd been there since October. And now it was January.

'And you?' he asked Eino. 'How do you come to be so far from home? Did you always dream about living in Paris?'

'Not at first. In the beginning I just wanted to go away, anywhere. I couldn't get along with them at home. And I hated school.'

'I liked school, but I was lucky. I had good teachers and tutors.'

'It doesn't depend on the teachers. I just didn't have the aptitude for it. Otherwise . . . What I wanted to do was to be an architect, or something along those lines – to make things and to build them. I was always good with my hands. I had a great-uncle like that; he'd sit all day long, whittling things with a penknife: animals, people – he could do anything. He taught me to paint, to draw; to hunt, and do woodcarving. For that kind of thing I loved being in the country. And for real work – to do hard work that satisfies your body. I helped a friend of my father's to build a house once. That was fine. That was a side of home life that I liked.'

'Me too,' Axel said. All his life he'd felt comforted and healed by the beauty of the countryside, although as far as any real work went, they'd had servants for that.

'In the town,' Eino told him, 'you just sit on a stool and don't do anything, and you're ready to die of tiredness at the end of the day. It isn't healthy.'

'You mean school?'

'School, and most businesses. My aunts had a confectionery shop – a big place, staff, everything tied up in ribbons and fancy wrapping, people making the boxes, importing ingredients, and so on. When I was a boy they let me design the boxes.'

'And all the chocolate you could eat, I suppose.'

'They say it's poison, you know – all sweet food: that it rots your insides, not just your teeth.'

'The favourite food of children.'

'Yes. Right from the beginning we develop a taste for what's going to destroy us.'

'Well,' Axel said, 'that's putting it rather strongly. If you live long enough, you can die of anything. It's simply a matter of time, isn't it?'

Eino laughed. Tears came to his eyes. The laughter began to sound wild. It made Axel wonder if he was sick or crazy, or even hungrier than he'd assumed. 'But the chocolate wasn't enough?' he said.

'I'd been taken to a museum once. My mother wanted to look at china – plates and vases, that sort of thing. And they had a section for Venetian glass. That made a big impression on me. I wanted to know how it was possible to form a hard material like that into shapes – to add colour to it, to make a glass flower or even a glass bowl. Then they told me that the men who made things out of glass did it by blowing molten bubbles. Of course I thought that was wonderful. I wanted to see it straight away. I kept asking to go. You know, I'd forgotten all this. It's odd how things suddenly pop into your head when you get to talking. That's right: I made them take me to a glass factory somewhere. As a matter of fact, I don't remember too much about that. It wasn't very interesting after all. The next craze was wanting to learn about architecture. That wasn't any good. I couldn't do the schoolwork. But I always had this idea that I'd build a house – a real one. Big. Not just helping to work on somebody's summer cabin. I still think so. There are plenty of good houses that were built without mathematics, aren't there?'

'Of course,' Axel said, although he had an idea that the big houses usually demanded a preliminary plan and a lot of calculation – measurements, investigation of the surrounding land, information about soil and drainage.

Eino said, 'My father always wanted a boat, all his life. He had the idea, but it was only a wish on his part. He never had the absolute certainty that one day he'd get the boat. But in my case, you see, I just know I'm going to build that house.'

'And that's why you came to Paris, to learn about –'

'No, that was a long time ago. What happened was that they sent me to Berlin to learn about the restaurant trade and I wanted to be a painter, so I just jumped on the first train out. A friend of mine came with me, but he moved on. I stayed put, and painted.'

'You're a painter?' It didn't seem possible to Axel that anyone his own age, anyone from his own country, and especially anyone he knew, could be a genuine painter. 'That's how you make your living?'

'If you can call it that. I do a lot of other things, too. Anything for cash.'

'Portraits?'

'Portraits, landscapes, billboards, valentines, playbills, ceilings. And you? You don't have to work, am I right?'

'I work in a bank.'

'I see. That explains it.'

'What?'

'The clothes.'

'It's only like any other uniform.' He smiled, thinking that Eino too was dressed in a kind of uniform; some looks were chosen, some imposed according to someone else's choice. He wasn't ready to say that he too was a painter, that he wasn't getting anywhere with it, and that after discovering how inferior all his work was, he wasn't enjoying it any longer.

He'd realized just before Christmas. The knowledge had ruined his holiday. He'd come in late after the office celebrations, sat down at his writing table, opened the presents from his family, and suddenly felt so homesick that he'd wanted to weep. There were books, and some extra money from his parents, cards and letters from aunts and uncles and cousins; a scarf his sister, Anna, had knitted for him, a pair of opera glasses from his uncle Karl, a photograph of all the family gathered together. And he'd given up all that family life for the sake of the dismal, misshapen daubs propped against the wall in front of him and beside the chair in the corner. He could see all at once that in putting the paint on the canvas he had been responsible for adding to the ugliness in the world. It would have been better if those objects had never been made. Nor was he a success, as he'd dreamed, in any other way. He was in the capital city of love, and was ready to die of loneliness.

'I couldn't work in a bank,' Eino said.

'Why not?'

'The routine would kill me.'

'It's actually full of variety. They keep moving you around from one department to another. It's quite interesting. Very interesting, really – only I always wanted to do something more, ah, artistic.'

'And the fixed hours. Once you've been your own boss, every other kind of job seems servile.'

'I don't look at it that way. You can't get anything much done without a certain amount of teamwork and cooperation.'

'Would you rather be the one giving the orders, or carrying them out?'

'I don't think it matters, as long as the work is important. Of course, I'm not like you – I was never very good with my hands, so there are some jobs I'd rather not try. I was better at all the mathematics and sitting at a desk.'

'I could only work for somebody I liked.'

'Most people feel like that.'

'Most people don't have the choice. They're glad to get any kind of work.'

'Do you go back for visits?'

'No. I write to one of my sisters, once in a while. Do you?'

'I've only been here a few months. But I write to them, all the time. They'd be worried if I missed a week. I expect your family believes in more independence.'

'We had a big fight,' Eino said. 'I haven't seen any of them for three years.' He put down his empty cup and breathed out.

He was about to say thanks for the coffee.

Axel asked, 'Do you think I could see your paintings sometime?'

*

When he looked around the walls at Eino's pictures, Axel knew for certain that he himself stood no chance of becoming a painter, even if he were to start all over again. Eino painted easily and quickly. The canvases hung around the room and leaning in rows against the walls, were clear, bright, attractive. Even if they weren't great, they were well presented. Axel liked them.

He also liked, and was extremely impressed by, the way Eino lived. They were the same age, yet Eino had dared to step straight into the bohemian life: he had a mistress named Marissa and a small child – a boy called Bruno – who was dark-eyed, like his mother.

Marissa approved of Axel immediately. His presence in their circle seemed to her an indication that Eino might soon work his way towards the respectability she longed for. She invited Axel to come see them whenever he liked.

He took to visiting them early in the evening, or – at the end of the week – in the late afternoon. If the weather was good, he'd stroll to a café with them and buy them all something to drink. If it was raining, they stayed at home; he might bring cakes with him, or flowers. One afternoon, at the beginning of their acquaintance, Axel came to call and found that Eino was out. He was embarrassed and said he wouldn't stay, but Marissa told him that he had to come in and sit down – she wanted to talk to him.

He sat on a chair while she brought out the bath for the child. She wouldn't let him help her with anything. 'You just sit there,' she ordered. 'You don't know how nice it is to have someone to talk to. Sometimes I'm so lonely, I start talking to myself. And I know where he is, too. He's with that woman. I suppose you know who I mean.'

'No,' Axel said. 'Who?'

'There's no need for you to try to protect him.'

'I don't know who you mean. You're the only woman Eino has introduced me to.'

'A rich woman who's got a studio full of other rich women. They're all trying to be painters and sculptors. I call it the Marie Antoinette club. She's in love with Eino.'

'But he loves you.'

'Then why doesn't he marry me?' she asked. The child shrieked as she began to undress it.

'Maybe he doesn't believe in the institution of marriage.'

'Men just say those things. It means it makes it easier to leave.'

'He wouldn't leave a woman with a child? Surely not.'

'And another one coming,' she muttered. 'I was a fool. I didn't want to lose him. I loved him too much.' She tugged at the child's arm and hissed, 'Be quiet,' into its screaming face. She didn't look like a woman who had ever loved anyone.

*

As he got to know Eino better, Axel met a good many people, most of them women. He began to assume things that Eino didn't tell him. He suspected, for example, that Eino was sleeping with the wife of the grocer down at the end of the street, and with a widow who occasionally hired him to do painting and repairs in her daughter's house; and with a few others. The woman whom Marissa thought of as the guilty one was – according to Eino – not on his list.

Axel met her one rainy day just before afternoon turned into evening. Rain poured down the high windows of her studio. She'd had the fires lit in the drawing-room and was about to pull the curtains. Everything in the room was plump and lustrous: the velvet cushions, the thick, plush sofa covers, brocade curtains: even the figured wallpaper. But the studio beyond was plain. The far wall was simple plaster, the door-frame in it unpainted and the floorboards bare. Three women were at work under the vaulted, glass-paned roof; they wore aprons like shopkeepers or butchers and had their hair pinned back severely. It seemed to Axel at first sight that they were like the three daughters of a fairytale: old, middle and young. The old one was an American spinster who painted badly but enthusiastically; the middle woman was good-looking – the young wife of an older man; a manufacturer of some kind, who was proud of her accomplishments. And the youngest was a black-haired German girl named Minna. She was very young: a large girl, not especially pretty, but she had something; as soon as you noticed that she was fairly plain, you decided she had a certain charm that made up for that. Her subject was sculpture. She was modelling a bust in clay when Axel was introduced to her. He nodded and smiled. At that moment he was more interested in the founder of the school and owner of the house, who showed them back to the warmer room and rang for tea.

'They stay on late, even when the weather's like this,' she said.

'Karen never has a free moment,' Eino explained.

'All my moments are free, my dear,' she told him. 'That's why you're never going to get anywhere with all that. Stop pushing and sit down.' She dropped into a chair and laughed. Axel and Eino took the chairs set in front of her, so she could see them both without turning her head. The positioning was a little like the seating in a small boat.

He began to forget about everything else as she talked. He thought he was falling in love with her: with the look of her clear skin and the pale colour of her hair; with her voice, her thoughts, the serenity of her manner and irony of her speech. He said so to Eino afterwards while they were walking through the rain. But Eino told him, 'No, it's just friendship. I thought the same thing myself at first, but you'll see: she isn't for love.'

'Of course she is. She's wonderful.'

'Oh, I agree. And she's beautiful too, but she's rather – not alluring, you know. She's like a nursemaid. One doesn't have romantic thoughts about her.'

'Speak for yourself. I think she's lovely.'

'Everything about her is so nice and tidy. All in its place, so controlled.'

'Yes. I admire that.'

'And – I'm not sure how much she likes men.'

'She likes you. I got the impression she liked me, too.'

'That wasn't what I meant. I think somehow she doesn't take certain things seriously. Anything much, really. Certainly not love.'

'You were flirting with her all the time.'

'I like her a lot. It aggravates me that she's never going to say yes.'

'So, she never has lovers? She's always been alone?'

'Well, that's the mystery. You think you've understood the way it is, and then suddenly there are these intriguing flashes of something else, and you wonder.'

'Tell me some more about her.'

Eino talked about Karen – what he knew about her family back in Sweden, and of her friends in Paris. The school, he said, had been going for six years and was a success, although it hadn't yet produced any outstanding work.

'And Karen herself?'

'She's a good painter. Nothing she ever does is bad or cheap or a poor imitation. But she doesn't have the eye. She doesn't see in a new way, or make a shape or a vision that seems to be a new form. She's a little better than I am, that's all.'

'But you're good.'

'I'm competent, yes. And that's good. But there are grad-ations, and you asked me. A really important school of art would be turning out students who broke the mould. Maybe not in six years, of course.'

'I don't understand,' Axel said, 'how you can talk about art like this, when you can paint the way you do.'

'That's why. I'm a practitioner. You're an appreciator.'

'Well, as far as that goes, some day if we get really drunk together, I'll show you my paintings.'

'You?'

'I think there are a few left that I haven't painted over.'

'What's wrong with now?' Eino said.

'There isn't enough time. We'd have to be drinking all day.'

'We'll make up for it in speed,' Eino told him.

They went out drinking for three hours. Axel still didn't want to show Eino the paintings. 'You'll think I'm such a fool,' he said. 'I wish now I'd never mentioned them. You'll see them, and you'll think: *how could this man be a friend of mine?*'

'Axel, if you don't show them to me tonight, I'll know you didn't trust me enough. And if you don't show them to me now, I'm going to be too drunk to see them. Come on.' Eino rose from his seat and plunged out into the night, dragging Axel after him. Axel tried to get his hand free in order to put up his umbrella, but Eino wouldn't listen to his complaints. They were both soaked to the skin.

Axel led the way upstairs, trudging ahead slowly. Eino prodded him from behind. 'Don't make so much noise,' Axel told him. 'You'll get me thrown out.'

'What for? You pay your rent, don't you? Besides, I can find you a better place than this.'

They reached the top. Axel struggled with the key, threw open the door and fumbled his way across the room. 'Heat and light,' he said. 'I want you to feel comfortable when you start to laugh.'

Eino said nothing. He stood near the door until Axel had everything prepared, and then looked at the paintings as they were thrust forward.

Axel did all the talking. He said, 'Oh God, they're so terrible, oh God. They're awful. They're just dreadful. You see?' He came to the end of the canvases and threw himself into a chair.

Eino walked silently around the room, looking at everything else, too. Finally he said, 'You shouldn't mind so much about it. What you can be good at doesn't necessarily have to be in one particular vein.'

'What could I do? I'm not good at anything.'

'You're a good friend.'

'How do you know?' Axel said thickly. 'You hardly know me.'

'I knew that the day we met. I always know who's going to be a friend. It's like knowing about women. Don't you?'

Axel belched and said that at the moment his luck with women was even more disastrous than his painting. 'I spend most of my evenings staring at them through a pair of opera glasses. I can tell you the name of every girl in the *corps de ballet* just from her legs. But that's the nearest I get. Anyway, even before I came to Paris, somehow I never seemed to end up with the ones I really wanted. Except once, that time – and then I threw it away.'

'That's all right,' Eino told him. 'I'll introduce you to some women.'

Axel stood up. He reeled against the chair, fell back and tried to rest his elbow against the book case. He missed the first time. 'That would be kind,' he said.

*

He used to visit Karen's studio on his way back from work. Sometimes they'd go out together and sometimes they'd arrange to meet Eino for a meal. They all knew, without saying anything about it, that Marissa wouldn't want to join their party. And Axel had stopped wanting to see her.

He found that he could talk to Karen about art more easily than to Eino. She liked wandering through the museums with him. One day he spoke of a Scandinavian Renaissance in the arts – painting, music, poetry: everything. And she said, 'I suppose you got all that from Eino.'

'No,' he told her sharply, 'I do have some ideas of my own.'

She laughed, and said, 'He's always talking about it, though. Isn't he?'

'He talks about all kinds of things.'

'But mostly about how the Scandinavian countries are going to be a single cultural nation and at the moment they're like Italy before the unification.'

'Oh, I wasn't thinking about all that political business.'

'When we first met, he couldn't praise city life enough – especially Paris. Paris and the arts of Europe. But recently he's begun to change. I think it has something to do with his need to get away from Marissa. Now he says that we've got to go back to nature and back to the origins of Viking society. To study the trees and streams and mountains. Doesn't he? He's always talking about natural shapes and fundamental design.'

'That's right. Why not? He's told me how to look for patterns everywhere. You wouldn't believe how many different shapes wind and water – '

'I detest nature,' she said.

'How do you mean?'

'Crude, uncomfortable, formless, without a comprehensible style. Most women hate nature. I like civilized life, modern ideas. Eino wants to go backwards. It's a kind of sentimentality. And the success of the venture would depend on a rebrutalizing of women – just as we've managed to bring things to the point where we're sometimes thought of as rational beings. What can one say to a man like that?'

'He reads a lot of Russian newspapers. They're always talking about – God knows what: German philosophy, that kind of thing.'

'I don't take that seriously. I think he's much more interested in those English notions – he wants to build a model farm and have a school for weaving and furniture-making, and do his own dyeing and make his own pots and vases and glassware. And silverware.'

'He does talk about building a house.'

'Precisely. My idea of a house is a little more like the governor's mansion than some pathetic old log cabin out in the pinewoods.'

'He says it's got something to do with national identity.'

'And what do you think?' she said suddenly. Her blue eyes looked back as if a trap had been sprung on him and she was watching from the outside. 'Do you think,' she asked, 'that it's natural for a woman to live alone, without a husband or children?'

'No,' he said. 'I don't.'

'Most people don't. But I love my life now. And I never used to be happy like this.' She turned her head away and walked on, smiling. Axel wanted to know why she hadn't been happy before, but it was as if he'd been told not to ask. If he tried to find out, he was sure, she'd smile again and steer the talk another way.

*

Occasionally when he'd call to see Karen, she'd be out and the students would brew him a cup of tea or coffee. His favourite pupil in the school became the young German girl, Minna. He liked her work, too; it was strong, simple and noble, the subjects usually full-length nudes, often of children. She was also good at sculpting animals in clay.

He saw her sitting alone one day at a café table. He thought she might be waiting for a man, but he wanted to say hello anyway, so he stopped. She told him she wasn't waiting for anyone; she often sat at that table by herself because she liked the building across the street and it pleased her to see how the light fell over it as evening approached.

'But it's freezing,' he said. 'Let's go someplace warmer. You could catch pneumonia sitting here.'

'Or something even more serious,' she said. 'Like what Karen's got.'

He thought at first that she was making some sort of joke. Karen always had a beautiful, healthy glow in her cheeks and a sparkle in her eyes. Sometimes she'd cough a little – that was just a kind of habit, like the repeated use of a gesture.

'She's consumptive,' Minna said.

'Impossible. She's the picture of health.'

'The picture, maybe. Not the reality. She's very ill. It's gone so far that she won't see the doctors any more. It's the reason why she left home. That's where she caught it.'

'I can't believe it,' he said.

She bowed her head sadly and looked back up. The building she liked had become part of the night while they'd been talking.

He took her to dinner. They discussed sculpture and Eino and her family back in Germany, who had all sworn they'd never speak to her again. Her mother had thrown a coffee-pot after her the day she'd left.

She spoke of the integrity of form and the meaning of line, shape and colour. 'It's all action,' she said.

A week later, he took her to bed. He told Eino, because Eino had introduced him to several women of easy ways and was constantly proposing to find him another. Now he didn't want any others. He didn't love Minna but he wanted to stay with her for a while. And he thought that she was in love with him; that made him happy.

'She's a nice girl,' Eino said.

'And a very fine sculptress.'

'Perhaps. And headstrong.'

'Not at all,' Axel said. 'She's sweet and compliant. A loving, docile character.'

'She walked right out on that family of hers, and they're a bunch of fire-eaters. That must have taken something. For a girl to leave home –'

'She had somewhere to go. She'd already written to Karen.'

'Even so. If you leave home for good, these havens and shelters are always temporary. Staying with friends and studying at schools won't make up for it. She isn't the kind that should be on her own.'

Axel suddenly had the feeling that Eino was trying to make him feel guilty. He didn't like it. He wasn't responsible for the girl. And it wasn't as if he'd been the first, although in fact that was something he hadn't considered until afterwards.

'I'd ask you back,' Eino told him, 'but Marissa isn't very well.'

'Because of the baby?'

'I suppose so. What's really doing it is that she whips herself into a frenzy of jealousy. Screaming and throwing things. I bang out of the house. Then I come back and she's screaming about where I've been, and then she cries for hours.'

'I'm sorry.'

'It's disgusting,' Eino said. 'I wish I were out of it. I'd walk out on her this minute if it weren't for Bruno. She's sent him to her aunt's.'

'It'll be better when the baby's born,' Axel said. 'Give her something to think about.'

'If it were anybody but Karen, it might make sense. I can't very well say she's the only one in town I haven't had.'

'Minna tells me Karen's sick,' Axel said. 'Is it true?'

'She's got that cough.'

'It isn't serious?'

'Of course not.'

Axel was relieved. He believed it because he had come to believe whatever Eino told him.

*

Just as the snows cleared and the rains started, Karen summoned them both to her tea table. The painting and sculpting ladies had gone. They were alone in the apartment except for the cook and maid in the back rooms beyond the curtain. Karen took out a bottle and glasses. She poured three drinks, lifted her glass and said, 'Minna's pregnant.'

Axel drank a large gulp. He thought that Minna ought to have come to him first.

Karen said, 'You've both been sleeping with her. Which one of you is going to marry her? She isn't a woman like Marissa, you know. That can't be allowed to happen.'

Axel looked at Eino, who remained head-down, staring at his drink.

'Another glass?' Karen asked.

Eino murmured, 'I can't marry her. Not while Marissa is this way.'

'Axel?' Karen said.

He took the second drink she was offering. He said that he'd have to talk to Minna herself before he could tell what he thought.

*

They were married in a rush. He wrote to his father and eventually received a letter back that expressed shock – which didn't worry him – and sadness, which upset him profoundly. The rest of the family wrote short, constrained letters. He felt that he'd been cut off from them forever. The cold rain beat on the window-panes outside as he stood staring down into the street or across the way at the roof-tops.

In the sixth month of her pregnancy, Marissa had a miscarriage. She nearly died. Eino stayed with her for a month afterwards, to see that she recovered her health and to try to make her tell him where Bruno was. Then he left her. By that time Karen had begun to cough up blood: the doctors said it wouldn't be long.

She received callers without rising to her feet. On some days she looked normal, on others all at once she was grey as a corpse and it was as if the colour had forsaken even her eyes. Axel came home one evening after seeing her and burst into tears. Minna put her hand on the back of his head. He was certain now, although she'd denied it, that the child she was carrying was Eino's and that Eino had been the one she'd loved all along; yet she was kind to Axel, as he was to her. He was fond of her. It wasn't what he wanted, but nothing ever was. Compared to the fact that Karen was dying, it didn't seem to matter, especially since he and Eino were such close friends.

Early in June Karen had a haemorrhage. She lived for four days after that. When Axel went to see her, she said, 'Look at me now, Axel dear. This is nature.' She smiled a terrible, delighted smile and whispered, 'I'm not supposed to laugh. It starts me coughing again.'

When her will was read, it turned out that she'd bequeathed a huge amount of money to found a combined school and artists' colony. It was all left in trust to Eino, who was to have sole power of decision over the disbursement.

'She must have loved you after all,' Axel said.

'Don't be stupid,' Eino told him. 'She knew I could spend it in a way that would do some good. I was always telling her what

I'd do if I had the chance. You'll help, won't you? You and Minna?'

'And Marissa?' Axel asked.

'Marissa sent me a letter as soon as she heard. Told me how glad she was that Karen had finally died; and said we could get married now, if I ever wanted to see my child again.'

'Do you think she's insane?'

'No, only insufferable. She was always a bitch. It's just that a long time ago she used to be good in bed, too.'

'She can't keep your child from you.'

Eino answered that she'd already succeeded for months, but that he'd hired lawyers. That was as good as setting fire to your money, but there was no other solution. He'd get the boy and then go back to Finland. And as soon as Minna had the baby and was ready to move house, she and Axel ought to join them.

Axel said he'd contribute in any way he could. But when he was alone, he thought carefully about the scheme. He didn't believe it would be a good idea to ally himself so closely to a business enterprise that would depend on the friendship of a man who had no experience in business. He decided that after the birth of the child, he'd take Minna back to visit his family, and ask them for help.

*

During the long, light northern summers Axel used to work on the accounts early in the morning. At night he'd write poetry, which was even worse than his paintings had been back in Paris twenty years before. When the days grew shorter and colder and darker, he worked at night. He kept a bottle near his right hand. He'd pour out the drink systematically, so that there was always something in the glass. He sipped slowly and got through a couple of bottles a day. The alcohol never impaired his ability to count, though it had ruined his teeth, his circulation and his sleep. Nor had it inhibited the nimbleness of his mathematical juggling, the subtlety of his sense of proportion. When he falsified the figures in the books, it was all done in perfect ratio. That was why he was never going to get caught.

While he drank and wrote down the numbers, he'd cough a little, as he always did in the months of snow, but he hardly noticed that any more. It seemed to be a part of the winter, or like a nervous tic that he'd lived with for half his life.

At one time he'd worked over the books with his cat, Bonaparte, sitting on his lap. Bonaparte was a dark, skinny, animal, short-haired and soft. When Axel sat by the fire to read or just to daydream, Bonaparte would arrange himself with his arms around Axel's neck or with his nose pushed up into Axel's armpit. And Axel could think better: the cat's warmth and its purring made him feel loved. But then, one summer, Bonaparte contracted the mange. Axel noticed that all at once his own hair was starting to fall out. And the children in the artists' colony caught ringworm.

The mothers in the community blamed the cat. That was nonsense, of course. It was much more likely that one of their odious brats had infected Bonaparte. After all, cats were very clean animals. Axel had probably said as much when he was drunk, although he didn't remember. There had been some kind of quarrel as the Philistines turned against him – that he did remember: using the name Philistine. And it was true; the wives and children and other relatives had nothing to do with art. They were living in the colony the way camp followers lived with an army – irrelevant to the war and often getting in the way.

A few days after the quarrel, he'd found Bonaparte outside on the doorstep, dead; he'd been torn to pieces. Maybe he'd been attacked by a wild animal, but it didn't seem possible that he'd be able to reach home with such injuries. Axel thought it more likely that one of the people he'd insulted had killed the cat out of spite and put him there, where Axel would find him in the morning.

And since then, he'd felt less guilty about the embezzlement. He should have had half the money, anyway. Karen had left it all to Eino because she'd thought that whatever kind of artistic movement they created out in the forests should be under the control of one person. She knew that Eino wouldn't be able to agree with anyone who had an opinion different from his own, whereas Axel could accommodate himself to other people's interests. Of course, she couldn't have known what was to happen to them.

From time to time Axel thought about her: her voice, her laughter, the way she'd looked in her green dress with the black velvet facings. He also thought that if he could dream up some way of doing it, he'd like to get back at Eino for having everything, while he had nothing. He'd had nothing since Paris and the scandal that had almost precisely coincided with his family's financial collapse – the landslide of bad luck that had swept them into bankruptcy, illness, emigration and death.

*

Eino's wife, Maria, worked on a hooked rug while she talked to him. She said, 'He's always drunk. All the time, awake or asleep.'

Eino made a small sound that didn't mean yes or no, but simply that he was listening. He moved his fingers along the side of a glass one of his students had made; the balance, the shape, everything was right. The young man had even invented his own design – a swirl of blue lay at the heart of the inner cup and appeared to swim in its white casing as the glass was turned.

'Isn't he ever going to leave?' she said. 'I don't know why you put up with the man.'

'Because we were young in Paris together,' Eino answered, without taking his eyes off the glass. 'He knew me when I was becoming what I am. He didn't become anything. He remained unfinished. Unexpressed.' And when Karen's will was read out, Axel had been put in the position of a dependant.

'You aren't the one that has to feed him and wait on him,' she complained, hitching the rug towards her.

'Is it such a hardship?'

'You aren't the one,' she repeated.

'Don't be ungenerous.' She wasn't normally so mean-minded against people. In her housekeeping she was thrifty – a good quality for a wife to have – but in her dealings with people she usually gave them some margin before deciding against them.

'And,' she added, 'I'm the one he tries to pester with his attentions.'

Eino laughed. He couldn't imagine the moth-eaten, shambling Axel trying to win any favours from Maria, who had grown heroically buxom after the birth of her last child.

'And your daughter,' she said. He didn't laugh at that. He turned in his chair to look at her, but she was staring down at her work. In a few minutes, she'd start up again. These conversations of hers could last for days. It took her a long time to drag all the evidence back and forth, to get to the stage where she could demand that he take action about something or other. Naturally he knew what she wanted this time. She wanted Axel to go.

He said, 'He's useful to the community. I was never any good at book-keeping and that kind of thing.'

'And how good is he?'

'He was trained for it.'

'I've sometimes thought he doctors the books.'

'What does that mean?'

'Fiddling around with the figures, skimming some money off the top.'

'It always balances out all right.'

'Of course,' she said. 'That's how they do it.'

Eino ran his eye over the row of glass objects on the shelf above his desk, at the chair to his right, the shawl hanging over the back of it, and the rug down on the floor. Everything he looked at had been made by craftsmen in the community – each article had its own unity and integrity. When one of his students finished a good piece of work, it was like a woman giving birth to a child she'd been forming inside her for months. Axel would never be able to know that kind of accomplishment. And he had no family, either.

'You have to make allowances for him,' Eino said. 'He's on his own and he's getting older.'

'That just makes him harder to get along with.'

'Please, Maria.'

'It's true. He doesn't contribute. We could teach one of the young ones to handle the money.'

'He's my friend,' Eino told her. 'I don't want to hear this.' He turned back to the desk and picked up his magnifying glass. It probably wasn't really true that he and Axel were still friends, but they had been once. He thought: *Being a friend has destroyed Axel so that he hasn't lived his life. He's lived a small part of mine.*

*

They walked out into the woods by the path they'd taken long ago when they first visited the family on the other side of the lake. At that time the farmer, from whom Eino had bought the land, lived modestly on his homestead with his wife and three daughters and two sons. One of the daughters was pretty; she'd come in to pour water in the bath-house. She'd had a shy smile and wore her hair in a long braid that hung down her back.

'I want to talk to you about something,' Eino said.

There had been a fresh snowfall the night before. Everything was coated, white, still. The trees were like ranks of statuary around them. It was beautiful, but Axel's pleasure in the way it looked was accompanied by a sense of how dangerous it was. For several years he'd believed that when he died it would be the cold that would kill him.

'It's about the girls,' Eino went on. 'My own girls too, so it seems. They're too young for you, Axel. I don't blame you for wanting affection, but why don't you find yourself someone nearer your own age? A nice widow, something like that.'

'I'm sick of leftovers,' Axel said. His voice was harsh and the tone sour.

'I know it can't be easy out here, but a few weeks back in town, say, and you could meet somebody.'

'Who would look at a man like me? You think I don't know what I've become?'

'A shave, some new clothes. Plenty of women would look at you.'

'All the desperate ones. Some miserable old maid that looks like an elk in a corset.'

'You'd have to sober up. It isn't too late for you to start off fresh, get married, have a family.'

Axel smacked aside a branch full of snow. The bough sprang up, releasing a cloud of powdery crystals. He said, 'I had a family once.'

'That's over.'

'Nothing's over till you die. I'm beginning to understand that. I've been having some dreams lately – you know, there was a long time when I didn't dream at all.'

'Look at that,' Eino said. He pointed to a place among the trees and rocks where one of the streams had melted and frozen again. The ice poured over itself in layers, its clear spaces mapped by ribs of depth and brightness: laced with white lanes, dark fissures, mines of shattered brilliance. 'I'd like to make a vase like that. Just like that. And put spring flowers in it.'

Axel looked. The place didn't seem very wonderful; just cold as hell, like everything else around him.

*

He used to think, back in Paris, how good it would be to breathe the fresh, cold air of his home. He'd stand by the windows and look out into the street, where the rain flooded down on the umbrellas of the crowds. Not even the rain could wash away the soot and grime. The air was no good. The rain itself came down dirty.

He thought that if they could get Karen to a better climate, she'd be all right. He tried to persuade her to go. She shook her head. Sometimes she was too tired to speak. Sometimes she'd actually refuse to see anybody. The school disbanded. Her servants were red-eyed when they opened the door to him. Eino said he'd tried to talk her into moving south and she'd told him that the doctors had already decided: it was too late for cures.

He met a student of hers in the museum one day: the old American woman, who started to sob, saying that it was too dreadful – a young life like that, and such a lovely girl; and when you thought of the real swine who were going to keep on eating and drinking for another forty years it almost made you despair. Yes, he agreed with her: there was no justice, no sense in it. He took her arm and walked through the galleries with her. She told him about how she'd fallen in love with paintings when she was a child; if she hadn't longed to paint, she'd have wanted to be an eye doctor, because vision – everything about its workings, even the fact that it was there at all – had always struck her as miraculous. 'And now that I'm old,' she ended, 'I'm losing it, of course.'

When he got back to the apartment, he told Minna about the meeting. She didn't appear very interested. She was reading a book on classical Greek sculpture. She kept turning over the pages of photographic plates. She said that everyone would miss Karen, naturally. He took up his post at the window again.

Karen died in the early summer. At the end she kept saying, 'I can't breathe.' Axel started to cough on the way to the funeral. As he left the cemetery grounds, he felt the cough coming on again. He disengaged himself from Minna, who was leaning on his right arm. 'Handkerchief,' he explained. He coughed, blew his nose and then raised his head and saw a woman turn the corner at the end of the street; she walked hurriedly and looked back. It was Marissa.

He told Eino. Eino said, 'She never gives up.' He'd left her, but she had the child, who was still down in the country with one of her aunts, or an aunt's family. Several lawyers had told him he didn't stand a chance of getting the boy back through the courts. 'If I knew where she was keeping him, I'd just grab him.'

'She could go to the police for that.'

'I'd take him home. Right up north. He'd be fine there, away from everything. It was the miscarriage that unhinged her.'

'She was always that way,' Axel said, 'only she used to love you.'

'I should have married Karen.'

'You should have married Minna. Shouldn't you?'

'Don't you start. That's why I couldn't stand it any more. Marissa kept saying that Karen had stolen her baby before it was born, and given it to Minna instead.'

*

When people went crazy, Axel thought, what you saw was usually simply the last stage of it, where everything broke.

He threw back a quick swallow of his drink and filled the glass again, coughing as he'd been doing for nearly twenty years. At first he'd believed he was imitating Karen. He'd noticed before how for a time surviving friends and relatives often mimicked the gestures or habits of speech they associated with someone dead. You could understand that – since the missing person was on their minds – their unspoken thoughts might announce themselves as movement. Minna used to say that people thought with their whole bodies: if you looked carefully, you could see it was true. But it might be more than that. It might be that the mimicry was intended somehow to keep the dead alive; that it was another reproductive process: like art, like memory, like the imagination.

He hadn't forgotten Karen. While he drank, it was as if he could remember talking to her just a few days before, being in France: in Paris, in her drawing room with her. 'And what did you think of that hideous exhibition?' she'd say; or, 'Tell me about the bank, Axel. Who got what wrong today?'

His memory of her was much clearer than his recollection of Minna. He recalled very little of the day when he came home and found the police and the stretchers, and the caretaker in hysterics. It was as though most of that day had been burned from his life, the heat from it blurring and melting the time before and after. He just remembered that it seemed to be raining forever as the time drew near for Minna to give birth.

He knew, of course. But all the pictures that should have gone with the information had been erased. He must have had to look at Minna afterwards, for instance, but he had no memory of it. He knew that Marissa, accompanied by Bruno, had climbed the stairs to the apartment. The caretaker had let them in. After that, most of the action could be pieced together only by what the caretaker was supposed to have heard. The police eventually came to the conclusion that Marissa, under the impression that Minna was carrying her lover's child, had entered the apartment, pulled out a pistol, shot the little boy, shot Minna, and then killed herself.

It took them a long while to figure all that out. In the beginning, they were only interested in Axel. They asked him suspiciously, accusingly: *Who is this woman named Marissa? Do you know her? If you don't know her, why did she kill your wife? Who is the child? Is the boy yours? How long have you known the woman? Did you love your wife? Did you quarrel with your wife? Was your wife a woman of easy morals, as some of these artistic people are? Did she leave a will?*

The questions were endless, coming down like the rain. He was ready to say anything to make them stop. He was prepared for them to take him out and put his head on the block. But Eino came and told them everything the right way around.

*

As he was drinking late at night he sometimes thought that it was curious: the catastrophe had made Eino stronger. It had even seemed to make him more intelligent; he'd come into focus after the killings. His speech, too, had changed. His talk was now incisive. When he spoke of the community's work, he cared about his subject and could make other people care, whereas before, he'd been a rough speaker, so bigoted that he could sound wholly ignorant. And, in contrast, the smooth speech of Axel's early years had grown rambling, disjointed, slurred.

He drank another glass. He finished the bottle. That night he had a dream.

He dreamt that he was standing at the entrance of a room that had a large table in it. Several people were seated around the table. There was talk and laughter, and an agreeable atmosphere of festivity. The host, at the end of the table, appeared delighted to see Axel and beckoned him in, greeting him warmly, and made him sit down next to him, where he had saved a chair. Axel felt extremely happy. His host then took up a decanter and poured out wine into a glass, which he handed to Axel. But Axel saw that the decanter had been emptied; he was the only one at the table who had any wine. He thought it would be rude to let the others go without anything. So he handed the glass back, in order that some of the wine could be given to the rest of the company. His host smiled, accepted the glass again, and, instead of doing what Axel had expected, turned to the sideboard nearby and set the glass there, where it remained throughout the course of the dinner.

There wasn't much more to the dream than that, but Axel was disturbed by it. He'd begun to feel out of place even when he was still in the dream. He'd obviously done something wrong while trying to be polite. The host hadn't exactly disapproved, but neither had he understood the reasoning behind the action of his guest.

In the morning Axel couldn't get up. One of the apprentices was sent over with some soup, but no one began to worry until the evening, when the doctor came – a young man whom Axel didn't trust or like.

'I'm all right,' Axel told him. 'No ringworm here.'

'You've got a fever.'

'It's the winter. I always do.'

'Well, you shouldn't. Not like this.'

Axel opened his mouth to argue, and an extraordinary thing happened: he leaned forward, gave a little cough, and was suddenly covered in blood. The doctor said, 'God in heaven.' Axel couldn't say anything; he was astounded at how easily it had happened, and almost without pain.

Eino came to see him. 'You'll get well,' he assured Axel. 'We'll feed you up.'

Axel stared morosely into Eino's face. He could get well, perhaps, but it was going to be a struggle if he had to put up with the horrible, healthy food they produced in the community – rough black bread and turnips, bean stew, cabbage forever. 'A little beefsteak and champagne,' he suggested, 'might do me some good. It wouldn't hurt the rest of you, either. No wonder you're such a dreary bunch.'

'Calm down, Axel. We'll get you better. I promise.'

'Maybe. Yes, maybe. But you should have stayed in the cities, you know. Karen was right about that.'

'We've talked that to death.'

Axel laughed. He asked, 'Where are you going to find spring flowers at this time of year?'

'What are you talking about?'

'Ice. I could go out into the snow right now and not feel it. I'm as hot as if I'd just come out of the sauna. We could go for a walk.'

'Tomorrow, maybe.'

'I don't know why you think I'd be interested in your wife. I wouldn't want her even for a holiday weekend. Hunched over her nasty handwoven things, nagging – '

'That's enough, Axel.'

'Anyway, I've got a wife of my own. Wonderful girl, full of character. Beautiful black hair. Fine artist. She was so good to me. I know she never loved me, but she was really nice to me. You can't imagine.'

Eino pushed his chair back and rushed out of the cabin. He returned in the morning to see if Axel was better, but the fever continued.

Axel lay in his bed and thought. He sweated and drowsed and wondered how he could pay Eino back for not helping him. Eino had everything, and now he thought he was such a great hero, too. He was busy changing the world. Finnish art and culture wasn't enough for him – on top of all that, he wanted to change Finnish politics. *Finland for the Finns*, he'd say: *Our art must be our own, from our own forms – rivers, stones, trees – and our ideas should be our own as well, not Swedish or Russian or German.*

It didn't make sense to bury yourself in the country if you wanted to do anything higher than farming. Art flourished among the bright lights. Down in the country all you could raise was beets and manure. *Man is a city-dwelling animal*: Axel remembered that from school. 'City-dwelling' was usually translated as 'political'. And Eino was just as wrong about that; to go forward, they needed to copy and import more ideas – to become international. A lot of small countries had become great because they'd gone out and brought the rest of the world back to their people, not closed the doors against outside influence.

Eino was wrong. On the other hand, Eino had succeeded. He hadn't lost heart because the French were always going to be better painters. He'd just gone ahead and done the work he'd planned for himself. And it was good, you had to give him credit for that; and not like anybody else's, either. Nevertheless, it wasn't art. It was tables and chairs. And furthermore – why was it that Eino, always so desirable to women, invariably settled down with the ugly ones? He'd never built that big house he'd wanted, either.

Axel dozed and woke again. The fire was high: someone must have come in and built it up while he'd slept, and gone away again. There was a soup tureen on the table beside him, a bowl of fruit, and buttered bread on a plate. He wasn't hungry. He turned away from them.

He remembered his family, the houses where he used to live; he thought about his parents: as they were when he left home to go to Paris, and before that, in his childhood. They'd given him plenty of good advice and help. Had he wanted to end like this?

Why had he been so obsessed by the idea of becoming an artist? If he'd decided just to have a good time instead, he could have been happy. Maybe there was something in him, like a weight, that would always drag him down. He knew that – probably – if he had kept his mouth shut all those years ago, he could have held on to the girl in St Petersburg, made several rich friends, gone to many splendid dinners and balls and other

celebrations: become known and liked by a crowd of interesting
people, and – possibly – have won her in the end, although that
wasn't likely: there had been other, more sophisticated young
men around, and also less sophisticated, if she'd had a mind to
try that too. Of course, she might have forced him into the stand
he'd taken. She might have wanted an excuse to break with him.
The attitude of the maid had suggested that. Not that any of it
mattered. In any case, he had lost. But most of the loss was his
fault. He should have caught hold of whatever he could get, and
enjoyed it.

He remembered his dream about the host who had offered
him the glass of wine. And suddenly he realized the meaning of
it: the host was God and He had given Axel the full glass he was
meant to drink. It couldn't be distributed among any of the other
guests because it was intended for him alone. It had been the life
he was supposed to live. And when he had refused it, it had to
go unused by anyone.

He wanted to cry out with anger and grief. He'd missed the
whole of his life. And he knew that – as he had once hoped – his
life had indeed been picked out, from the beginning, to be the
life of an artist, which wasn't like the life of other men. An
artist's life was his work. He thought: *How disappointed God must
be in me. How disappointed I am in myself.* He hadn't believed in
God for years.

He knew what he should do: he should get out and go to the
south – the real south, where he'd be able to recover his health.
But he couldn't now. He'd left it too late.

*

After two days, he thought he was better. He wanted to get up.
Eino came to visit him and sat by the bed; he told Axel the doctor
had said he was to stay indoors, although if he wanted to move
to the writing-table or the sofa, that would be all right. Axel got
up out of bed and fainted.

When he came to again, he was sure he was near death.
'You'll get well,' Eino told him.

'Of course I won't. I'm going to die. You're the one who's going to live. And you deserve to, because you didn't refuse the glass. I should have known how important it was.'

Eino looked around him. He shot a glance towards the foot of the bed, at the side, where Axel used to stash his empty bottles. 'What glass?' he said.

Axel pretended to sleep. A picture came to him, like a dream, of Maria sitting by the fire and working on a piece of material. He thought it was sure to be one of her hooked rugs, but when he looked more closely he saw with horror that it was a long, grey chain of little people that she was knitting. She was producing the future. Then he was staring at the wall and realizing that he'd fallen asleep after all.

He'd been right in the first place to distrust the idea of living in one of these artists' colonies. He ought to be near the bustle and variety of a modern city, not buried in some fantasy of Eden, where the food had no real taste and the people were all the same. The women, the girls, were like the lumpy food: standing there with their mouths open while you tried out a little persiflage – nothing too complicated, no elaborate scrollwork or classical vocabulary – and then giggling or laughing loudly. Their laughter was like the quacking of ducks, the braying of donkeys. It took an effort to believe that they were human. He used to be accustomed to good society – not at the top, but men and women who could hold a conversation. Even Eino wasn't up to that. He'd thought Eino was some sort of rough-hewn genius, but actually he was only an obstinate craftsman with a love of the peasant traditions.

Suddenly it infuriated him that not only was he going to miss being an artist and living an interesting life, but that he'd tied himself to someone else who was, in his own way, second-best. It was like being a wife who finds out twenty years too late that she's chosen the wrong man.

'He's starting to go a little crazy,' Eino said.

'He was always like that,' Maria told him. 'Even before he started to drink so much.'

'This is different. I suppose it's the illness.'

'What does the doctor say?'

'As much as he knows, and that isn't much.'

'I think,' Maria said, 'there are some artists who go off their heads. And there are other people who go crazy because they aren't artists. That's Axel. He doesn't have any talents, not for anything.'

'He's got a talent for friendship.'

'Oh?' she said. 'Are you sure?'

'Let's leave all this,' Eino said, 'till we know when he's going to get better.' He went to visit Axel again. He was astonished by the change in him.

Axel was sitting up in the chair. He was fully clothed and wearing his heavy outdoor boots. His coat, scarf and hat were on the table next to him. His face looked deathly. He said, 'I was waiting for you, Eino. I wanted to take one last walk with you.'

'I don't think you should, Axel.'

'I need to. If I can't get all the way back, you can bring me home. Or you can leave me.'

'I don't think the doctor would like it.'

'You know that doctor – that doctor only likes healthy people. He can't do anything for me. You're the one who can help. You can take me for a walk.' He stood up and reached out quickly to touch the table.

Eino thought they probably wouldn't make it past the two neighbouring cabins. He said all right.

They started off down the path that led into the woods. The sun was out. There was no wind, but it was a day of intense, dry cold. Axel started to talk.

'I remember going through the museums in Paris with you,' he said. 'I was fascinated by the things you told me; your whole life. One day you said you'd been living on pumpernickel sandwiches recently and that meant two slices of bread with a piece of pumpernickel between them. I was so shocked by everything and so pleased. You took me to meet the Italian who used to be a glass-blower and you ran your fingers down the outside of a vase and said you could tell the lead content that way. I couldn't believe it. Then you laughed and said it was like everything else, you had to have a feeling for it. You said that the forests of Finland were better than the finest museums and I believed you. I came here. I remember that girl, the farmer's daughter; when she bent down to pour out the water; her shoulders and back. I thought maybe humanity was still possible for me. But you told me you'd always been interested in glass more than anything else, because it was the medium closest to ice. Eino, the first winter we were here, I had my warning. I was walking along this very trail, right about here – and something fell from above, just in front of me: plop! and there it was – a bird. It had died in the air. It must have been lost too, at that time of the year. I'd heard such a thing was possible, but to have it happen to me, after everything else – no. This beauty and nobility of nature you'd been telling me about; I thought it was all lies. It seemed to me that nature was pitiless: it was engaged in a constant effort to annihilate what was already there, in order to produce new forms. Or to come up with one more form just like the last one. It was only interested in moving onward. I began to understand the character of Judas. I knew that he must have been a man who watched his friend with sympathy until the moment when he realized that the friend was wrong and stupid, and that none of his ideas would work, and shouldn't be allowed to, anyway.'

'Stop talking, Axel,' Eino said.

'How dark it is in the winter, all the time. The snow. Of course the snow has its own brightness, but the light goes out of the sky. It isn't fair. The cold goes on too long. It makes me feel horrible sometimes.'

'You'll feel better in the spring.'

'How am I going to feel better? I've got what Karen had.'

'The doctors are learning new things every minute. Some day people won't have these diseases.'

'But what makes anyone catch diseases? Some do and some don't. That's heredity. Or is it? Nobody understands that, either. What do we know at all? What have we ever learned?'

'Well,' Eino suggested, 'there's photography. That's quite an extraordinary thing, isn't it? Much more complicated than most machines.'

'Yes,' Axel said, calmed. 'Yes, that's right. That was a great discovery.'

'And there are the arts.'

'Oh, that was the one thing I could always understand. I just couldn't do it, that's all. And I don't know any more why people try to do anything in life. None of it has any meaning without beauty, and beauty goes – it just evaporates. Look, like snow. Like youth, Eino. Like all of us, everything. What was it for?'

'For the ones who come after us.'

'The hell with them. It's going to be the same for them as it's been for us.'

'No, it's going to be better. We'll leave them that inheritance.'

'That's idiotic. One good war can wipe out what ten generations create. In times of need, everything goes by the board. If life gets hard enough, people eat anything. They'd eat the paint off the Sistine Chapel. They'd eat the face off the Botticelli Venus.'

'Stop talking so much,' Eino said. 'You're tiring yourself out. I think we should go back.'

Axel stopped. They had come almost to the end of a plantation where the regularly spaced trees were so encrusted and massy with snow that they no longer resembled living, growing things; they looked like structures built for some purpose, as if to guard a fortress or line the approach to a palace that wasn't there. Now that the day was giving out, a bluish light seemed to come from all the weight of ice on them.

Axel took a few more steps forward. Beyond the trees lay a long, open stretch of land that was absolutely even and blank. 'You want me to leave,' he said. 'All right. I'm leaving.'

'It's too cold to stay out here, Axel. Come on.'

'Look, Eino.'

'If you don't come now, I'm going to knock you out and carry you back.'

'Look. Don't you see?' Axel stumbled forward. A gigantic, bursting whiteness flowered everywhere around him, over the entire country, over the world: a white like the blossoming of trees in the spring. Everything else gave way to it, even the thought of colour. He would have laughed, if it hadn't been so cold. It was cold enough to snatch the breath from your body and keep it.

'You were always pointing things out to me,' he said, 'and I never saw: forms, shapes, patterns. I thought I knew what you were talking about. But now I'm seeing them, Eino. Look, there in the snow – it's the wing of a dove. Perfect. And over there another one, like a fan of feathers, and next to it all the white flowers. And this house around us: the house – don't you see?'

Eino followed, keeping his hands ready in case Axel started to fall. They walked far out into the open: into an immense, white-filled space that was flat and silent. 'No,' he said, 'I can't see anything.'

'But it's everywhere. I'm seeing them, Eino. I'm seeing everything. God, what a feeling. Like a sword going into me. All this beauty.'

'Axel, we've got to get you back to the house.'

Axel stood away and faced Eino. He coughed a little.

'We can talk about this later,' Eino said.

'Wonderful forms,' Axel whispered. 'Beautiful shapes.' He began to wave his arms, lost his balance and toppled straight backward on to the ground, where he lay motionless, arms and legs outspread. His eyes, as still as ice, looked towards the sky.

In the Act

As long as Helen was attending her adult education classes twice a week, everything worked out fine: Edgar could have a completely quiet house for his work, or his thinking, or whatever it was. But when the lease on the school's building ran out, all the courses would end – the flower arranging, the intermediate French and beginning Italian, the judo, oil painting and transcendental meditation.

She told Edgar well in advance. He nodded. She repeated the information, just in case. He said, 'Mm.' Over the next two weeks she mentioned the school closure at least three times. And, after she and her classmates had had their farewell party, she told him all about that, adding, 'So, I'll be at home next week. And the week after that. And so on.'

'Home?' Edgar said. 'What about your adult education things?'

She went over the whole history one more time. At last he was listening. He looked straight at her and said, 'Oh. That means you'll have to find something else to occupy yourself with on those afternoons.'

'I suppose so. I might stay home and paint here.'

'I'll be busy up in the lab.'

'I could make a kind of studio down in the cellar.'

'I'll be working. I need absolute peace and quiet.'

'Well, painting isn't very loud.'

'Helen,' he said, 'I'd like to have the house to myself.'

She never got angry with him any more; that is, she'd discovered that it did no good: he'd just look at her coldly as if she were exhibiting distressing habits usually encountered only among the lower species. Raising her voice – when she'd been driven to it – produced the same reaction from him. She'd learned to be argumentative in a fudgy, forgiving drone she'd found effective with the children: enough of that sound and the boredom level rose to a point where people would agree to anything. Edgar had a matching special tone for private quarrels: knowing, didactic, often sarcastic or hectoring. Whenever he used it outside the house, it made him disliked. It was a good voice for winning arguments by making other people hysterical. His hearing seemed to block off when it started.

She said, 'If you'd like the house to yourself, you can have it. Maybe you wouldn't mind fixing some supper for us while you're here. That way, I'd have something to look forward to, soon as I get in from walking around the block five thousand times.'

'There's no need for that.'

'OK, you can take me out. Twice a week. That'll be nice. We could see a lot of new movies in just a month.'

'You're being unreasonable.'

'Of course I am. I'm a woman,' she said. 'You've already explained that to me.'

'Let's not get into that.'

'Why not? If I'm not even allowed to paint downstairs somewhere for two afternoons a week? I never come up to the attic, do I?'

'You're always tapping on the door, asking me if I want a cup of coffee.'

'Only that once.'

'It was a crucial moment.'

'Well, now you've got your thermos bottle and everything, you're all set up there.'

'You came up other times.'

'That big noise – explosion, whatever it was: of course I did. I was worried. You could burn the house down.'

'I think this is time number fourteen for telling you that the experiments are not dangerous.'

'Fourteen? I'm sure that must be right. You keep track of things like that so well. Each time I conceived, it was a positive miracle of timing. I can remember you crossing off the days on the calendar.'

'You're trying to sidetrack me.'

'I'm trying to get you to allow me to stay in my own house.'

'I really do need complete freedom to work. It simply isn't the same when somebody else is in the house. Even if you didn't try to interrupt me again.'

'The only other time I knocked on the door was when there was all the screaming.'

'I told you,' Edgar said. 'I got the volume too high.'

'It sounded like real people.'

'It was a tape.'

'For heaven's sake, Edgar – where can I go?'

'See some friends? Look around a museum or two. Find another one of those adult education places.'

All at once she felt hurt. She didn't want to argue any more, even if there was a hope of winning. She was ready to walk out and tramp up and down the streets like a child running away. She said, 'I'll try,' and went into the living-room. She walked around the corner, into the alcove where the desk was. She sat down in the plump, floral-patterned chair, put her knees up and curled into a ball. She heard his feet going up the stairs, then up the next flight to the attic. He wouldn't be wondering whether he'd made her miserable. He'd be getting out the keys to unlock the attic door, which he kept locked all the time, and if he was inside, bolted too. He'd be sighing with pleasure at the prospect of getting back to his experiment. Of course he was right: she'd have to find something to do with her time. But just for a few minutes, she'd stay in the flowered chair, with her arm over her eyes.

*

The next morning, she was angry. He read through his news-paper conscientiously, withdrawing his attention from it for only a few seconds to tell her that she hadn't cut all the segments entirely free in his grapefruit – he'd hit exactly four that were still attached. She knew, he said, how that kind of thing annoyed him.

She read her letters. Her two sons were at boarding school. Edgar approved. She herself would never have suggested sending, or allowing, the boys to go away: in fact, the suggestion had come from them. They had suddenly clamoured for the expensive snobberies of the East Coast; they needed, they wanted, they couldn't live without education at the last of the all-male establishments. Helen's attendance at adult education classes dated from the time of their emigration.

Both of the boys had written to her. Usually she was delighted by whatever they had to say. This morning their news seemed to be nothing but boastful accounts of how they had won some sports event or beaten another boy at something, shown him who was who: and so forth. She was probably lucky they were far away. That would have been two more grapefruits she wouldn't be able to get right.

When she passed the letters over to Edgar, he was soberly pleased with the boys' victories. He wasn't too bad as a father. He wasn't actually too bad anyway, except that sometimes he irritated her to distraction. She still couldn't believe he was asking her to get out of the house every Tuesday and Thursday, so he'd have the whole place to himself.

'What's wrong with the coffee pot?' he added.

She snapped back out of her thoughts. 'I was wondering about adult education classes,' she told him.

'Fine. More of that flower arranging, or maybe a new language.'

'Yes, maybe. Who would I talk to in a new language?'

'Well, the teacher. Anybody else who speaks it.' He went back to the paper. Soon afterwards he took his last sip of coffee, looked around for his briefcase, and left the house for the pathology laboratories where he had his job. They did a lot of work for the police as well as for hospitals and private clinics. His speciality was haemoglobin.

With the dusting and vacuuming she worked off some of her vexation. Then she sat down with a cup of coffee. She phoned about the plumber's bill, the bracelet link that was supposed to be done but still wasn't, the garage. Nothing was ready. She was about to call up her friend, Gina, to complain about life in general, when she had a better idea: she'd go up to the attic.

She had a key. Long before the day when there was the explosion or the one when she'd heard the screams, she had wanted to see inside his laboratory. The loud noise had at first scared her off from the idea of trespassing, and then reinforced her initial desire: to go in and take a look around – make sure everything was all right up there. The screams too, at first frightening, had made her eager to see, to know; for a few moments she had been convinced that there were real people up there. Not that Edgar would be carrying out any experiment that would cause pain to someone, but – she didn't really know what she thought about it all.

The way he locked the door before he came downstairs; the way he locked up as soon as he entered the lab and shut the door behind him, shooting the bolt across: it made her nervous. If there was nothing inside that could harm her, it was an insult to keep her out. On the other hand, if there was something dangerous up there, did she dare go in and find out about it?

The key was one of the extras from the Mexican bowl that had been shoved over to the end of a workbench in the cellar. The bowl was filled with old keys. Helen had looked through the whole collection when they had moved in; she'd assumed that they came from other houses or even from workplaces long vanished. There were about fifty keys, some large, long and rusted, like the sort of thing that might be needed for a garden gate or a toolshed. After the screams, when her frustration and curiosity about the lab had reached a sudden peak, she'd remembered the bowl of keys. Some could be discounted straight away, but about a dozen were possible.

The one that fitted was an ordinary brass key. She'd unlocked the door, pushed it open slowly, peeked in and locked up again. She hadn't stepped over the threshold. Now, standing in the middle of her living-room rug, she wondered why she hadn't gone in and had a thorough look at everything. She seemed to recall that what was in the room had been fairly uninteresting: tables, benches, racks of test tubes, a microscope, a couple of bunsen burners, two sinks, a bookcase against the wall. Never mind: this time she'd go through the place carefully.

She got the key and started up the stairs, moving fast. She had the door open before there was time to think about it.

The room looked slightly different from when she'd last seen it, and more crowded. There were more bottles, jars and test tubes. Standing racks had been added at the far end, where the empty steamer trunks used to be. She also remembered a rather nice sofa; more like a *chaise longue*. Edgar had occasionally stayed up in the lab overnight, working while she'd watched the late movie downstairs, or read a detective story. She'd always thought the sofa was too good to leave up in the attic, but Edgar had insisted that he needed it. Now she couldn't see it. But, as she moved forward, she noticed with surprise that a bathtub had been added to the collection of sinks and troughs; it was an old, high-standing type. She couldn't imagine how Edgar had managed to get it in there. He'd have had to hire people. *Out of the van and to the front door*, she was thinking; *up the stairs*. She began to worry about the weight. Even though the house was well-built and strong, and most of the heavy equipment stood around the sides, it wasn't a good idea to fill up a place with too many heavy objects. Edgar had undoubtedly gone into the question of beam-stress and calculated the risks; he'd have found out all about the subject. Of course, every once in a while, he was wrong.

She looked into the first alcove: empty. She turned into the second, bigger one. There was the sofa. And there was a bundle of something thrown on top of it, wrapped in a sheet. She was about to pass by when she saw a hand protruding from one of the bottom folds of the sheet.

She let out a gurgled little shriek that scared her. She looked away and then back again. Propped against the edge of the sofa's armrest was a leg, from the knee down. Next to it lay an open shoebox containing fingers. She began to feel that her breathing wasn't right. She wanted to get out, but there was still the question of what was under the sheet. She had to know that. If she ran out without looking, she'd never summon the courage to use the key again.

She counted to ten, wiped her hands down the sides of her skirt and told herself that whatever the thing was, it couldn't be worse than what they were liable to show you nowadays on television, even in the news programmes. She reached out and pulled down the edge of the sheet.

It was pretty bad: a head with the face laid bare. The muscles, tendons and other bits across the face were mainly red or pink, a few of them darker than she'd imagined things like that were supposed to be. But they weren't wet; there was no blood. She bent her knees and looked more closely. From inside the still open skull she caught the glint of metal. There were lots of small wheels and bolts and tubes inside, like the interior of a watch or a radio.

She straightened up, rearranged the sheet and gently put out a hand towards the half leg. She felt the skin below the place where the joint should have been attached to some knuckly part of a knee.

A chill ran over her scalp. The skin, though unwarmed, was creamy, smooth, soft and silky, uncannily delicious to the touch. She pulled back her hand. For about five minutes she stood just staring at the wall. Then, she understood. The body wasn't real. Naturally, it couldn't be real: a dead body would have to be refrigerated. Therefore, that thing there on the sofa in pieces was not a corpse Edgar had taken from the pathology morgue; it was a body he had built himself out of other materials. Why on earth he'd want to do such a thing was beyond her.

She left everything in place, closed the door behind her and locked it with her key. Later in the day the answer came to her: her husband must be pioneering research on victims of road accidents. She had read an article several years before, about a medical school that simulated injuries by strapping life-sized replicas of people into cars; after smashing them up, they studied the damaged parts. The project had been funded by an insurance company. No doubt Edgar was working on something similar, although greatly in advance of anything she'd heard about. That skin, for example, was fantastic. And all the intricate bands of muscle and everything – the thing was very complicated. She still didn't understand what the clockwork mechanism in the head would be for, but maybe that would have something to do with a remote-control guidance system. The whole business was explainable. She stopped feeling scared. Nevertheless, she was thankful that the eyelids had been closed.

Edgar worked hard up in the attic for several days. She thought she'd give him a week and then go up and check on the progress he'd made. In the meantime, she looked into the possibilities of new adult education schools. She had lunch with Gina, who was worried about her daughter's weight problem and who poured out a long story to her about psychologists, behaviourists, weight-watchers and doctors. Helen listened sympathetically; she was glad to have such a convoluted narrative to concentrate on – there was no room for temptation to talk about what was troubling her: Edgar and the activity he was engaged in up in the attic.

Two days later, Mr Murdock from the old oil painting classes asked her to tea with Pat and Babs. The three of them cheered her up. Mr Murdock had already left the new classes they'd joined; the other two were going to, but for the moment they were sticking it out in order to be able to report back all the latest stories about the odious Miss Bindale. Miss Bindale was driving every-one away: she might end by causing the teacher to resign, too. It was a shame, they all said: one person could spoil everything. Mr Murdock recommended a language school he'd gone to for French. The place wasn't so much fun as their adult education school – it was more serious, the classes were mostly for busi-nessmen and unless you applied for the weekend, everything was in the evening. Pat said, 'It'd be a really good way to meet men. If you don't want the address, I'll keep it myself.'

'You'll never get anywhere if it's a language,' Babs told her. 'Car maintenance, that's the one. There aren't any other women at all.'

'Or karate,' Helen said.

'I wouldn't try it. You pick the wrong type there – they'll throw you against the wall and say it was an accident because they forgot to leave out some basic move. No thanks.'

Pat said that a friend of hers, named Shirley, had gone to a couple of other adult education places and had given her the addresses; four different ones. 'I liked the first one, so I never tried the others, but I can send you the addresses. I'll take a good look around, see where I put that piece of paper.'

Edgar spent the whole of the weekend up in the lab: Saturday night and Sunday too. He came down for meals. On Friday he'd brought her flowers, given her a talk about why the work was going to be necessary; when, where and how he'd expect his meals during the period; and how he appreciated her coopera-tion. She said, 'Yes, dear,' to everything, put his red roses in a vase, took it into the living-room and told him they looked lovely. She preferred daffodils, chrysanthemums, tulips, daisies, stocks, sweet peas, asters: almost anything. And if they had to be roses, any colour other than red.

He stayed in the bedroom Friday night, making sure that she didn't feel neglected. He wanted her to be satisfied with the arrangements. She was not only satisfied; she was surprised.

She carried out her appointed cooking tasks with grim cheer-fulness. She could hardly wait until Monday, when he'd be out of the house and she could go look at what he'd been doing.

On Sunday she knew that he'd achieved some kind of break-through in the work. He was transformed, radiant. He looked tired, but serene. Whatever it was, was finished. However, he didn't say anything about coming downstairs. He stayed up in the attic that night.

The next morning she waited a while after he'd gone. She was going to give him enough time to get all the way to work, and more: in case he'd forgotten something and had to come back for it. She wanted to be able to look at everything and not feel rushed. Whatever he'd completed was still up in the attic – all he'd taken with him was his briefcase.

She did the dishes, made the bed, checked her watch. She looked out of the window, although she didn't need to: it was one of those unnecessary things people do when they're anxious about something. She got the key.

The attic workroom looked the same, as far as she could see. She stepped in, closing the door lightly, so that it touched the jamb but didn't click into the frame. She walked forward. Her eyes jumped from place to place.

She peered into the first alcove: nothing. She hurried to the second; there was the sofa. And on it lay a young and beautiful woman: the creamy skin was as it had been before. The face had been fitted with its outer coating; everything there was in place: the lilac-tinted eyelids with long, dark lashes, the cupid's-bow mouth, the small, pert nose.

The face lay in the centre of a cloudlike nest of twirly blonde ringlets. A blue ribbon peeped out from a bunch of them at the back. The dress she wore was pink and cut like some sort of ballerina costume: the bodice like a bathing-suit top, the skirt standing out with layers of net and lace and stiffening. Her feet and legs were bare. The toe-nails, like the nails on the fingers, had been painted red.

Helen reached out towards the left leg. She ran her hand over it, stopped, and then quickly pulled back. The skin was warm. She moved along the side of the sofa, to where she could be near the head. 'Wake up,' she ordered. There was no response. Naturally: this wasn't a person – it was some kind of doll. It was so lifelike that it was almost impossible to believe that; nevertheless, her husband had built it.

As she stood there, trying to imagine why Edgar should have made a doll so detailed in that particular way, with painted nails and a blue satin bow and everything, she began to wonder how lifelike the rest of the body was. That was an important question.

If she hadn't seen the thing in its partly assembled state the week before, she wouldn't have known this was a replica, a machine. But having seen it complete, there was – all at once – no doubt in her mind that her husband had invented it for his own private purposes: otherwise, why make it so definitely non-utilitarian?

She thought she'd better know what she was up against. She examined the doll thoroughly, taking off the pink dress first, and then the black lace bra and underpants. She started to lose her sense of danger. She was getting mad. Who else, other than Edgar himself, could have chosen the pink dress and black underwear? He couldn't walk into a dress shop in her company without becoming flustered, yet she could picture him standing at a counter somewhere and asking for the clothes, saying in his argument-winning voice, 'Black lace, please, with a ribbon right about here.' He'd known the right size, too – but of course he'd known that. The doll had been built to specification: his specifications. *Oh*, Helen thought, *the swine*.

And the thing was so real-looking. She was sitting on the edge of the sofa and fiddling around with the doll's head, investigating the way the hair grew, when she felt her finger push down on what must have been a button behind the left ear.

The doll's eyelids rose, revealing a pair of enormous blue eyes. The lips parted in a dazzling smile, the torso began to breathe.

'Oh,' Helen said. 'Oh, dear.'

'Oh, dear,' the doll repeated gently. 'What can the matter be?'

Helen thought she might be going crazy. She asked – automatically and politely – 'Who are you?'

'I'm fine,' the doll told her. 'How are you?'

'Not how. Who?'

The doll smiled lovingly and relapsed into an expression of joyful delight. The eyelids blinked every once in a while. Helen watched. The action had evidently been programmed to be slightly irregular, to avoid an impression of the mechanical. Still, there was something hypnotic about it. The lips were silent. The voice too must be on a computer: the doll would only answer if you spoke to it. The voice-tape scanner didn't seem to be quite perfect yet, either.

She was trying to push the button again, to turn off the

eyelids, when she hit a nearby second button instead and sent the machine into overdrive. The lids drooped, the arms went up and out, the knees flew apart, the hips began to gyrate in an unmistakable manner, and the lips spoke.

Helen shot to her feet, stumbled back a few steps and crashed against the wall. She folded her arms and stayed where she was, staring with mesmerized intensity while the doll went through the cycle it had begun. Probably there were many other things it could do – this would be merely one of the variations. Out of the rosebud mouth came a mixture of babytalk and obscenity, of crude slang and sentimentality.

She gripped the sides of her arms and waited sternly until the exercise appeared to be over, though the doll was still begging in sweetly tremulous whispers for more. She stepped forward and slapped it across the face. 'Darling,' it murmured. She scrabbled among the golden curls, grabbed the ear and pushed every button she could see. There were five, all very small. They looked like pinheads. There were also two tiny switches she decided to leave alone. She'd seen enough. She was quivering with rage, shame and the need for revenge.

When she thought about wearing herself out doing the shopping and cooking and scrubbing, she prickled all over with a sense of grievance. She'd been slaving away for years, just so he could run up to the attic every evening and keep his secrets. And the boys were turning into the same kind as their father: what they wanted too was someone menial to provide services for them. And then they could spend their lives playing.

She saw herself as a lone, victimized woman beleaguered by selfish men. Her anger gave her a courage she wouldn't otherwise have had.

She ran out and across the hall to the other side of the attic – the side that wasn't locked. There were the trunks and suitcases, including the nice big one with wheels. There too was the chest full of spare blankets and quilts. She pulled out two of the blankets and took them into the lab. Then she carried the suitcase downstairs to the front hall.

She went up to the attic again, dressed the doll in its clothes, rolled it into the blankets and dragged them across the floor and down the stairs. She unzipped the suitcase, dumped the doll inside, folded the legs and arms and began to pack it tight, zipping the outside as she stuffed the pink skirt away.

She went up to the attic one more time, to put the blankets back and to shut the door of the lab.

She got her coat and handbag. The suitcase was easy to manage until she had to lift it into the back of the car. That wasn't so easy. Edgar was the one with the big car. Still, she could do it. All she'd have to worry about would be steps. The doll seemed to weigh exactly the same as a real woman of equivalent height and size.

There were three choices: the airport, the bus depot and the train station. The train station was large and nearer than the airport. She'd try it first.

Everything went well. She found a parking space straight away and was able to wheel the suitcase across the road, on to the sidewalk and through the doors, up an escalator and across several waiting rooms, to the locker halls. There was a whole bank of extra-large lockers; she heaved the case into one of them, put in enough money to release the key, and went to get some more coins. She ended up having to buy a paperback book, but the woman at the cash register agreed to let her have two big handfuls of change. She fed the money meticulously into the slot. The suitcase would be paid up for over two weeks.

*

Ron was getting out of his car when he saw the woman slam her car door and start to wheel the suitcase across the parking lot. She looked possible: the case seemed heavy.

He followed, walking casually. He had a repertoire of walks calculated to throw off suspicion. He hadn't had to learn any of them – they came naturally, like all his other athletic talents. That was what he was always telling Sid down at the gym: *I got natural talent. I don't need nobody teaching me nothing.* He still couldn't understand how Sid had knocked him out in the third round. He

hadn't given up the idea that something had been slipped into his
Coke. Sometimes there was a lot of heavy betting going on, even
when you were just sparring.

She looked like a nice, respectable woman; pretty, took care of
herself. The kind that said no. Her clothes cost something, which
was a good sign; so was the trouble she had getting the wheels of
the case up on to the kerb. Of course, she could be getting on a
train.

He followed her all the way around the corner to the lockers. He
watched, standing against the wall and pretending to look at his
paper. When she was through, he followed her far enough to see
that she was coming back. She put a lot of money in the locker:
good – the case would be there a while. But he'd probably better
get it quick, before somebody else did.

She left the building. That might mean she was going for a
second suitcase that she hadn't been able to handle in the same
load. He looked around, folded his paper, held it to cover what he
was doing, and stepped up to the locker. He took a metal slide out
of his pocket and stuck it into the keyhole. It was a cinch.

Some people could never have looked unsuspicious while
wheeling away stolen luggage, but you had to believe in yourself:
that was the main thing. Ron did his best. He didn't hurry. He got
the bag into the back seat of his car and started off. Her car, he
noticed, was already gone.

Normally he'd have stopped just around the block somewhere,
to go through the contents; but the traffic was building up. He
decided to drive straight on home. He was beginning to get
curious about what was inside. The suitcase was really heavy. The
moment he'd pulled it from the locker he'd thought: *Great – gold
bars; silver candlesticks*. A lot of people had those lockers. She
hadn't looked like that type, but how could you ever tell? She
could be helping a pal, or a husband. A guy he knew had found
some cash once – a whole overnight bag full of the stuff. And all of
it counterfeit, it turned out; he'd done time for that.

He got the bag out of the car, into the apartment block where
he lived, up three floors in the elevator, down the hall to his

bedroom. He broke the locks as soon as he'd thrown his jacket over the back of the easy chair. He unzipped both sides.

A powerful odour of mothballs was released into the room as the lid sprang open, disclosing a blonde woman in a pink dress. She was huddled up like a baby rabbit and he was sure she was dead. He'd be suspected, of course. He'd have to ditch the case someplace, fast. He put his hand on her arm to squash her in again. The arm was warm. He jumped away. He closed the curtains and turned on the lights.

He couldn't put her back. She might be alive now, but soon she'd suffocate. It was a good thing he'd found her in time. When he thought of that respectable type who'd shut her in the locker, he was amazed.

He got the plastic sheet he'd used to cover his Norton Atlas before one of his friends had borrowed the machine and smashed it to pieces. He spread the sheet over the bed and lifted the woman on top of it. He thought she looked fabulous, just like a dream. She seemed to be unharmed except for a mild discoloration on her left cheek, which might have been sustained in the packing. There was no blood that he could see. He thought he'd better do a complete check, to make sure she was all right. He took off her clothes. The dress was a bit weird, but she had some pretty classy underwear. Under the underwear was OK, too. He thought he might have some fun with her, while he was at it. He'd saved her life, after all: she owed him.

He was beginning to wonder what was going on – despite the warmth, she didn't actually seem to be breathing – when, accidentally, as he was running his hand through her hair, the side of his thumb hit two tiny, hard knobs of some kind and his problems were over.

The woman sighed and stretched out her arms. Her hands came softly around his back. Her eyes opened, her mouth smiled. She said, 'Ooh, you're so nice.'

*

Helen was curled up in her favourite living-room chair when
Edgar came in from work. She was reading the paperback she'd
had to buy at the station; a nurse novel called *Summer of Passion*.
She heard the car, the slam of the door, his feet crunching on the
gravel of the driveway, the door being opened and shut. He
called out, 'Hi,' going up the stairs. She answered, and read to
the end of the paragraph: *at last Tracy knew that she had found the
man of her desires and that this summer of passion would live in her
heart forever*. Helen yawned. She put the phone bill between the
pages of the book and stood up. Edgar was taking his time.
Maybe he was running around the attic in circles, every time
coming back to the empty sofa and not believing it. She didn't
feel sorry. She felt mean-hearted, even cruel, and absolutely
satisfied. Let him be on the receiving end of things for a while. It
might do him some good.

The attic door slammed. He'd figured out she had to be the
one to blame. He came thundering down the stairs and across
the front hall. She put the book down on the coffee table. Edgar
dashed into the room, breathing loudly. His hair was sticking
up, as if he'd been running his hands through it. 'Where is she?'
he demanded.

'Who?'

'My experiment. You know what I'm talking about.'

'Oh? It's a she, is it?'

'Where is she?' he shouted. 'You get her back here, or you're
going to wish you'd never been born.' He took a step forward.

'Oh no, you don't,' she said. 'You lay a finger on me, and
you'll never see her again.'

'What have you done with her?'

'That's my business. If you want her back, we're going to have
to talk it over.'

He looked defiant, but he gave in. She took up her stance by
the red roses, he struck a pose in front of the Chinese lamp with
the decorations that spelled out Good Fortune and Long Life. He
said, 'You don't know what you've done. It's a masterpiece. It's
as if you'd stolen the Mona Lisa. The eyes – my God, how I

worked to get the eyes right. It's a miracle.'

A *woman*, she thought, *can get the eyes and everything else right without any trouble: her creative power is inherent. Men can never create; they only copy. That's why they're always so jealous.*

'What's her name, by the way?' she asked.

He looked embarrassed, finally. 'Dolly,' he said.

'Brilliant. I suppose you're going to tell me this is love.'

'Helen, in case you still haven't grasped it after all these years – my main interest in life is science. Progress. Going forward into the future.'

'OK. You just let me know how long it's going to take you to come up with the companion-piece.'

'What?'

This was her moment. She thought she might begin to rise from the floor with the rush of excitement, the wonderful elation: dizzying, intoxicating, triumphant. This was power. There was even a phrase for it: drunk with power. No wonder people wouldn't give it up once they got hold of it. It was as if she'd been grabbed by something out of the sky, and pulled up; she was going higher and higher. Nothing could hurt her. She was invulnerable.

'I want,' she said, 'what you had – something nice on the side. A male escort: presentable, amusing, and a real stud.'

'No way.'

'Then I guess it's goodbye, Dolly.'

'If you don't tell me –'

'Don't you dare touch me,' she shrieked. 'It's all right for you to play around in my own home, while I'm down here doing the housework, isn't it?'

'I don't think you understand.'

'I don't?'

'It's just a doll.'

'Pubic hair and nipples everywhere you look – that's some doll. And what about that twitch and switch business she does? That's a couple of giant steps ahead of the ones that just wet their pants and cry mama.'

'It may turn out to have important medical uses. Ah ... therapeutic.'

'Good. That's just what I'm in need of.'

'Helen,' he said, 'let's forget all about this.'

'OK. It isn't that important to me. I can find a real man anywhere. But if you want your Dolly back, you can make me a perfect one. That's only fair. One for you and one for me.'

'I don't know why you're so steamed up.'

'I'm not that crazy about adultery, that's all. Especially if I'm the one who's being acted against.'

'There's no question of adultery. In any case – well, in any case there's no moral lapse unless it's done with another person.'

'No kidding? I thought the moral lapse was there even if you only did it in the mind.'

'Let me explain it to you.'

'Fine,' she told him. 'Just as long as you keep working at my gigolo. And if there aren't any lapses, we're both in the clear, aren't we?'

*

The instant Dolly opened her eyes, Ron fell in love with her. Everything was different. Everything was solved. He'd never thought it would happen to him. He hadn't believed in it: Love. It was going to come as a big surprise to his friends down at the gym – they'd all agreed long ago that life was a lot better without women. They'd just have to get used to her. She was part of his life now. The fact that she was a doll he regarded as an advantage. You didn't need to feed her or buy her drinks or stop the car so she could keep looking for a rest room every five minutes. She was unchanging. The extraordinary skin she possessed cleaned and preserved itself without trouble; the mark on her cheek faded even before the smell of mothballs had worn off. A fresh, spring-like fragrance seemed to breathe from her body. His friends would have to accept her as they'd have had to if he'd gotten married. That was what things were going to be like – like having a wife, except that not being human, of course, she was nicer.

That first day, he figured out how to use all the push-buttons. He knew her name because she told him: she got right up close to his face, winked, gave a little giggle and whispered, 'Dolly wants to play.' She was so good at answering his questions that it took him some time to realize she was repeating, and that if he asked a particular question, she'd always give the same response, or one of several set replies. A similar repetitiveness characterized some of her physical reactions, but he didn't mind that. And when you thought about it, her conversation wasn't much more limited than most women's. She sometimes said something that didn't fit, that was all – never anything really stupid. And if she came up with the wrong wording, that wasn't her fault. It almost never happened. Her answers were so good and she was so understanding about everything, that he believed she knew what he was getting at; even if she was a doll, even if she wasn't real in any way. To him she was real. When he looked into her beautiful eyes, he was convinced that she loved him. He was happy. He was also sure that there were no others like her. There could be only one Dolly.

He told her everything. All about himself, what he wanted out of life, what his dreams of success used to be, how he'd grown up: all the things he used to think. He didn't know what he thought any more and he didn't have any dreams left. He cried in her arms. She stroked his hair and called him darling. She said, 'Hush, darling. It's all right.' He believed her. He talked to her for hours. He knew that if she could, she'd speak as freely as he did.

*

Edgar applied for emergency leave from his job. It knocked out the holiday they'd been planning to take with the boys in the summer vacation, but he needed the time. He worked all day and most of the night. Helen brought up his meals on a tray. She tried to make comments once. He screamed at her. He shouted threats, oaths and accusations, ending up with a warning that if she didn't shut up about absolutely everything, he wouldn't be responsible. She smiled. She said in her gooey, peacemaker's voice, 'What a pompous twerp you've turned into, Edgar.' It was all out in the open now.

And he no longer felt guilty about his infidelities, mental or physical. It served her right. He wished that he'd been more adventurous, all the way back to the beginning, when they'd married: he wished he'd led a double life – a triple one. It was galling to be so hard at work, wasting the strength of his body and brain on the creation of a thing intended to give her pleasure. He could do it, of course; he had mastered the technique and the principles. But it was infuriating. It seemed to him now that there hadn't been a single moment when she'd been anything but a hindrance to him. She nagged, she had terrible moods, she wasn't such a wonderful cook, every once in a while she made a truly embarrassing scene – like the one at Christmas with his uncle – and she could wear really dumpy clothes that he didn't like. She'd keep wearing them after he'd expressly told her he didn't like them. And he didn't think she'd brought the boys up that well, either. They got away from her just in time.

He had needed Dolly in order to keep on living with his wife. If he couldn't have Dolly back, there was no point in going on. Now that there was no longer any secrecy, there was probably no more hope for his marriage. Still, as long as he could recover Dolly, there was hope for him.

When he thought about Dolly, he was ready to go through any trial, do any amount of work. He missed her. He missed the laugh in her voice and the look in her eyes when she said, 'Let's have a good time. Let's have a ball.'

He lost his concentration for a moment. The scalpel slipped. The voicebox let out a horrible cry. He waited to see if Helen would come charging up the stairs to crouch by the banisters and listen. Nothing happened. Now that she knew, she wasn't worried. She'd wait and be silent.

*

At the beginning Ron was satisfied with keeping Dolly in his bedroom. But as he began to depend on her, he felt the desire to take her out. He'd found the buttons to make her walk and respond to his request for her to sit down or get up. A mild pressure on her arm would help her to change pace, turn a corner. Naturally the pink dress wasn't right for outdoor wear. He bought her a T-shirt and a skirt. She looked great in them. But the shoes were a problem: you had to try them on. He didn't want to spend money on the wrong size. He asked his friend, Charlie, in a general way, what to do if you didn't know your size and couldn't put the shoes on to find out: if you were buying a present, say. Charlie told him to try L. L. Bean. 'All you need to do,' he told Ron, 'is send them a tracing of your foot.'

He had a lot of fun making the tracings with Dolly. He sent away for a pair of flat shoes. When they arrived, he walked her around the room in them for a long time, examining the skin on her feet at intervals. He didn't know what would happen if her skin got badly broken or damaged. He had no idea where he could take her to be fixed. He asked if the shoes felt OK; she said everything was just fine and she loved him – he was wonderful.

He sent away for a pair of high heels and some rubber boots as well as socks, a parka, a shirt and a sweater, a pair of corduroy trousers and a blue and white flannel nightgown with ruffles around the neck. He also went out and bought some fingernail polish. Her nails appeared to be indestructible, but the polish was chipping. The girl behind the counter gave him a little lecture about the necessity of removing the old polish before putting on a second coat. She sold him quite a lot of cosmetic equipment. He thought, since he was there, he might buy eye make-up and lipstick, too. 'Does it come with instructions?' he asked. The salesgirl sold him a book with pictures and an expensive box full of tiny brushes.

He got hold of an airport case that contained a roll of traveller's cheques and five silk suits. He won on the races and after that, at the tables. Dolly was bringing him luck.

He took her out. People turned to look at her because she was so beautiful, not because they thought something was wrong. He felt like a million dollars walking down the street with her. It was too bad that he couldn't get her to eat or drink, because then he'd be able to take her into a restaurant or a bar. But just walking along, arm in arm, was nice. One afternoon he bumped into Charlie, who took a look at Dolly and nearly fell over. 'Jeez, Ron,' he said, 'what a doll.'

Dolly wrinkled up her nose and giggled. She squirmed a little with excitement. Her eyes got bigger.

'Jeez,' Charlie said again. 'You going to introduce me?'

'Charlie, this is Dolly,' Ron said. 'Say hi, honey.'

'Hi, honey,' Dolly said. She put her hand in Charlie's.

Charlie said, 'Oh, boy. You been holding out on us, pal. Hi there, Dolly. I don't know why my old buddy Ron here didn't tell me about you before.'

'We got to be going,' Ron said.

'Oh, come on. You don't have to go, do you, Dolly?'

'Yes,' Ron said. 'Say goodbye, sugarpie.'

Dolly twiddled her fingers at Charlie. She gave him a breathy, hicupping laugh and then whispered, 'Goodbye, sugarpie.'

'Oh, boy,' Charlie said again.

Ron pulled her away fast. She clip-clopped beside him quickly in her high heels, her hips swaying, her large eyes roving happily.

It hadn't gone too badly, but he didn't trust her for extended conversation. He figured they'd better put in some practice first.

He took on a job delivering goods for a friend. Everything was packed up in boxes. Maybe the boxes contained stuff he shouldn't know about. Normally he wouldn't care, but now he kept thinking about Dolly: what would happen to her if he got caught? She'd be found by somebody else, who'd take her away and keep her, just the way he had.

He stopped checking out the airport lockers. He began to look through the papers for legitimate work. Down at the gym they thought he was crazy – at least, they did at first. Word had gone around about Dolly; everybody asked about her. When was Ron going to bring her in to meet the gang?

He coached her for a while and then took her down to the gym. They all loved her. And they thought she was real. They said they could understand how Ron would want to settle down to something steady, if he had a girl like that. An older man named Bud actually clapped him on the shoulder and said something about wedding bells.

Ron wondered if maybe he could get away with introducing her to his sister and her family. He didn't see why not. He phoned Kathleen. She said sure.

'Only thing is,' he explained, 'she's on this very strict diet, so she won't eat anything. I thought I'd better tell you.'

'Well, I can fix her a salad.'

'No, it's sort of everything. She's allergic.'

Kathleen told him not to worry. He put Dolly into the car, together with a change of clothes and her rubber boots. He drove carefully, thinking all the time that if they crashed, or if she were to cut herself in some other way, he wouldn't know what to do, where to take her. He didn't even know what was inside her; if she got hurt seriously, whatever was in there might all leak out.

Kathleen decided, as soon as she saw Dolly: she didn't like her. Her husband, Ben, thought Dolly was great. The children liked her too, but they didn't understand why she wouldn't pat their dog, when it was evidently so interested in her and kept sniffing around her. Ron grabbed the dog and kept it by him. Later in the afternoon while they were walking along the path by the creek, the dog ran ahead and almost made Dolly trip over. At that moment Ron thought it couldn't work: his friends at the gym were going to accept her, real or not, but his family never would.

Before he drove off he sat Dolly in the car, walked back to where Kathleen was standing, and asked, 'Well? Do you like her?'

'Sure. She's fine,' Kathleen said. 'A little dumb, maybe.'

'But nice. She's got a heart of gold.'

'I guess it's just – if people are really silly all the time, it's too much like being with the kids. I start to get aggravated.'

All the way back to town he felt angry. It wasn't right that he should have to hide Dolly away like a secret vice. She should be seen and admired.

The next day he took her on an expedition into town: through the parks, into the big stores, around one of the museums. The weather was good, which was lucky. He didn't know how she'd react to rain or whether she'd be steady on her feet over wet sidewalks. Of course, he didn't know how a prolonged exposure to sunlight was going to affect her, either, but she seemed all right. Her feet, too, looked all right.

He took her by public transport, since that was part of the idea. They rode on the subway, then they changed to a bus. He had his arm around her as usual, when one of the other passengers got up from the seat behind them, knocking Ron's arm and the back of Dolly's head as he went by. Ron clutched her more tightly; inadvertently he hit several of the control buttons.

Dolly's arms raised themselves above her head, her eyelids flickered, her legs shot apart, her hips began to swing forward and back. 'Ooh,' she said, 'you're so good.'

He tried to find the switch. He panicked and turned it on higher by mistake.

She went faster, gasping, 'Ooh, you feel so nice, ooh do it to me.'

He fumbled at her hairline while people around them said, 'Come on, Mister, give us a break,' and, 'That's some girlfriend you've got – can't you do it at home?'

He found the switch just as she was telling him – and the whole bus – the thing she loved best about him.

The driver put on the brakes and said, 'OK, Mac, get that tramp out of my bus.'

Ron refused. If he got out with Dolly before he'd planned to, he'd never be able to walk her to where they could get a cab or find another bus. 'She can't help it,' he said. 'She's sick.'

The driver came back to insist; he had a big beer-belly. Ron got ready to punch him right in the middle of it and then drive the bus away himself. Dolly slumped against him, her face by his collarbone, her eyes closed. 'It just comes over her sometimes,' he said. That wasn't enough of an explanation, apparently. He added, 'She had a real bad time when she was a kid.'

The bus went quiet. Everyone thought over the implications of what Ron had said. The driver went back to the wheel. The bus started up again. Still no one spoke. The silence was beginning to be painful. Ron didn't know why he'd chosen that particular thing to say, even though it had worked – it had shut everybody up fine. But it left him feeling almost as strange as everyone else seemed to. By the end of the ride he'd begun to have a clear idea of the appalling childhood Dolly must have lived through. And he promised himself to take even better care of her than before, in order to make up for her sad life.

When his stop came, he carried her out in his arms. She appeared to be asleep. A few of the other passengers made hushed exclamations and murmurs of interest as he left.

He had to admit that there was always going to be a risk if he took her out in public. Driving alone with her in the car wouldn't be such a problem. He wanted to take her to the beach: to camp in the dunes and make love on the sands at night. He thought her skin would be proof against the abrasions of sand, the burning of the sun, the action of salt water. But he wasn't sure. The more he thought about her possible fragility, the more he worried. If he were hurt, even severely, he could be put together again: but could she?

*

Helen did the shopping, cooked the meals and began a thorough cleaning of everything in the house: the curtains, the chair covers, the rugs. She wouldn't have a spare moment to use for thought. She wanted to maintain her sense of outrage at a high level, where it could help to keep her active. She had no intention of breaking down into misery. She vacuumed and ironed and dusted. She washed and scrubbed. Once, just for a moment, her anger subsided and she felt wounded.

Edgar had done all that, she thought – he'd been driven to it, because she wasn't enough for him. She obviously hadn't been good enough in bed, either, otherwise he wouldn't have needed such a blatant type as compensation for her deficiencies. Her only success had been the children. She should really give up.

She caught herself just in time. She fought hard against despair, whipping her indignation up again. If things were bad, you should never crumple. Do something about it – no matter what. She stoked her fury until she thought she could do anything, even break up her marriage, if she had to. She was too mad to care whether she wrecked her home or not. *Let him suffer for a change*, she thought.

She could sue him: win a divorce case hands down. You could cite anybody nowadays. There had been a story in the papers recently about a man whose wife, without his knowledge, and – if he'd known – against his will, had had herself impregnated by a machine in a sperm-bank clinic. The husband had accused as co-respondent, and therefore father of the child, the technician who'd switched on the apparatus. The fact that the operator of the machine was a woman had made no difference in law. And soon you'd be able to say it was the machine itself. Helen could name this Dolly as the other woman. Why not? When she produced the doll in court and switched on the buttons that sent her into her act, they'd hand the betrayed wife everything on a plate: house, children, her car, his car, the bank accounts – it would be a long list. If she thought about it, she might rather have just him. So, she wasn't going to think about it too hard. She kept on doing the housework.

Up in the attic Edgar worked quickly – frenetically, in fact – although to him it seemed slow. When the replica was ready, he brought it downstairs to the living room and sat it on a chair. He called out, 'Helen,' as she was coming around the corner from the hall. She'd heard him on the stairs.

'Well, it's ready,' he told her.

She looked past him at the male doll sitting in the armchair. Edgar had dressed it in one of his suits.

'Oh, honestly, Edgar,' she said.

'What?' He sounded close to collapse. He probably hadn't slept for days.

She said, 'He looks like a floorwalker.'

'There's nothing wrong with him. It's astounding, given the short time – '

'He looks so namby-pamby. I bet you didn't even put any hair on his chest.'

'As a matter of fact – '

'You didn't?'

'The hair is extremely difficult to do, you know. I wasn't aware that all women found it such a necessary item. I understand a lot of them hold just the opposite view.'

'And the skin. It's too smooth and soft-looking. It's like a woman's.'

'Well, that's the kind I can make. Damn it, it's an exceptionally lifelike specimen. It ought to give complete satisfaction.'

'It better,' she said. She glared at the doll. She didn't like him at all. She moved forward to examine him more closely.

'And now,' Edgar announced, 'I want Dolly.'

'Not till I've tried him out. What's this? The eyes, Edgar.'

'They're perfect. What's wrong with them?'

'They're blue. I wanted them brown.'

'Blue is the colour I know how to do.'

'And he's so pale. He almost looks unhealthy.'

'I thought of building him so he'd strangle you in bed.'

She smiled a long, slow smile she'd been practising. It let him know that she realized she was in control of the situation. She asked him if he wanted to check into a hotel somewhere, or maybe he'd stay up in the attic: because she and her new friend planned to be busy in the bedroom for a while.

'Don't overdo it,' he told her. 'It's possible to injure yourself that way, you know.'

'You let me worry about that.' She asked for full instructions about the push-button system. She got the doll to rise from the chair and walk up the stairs with her. Edgar went out and got drunk for two days.

She tried out the doll at all the activities he was capable of. She still didn't like him. He didn't look right, he could be uncomfortable without constant monitoring, and his conversation was narrow in the extreme. His sexual prowess was without subtlety, charm, surprise, or even much variety. She didn't believe that her husband had tried to shortchange her; he simply hadn't had the ingenuity to programme a better model.

As soon as Edgar sobered up, he knocked at the door. He was full of demands. She didn't listen. She said, 'Who was the nerd you modelled this thing on?'

'I didn't. He's a kind of conglomerate.'

'Conglomerate certainly isn't as good as whoever it was you picked to make the girl from.'

'I didn't pick anyone. Dolly isn't a copy. She's an ideal.'

'Oh, my. Well, this one is definitely not my ideal.'

'Tough. You made a bargain with me.'

'And you gave me a dud.'

'I don't believe it.'

'He's so boring to talk to, you could go into rigor mortis halfway through a sentence.'

'I didn't think you wanted him to be able to discuss the novels of Proust.'

'But that could be arranged, couldn't it? You could feed some books into him?'

'Sure.'

'And he isn't such a high-stepper in the sack.'

'Come on, Helen. Anything more and you'll rupture yourself.'

'Reprogramming is what he needs. I can tell you exactly what I want added.'

'You can go jump in the lake.'

'And I want him to teach me Italian. And flower painting and intermediate *cordon bleu*.'

'No demonstration stuff. I can do a language if you get me the tapes, but they'll have to be changed when you graduate to the next stage. There isn't that much room inside for extra speech.'

He was no longer angry or contemptuous. He looked exhausted. He made all the changes she'd asked for on the doll and added a tape of Italian lessons. She tried everything out. The renovated model was a great improvement. She felt worse than ever.

'Where is she?' Edgar pleaded, looking beaten, unhappy, hopeless.

Helen gave him the key to the locker.

*

Ron stopped taking Dolly to the gym when the boys began to pester him with too many questions. They pressed up around her in a circle, trying to find out what she thought of everything; that got him nervous and mixed her up. And then they started on him. What they most wanted to know was: where did she come from?

He had no answer to that, but no ideas about it, either. Lots of things – some of the most important things in life – remained completely mysterious. That didn't matter. It made more sense just to be happy you had them instead of asking questions about them all the time.

But one day while they were making love, instead of waiting for the end of the cycle she was on, Dolly went into a totally different one. Ron guessed that he must have given her some verbal instruction or physical signal. She started to do things he hadn't realized she knew about. He'd never done them himself, only heard about them. He did his best to keep up. She laughed with pleasure and said, 'Does Edgar love his Dolly?'

'Who's Edgar?' he asked.

'Edgar's Dolly's honeybunch, isn't he? Dolly's so happy with her great big gorgeous Edgar, especially with his great big gorgeous – '

'I ain't Edgar,' Ron yelled at her. He did something calculated to startle and possibly hurt her. She told him he was wonderful, the best she'd ever had: her very own Edgar.

It wasn't her fault. She didn't know any better. But it just about killed him.

He began to feel jealous. He hadn't wanted to think about how she was made – he'd assumed that she'd been made by machines. But now he had it figured out: she'd been custom-made for one person – a man named Edgar. It still didn't occur to him that this Edgar could have built her himself. He didn't think of things as being made by people. He thought of them as being bought in stores. She would have come from some very fancy place like the big stores where rich people bought diamond necklaces and matching sets of alligator-skin luggage, and so on. You could have all that stuff custom-made.

Someone else had thought her up. She'd been another man's invention. And Ron hadn't been the first to love her; he was sure about that. A sadness began to grow in him. The fact that she couldn't hold a real converstion still didn't bother him, nor that the things she said were always the same. What caused him pain was to hear her calling him by another's man's name. He began to think he could live with that too if only in some other phrase she'd occasionally call him by his own name, too.

The sadness began to overshadow his love to such an extent that he thought he'd have to do something about it. He got the suitcase out from the back of the closet and went over the inside. There was a piece of white cardboard tucked into one of the shirt-racks in the underside of the top lid. Someone had written a name and address on the card, together with a promise to reward the finder for the return of the case. The name matched the initials on the outside. The first letter of each was E; E for Edgar, maybe. People were so dumb, Ron thought. He'd never put a name or address on anything he was carrying around. Somebody could decide to come after you and clean up.

He put the card in his wallet but he still hadn't really made up his mind.

The next morning everything was decided for him while he was making breakfast in the kitchen. He'd cracked a couple of eggs into the frying pan and was walking over to the garbage pail with the shells. One of them jumped out of his hand. He scooped it up again and threw it out with the others. He meant to wipe a rag over the part of the floor where it had landed but the eggs started to sizzle in the pan. He stepped back to the stove. And at that moment, Dolly came into the room. Before he had a chance to warn her, she was all over the place – skidding and sliding and landing with a thump.

He picked her up and sat her down on top of the folding stool. He asked, 'Are you OK, honey?' She smiled and said she was fine. But he could see, in the middle of her right arm, a dent. He touched the centre of the injured place lightly with the tips of his fingers, then he pushed the flat of his hand firmly over the higher edge of the indentation; he hoped that the pressure would bring the hollow back up to its normal level. But nothing changed. The thing he was afraid of had happened.

'Dolly's hurt,' she said. 'Dolly needs a four-five-four repair.'

'What's that?'

'Dolly needs a four-five-four repair on her arm.'

'Uh-huh,' he said. He didn't know what to do. All through the day he watched her, to see if the dent got bigger. It didn't; it stayed the same, but at regular intervals she reminded him that she needed to have the arm seen to.

He knew that it was dangerous to keep putting off the moment of action. He should find out what she'd need to have done if something worse went wrong. He could only do that by getting hold of whoever knew how to fix her; and then by trickery, threats, bribes, blackmail or violence, making sure he got the person to help him. If he could find somebody to teach him how to carry out all her repair work himself, that was what he'd like best.

*

When Edgar began his drive back to the house, Helen was sitting on the living room sofa at the opposite end from the male doll, who was teaching her how to conjugate the verb *to be* in Italian. While she was answering the questions put to her, she stared up at the wall, near the ceiling. She was already tired of him. The renovations had been minimal, she decided. Edgar wasn't able to programme a better man, more intelligent, attractive. Perhaps no alterations would make any difference; maybe she just wanted him to be real, even if he was boring. Edgar evidently felt the other way: what he'd loved most about Dolly was that she was perfect, unreal, like a dream. The element of fantasy stimulated him.

For Helen, on the contrary, the excitement was over. Even the erotic thrill was gone. Owning the doll was probably going to be like driving a car – you'd begin by playing with it for fun and thinking it was a marvellous toy: but you'd end up putting it to practical use on chores like the shopping. From now on she'd be using the doll only as a routine measure for alleviating frustration. As soon as Edgar got Dolly back, there'd be plenty of opportunity for feeling frustrated and neglected.

She remembered what Edgar had said about the possible therapeutic value of such a doll. It could be true. There might be lots of people who'd favour the companionship of a non-human partner once a week. Or three times a day. No emotions, no strings attached. She thought about her sons: the schoolboy market. There were many categories that came to mind – the recently divorced, the husbands of women who were pregnant or new mothers, the wives of men who were ill, absent, unable, unfaithful, uninterested. And there would be no danger of venereal disease. There were great possibilities. If the idea could be turned into a commercial venture, it might make millions. They could advertise: *Ladies, are you lonely?* She might lend the doll to Gina and see what she thought.

'*Dove?*' the doll said.

'*Qui,*' she answered.

The front door opened and banged shut as Edgar's footsteps pounded through the hall. He was running. He burst into the living-room and roared, 'Where is she? I want the truth this time. And I mean it.'

'The doll?' Helen said. 'I gave you the key.'

'Oh, yes. But when he got there, the cupboard was bare. There's nothing inside that locker. It's empty.'

'It can't be. It's got two more days to go. Edgar, that was the right key and I put the suitcase in there myself. They aren't allowed to open those lockers before the money runs out. I put in so many – '

'But she isn't there.'

'She's got to be. You must have tried the wrong locker. Or maybe the wrong part of the row. All those things look alike.'

'I looked everywhere. I saw the right locker. It was the right one, but there wasn't any suitcase in it. If there was ever anything in it, it's gone now.'

'Well, if it's gone,' she said, 'it's been stolen.'

'It can't be stolen. No.'

'That's the only explanation I can think of. That's where I put her, so she should still be there. I guess it happens sometimes that they get people forcing the locks, or whatever they do.'

'How could you be so careless? To put her in a public place, where anybody could get at her.'

'I didn't want to try to hide her in the house. I thought you'd find her.'

'But how am I going to get her back?'

'I don't know.'

'You'd better know. If I can't find her, Helen – it's the end.'

'You could make another one, any time.'

'Impossible.' He shook his head slowly and sat down in a chair. He still had his coat on.

Helen said, 'I guess we could share Auto.'

'Otto?'

'His name,' she said, looking at the doll. 'Automatico. Auto for short.'

'*Buon giorno*,' the doll murmured, making a slight bow from the waist.

Edgar said, 'Hi,' in a loud, unpleasant tone.

'*Come sta*?' the doll asked.

'That's all right, Auto,' Helen said. 'You can be quiet now. We've got some things to talk about.'

'*Bene, signora.*'

Edgar stared at the doll and snorted. 'That's really what you wanted? The guy's a pain in the ass.'

'He's getting to be very boring. He's about as interesting as a vibrator.'

'I did just what you said.'

'But I'm getting sort of sick of him. I always know what's coming next.'

'I could programme him for random selection – that's the best I can do.'

'Maybe what I needed was you.'

'It's a little late.'

'It was a little late even before you started work on that thing. It began way back, with the computer – didn't it? Remember? When you stopped coming to the table. You'd make me bring in your meals and leave them. You can get a divorce for it nowadays: you cite the computer.'

'I could cite Auto here.'

'Not if you made him. I don't know what they'd call that – complicity or connivance, or something.'

'I think I'll go out for a walk.'

'What's your opinion of putting a doll like this on the market? It could become the new executive toy.'

'Certainly not.'

'Why not? We could make a fortune selling them. You think we should give them away?'

'Why stop with selling? You could run a rental service. Go into the call girl business: charge for every time.'

'That's no good. If we didn't agree to sell them, they'd get stolen. People are going to want their own. Would it make a difference to let them out in the world – could somebody copy the way you do them?'

'Not yet. It's my invention. But if there's money in it, you can bet there'd be people after the process. Life wouldn't be worth living. We might not even be safe. That's one of the reasons I decided from the beginning, that if I had any success with the project, I'd keep it to myself.'

'You said the dolls could have a therapeutic value.'

'Yes, well . . . you had me cornered. The therapy was for me.

Just as you suspected. I only wanted to make one.'

'But all those techniques and materials – the skin, the vocal cords – everything: they could be used in hospitals, couldn't they?'

'No. It's all artificial.'

'But it responds to touch and sound. If the dolls can do that, so could separate parts. You could fix almost any physical injury.'

'Theoretically.'

'It's possible?'

'In theory.'

'Then you've got to. I didn't think that far, before. If it's really possible, it's our duty.'

'Jesus God, Helen. You take the cake. You just do.'

'Me? Who had the idea for this in the first place?'

'Not as a business.'

'Oh, I see. That's what makes the difference, is it?'

Out in the hall the phone rang. Helen turned her head, but didn't move. Edgar said, 'Aren't you going to get it?'

'I want to finish what we're talking about.'

He stood up and went into the hall. She called after him, 'Why don't you take your coat off?' He picked up the receiver and barked into it, 'Hello?'

A muffled voice came over the wire, saying, 'I got something belongs to you.'

'Oh?'

'A suitcase.'

'Yes,' Edgar said quickly. 'Where is it?'

'Something was inside it. Something kind of blonde, with blue eyes.'

'Where is she?'

'I'll do a deal,' the voice said. 'OK?'

'We can talk about that. Bring her here and we'll discuss it.'

'Oh, no. I'm not bringing her anyplace.'

'You don't understand. It's a very delicate mechanism. She shouldn't have been away so long. She could be damaged.'

'She looks fine.'

'She could be damaged and it wouldn't show. Internal injuries. I've got to have a look at her. She's supposed to have regular inspections.'

There was silence at the other end. Edgar was covered in sweat. He couldn't think up any more reasons to tell the man why Dolly should come back. He said, 'What's your name?'

'Ron,' the voice told him.

'Well, Ron, you'd better believe me. If it goes beyond a certain stage, I can't fix anything. I've been worried out of my mind. She's got to come back to the lab.'

'Are you the guy that, um . . .'

'I'm the designer.'

'Uh-huh. OK.'

'Now.'

'Right. I'll be over.' He hung up.

Edgar banged down the phone, threw off his coat and started up the stairs. Helen came out of the living-room behind him. 'Where are you going?' she said.

'He's got her.'

'Who? What have you done with your coat?'

'A man that called up. Ron. He's bringing her over here now.'

'Are you going out?'

'Of course not. Dolly's coming here.'

'Well, come back and sit down,' Helen said. She picked up his coat and hung it in the hall closet.

'I'm the one who knows about her,' he muttered. 'He can't do anything without me.'

Helen pushed him into the living-room and sat him down in a chair. She took Auto out, around the corner. She steered him to the downstairs guest room where Edgar's grandmother had once stayed after her leg operation. She stood him up in the closet and closed the door on him.

She waited with Edgar for ten minutes. As soon as they heard the car outside they both ran to the windows. They saw Ron get out of the car. He was wearing blue jeans and a red T-shirt. Helen said, 'Well, he's a bit of a slob, but that's more the kind of thing I had in mind.'

'What?'

'To wind up and go to bed with. That man there.'

'Mm,' Edgar said. He was wondering if he'd be strong enough to tackle a man like that, who looked as if he could knock people down. He began to think about what must have happened all the time Dolly was away. A man like that wouldn't have let her alone, once he'd seen her. Of course not. Edgar was ready to kill him, despite the difference in size.

Ron got Dolly out of the car. He handled her carefully. He walked her up the front steps. He rang the doorbell.

Edgar jerked the door open. The four of them stood looking at each other. Edgar said, 'Hello, Dolly.'

'Hello there, Edgar-poo,' Dolly answered.

'How are you?'

'Dolly's just fine when Edgar's here.'

Helen leaned close to Ron. She said, 'I'm Helen.'

'Ron,' he said. 'Hi.'

'Why don't we all step into the house?' She led the way. She put the three others into the living-room, brought in some coffee and sandwiches, and said she'd take Dolly into the next room.

'She stays here,' Ron declared.

'She makes me nervous. I'm just going to put her in the guest room. You can come see.'

Ron went with her. Helen opened the door to show him the empty room. She smiled at him. 'See?' she told him. He laid Dolly down on top of the bed. He looked all around the room and stepped back. Helen closed the door.

Ron followed her back to the living-room, where Edgar had changed from coffee to whiskey. Edgar said, 'Want a drink?'

Ron nodded. He knew he had the upper hand, drunk or sober. Even over the phone Edgar had sounded like a drip. Maybe he'd put Dolly together, but she was Ron's by right of conquest. Possession was nine-tenths of the law: that was what they said. Let Edgar what's-his-name try to take her back. Ron had a good left as well as a good right: he'd show this Edgar. And the woman was giving him the eye; he might be able to get her to back him up. Now that it occurred to him to notice, he knew who she was, too. She was the woman who'd put the suitcase into the locker.

Edgar began to talk, to plead, to describe the vague glimmerings of the dream he'd had: when Dolly had first come to him as a mere idea. He began to sound so desperate, he'd been so choked up at the sight of Dolly, that Ron pretended to soften. It didn't do any good to scare people too much while you were still trying to line them up; they could go and do something crazy. He said, 'Look, Ed, I guess I can see how it is. You feel the same as me. But I can't let her go. You understand? I never thought I'd say it, but we're going to have to do some kind of a deal about sharing.'

'Share Dolly? Not for anything.'

'That's the way it's got to be. Or – you can make up your mind to go on without her. I'll just put her in the car and drive her out of your life again. It could be a long time till I needed to bring her back to you. You built her to last, didn't you?'

'I? Yes. I'm the important one. I'm the creator. You two – what are you? I created them.'

'You create, maybe,' Helen said, 'but you don't appreciate.'

'That's right,' Ron told him. 'You couldn't ever love Dolly like I do.'

'I invented her, man. She's all mine – she's all me.'

Helen said, 'If you could hear what you sound like, Edgar.'

'I sound like a man who's been treated badly. Helen, you used to understand me.'

'Oh? That must have been nice for you. And did you understand me?' She stood up, went to the liquor cabinet and said, 'You still haven't brought in the Cinzano. I'll get it.' She marched from the room.

Edgar said to Ron, 'It's true. You're the one who needs me.'

'Right. That's why I'm willing to talk about it. You don't have to bother with this. You can make yourself another one. Can't you?'

'No.'

'Sure. You make one, you can make two.'

'I made a second one. It was no good.'

'What was wrong with her?'

'It was a male replica. For my wife.'

'Yeah?'

'It was her price for telling me where she put Dolly.'

'No shit. And she didn't like it?'

'It isn't real enough, apparently. She says she's bored with it.'

'Maybe you're only good at them when it's a woman.'

'No – I know what the trouble is. It's that I put all my best work, all my ideas and hopes, into that one effort. Dolly was the only time I could do it. I'm like a man who falls in love just once and can't feel the same about any other woman.'

Ron didn't believe it. He thought Edgar wouldn't want to give anything to other people: that was the reason why he'd fail.

Edgar made himself a fresh drink. Helen, having found her bottle of vermouth, carried it to the guest room and parked it on the dresser while she took off Dolly's clothes, got Auto out of the closet and then stripped him too. She put him on top of Dolly, arranged both dolls in appropriate positions, and pushed the buttons behind their ears.

She took the bottle into the living-room. She poured herself a drink.

Ron said, 'OK. I get it. But you've got to see it my way, too. We do a deal, right?'

'I might go back on it,' Edgar said.

'And then I'd come after you. And I've got a lot of friends, Ed. They don't all have real good manners, either. You think about that.'

Helen drank three large gulps of her drink. She could hear the dolls. After a few seconds, the others heard too.

'What's that?' Edgar said.

'What's going on out there?' Ron asked. 'Who else is in this house? You trying to pull something on me?'

'Let's go see,' Helen suggested. She bounced towards the door and danced into the hallway. The raucous noise of the dolls drew the two men after her.

She smiled as she flung open the door to show Auto and Dolly engaged on what must have been round two of the full ten-patterned cycle: he whispering, 'I could really go for you, you know,' and she panting, 'Oh, you gorgeous hunk of man,' as he began to repeat, 'Bellissima,' with increasingly frenzied enthusiasm.

Edgar and Ron called out curses. They rushed past Helen and grabbed Auto. They tore him away from his exertions. They got him down on the ground and began to kick him. Then they hit out at each other. Helen took the opportunity to batter Dolly with the bottle she still held. Vermouth sloshed over the bed, on to the fighting men. Edgar slapped her across the face. The dolls, against all odds, continued to try to fornicate with anything and anyone they encountered, still mouthing expressions of rapturous delight, still whispering endearment and flattery; whereas Helen, Ron and Edgar roared out obscenities: they picked up any weapons they could find, laying about with pokers, shovels, baseballs bats. Pieces of the dolls flew across the room. Springs twanged against the walls and ceiling. Reels of tape unwound themselves among the wreckage. And the battle went on; until at last – their faces contorted by hatred – husband, wife and stranger stood bruised, bloody, half-clothed and sweating among the rubble of what they had been fighting over: out of breath in the silent room, unable to speak. There was nothing to say. They stared as if they didn't recognize each other, or the room they were standing in, or any other part of the world which, until just a few moments before, had been theirs.

The End of Tragedy

Mamie joined Sal at Luigi's after the Friday evening perform-
ance. Sal was already sitting down, eating cherry cheesecake.
Friday was the one day she went off her diet intentionally.
Friday was also their payday.

Mamie didn't need to lose weight. She'd never liked sugary
foods much, and though recently she'd started to drink at least
one glass of something every night, she burned it off in the
daytime. She was the pretty one: baby face and nice legs. Her
only genuine acting talent was for screaming. It was a gift she
hadn't known about until she'd gone to audition for a play based
on a murder mystery.

'Can you scream?' the stage manager had asked her. He was
leaning against a wall backstage, while he drank coffee out of a
paper cup and watched the stage-hands strike a set from the
matinée.

'Sure, I guess so,' she'd said.

'Let's hear it.'

Mamie had looked around at the crowded stage, up at the
lights and sandbags. She'd suddenly felt angry and desperate
and as if she was never going to get anywhere in life or do
anything. She screamed.

There was dead silence afterwards. And a voice from somewhere said, 'Mother of God, what was that?'

'You're hired,' the stage-manager told her. It was her first
break. She played the maid who found the body at the end of
Act I. She didn't have any words to say, only the scream. But she

got so good at it that she made an impression on the management and they recommended her to the company where she met Sal. That was one of the few times she hadn't had to go to bed with someone in order to get a job.

Sal thought she was crazy. Sal had never slept with anybody for anything except fun. 'It's because you're too nice,' she said, 'and you don't think you can get what you want any other way.'

'I'm not very good at anything else,' Mamie told her. 'I'm just beginning to realize: I'm probably never going to be very good as an actress.'

'You certainly never will if you go around with that attitude. Think big, Mamie.'

Sal was smart and a quick study. She could sing, she could dance; she had a strong vocal delivery. But she didn't have the looks. She'd grown up in Iowa, although you'd never have guessed she wasn't a girl from the city. With Mamie, you could still tell she was a country girl. If you listened hard to the accent, you could even place her: West Virginia. She hadn't had many friends growing up. At her school the girls had either felt sorry for her because of her family, or despised her; or, later, been jealous because of the boys. And she'd had only two other close friends in the theatre besides Sal: one had married and the other had decided to stay with the telephone job she used to take between parts.

Mamie had been in hundreds of plays. She had even had lines in some of them. But neither she nor Sal had ever had the lead. They'd been in the company for five months while other girls had dropped out for various reasons: broken legs, proposals, suicide attempts, illnesses, parents who caught up with them, boyfriends who needed a girl who stayed put.

They'd studied cooking in Memphis, taken modern dance lessons in Peoria, attended a Japanese self-defence class in Kansas City. The Kansas City run had been the best. That was when Sal had asked Mamie to teach her the scream.

'We'd better go somewhere out in the open,' Mamie had said.

They'd taken a picnic to one of the places they'd seen on the way to their classes. They had plenty of time on their hands, since Sal was trying to be faithful to a drummer whose band was playing in Chicago, and Mamie had just broken up with a tennis instructor and thought she was falling in love with their self-defence teacher, whom they called Mr Moto because they kept disagreeing about his real name.

Before they ate anything, Sal wanted to hear the scream. Mamie stood away from the tree under which they'd spread their tablecloth. She screamed three times.

'Now, you,' she said.

But Sal's screams had nothing special about them. They were either completely ordinary, or sounded false. Mamie screamed with an immediate, thrilling release of mindless terror.

'How do you do it?' Sal asked. 'Where do you start?'

'That's just it. You don't start. It comes all in one piece, from way down deep inside. It hurt my throat a lot in the beginning, but when I got used to it, I really started to enjoy it. Now it makes me feel good.'

'It's horrible to hear. It's totally unnerving.'

'If you practise, you'll pick it up. You've got to think it, sort of. And then you just let her rip.'

'Let's eat first,' Sal had said. And she'd never bothered with the scream after that. It remained the one thing Mamie could do better than other people.

Each of them had worked in companies where they'd been underpaid, not paid, and run out on. The costumes had gone astray between one town and another, the props had broken, someone had sold the scenery and disappeared with the proceeds. The troupe they were with now was pretty well organized and it paid promptly. Friday was always a big occasion. They still couldn't forget the times when the funds had never come through. Mamie had even gone with men for money, although they hadn't put it that way and she didn't think of it like that. It had always been: 'Can you lend me something till the end of the week?' The answer would be, 'Sure, and how about coming out for a meal?' And afterwards, going back to their place with them and somehow forgetting to pay them back, which she knew they didn't expect her to do anyway. She hadn't worried about it. There weren't many men she couldn't make herself feel fond of after a couple of drinks. Once in a while an evening would turn out to be a lot more unpleasant than she'd imagined, but that could also happen with the ones who seemed to be quiet and well-behaved.

The main effect promiscuity had had on her was to make her more susceptible to the idea of love. True love, she was certain, would wipe out other experiences. Love was like gambling in that respect – the big win cancelled all your losses. And when true love came, she'd give up the stage. Love was the greatest role of all: everybody knew that.

*

Mamie came in late because she'd been trying to catch a last look at the man out front. She sat down opposite Sal and started to go over the menu, which she already knew by heart.

Luigi himself, whose real name was Harry, took their order. He winked at Sal. After he'd gone, Mamie whispered, 'He's got a thing about you.' Sal made her horror-movie face and let it freeze for a couple of seconds.

Their wine arrived, and the cannelloni. Sal said softly, 'He was there again tonight. Same seat, same row. Talk about having a thing about somebody.'

'Probably came in to get out of the rain.'

'It isn't raining. You're the one he keeps staring at.'

'How can you tell?'

'Well, can't you? Anybody like that looked at me, I'd be able to tell.'

'I'm half blinded by those lights,' Mamie said.

She'd spotted him the first time he'd been to see the show. She noticed him because he looked just like the kind of man she'd always wanted to meet – the kind you saw in the movies and just as good-looking, except that he didn't look like an actor. He looked more real.

The second time he turned up, all the girls started to talk about him. It wasn't such a rotten show, but nobody could say it was *My Fair Lady*, either. The takings were low, the house was at least half empty. It was strange to find someone coming back for more, especially a young man. This Friday night would be his fourth time in two weeks.

'I wish he'd make up his mind,' Sal said. 'If he's a talent scout, he should have known on the first night. And if it's anything else – well, I guess he ought to know that pretty quick, too.'

'Do you get the feeling you're playing up to it?'

'Are you kidding? The whole back line of the chorus is knocking itself out. I'm exhausted. Aren't you?'

'I guess so.'

'In fact, I'm so tired, I think I'm going to need some more of that cheesecake.' She waited for Mamie to say something, but Mamie never made any comments about food on a Friday; that was their agreement.

*

Next day at the Saturday matinée he was sitting there again. And afterwards, as Mamie came out of the stage door exit, he was waiting for her. She could see him clearly for the first time, standing close and directly in the light. He looked so wonderful she couldn't believe it: like an ad for something.

He said, 'Miss Davenport? I hope you don't mind my coming backstage like this, but I really did enjoy your performance.'

'Oh,' she said. ' 'Course I don't mind. It's nice when people come around to say they've liked the show. Makes us girls feel appreciated.'

He smiled, showing beautiful teeth. 'My name's Carter Mathews,' he said. It sounded like a made-up name, but in her line of work she was used to that.

'And you know mine,' she said. 'Rhoda Davenport. Hi.'

They shook hands. He asked her to come out for a cup of coffee, or a snack, a drink, or dinner, or anything at all. 'Maybe supper after the evening performance?'

'That would be best,' she said. 'We're always kind of rushed on a Saturday.'

'Fine. I'll meet you here after the show and take you out for a big meal somewhere, put you in a cab afterwards. We can have a nice talk.'

She spent the break between performances with Sal. They went to their Saturday cafeteria. Sal ordered a salad without dressing. She said, 'Look, Mamie, I've been thinking. You don't want a salad?'

'Just the sandwich. I've got a date. I've got a date like you never saw in your life.'

'What's his name?'

'Carter.'

'His first name.'

'That's his first name.'

'Hotsy-totsy. You're in the big league now. I guess his last name's George or something? The nurse read the certificate backwards?'

'You wait till you see him.'

'What's he like?'

'Delightful, delovely, de works.'

'Hair and eyes?'

'Uh-huh.'

'Mamie, what does he look like?'

'Hollywood smile. Very kind of alert-looking. You know. Sort of light brown hair. Grey eyes. Real nice. I mean, honest.' Just to tease, she kept back the information that he was the man from the audience.

They talked for an hour about Carter and whether he was going to be The One. Mamie tended to jump into affairs with both feet flying and then to cry on Sal's shoulder for weeks about what a bum she'd picked, again.

Sal broke down and ordered the Roquefort dressing and a couple of doughnuts. She said, 'I've been thinking: that girl we met last spring. Well – not girl. Suzanne.'

'That's a cheerful subject.'

'What I was thinking, was: I don't want to end up like that.'

'No reason why you should. Just don't do it.'

'I don't mean killing myself. I mean before – how discouraged she was; never getting any good parts, sleeping around with guys that said they'd help her and didn't. Hitting the bottle, taking sleeping pills, and a whole lot of other things too, I guess. Getting old, and nothing to show for it.'

'It's a hazard of the profession, that's what they say. Never a dull moment, and no security. Isn't it better than being stuck behind a sink all day?'

'The older I get, the more I figure maybe the stove and the sink wouldn't be so bad. Especially when I wonder about kids. I keep thinking, every once in a while, how nice it would be.'

'Well, find a man first. After that, it's up to you.'

'Trouble is, I'm too used to thinking myself into a part.'

'So, you might find out after about a year, you were sick of that part and wanted to try another one. Where would you be then?'

'Stuck,' Sal said.

*

He was there at the stage door, right on time, and took her out to dinner. Everything seemed easy and relaxed. Then he said, 'I guess you know that what I was really interested in was taking you out like this and having some fun. You don't mind?'

She giggled, a bit drunk. She'd shot up to the ceiling on half a bottle of white wine and felt great. She said, 'Well, I did sort of suspect something like that.'

'But now that we're getting so friendly and I can tell what a nice girl you are, I wonder if you could help me out. See, that's why I was going around looking at shows in the first place. I mean – not really, but I don't usually get the time to enjoy myself like that, and I didn't know how to begin. I was thinking of maybe going to a private detective.'

'You've lost me,' she said. 'What are we talking about?'

'A job. But it isn't important. I'm just going to have to find somebody at some point.'

'What kind of job?'

'I guess you could call it impersonation, but there wouldn't be anything shady about it. All completely straightforward.'

'Guaranteed legit?'

'Oh, definitely. Like I said. Maybe it could be described as entertainment; you know, sometimes a family gives big week-end parties and they need a girl to make sure it runs smoothly and looks good – sort of like being a receptionist.'

Mamie put her glass to her mouth again. She'd met one woman who had hired herself out as a go-go organizer for parties back in the late sixties, and even back then it hadn't been above-board.

'What I actually need,' he said, 'is just a girl who'll pose as my fiancée when I go visit my cousins.'

She could see from his face that he didn't mean anything weird, but she didn't know what to answer.

He said, 'I guess it sounds silly.'

'Why? Why do you need the fiancée?'

'It's to take the heat off of somebody else.'

'What?'

'It's so dumb. There's this girl who was the girl next door when I was growing up. They kept trying to push us together all the time. And she's all right, just – we aren't interested in each other. Well, for a while I used to go out with her because it kept our parents happy and we could both go where we liked and do what we liked, and we'd just give each other alibis. Then she got mixed up with a married man, so she needed me as a cover. And I had my eye on somebody else too, so it was convenient for both of us. You see how the thing worked?'

'Sounds pretty good.'

'Now she wants to get married to this guy, but her parents aren't going to accept it while I'm still on the loose. I know them.'

'What about your parents?'

'They died three years ago.'

'Both of them?'

He nodded. He looked so sad all of a sudden that she didn't want to ask him any more.

He took her back to her room and kissed her at the door. As he said goodnight he made her laugh, and, while she was still laughing, he walked over the threshold with her and kicked the door shut behind them.

'You've left the cab downstairs,' she told him.

'Maybe you'd better come to my place,' he suggested. 'I could tell you all about how to be my fiancée. I'm too drunk to be dangerous. In fact, I'm kind of shy anyway. But I don't want to have to say goodnight yet.'

She said OK. They got back into the taxi and went to his hotel. She marched straight to the side stairs and he met her on the landing after he'd picked up the key.

As soon as they got into his room it turned out that he wasn't drunk at all. Everything started to go a lot faster than she'd had any idea it would. They were in bed and she could see her clothes on the chair and on the floor. He wasn't a bit shy or even very nice. He was actually a little rough. She was still high enough not to be scared, but she bruised easily, and he was pinching and scratching and biting her.

'You're bruising me all over,' she said.

He told her to shut up.

'You're hurting me.'

'Shut up,' he said, 'or I'll hit you.'

That shut her up. She turned her head to the side. She should have known better. It didn't happen often that she was completely wrong about a man, but every time it did, it seemed that it was the kind of stupid mistake she always made, and always her fault. The number of men, she thought, she'd said yes to just because she was lonely; and afterwards you could tell they didn't even like you much. She was nearly ready to cry.

He lit a cigarette and put his left arm behind his head. He said, 'You're very inhibited for an actress.'

'What did you think I was – a professional?'

'I just thought, most of the actresses I know are into everything.'

Including impersonation, she thought. Who knew what the story was there? He was obviously a good liar and better at acting than she was. His whole bedroom technique was worked out like a part: a solo part. A star part. He could screw for the Olympics.

She began to feel worse and worse. She reached down, found her slip, slung her legs over the side of the bed and put the slip on over her head.

'What are you doing?' he said.

'I think I'd better be going.'

'What for?' He pulled her back and tried to turn her around. She didn't want to look at him.

'What's the matter? I thought you were having a pretty good time. Stick around. I'll introduce you to the whole of the repertoire.'

She tried to stand up again, saying, 'I think I might be too amateur.'

'Come back here. I want to talk to you about being introduced as my fiancée.'

'Oh? That's for real?'

'I told you.'

'I thought maybe you'd just made it up.'

'Why would I do that?'

'I don't know. People make things up sometimes.' Sometimes they even said they loved you when you didn't need to hear it. That was a thing he hadn't done. Maybe he'd figured that with a girl like her, he wouldn't have to bother.

He said, 'You've got the feeling you're being used, huh?'

'That doesn't worry me. That usually works both ways.' What worried her was the lack of friendliness. It had reminded her of auditioning: when she'd be afraid that her performance was breaking up, and would become aware of the contempt aimed at her from out in the darkness where the judges were sitting, watching her go through her paces.

'Come back over here,' he told her. 'We'll get acquainted.'

All of a sudden he was sweet and loving to her. He said he was sorry he'd upset her; he hadn't been with a woman for so long that he'd forgotten how to behave. She didn't believe that. And then she didn't care. She didn't even care that she was giving too much away. She knew all at once that he was The One, as she and Sal used to call it; so, everything was all right, even though she didn't know him very well yet.

They laughed about the job of posing as his fiancée. And he asked her about the other shows she'd been in. They laughed over them, too. He told her something about himself and his work; he was a lawyer. That impressed her. He'd come to town on business, to get someone to sign a paper for his firm; she kept forgetting the real name of the place because he liked to refer to the partnership as Eargerm and Stripling: the names had something to do with an office joke. They were the ones who had paid for the hotel the first time, when he'd been to see the show and decided that he wanted to have another look.

She told Sal everything, naturally. Sal said, 'How you land yourself in these situations. He sounds like a real firecracker.'

'He's great. He sort of took me by storm. I didn't think he was very nice at first. But he was just nervous. Can you imagine?'

'No,' Sal said seriously. 'He doesn't look in any way, even remotely, like the nervous type. Are you sure he's OK?'

Of course she was sure. She was sure for six weeks. And at the end of four, she was pretty sure she was pregnant. When he asked her to come back to his home town to meet his relatives, she walked out on her job straight away. 'And afterwards,' she said, 'I'll move, so you won't have to keep travelling back and forth. I could move in with you.'

'Or we could find you another place of your own,' he told her. 'We'll see.'

'All right,' she said. By that time she'd know definitely about the pregnancy. By that time anything could have happened.

*

He did the driving. It was a new car and he owned it. His looks, his manner, his clothes: you could tell that everything about him was all right – respectable, coming from a good family that went back generations. He had his touchy side, but a lot of people had a funny temper.

It had been a long time since she'd been out of the city. She looked at the landscape moving past and felt happy. She loved him. She was convinced that this time she'd get married.

He didn't talk much except to tell her about the family she'd be meeting: Katherine and Waverley Chase, who had been his parents' best friends; and their three sons: Russell, Randall and Raymond. Russell had been married to Carter's cousin, Julie. And for a few years when they were young, Carter and Julie and the Chase boys had all gone to the same school; until his parents had moved away.

'They're cousins by marriage?' she asked.

'They aren't anything. They were neighbours and my cousin married into their family. But we'll be staying with them.'

They checked in overnight at a motel that had an indoor skating rink as well as a large, heated pool and a room full of computer games. The restaurant wasn't bad, either; there was a help-yourself salad bar plus the usual waitress service. According to a cardboard notice on the table, private rooms were available for receptions; catering could be arranged. The building seemed to be the social centre for several small towns in the neighbourhood. Many of the diners were dressed up in Saturday night clothes: the women, in teetery heels, sported glitter and sleazy, backless dresses. One young couple, who were sitting in a booth near their table, had gone further than the rest and made themselves into living paintings: their hair had been striped with colours as bright as the feathers of a cockatoo, and made to stand out like sunbursts around their heads. The boy wore a great many earrings on each ear; the girl had a white, powdered face, red eye-shadow, black lips and green fingernails. In every other way the two were rather conservative – dressed in black leather and not flaunting their unusual appearance but sitting quietly together, his arm over her shoulders. He was reading a copy of *Popular Mechanics*, she was doing a crossword puzzle in a book. They were relaxed and unselfconscious with each other, like an old married couple.

Mamie thought they were terrific. They looked like fun. But Carter said, 'I'm surprised they let those two in. What a pair.' And all at once she understood that the dividing-line he had drawn between himself and a couple like that was final. He'd never associate with them. So now she too would have to keep at a distance from such odd-looking characters. He had already told her what subjects she should try never to bring up when they arrived at the Chases'. 'Don't do this,' he'd said, and, 'Don't do that.'

They went back to their room. She put fifty cents in the bed massage and laughed hysterically as the mattress lumbered ponderously from side to side.

'What's it supposed to do?' she yelled. 'That's the slowest bump-and-grind routine I've ever seen.'

'Not so loud,' he told her. 'There are people next door.'

'Come on over here. I've always wanted to try out one of these.'

He went to brush his teeth. When he was finished, the bed had come to the end of its shimmy. He sat down on the edge.

He said, 'I think we'd better get a few things straight. We'll be there tomorrow.'

She looked up.

'Is your real name Rhoda?'

'My name's Mamie Hart.'

'Mamie?'

'For May. The month I was born.'

'Well, I guess it doesn't matter. I'll introduce you as Rhoda, if you like.'

'Not enough class, huh? One of my aunts was called Maybelle – it's supposed to be French. We called her Mabel. And my grandparents were named Herz. They changed it to Hart.'

'Is that a Jewish name?'

'Not that I know of. What is this? You want to see a racial purity badge or something? Sal used to say she got this kind of crap from people all the time. What would it matter, anyway? Jesus fucking Christ.'

He slapped her hard on the right side of the head. 'I told you not to use that word,' he said. 'If you want to trade obscenities in a bar-room brawl somewhere, you go right ahead. That's the place for them. You're a little old for me to have to wash out your mouth with soap.'

She burned all over. Tears had run from her eyes at the impact of the blow. She said, 'You know what an obscenity is? An obscenity is what you just did.'

'That's another thing. We've got to do something about your cheap dialogue. You've been in too many corny plays. You can't remember how real people talk.'

'I've got a very good memory. I'll remember this.' She pressed her hand against her face. Luckily he'd hit her fairly high up. She might have a black eye afterwards, but the teeth were all right. The teeth were money.

'As far as I'm concerned,' he said, 'you can be anything, and your name could be anything. It isn't me. It's some of the people you'll be meeting. I thought I'd better prepare you. Psychologically. You might find it hard to act your part.'

'Oh? What part is that?'

'There's something I should have explained. I should have told you a lot of things, but it started to get harder and harder to begin. What I said about this other girl – well: it isn't exactly like that. It's a long story.' He reached out to put his fingers against her cheek. She drew back a little. 'That's all I need,' he said; 'you turning up there with a black eye.'

'That's the only thing you're worried about, isn't it – that it's going to show? You don't care if you hurt me, only if it makes a mark.'

'Sure, I care. I'm just getting kind of nerved up, now we're so near. I don't want to drag you into it. What I needed was a hired professional. I should have gone to a private detective and paid them to find somebody.'

'What are you talking about?'

'My cousin Julie, who was married to this guy, Russell Chase; they call him Ross. We grew up together. She was my favourite cousin. Our families moved twice. When we were just kids, there wasn't anybody else around at all.'

'You slept with her.'

'You don't understand. She was my favourite cousin.'

'And you slept with her.'

'I guess so.'

'You can't remember whether you did or didn't?'

'There wasn't any need for it. We were completely . . . but we did, yes. When we were in our early teens, really still children. She was actually only twelve. Then my parents moved. I didn't see her for years. We wrote to each other. I used to think . . . We didn't meet again till she was getting married. I was invited. And I knew then. I realized at the reception. I almost started to make a speech, try to take her away with me. When I kissed her, we knew that the wedding was a big mistake. I looked around and there were all our relatives and all of his, everybody dressed up, eating and drinking, the noise: I thought I was going crazy. I asked her to go with me right then, that minute. And she said, "I can't."'

'So, you started sleeping with each other again,' Mamie said. It was what she would have expected; she'd been in plays like that.

He sat up and lit a cigarette, took one long drag and then stubbed it out in the ashtray. He said, 'We would have. I'd have made her get a divorce and it would have been all right. But we didn't get the time. They acted too fast. What they wanted was the money. It was divided in our family so there was part of it she got for her lifetime and then it reverted to me unless she had children. One of those complicated Trust things. I don't know what old man Chase did with their own money and investments, but they needed somebody to bail them out and they had to get hold of it in a way that meant nothing could become mine before a certain time. Anyway, that's it.'

'That's what?'

'That's why they killed her.'

'They went to jail for murder and now they're – '

'They killed her and got away with it. Nobody else suspected.'

'Carter, how can you know that?'

'I'm sure of it, positively. They were out mountain-climbing. Said she got too near the edge. Well, I don't believe it. I got a so-called suicide note from her. Very good job of copying her handwriting, but it just isn't the way she said things. And she'd have used some of our special names, and so on. That was why I wanted somebody to try to get them to confess. I thought: if I got a girl to – '

'Me?'

'Maybe it was only Ross. Or maybe the whole family was in on it.'

'Look,' she said, 'this is something crooked, isn't it? I've never been mixed up in anything crooked in my life.'

'I told you, Rhoda, it's on the level. All I want is for you to get them feeling guilty and losing their nerve.'

'But how could I do that?'

'Didn't I tell you? You look just like her. Like my cousin, Julie.'

'I feel sick,' she said.

'You relax. They're the ones that are going to be feeling bad. You just enjoy yourself.'

'Supposing these people did kill somebody – why wouldn't they kill me, too?'

'Because this time I'm here to protect you.'

*

'Katherine,' he said, 'this is Rhoda Hart. Waverley, Randall, Ray, Ross; Rhoda.'

Mamie shook hands with them all. She didn't understand why he'd used half of her real name and half of her stage name – especially why he hadn't done it the other way around, since

Hart had seemed to be the one he'd had doubts about. ('I just forgot,' he said later. 'I was concentrating so hard on whether you'd be OK. And then it was too late.')

They sat down. She felt herself being sized up by the mother. One of the sons, the one named Randall, handed her a sherry. There was a log fire burning in the fireplace. Katherine Chase asked, 'What part of the country do you come from, Miss Hart?'

'From the middle,' she said. 'Not really east or south. But not really anywhere else, either; in the mountains, from one of those small towns where everybody just wants to get out. It's funny how there's still any population in those areas. Nobody ever goes back.'

'"How you gonna keep 'em down on the farm?"' Waverley boomed. His wife swivelled her head around and glared at him.

'That's right,' Mamie said. 'Once you've had theatres and museums and nice restaurants and good clothes, going out and having fun – well, even if you want to settle down, it isn't going to be that kind of life again.'

'You never go back?' Randall asked. He'd treated her to a long look and touched her hand as he'd passed the glass to her. The important one, Russell, had barely given her a glance.

'There are a couple of people I send Christmas cards to,' she said. 'But my family's all gone now.' She stopped. There was a silence no one had foreseen. Suddenly it was absolute. She remembered her childhood. Her eyes filled with tears. She couldn't look at anyone.

'Yes, well,' the third brother, Raymond, said. 'Can I offer you a peanut? Or some of these things – what are they?'

'Cheese biscuits,' Katherine said.

'They look like something that's been burned by mistake.'

'No, thank you,' Mamie said. She smiled at Raymond. And as she did, out of the corner of her eye she saw Russell look up and stare at her.

The lunch went well. Waverley and Randall both got moderately drunk. Everyone except Russell retired afterwards for a nap. He stayed downstairs; 'to do some work,' he said.

The house was large enough so that she and Carter had been given separate rooms without having it look as though they were being kept apart for reasons of morality. Another one of his last-minute decisions had been to introduce her as a friend, not a fiancée. But their rooms were adjoining.

They went into her room and sat on the bed.

'If he's guilty about anything, he sure doesn't act it,' she said.

'Why would he be guilty? He doesn't feel sorry and he isn't scared that anybody knows. I still can't make up my mind about the others.'

'If guilt isn't going to worry him, there's no point in me being here. How's he going to go crazy if he doesn't care?'

'We've only been here a couple of hours. Give him a chance.'

'I like the one that offered me the peanut.'

'Raymond.'

'But she hates me. And she's got me numbered, all right. The others don't mind. But men don't, usually.'

'They do. They just show it differently.' He lay back on the bed and closed his eyes. He said, 'They're taking us out to the country club. Try to dance with all three of them.'

'You sound like a real promoter. Like one of those greaseballs that come up and say: you want a girl, a nice girl, a schoolteacher, my sister?'

'I could hit you again, you know.'

'And I could run downstairs and tell them all about your sneaky suspicions.'

'I'd say you were just some girl I knew, who kept hallucinating. I can make things up pretty fast.'

'But they've got to be thinking something. If I look just like her.'

'Maybe they haven't seen the resemblance yet.'

'Isn't it obvious?'

'Maybe not as obvious to them as it is to me.'

'Do you have a picture of her?'

'No.'

'Your favourite cousin? The girl you were in love with? You don't have a picture of her?'

'No.'

'Why not?' He was trying to make her think he was falling asleep. 'Why not?' she repeated.

'I tore them all up when she died,' he said.

*

For a while she believed the torn-up picture story. He could make her believe in anything for a while. And then he'd come up with some other mystification and blame her for being slow to understand what he meant. He'd criticize or correct her about something: her speech, her lipstick, the fact that her skirt was wrinkled. He had chosen and paid for most of her clothes himself, but she sometimes wore the wrong shoes or tied an old kerchief around her neck. He noticed everything like that.

She followed his orders and reported back to him. There were periods when he'd grow sulky or quiet; he'd sit on the side of the bed in his room and fix his eyes on the wall. All she wanted now was to make love, but he'd move out of her embrace when she tried to hold on to him. He told her it was better not to, while they were still in the Chases' house.

'You could try re-routing it on to the boys,' he said.

She didn't understand. One day he said, 'You aren't doing very much to make them interested in you.'

'What am I supposed to do? They think I'm your girlfriend, don't they? They aren't going to make a pass at somebody else's girl.'

'Of course they are. That's half the fun, taking a girl away from somebody else. Tell them a hard-luck story. Tell them anything.'

'I guess I should just lay it on the line and ask, "How did you all kill cousin Julie?"'

'For Christ's sake, no. Don't say anything about her.'

'He doesn't like me, you know. Ross doesn't.'

'First it was Katherine, now it's Russell. Everybody likes you fine.'

'No. The others do, all right. But he hardly even looks at me.'

'He's just a little under par with girls.'

'He swept your favourite cousin off her feet, didn't he? He must have something.'

'She was on the rebound. She was so hurt, she thought she needed a wet rag like that. She'd have turned down Randall and Ray.'

'And you?'

'See if you can get him to confide in you. Be a good listener. You know – all those things your mother told you.'

'My mother told me not to do it, but if I was going to do it, to make sure he had a bank balance first, and then get pregnant and go to his mother and cry.'

'Was that what she did herself?'

'Of course not. She married for love and he didn't amount to anything. That's why she wanted me to have a better life.'

*

She stood at the top landing and looked down. The carpeted and banistered stairways stretched away in three directions. Potted plants filled the landings with exuberant growth. They were placed in front of huge, ornate mirrors and thus appeared to spread their jungle-like foliage twice as widely as they actually did. The stairs too ran up and down in the mirrors as you approached your reflection.

She'd always wanted to live in such a house. In the part of the country where she'd grown up there were a few houses like that, but she'd never been inside one. Once she got to the city, she saw a lot of beautiful places: never any back home. She hadn't been up on the knoll; her life had been down at the bottom of the hill in one of the little brick boxes near the railroad tracks. Her mother had been proud to think that one day the miserable thing would be theirs. That was what the family had hoped for.

It hadn't worked out that way. Her mother had died early. And Mamie had had no money behind her. She figured that if she had to drop down into real poverty, it would be better to do it in a big place, where nobody knew her. Possibly it would be more fun, too.

She'd been right. But it hadn't always been fun. And the shack near the railroad was Home Sweet Home compared to some of the places she'd been in: like that hotel where – if you got behind in the rent – the manager would come around and you could either pay up or go to the washrooms with him; and that didn't cancel the debt, either – he'd just defer it.

'Are you interested in fish, Rhoda?' a voice said below her.

She looked into the long mirror by her side and saw Russell's head reflected between the green leaves of rubber plants. She turned.

'To eat?'

'To look at while I feed them.'

'Oh,' she said. 'Sure. What are they, in a tank?'

'In an aquarium. I'm taking care of it while the school's on vacation.'

He drove her out to the deserted school. A light snow was falling. Indoors the radiators clanked. She hadn't been prepared for the different scale of the furniture, and was astonished at how small the desks and chairs were.

He walked her through into a hallway that smelled of sweeping compound. Paintings and crayon drawings, a thumbtack in each corner, covered the walls. Some of the pictures were hung fairly high up, but most had been set at the eye-level of a small child.

They entered another, larger classroom where, at the far end, an immense aquarium stood in an alcove that had evidently been made for it. The water bubbled gently, the fish propelled themselves slowly around and around. It was the biggest fish tank she'd seen outside a bar.

'Some interesting specimens,' he told her. She watched him shake the food into the water and check some gauges at the back. He wrote in a notebook, returned it to his pocket and moved his reading glasses up to the top of his head. Then he came and stood beside her, telling her the names of the various fish.

She put her fingers against the glass and pointed. 'That one?' she asked. 'And that one there?'

He put his arm around her. He kissed her neck. He slid his hand up under her sweater. She was about to push him away when she remembered Carter.

She let him keep going. He asked her in a whisper if it was all right. He didn't seem to her at all like someone who could ever have killed anybody. He seemed much more like a man who'd lost his wife and was dying of loneliness. She felt sorry for him. She said yes, it would be all right. He put their coats on the floor and flicked out the lights. She took off his glasses, which he'd forgotten he still had on.

On the drive back, he said something about not wanting to upset anything between her and Carter.

'Don't worry about that,' she told him. 'There hasn't been anything between us for a long time.'

'I thought you and he were together.'

'No. I think he was feeling kind of low after his girlfriend left him. He just invited me along for company.'

She asked him to tell her about himself. He talked about marine biology and the study of ancient oceans from the fossil evidence.

He wanted to know about her, so she told him more or less the truth, leaving Carter out of it. Then she laughed. She said, 'I can't get over all those tiny little chairs and tables. It looked like pixieland in there. But it was nice.' She hugged him. She felt that he was a friend now; there was no question that he liked her. He liked her a lot. It wasn't like the beginning with Carter, where she kept feeling afterwards that in spite of everything, maybe she hadn't quite made the grade.

'Once,' he told her, 'when they were repainting in the town hall, everyone had to use the school for meetings. All the stuffed shirts and obstructionists had to sit at the kiddies' desks. They had their knees jammed inside and their thighs bulging over the seats, and there they were, muttering and scowling and trying to find someplace to rest their elbows. God, they looked silly. And still taking themselves so seriously, and the great importance of their jobs. That was wonderful. A friend of mine on the local paper even got some pictures, but they wouldn't let him print them.'

Before he stopped the car, he asked her if she knew how to get to his room.

*

At the end of the week Carter took her back to town. It was supposed to be for a few days only; he'd return to his apartment in Chicago and let Ross make plans to start visiting her. Russell had said he wanted to see her before the geological conference he was to attend at the beginning of the month.

She still didn't understand what was going on. Sometimes Carter made her so confused that she stopped listening to what he was saying. She got ready to move out of town; that didn't take long. She had few possessions other than the clothes he'd bought for her. Now that she wasn't working and had the time, she couldn't fill up her days. She knew that she ought to think and plan ahead. But she just sat; or, sometimes, she went for walks.

She was out walking one day and started to feel so tired that she wanted to sit down. She was in the middle of town: not a bench anywhere in sight. Her head began to hurt. She saw a church in the distance and made for it.

She slumped into a pew at the back and kept her head down. For a while she thought she was the only visitor to the building, but gradually she became aware that someone else had been up at the front when she'd entered. Sounds came to her of the person shuffling around, then footsteps went down the side aisle and stopped a few yards away from her. She moved her eyes slowly until she was able to see a long, black skirt and heavy shoes: some sort of man of God. She didn't raise her head because she knew that the headache would keep getting worse unless she stayed still. It hurt so much already that she didn't realize she might be sitting in an attitude of worship.

She thought of how, pretty soon, she was going to have to tell Carter about the baby. She had no idea how he was going to take the news. She herself was sometimes glad about it – since it was a hold over him; yet sometimes she thought no, he'd go to other women because of it. And when she considered that possibility, she didn't want to be pregnant.

The pain began to disperse, and at last went altogether. She got to her feet. On her way out she saw the man, a priest or preacher, standing near the entrance. He beamed at her. He'd probably thought she was praying, instead of just trying to get rid of a headache. She went back to her room and to the telephone.

Carter called her up. He told her to go out with Russell. He rented an apartment for her. She took the bus in to the theatre to say goodbye to all the girls and moved, promising to send the address and phone number.

*

Carter paced up and down in the new place he'd found for her. He said he could no longer see how this scheme was going to work out. He didn't know what to do. He'd had a dream about Julie in which she'd stood at the edge of a mountain view and pointed at him and said he wasn't fulfilling his promise.

He kept her up late talking when she was falling asleep with weariness. He was impatient and abrupt and made her cry. One evening she said she couldn't stand any more. 'I keep doing just whatever you say,' she told him. 'I'm beginning to think this whole thing is nothing but lies. And you aren't nice to me.'

'I want you to ask him over for the weekend or something. His hours are pretty free outside of those meetings and research trips.'

'I think I'm pregnant,' she said.

He was delighted. He said, 'Ask him over and tell him.'

'It's yours. You know that already.'

'But he won't know.'

'Carter, why do you want all this?'

'They killed her. I keep telling you. Don't you believe me?'

'I believed you when you said you liked me, and when you told me the story about the girl next door, and I believed you about your cousin. Now what else do I have to believe?'

'And that they murdered her.'

'And how they pushed her off the mountainside, sure. But

most of all, I believe it that you hit me in the face that time. And I think you're planning something bad for me.'

'Not for you,' he said. 'Nothing bad for you. For them.'

'But everything's changed now.'

'It's perfect. You get married to him, and then we've got him.'

'How?'

'He'll trust you then.'

'Carter, if he really did kill anyone, maybe I'll be in danger.'

'They killed her for the money. You'll be fine.'

'Listen: you're a lawyer. If I get married to him, the baby's going to be his – isn't that right?'

'What did you want to go and get pregnant for in the first place? You aren't usually so careless, are you?'

'I guess I forgot.'

'Or maybe you were following your mother's advice and thought I'd marry you myself.'

'I should never have told you that. It isn't nice of you to use things against me. You shouldn't do that to people you love.'

'Who's talking about love?' he said. 'Pick up the phone, Rhoda. I think you should give Ross a call.'

'Maybe I should tell him everything.'

'Don't try it. I told you: I'm a lot better at this kind of thing than you'll ever be. You just do what I say, and we'll come out of it OK in the end.'

'You mean, we'll get married?'

'Eventually, yes. Of course. Didn't you know that?'

'But if I'm already married to him? A divorce takes a long time.'

'I'm the lawyer, remember. I can take care of that side of things.'

He dialled the number for her and pulled her to his side. As he gave her the receiver, he put his hand over her left breast and kept it there. Her heart thumped so hard that she couldn't think straight. She laid her hand over his and turned to look at his face. He mouthed words to her. She said, 'Hello? Could I speak to Russell Chase, please?'

*

When she told Russell he smiled a little, grinned, and then threw his arms around her. She burst into tears of remorse.

He took charge. He talked and talked: about how this was the best way, in some countries it was still considered the only way to get married, and he was sure he'd be good with children; he'd always thought babies were very interesting – he'd always wished that he hadn't been the youngest in his family.

He made her blow her nose and told her that they'd go down to the Town Hall in the morning.

'Did you want a church wedding?'

'No,' she gasped, 'definitely not a church wedding. It wouldn't feel right. Tell you the truth, I've never felt easy about church. Where I come from, it's all Holy Rollers and pointing the finger of sin, and the whole thing makes you feel kind of horrible even before you've thought of doing anything wrong.'

'That's just as well. I wouldn't want to go through it a second time, either. I don't know if you know: I was married before. There's so much we've got to catch up on, find out about each other.'

'Carter told me,' she said. 'And she died in some kind of accident?'

'Yes.'

'I'm sorry.'

'Yes. I'll tell you some day. I guess everyone takes it for granted in peacetime that only old people die; but it isn't true. Anybody can die, from any cause. It's a shock when it happens to someone your own age, or younger.'

He asked if there was anyone from her family she'd want to invite to the ceremony. She shook her head. She said, 'My family isn't – wasn't – anything like yours. I mean, you can tell I'm not a college girl. But my father was an honest working man. He had a job with the railroad. It's just that after my mother died, he started to drink a lot. So, finally one night he drank too much and slipped and hit his head. I don't think they were the kind of people your mother would approve of much.'

'Mother is marvellous, but she's a terrible snob. You must

have noticed. She's a snob about everybody and everything. Just ignore it.'

She agreed to all the wedding plans. A few hours later, however, she thought again. She phoned Carter.

'Stop crying,' he snapped at her. 'I can't hear half of what you're saying. And anyway, I told you already: not on the phone. I'd better come over.' He hung up immediately, without saying goodbye.

She felt tired and seasick and as if she'd never be able to stop wanting to cry. When she opened the door to him, he blew smoke into her face from his cigarette and didn't kiss her or touch her. 'Sit down,' he ordered. 'What is it, Rhoda?'

'I can't go through with it.'

'Doesn't he like the idea of being a father?'

'He loves it. He's so nice. I can't do it.'

'He's so nice, he pushed Julie out into empty space and watched her fall a hundred miles down, without batting an eyelid.'

'It's your baby. Don't you have any feelings about it?'

He crossed to the sofa, tossed his coat over the arm and sat down next to her. He put out what was left of his cigarette. 'You know why I chose you,' he said.

'Sure. You knew I needed the money.'

'I knew you needed the money, and you'd need me, and you'd get used to nice things fast. And you look right.'

'Like her,' she said.

'Only a little. Only the same general type, and that's how people spot resemblances: by the type. If anyone wanted to compare you both detail by detail, you actually look completely different. And you're a lot prettier, of course.'

'But you loved her.'

'Not really. A little. It's nice to have cousins – somebody who's midway between friends and brothers or sisters. She didn't deserve that. They did it because of the money. We were supposed to inherit it fifty–fifty, but then my grandfather ... You know, sometimes people try to be so helpful when they should just keep their big mouths shut and not go telling about some escapade you thought was amusing. Old people don't always have the same kind of humour. But she was fine; she turned up trumps – said we'd split it just the way he intended in the first will. And she was all ready to hand it over when the Chase family decided to take a skiing holiday way up in the mountains. That's another thing: she was really good at all those winter sports. She'd never have lost her footing. They thought it was such a good choice because it would look natural: but not to me.' He put his elbows on his knees, his head in his hands, and sighed. 'That's the way it was. They cleaned up. Pulled their lousy bank out of the red, and everything. But I swore to get it back. I didn't know exactly how. What I had in mind was getting some kind of evidence to threaten them with.'

'Like what?'

'I don't know any more. I was going to play it by ear. Then I fell in love with you. I didn't mean to. I never fall in love with anybody. It's ruined everything.' He leaned over and laid his head in her lap. He sighed again, loudly, several times. It sounded like sobbing. She smoothed her hand over his hair.

'Are we going to get married?' she asked.

'Afterwards.'

'After what, Carter?'

'After we get the money.' He sat up and reached for another cigarette.

She got to her feet. She said, 'You couldn't love me and let me sleep with another man. You couldn't want me to get married to another man. Not if you loved me.'

'It's only for a little while. And you'll still be mine. Tell him you can't, because of the baby. Maybe you shouldn't, anyway. It might be bad for you.'

She started to answer and began to stammer. She couldn't go on. He took her arm and pulled her down beside him. 'Think of the life we'll have afterwards,' he said. 'And our kids, too. All the things we can do.'

'But we could be happy now. We could have a good life. Why can't you forget about it?'

'Why should I?' he shouted. 'Why shouldn't I have all the good things I was meant to have?'

'You can work for them. We both can.'

'Not that kind of money. That kind you've got to inherit.'

'It's too bad you're a man. Otherwise, you could marry for it.'

'Oh, I could still do that. Couldn't I? Everything in perfect working order.'

'You wouldn't.'

'Too much time and effort. This way's better.'

'Not for me. If we love each other, we should do it the right way.'

'Get married, be poor, and get to be as unhappy as everybody else?'

'Lots of people are poor. I grew up that way. It wasn't so bad.'

'Wasn't it?'

'It was better than what you've got in mind. Anyway, you talk about being poor, but you've got a good job.'

'It takes me everything I earn just to keep up the payments on my apartment. Christ, I don't even like the place. When would we ever take a vacation, or get a house? And with a baby, too?'

'But I'll be his wife. Every night – '

'Well, you did it once. More than once.'

She'd forgotten what she had or hadn't done, or how often. She remembered that he'd made her so miserable and angry that she'd have done anything.

'That isn't important,' he added.

'Marriage is even more. It's more than you think. I've seen it happen with a lot of girls. You think it's just like an official version of the usual thing, but it isn't.'

'It's only the piece of paper and how people think about it. Society's approval.'

'It's everything,' she said. 'It's the whole family. It's stronger than you've got any idea. And no amount of money is worth giving up happiness for.'

'It's mine,' he insisted. 'And I can't take that job much longer. I've worked my ass off in that place. When you start out, they work you right around the clock. They work you into the ground.'

'But that's over. You told me, you're going to be a junior partner.'

'Big deal. So I can have thirty more years of working myself into the grave for them. I want to get out. All the way out, and be free.'

'Being a lawyer,' she said, 'is a nice job, well-paid, steady.'

'Nine to five every day, to the end of my days?'

'I don't understand what you think is so bad about it.'

'You saw their house – that's only part of it. And the bastards have thrown more than half of it away. Russell gets through money like a drunken sailor. Every minute we waste, there's less of it left. Do this for me, Rhoda. Please. I promise it'll be OK in the end.'

'How can it be? How are we even going to see each other if I'm married to somebody else?'

'I'll work something out,' he said. 'And don't look so sad. Think of it like going into enemy country as a spy during wartime. You've got to be brave.'

'And be a good actress,' she said. She gave up. She gave in. She married Russell.

*

When she was seven months pregnant, Mamie thought she couldn't take anything any longer. She missed Carter all the time. She had no friends except Russell, and he – she was now sure – didn't intend, as he had first promised, to move out of his parents' house. 'It's so comfortable,' he said. 'Plenty of room for all my specimens and for the periodicals, too. We'd need a huge place if we moved. Don't you like it here?'

'I'm like a guest. I never even wash a dish.'

'You're the first girl I ever heard of who liked washing dishes.'

'You know what I mean.'

She asked if she could go back to town just for the weekend to see a friend. He agreed straight away. He trusted her completely. When they had signed the joint insurance papers, he'd had himself insured for so much that if he died, she'd never have to take a job again. She'd be a rich woman. It worked the other way around too, of course, but that was only sensible if he was ever going to find himself in the position of having to bring up a child on his own.

She made a reservation at the kind of hotel she'd never stayed in before. And she started to telephone Carter before she'd even unpacked. She couldn't get through to him either at his apartment or at the office. She tried for hours, then she went out for a walk.

It was a cool day. In the park the flowers looked wrong for the time of year. Mothers and babysitters, dressed in coats and sweaters, sat on the benches while the children they were looking after played nearby. She should have been feeling good.

She thought of sitting down on a bench, but kept walking. Her fur coat was unbuttoned, the large swell of her body bulging through the opening, but she didn't feel cold; the heat generated by the foetus added to her own warmth. If she sat down anywhere, she knew someone would come up to her and ask about the baby. Now that it was so prominent, everyone did. They were just being friendly, but she sometimes wanted to say, 'Go take an interest in somebody else's stomach.'

She walked down into a section of town she knew from touring days. She thought about Sal, who was in another company now. She remembered the name of the company. It would be nice to see Sal, she thought. She bought a newspaper; there, among the ads on the theatre page, she found the address: the place where Sal's show was playing. She waved down a taxi, went to the theatre and bought a ticket for the orchestra. Now that she had money, she didn't think twice about buying an expensive seat.

The place was nearly deserted. A few old ladies, sitting two-by-two and wearing their hats, were bunched together in the front rows. She remembered those matinée audiences: how there were always two old ladies, usually in the front row, who would talk to each other all through the show in voices just as loud as your own.

The play was terrible. It was about an American sculptor living in Italy with his wife. Once he'd been good, but now he was reaching middle age and losing his talent, and he'd fallen in love with the Italian girl who was acting as his model. In the second act he had a long soliloquy about art and Michelangelo and the reasons why he'd wanted to go to Italy and why he felt such disdain for himself in the face of all the great works around him. Several times Mamie was afraid she was going to fall asleep, but she was kept awake by the thought that she'd see Sal come on stage again. Sal was playing the maid; she didn't have anything to say other than, 'Si, signor,' until the last act, where she made the most of a speech in broken English, telling the sculptor that the signora had left and there was a letter she'd wanted him to have.

Mamie went backstage afterwards. Sal came bounding out the door with her arms open.

'I saw you,' she yelled. 'My God, I couldn't believe it. I nearly dropped the coffee-pot again. Jesus, Mamie, you're pregnant.'

'I couldn't get out on the mat with Mr Moto any more, that's for sure.'

'Mr Moto, oh, my God: that was such a long time ago. Where was it?'

'Kansas City. It was the only sport I was ever really good at. Except dancing, of course – but that's an art. That's what Mrs Beebie kept saying.'

'Hell, yes. I remember. I was always a total bust at that karate, but I had a big crush on him.'

'Me, too. I just wish I could remember his real name. Are you doing anything before the next show?'

'You're kidding. I've got enough spare time to learn Outer Mongolian.'

'Let's go eat,' Mamie said. 'My treat.'

'You bet it is, in that coat. What is it? That's the minkiest mink I've ever seen.'

'It's a sable,' Mamie said. She could feel herself smirking a little. *And why not*, she thought.

They went to a restaurant Sal picked out. 'The sky's the limit,' Mamie said. 'Anything you like, and have it twice. If you're on a diet, this is the day to forget it.'

They went through the menu and ordered. Sal started on a bottle of wine, which Mamie refused, saying that it made her feel sick. 'And being in very smoky places,' she added.

'And the ring!' Sal exclaimed. 'Oh, wow. Eat your heart out, Elizabeth Taylor.'

Mamie stretched her hand across the table so Sal could get a better look. 'I thought you were great in the play,' she said. 'You were the only good thing. That big speech in the second act – '

'When he gets the throb in his voice, uh-huh. He's such a jerk. But this time it isn't his fault. I couldn't say those lines any better. And the empty house isn't much help. I'm afraid this one's just your archetypal turkey.'

Sal began to talk about herself. Mamie pumped her with questions until they'd eaten their way to the dessert. Sal said, 'What have you got in there – triplets? And I was the one that wanted kids. So how's old Carter?'

'It isn't Carter. It's his cousin's ex-husband. That's how these things happen: shazam.'

'How about that. I could use some shazam myself for a change.'

'Things bad?'

'I'm sort of down around low tide.'

'If it's money, ask.'

'No, the money's only the way it always is. I guess it's just this time of year. Thinking about love. You know. Even now it's gotten so cold out. You can't help thinking.'

Yes, Mamie said, she knew.

Later in the evening, when Sal was making up to go on stage, she tried to get hold of Carter again. But he must have been out of town for the weekend. She had to go back without seeing him.

She thought about him all the way to the house. She wondered if he was alone, or with somebody else. There was no shortage of women in town. When she remembered how the girls used to talk backstage, how they were all dying for it, she was sure he'd be with someone, another girl: somebody better. And maybe he'd be saying he loved her, bringing her flowers, buying her presents.

He'd only ever given her one thing, at the beginning: a keychain with an enamelled butterfly at the end of it. He said he didn't believe in presents. All the clothes he'd bought her for the visit to the Chases had been in the nature of a theatrical wardrobe; they were for business and professional purposes.

She loved the keychain, but he'd never bought her anything else. She hadn't expected him to, yet most men would have. She didn't think about it until one day when they were passing by a jeweller's shop and she lingered to look in.

'This is cheap stuff,' he said.

'That's the kind I can afford.' Her eye ran over the watches, clocks, plated cups, flashy earrings and chunky fake bracelets. Then, in one of the front corners she saw a collection of silver charms. She leaned closer.

'Come on,' he told her. She switched her attention away from a silver heart and was suddenly looking at a charm made of the two masks of drama, comedy and tragedy.

'Look. Look at that,' she said. He admitted that they weren't bad, but he wanted to move on.

She said, 'Let's go in. Just to see how much.'

She walked in without him and he followed. When the man behind the counter brought out the charm, she still thought it was perfect, and it wasn't expensive. That was the point where Carter should have offered to buy it for her. He shook his head. She bought it herself.

After they were out on the street again and had walked halfway to the restaurant they were going to, she took the charm out of its box and examined it.

He snatched it from her hand, stared at it, and began to tug at the two halves.

'What are you doing?' she said. 'You'll break it.'

He wrenched the two masks apart and threw one into the street.

'What are you doing?' she said again.

'I don't like the idea of you wearing that unlucky thing.' He handed her the piece that was left: the comedy mask.

'But it looks silly now. They're meant to go together. It's one of the things you've got to have in pairs. Like men and women.'

'Sometimes I think we'd be better off with only one of those, too.'

'What am I going to do with just one?'

'I don't know. Wear it as an earring. You could start a fashion. One earring.'

'That's already a fashion.'

'OK, start another one. The hell with it.'

She stepped off the kerb and searched up and down, trying to find the other mask again, but he took her by the hand and yanked her along with him, away from the place where she'd heard it land.

'You don't buy me anything,' she said, 'and when I get something for myself, you tear it to pieces.'

'I'll buy you something else.'

'But why did you do it?'

'What do you want a bad-luck thing like that for?' He dragged her into a large, expensive store, looked around aggressively and grabbed a silk scarf that was draped over the handle of a crocodile bag. It was part of the display.

'You like that?' he asked.

'Well, of course,' she said. It was one of the biggest silk scarves she'd ever seen and covered with prints of flowers in all different colours. 'But it's too expensive.'

A salesgirl was at his elbow straight away. She'd left her counter as soon as she'd seen them touching the scarf. He asked the price and Mamie was right – it cost more than a good dress would be. He bought it for her.

It became her favourite piece of clothing. She wore it around her neck or shoulders, or tied around her head, or at her waist.

Russell liked it, too; it always paid, he said, to buy the best. And Mamie thought: *Everything always pays, if you've got the money for it.*

*

She still hadn't seen him by the summer. And then the baby was born.

She was entirely absorbed in her child, as if hypnotized. At times she was also unhappier than she had been since she'd left West Virginia. It was like the year when her mother and father had died. She would cry for long periods. She didn't want to go out of the house. It wasn't that she was afraid, just that she didn't want to leave the baby. Russell was understanding, and Katherine suddenly seemed sympathetic – still cold and reserved, but she didn't lecture about her own experience as a mother or attempt to criticize: she tried to be encouraging and to talk about practical, ordinary things.

At night Mamie had anxious dreams. She kept remembering her mother, who had never talked about anything that had to do with the process of reproduction, and hadn't even told her daughter the facts of life; Mamie had had to get the information from school and gossiping with friends. But now she wondered about her mother: *Did she feel like this? Did she walk up and down with me to stop me crying; did she sing me to sleep?*

Russell spoke to her about taking a winter vacation in the sun somewhere. The grandparents started a savings account for baby Waverley, whom they called Bobby. And, for the baby's sake, the grown Waverley, her father-in-law, gave Mamie some stocks and shares, including shares in the bank. She had a private income now, as well as her bank account.

Sometimes Russell would ask her to lend him money until a cheque came through. She had plenty; she didn't mind. But one day Randall told her that somebody ought to have a word with Ross about his gambling.

'It's just a little roulette, isn't it?' she said.

'It's always a lot, and he keeps thinking he's got this system.

He's been like that ever since school. I think he should see a doctor about it. It's like throwing it away. Julie – '

'Yes?'

'Julie tried to stop him, but she couldn't, either. Maybe you can. Now that he's a father – well, he should show some responsibility.'

She asked Russell later, 'Do you gamble a lot?'

'Just for fun.'

'Randall told me I was supposed to get you to stop.'

'He's probably right. But it's the excitement. You can get hooked on it.'

'It doesn't matter, as long as you break even. You wouldn't keep playing if you lost all the time, would you?'

He said, 'One loss never counts when you know you can win it back a hundred times over on the next round.'

'You lose a lot?'

'Don't worry about it. I've got plenty to pay with.'

'Some of those casinos are run by pretty tough people, you know. I've heard they can actually hire men to take out a contract on customers that don't pay up.'

'But I always do pay up,' he told her. He sounded completely relaxed about the subject. She shrugged and said that everything was all right, then.

As soon as she was through with her special exercises and the check-ups, and felt that she was back to normal again, she asked to go into town to show the baby to Sal. She did mean to see Sal at some point, but the real reason for the trip would be to meet Carter.

*

She didn't take the fur coat or the diamond. This time she wore corduroy pants and a parka. She carried a duffelbag for her clothes and a neck-sling for Bobby.

She took him to the theatre first, to show Sal. Sal was speechless for a moment. And then she changed expression in a way Mamie had never seen outside the movies: she looked transfigured. She wanted to hold the baby. She called the other girls over. Three of them, including Sal, cried when Mamie got ready to go. They didn't want him to leave.

She went to a big department store she knew, had a snack in the restaurant and then moved to the ladies' room, and on to the large entrance hall next to it, where there were chairs and couches. She sat down and changed Bobby and breast-fed him. She kept looking at her watch, but it didn't matter. Carter could wait.

She walked. And she didn't begin to hurry when she saw that she was getting near the park.

Carter was sitting on one of the benches. He was smoking a cigarette. He looked as if he'd been waiting a long while. He was thinner than the last time she'd seen him. He stood up as she approached. 'Did you have to bring the kid?' he said.

'I wanted to show him off to my friends. They loved him. And besides, I still need to feed him.' She sat down on the bench. 'You don't have to look if you don't want to. You might turn to stone or something.'

He sat down again and took a quick look at the baby, asleep after its meal. He grunted. He said, 'You didn't find out about the money.'

'How can I ask? I don't want to get him mad at me. You don't know what he's like. He's got this way of . . . He doesn't like to be criticized and if you say anything, you can feel his trust in you sort of seeping away. And then you're the one that feels bad.'

'I can picture it. He's got a lot of spoiled little rich-girl tricks. Raymond's a bonehead and Randall's a pompous idiot, but Ross is the pick of the bunch.'

'I put my foot in it already, when I asked about the gambling.'

'What?'

'Randall said I should try and stop him.'

'He's gambling my money away?'

'He gambles a lot. But he's got plenty, you know that. The whole family's loaded. What are you worried about?'

'What was the other thing? The other thing you wanted to talk about?'

'About what you'd do if anything happened to me.'

'Nothing's going to happen to you.'

'What I mean is, there wouldn't be any way you could prove you were Bobby's father. He'd be brought up by the Chases. You knew that before, but now he's actually here. Look.' She touched the baby's cheek. It sighed, yawned, opened its eyes, moved its arms and trampled in the air with its feet. She held out a finger. Bobby grabbed it. She made kissing noises at him.

'He's kind of cute,' Carter said grudgingly.

'Hold your finger out.'

The baby clasped his finger in its hand and chortled.

'It's the way they learn,' she said. 'They're exercising all the time – with their voices, too. One of those books said that babies make noises even when they're in an empty room, to judge the distances – like echo-sounding. Isn't that smart? I've read so many books. I never knew how interesting . . . I mean, we all started like this. We were all this size.'

Carter touched the baby's face, its arms, its legs.

'You hold him,' Mamie said.

'No.'

'Yes. I'm getting tired. They weigh a lot and I don't think these sling things are the best way to lug them around.' She handed Bobby over, first showing how to protect his head. Carter held the baby in his arms and looked down. He looked for a long time and turned his head away. 'Jesus,' he whispered, 'what a mess.'

She felt secure at last. It was a mess, all right, but now he had to get them out of it. She was sure that somehow he was going to succeed in fixing everything up, and even work it so they'd keep the money, too. 'I'll miss him when we go sailing,' she said. 'Or skiing. They haven't made up their minds yet. I wanted to take him with us, but they all say it's better not to. And then they can get him on to the bottle while I'm drying out.'

'What?' Carter said. 'I wasn't listening.'

'We're going to wean Bobby while he's with the nurse and we're on this vacation.'

'Has he made a will?'

'We both did. At the same time we made out all the new insurance papers.'

'New? You didn't tell me that.'

'It's only the normal thing. Especially if you've just started a family.'

'How much are you insured for?'

'Oh, thousands and thousands. The limit.'

'Just like Julie.'

'But so is he.'

'That isn't going to matter, if he's the one pushing you over the railings.'

'I don't believe it.'

'That's how it happened to her.'

'Then they wouldn't try the same way again, would they?'

'People who commit murders usually stick to a pattern.'

'Have you ever killed anyone?'

He turned his head again. He said, 'If I had to get rid of somebody who was in my way – somebody who deserved it – I wouldn't feel guilty. Would you?'

'Yes. That's how people get caught. They want to talk about it. Because they feel bad.'

'I bet some of them feel better afterwards. Everybody wants to kill at least one person. Don't you?'

'Of course not.'

'Maybe not at the moment. But think back to when you were working in the theatre. Nobody you hated?'

'Two people.'

'I've got four at the office. And if you could have gotten away with it, wouldn't you have liked to?'

'Just for that moment of destroying them. But afterwards, think what it would do to you. How lonely and miserable you'd feel.'

'Not me.' He handed Bobby back to her. 'You've got to be the one to do it,' he said. 'It'll be easy for you. They won't suspect you for a minute, the mother of such a cute little baby.'

*

'Did you enjoy your trip?' Katherine asked.

'It was great. The girls all loved him. They cried. He was the only one that didn't. He was so good. Where is everybody?'

The others were out. Katherine asked her to take the baby up to the nursery and then come down to the study to have a cup of coffee and a chat.

Marilyn brought the coffee on one of the big silver trays. She came back with a plate of sandwiches. It still gave Mamie the creeps to have servants bringing things in and taking them out all the time. At the beginning, she'd thought it would be wonderful: gracious living like the advertisements. But what it meant in practice was that you could never be alone. And in her white uniform Marilyn looked more like a nurse than a maid.

Katherine said, 'I wanted to talk to you, Rhoda, before we go away. Of course there's time enough – a couple of months. But I always think it's best to settle up as you go along; not to let things slide.'

Mamie nodded. She didn't think she was ever going to like her mother-in-law, but she was no longer afraid of her. She could even see that Katherine was a lonely woman. She also knew that she herself had the approval of all the men in the family and that that was what counted with the Chases, even with Katherine.

'I've always been proud of my boys. Raymond and Randall were so good at sports . . .'

Loose-living studs, Mamie thought, *both headed towards the same path their father had taken and the same sauce he was pickled in.*

' . . . and now at the bank.'

Checking in late in the morning and out early in the afternoon, with a so-called business lunch in between, and playing around with their secretaries, sometimes right in the office.

'And Russell . . .'

Russell, the baby. It didn't show too much; his father had made him join all those games like the others, so he was in pretty good condition physically. But he hadn't escaped his mother.

'He was the really bright one at school. He always had his own ideas about the way things should be. We thought he'd go to the top. But – I do see he was right: he convinced us that the study of nature was just as important. Of course we know it is. It's just that sometimes it seems to me a shame that somebody who has a talent for a thing – that he should have avoided developing it. I expect you know he sometimes plays roulette and twenty-one.'

'Yes. He's interested in working out his systems.'

'I used to believe so. But it's an odd thing: you can go along believing something for years, and suddenly you know the truth in a flash. We all used to think this sort of gambling fever would come over Ross in waves – he'd go out and lose a lot and then come back and devote himself to the invention of a new set of numbers. I used to think the craving struck him when he was unhappy: that it was an addiction like alcohol.'

Everybody had an addiction, Mamie thought. Her father-in-law and the two other sons had liquor, sometimes women; Katherine had her position in the community. And she herself had Carter.

'I wasn't looking at the facts,' Katherine said. 'The facts are simply that gambling is the quickest way there is of throwing money away. Our family is a banking family and all the men in it, except Russell, work in the bank. He never wanted to – that was all right. But his choice of work didn't stop his feeling against it: guilt, or rebellion, or whatever it is. I don't understand it.'

Neither did Mamie. It seemed crazy. Most people would do just about anything for money. Money could change your life. She could certainly understand the excitement of gambling, but only if you were poor. Rich people didn't need to gamble; they had it already.

Katherine said, 'He needs someone to take him in hand. Now that you're both parents, it's important for you to think of the future.'

'I don't know much about money,' Mamie said.

'But perhaps you could speak to him. I think you ought to.'

'All right. I will. And maybe you could help me with something.'

'About finances?'

'No. It's something I can't ask Ross about. It's about his first wife, Julie.'

'Yes?'

'I just want to know about her. I don't have the feeling that something's being kept back from me, or anything – it's just that I can't ask him. What was she like?'

'Very attractive. Intelligent, well-read, good background, knew how to dress; perfect manners.'

And Carter loved her.

'I didn't mean that,' Mamie said. 'I want to know what she was like as a person, why Ross married her, whether she was at all like me, or whether she was my opposite.'

'Not quite your opposite, but certainly very different. She gave the impression of being always cheerful and efficient, in control. She'd had a very good job, a responsible position in a large firm. She was one of those girls who could be a managing director if she wanted to. Very outgoing, pleasant, put people at their ease.'

Mamie could imagine Sal saying, 'Miss Vogue'; that was the way they referred to certain people, and clothes, and parts in plays, where all the details were neat and matching and everything looked as if it had been designed by a machine.

'But,' she said, 'we look alike.'

'No, not at all.'

'Oh?'

'No. She was tall, above average height. Dark brown hair and – '

'Do you have a photograph?' Mamie said.

'Yes, I think so. Of course. All the wedding pictures, and from the summer, and that Christmas before the accident.'

'Tell me about the accident.'

'She just slipped. It was dreadful.'

'Was it on snow or on a rockface?'

'I think it must have been a slippery place, maybe ice, or just snow that was packed down.'

'Weren't you there?'

'We were all there, except Waverley – he wasn't feeling very well that morning. I was trying to keep up with the boys, and Ross and Julie were behind us. It was a frightful thing. He said he just looked back and she was in the air, falling away. It took him a long time to get over it.'

'Could I see the pictures?' Mamie asked.

Katherine led the way upstairs to her room. She brought out a pile of photograph albums, found the one she wanted and took it over to the windowseat.

Mamie sat down too. She held half the large album while Katherine turned the pages and told off the names and talked about the places. There were lots of pictures of Julie: tall, self-confident, with the dark hair and the fashion-model look.

'Why did you think,' Katherine asked, 'that you looked alike?'

'It was something Carter Mathews said that time he was here. Maybe he meant it in some other way.'

'Such a good-looking boy. But unreliable.'

'Um.'

'And quite notorious with women, always has at least three or four on a string at the same time.'

'Yes,' Mamie mumbled, 'I kind of got that impression about him.'

*

She wore the comedy mask on a thin silver chain around her neck. The morning after she'd come back from seeing Carter she was leaning down and forward near a chair Russell was sitting in, and he asked her, 'Is there only one of those masks? I thought the other one was right behind the – '

'No,' she said, 'there's only one. The comedy one.'

'You don't like tragedy?'

'I lost the other one.'

'I suppose it wouldn't be too hard to replace it.'

'I don't want to. I like it the way it is, now. I'm used to it like this.'

'I don't mind tragedy. It shows the character.'

Thinking of her mother, she said, 'Unless there's too much of it. Then people start to lose their personality. They go dead.'

'I don't call that tragedy.'

'What do you call it?'

'Just bad luck.'

'Uh-huh. There's a lot of it around.'

'But not for us,' he said, smiling fatuously at her. She made him knock on wood. She ran the mask back and forth on its chain until it zinged.

He said, 'My old teacher at the institute would get a kick out of that. The one time I got away from home – and he spent half his time telling me about America. He was always saying that Americans sentimentalized and falsified everything in order to make life more comfortable. No more tragedy, only fun. And the idealists had the concept of worthy effort – that was their form of fun.'

'Well, if you could get rid of the bad parts, wouldn't you?'

'You get rid of them by living through them.'

Mamie laughed. 'Sure,' she said.

'You don't think so?'

'I don't know. All I know is what we used to say in the profession: comedy ends in marriage, tragedy ends in death.'

'You could take that both ways. Are you saying that once you're married, the comedy's over?'

'No, it's –'

'And once you're dead, the tragedy's over?'

'Once you're dead, everything's over.'

'You believe that?'

'All I said was: that's the way they end.'

'Or it could mean intent – that the purpose of comedy is marriage. And the purpose of tragedy –'

'I'm getting mixed up now,' she said. She was also getting bored. He never teased her or laughed at her like Carter; he genuinely didn't think she was dumb. And she was gratified by the way he took her opinions so seriously; but sometimes he could go on and on until she wanted to jump up and start kicking the furniture. Her mother had said: *Marry a rich man and you'll never have to worry*. But it wasn't enough, even though her position had changed. When she was with Russell, she was in control. When she was with Carter, he was the one who had the power, because she was the one who loved. She was tied to both men without really knowing either of them. And she had two lives that she couldn't live right. Every minute she had to watch her step, to try to remember what she was supposed to be doing.

Russell had read a lot of plays and he could talk about them, but he didn't like going out much. She thought he'd rather stick with the plays in books. He even said once that the theatre wasn't like real life. Of course it wasn't, she'd said, any more than a painted portrait was a real face. They were both pictures. And there were good pictures or bad pictures – that was the only important question. He said something about artificiality. She didn't know where to begin on that argument. The house she lived in, her marriage, her whole life was artificial.

He'd go to movies. Occasionally he'd suggest going out for a meal and a film, but that was for her sake. He didn't find pleasure in the town; he preferred to see movies on television. What he really loved was his job. He also liked, and enjoyed playing with, and began to love, Bobby. When Mamie watched the two of them laughing and making faces at each other, she became fond of Russell and was happy in his company. At those moments she almost believed she belonged with him. And she started to get used to being married, and to think of it as normal.

He tried to tell her about biology – how large the scope of it was, and what it could explain. She listened as if fascinated. Sometimes, in fact, she found herself becoming interested, but usually it was because she thought that Carter would like to hear it.

'It's beyond all other things,' Russell told her. 'It's the basis. Whatever the future holds, there are millions of years behind us, and they're part of us: we're the product of them. All our instincts, everything.'

'Our thoughts?' she asked.

'Maybe not. But our dreams, certainly. They're the same as they always were. What kind of dreams do you have?'

'Oh, I don't know. Nice ones. And the bad ones. I guess being chased, or caught in a fire, or drowning or something. But that was only – I used to have horrible nightmares when I was little. Everybody does, don't they? And then I grew out of it. What kind of dreams do you have?'

'I have one that repeats,' he said. 'I'm standing alone in a high place. It's getting dark, there's someone behind me I can't see. And I'm afraid to turn around.'

'And that's all? That's the whole thing?'

'That's enough. It's very creepy and it usually wakes me up in a sweat. You'll see. Or maybe they'll stop, now that I've got you with me.'

'That would be nice,' she said.

'Cured by a woman's love. If comedy ends in marriage, where does it begin?'

'Laughing. Jokes.'

'And tragedy?'

'What?' She'd forgotten where they'd left the conversation.

'Tragedy begins at home,' he said.

'That's charity, Ross.'

'Oh, yes. Charity.'

She thought he might have meant to imply something about her, but he started almost immediately to look through a book he had with him; he wanted to show her a picture. He spoke of trained, scientific observation; about animals, birds and insects. 'You see these creatures,' he said, 'and they're capable of astonishing things – amazing. We call it instinct, but they're so inspired, they seem to know about cause and effect. And look here: the way the colour of the skin and fur and feathers has evolved to suit the climate and the habitat. It all seems to be so much more intelligent than ordinary thought. And simpler.'

*

She asked Russell to take her out for a drive in the country. It was like arranging a meeting with Carter. She wanted to talk to him outside the house.

She said, 'There's something I've got to ask you. You remember, Randall told me to tell you about gambling? Well, now your mother's leaning on me. I just wanted to know what's behind it.'

'When I was in high school and made my big decision to go into biology, you should have seen all the tricks they tried. They actually sent me to a doctor. They'd have sent me to a psychiatrist except that it would have ruined my career to have that on my record.'

'Why?'

'Well, who goes to psychiatrists? Crazy people – right? You can be as crazy as you like, but once you've seen a psychiatrist, it's official. Everybody knows it and they won't hire you, not even in a bank. In a bank what you should be worrying about is theft and embezzlement.'

'And gambling?'

'We call it investment. You want to know why they're in such a sweat? Because if I sold my shares on the open market, the family would drop from a 60 per cent majority shareholder down to 48 per cent. So, if the other 52 per cent wanted to vote in a block, they could start kicking people off the board. That kind of thing.'

'Would you?'

'I might. Or I might give them the choice of buying me out at a slightly higher price. That's what people usually do.'

'You seem to get along OK with them.'

'Sure.'

'It would just about kill your mother, wouldn't it? And your father?'

'They feel that way about everything. It might be good for the bank to have a couple of new people giving orders. Why not?'

'She said a peculiar thing, too. She said you were trying to throw your money away, and gambling was the quickest way of doing it.'

'I hadn't thought of that. Was that all you wanted to talk about?'

'Yes. I don't know what to do when they say, "You tell Russell this," or, "Tell him that." I mean, I can't just say, "Tell him yourself," can I?'

'Try it. See what happens. Or – no, it's better if you don't; this way, I can find out what's on their minds.'

'Think of myself as a soldier operating in enemy territory? Or as an actress playing a part?'

'That's right.'

'Why do they assume I won't pass everything on to you?'

'They probably can't believe we talk together like other married couples.'

'Why not?'

'I don't know.'

'Is it something about me?'

'Or me. I'm the one they always had trouble with. I won't fit in. There are a lot of wives who sit and listen to other people's good advice and they start to think to themselves that maybe their husband really does need to be changed around; so they don't say anything to him, they just start heckling him the way the others told them to.'

Julie did that, Mamie thought.

*

Carter was waiting for her in the cocktail lounge. She missed her step as she came up to him and he caught her quickly. She'd forgotten how strong he was; it was like the kind of sudden tackle you might see in a football game. He kissed her cheek.

'That all I get?' she asked.

'You've been drinking. You aren't supposed to drink, are you?'

'I'm all dried out now. I can have a drink or two.'

'You've had so many, you can't walk straight.'

'Two drinks, that's all. I'm fine. It's so fucking dark in here, like all these places. Your favourite word, for my favourite activity. Want to hit me? Want me to say it a little louder?'

'I think we'd better go someplace less public.'

'Fine by me. I'd like a drink first.'

'OK. One.' He went to the bar and brought her back a gin and tonic. 'All right?' he said, as he put the glass down in front of her.

'Sure. Same likes, same dislikes. Here's to our wonderful future.'

'I thought you were going to bring the baby.'

'To a place like this?'

'I thought we'd go somewhere else. We could have gone to my place.'

'I'm not supposed to be seen there, am I?'

'Drink that up. We've got to talk. What's gotten into you all of a sudden?'

'I've been seeing some very interesting photographs.'

'Of me?'

'Maybe. Which ones did you have in mind?'

'Well, I did a lot of crazy things when I was around college age. I even made a porno movie with a few friends.'

'Oh-ho?'

'We were all stoned, but we made a lot of money out of it.'

'Is that a fact? I expect you're sorry about it now.'

'Of course not. What's a picture? They could cover the front page with pictures of me doing it with an elephant. I wouldn't mind.'

'Jesus, I'd die.'

'I still think it's funny. I think it's even funnier that some of those guys are busting themselves trying to get the prints back. But you're right; the girls felt differently. They had a great time going along with everything until later. And then all of them – every single one – started to freak out about it: the idea that somebody they knew might see it. Or that lots of people could see it, who'd never met them, and somebody might spot them on the street or in a store or waiting for an elevator some day and say, "I've seen you before, and guess where?"'

'That's terrible. I think that's awful, Carter.'

'It had a pretty bad effect on them. I don't understand it. If they felt that way, why did they join in? What the hell?'

'Maybe after they fell in love and got married, they could be afraid of being blackmailed. They wouldn't want their husbands to know. You don't want people you love to know things about you that aren't nice.'

He threw down the book of matches he'd been playing with. All the matches were splayed and ripped; the cover was almost shredded. She couldn't make out his expression, even though her eyes had adjusted to the dim light. It might have been the look of a man who blackmailed women.

'Let's go to my place,' he said.

It was the first time they'd been together since shortly after her marriage. He told her she was more beautiful than before the baby; she was more fun. They went out once for a meal and came back again. She stayed most of the night. She could have stayed right through till morning and for the whole of the day, but she needed alibis just in case: the hotel bills, the theatre ticket stubs, and so on. As he walked her up to the hotel doorway, he said, 'Better than the photographs?'

'They weren't of you. They were of your cousin, Julie. The one who looks just like me, remember?'

'Here,' he said, touching the side of her face. 'That's what I saw. It seems a lot less pronounced now that I know you.'

'Come on, Carter. We're as different as black and white.'

'Black and white can look very similar. I told you: resemblance doesn't depend on that. Especially in a photograph.'

'Funny how you thought it had to be pictures of you.'

'It's probably just as well I told you. Things like that have a habit of popping up when you don't expect them. The horselaugh out of the past.'

'I brought you some pictures, too,' she said. 'I'll show you tomorrow.'

The next day, when they were in bed together, she reached over to the night-table for her handbag, opened it and brought out a large envelope full of photographs of the baby. She began to hand them to him one by one.

'Nice,' he told her. 'Look at us. All three of us here, and not a stitch on. Next time you come, bring him with you. I'm tired of being so careful.'

'It isn't worth taking the chance. You know what could happen legally.'

'Did they tell you where you're going on the vacation?'

'Some tiny little place in Switzerland. Or maybe it was Austria.' She told him the name.

'That's the same place,' he said. 'It's where they pushed her over the side.'

'No, it isn't. The name under the photographs is different.'

'It's the same area, right down the valley.'

'But not the same place. Not the same village. Is it?'

'Not exactly. It's right near it.'

'But not the same. That's what you said at first, wasn't it?'

'It doesn't sound good to me. Maybe the bank is on the rocks again, or Russell's in debt. You're insured right up to your ears.'

'So is he. It's the usual thing.'

'Who does your will leave everything to?'

'The new one leaves it to Bobby. Russell gets the interest till he's grown up.'

'And if Bobby dies?'

'Bobby?'

'Babies can get sick and die before you even realize anything's wrong. We should have gone through all this before.'

'But we did. We've been over and over everything. It goes to Russell. How could I leave it to you? I couldn't.'

'You could go to another lawyer and make a second will. And that's what I think you'd better do.'

*

She got out of bed and began to put on her clothes. She went into the bathroom, then to the kitchen. Carter came in after her and handed her a coffee-cup. He poured out some coffee for her, and some for himself.

He said, 'That's a horrible dress.'

'Russell likes it. He chose it himself. It's better than just that towel.' She started to get annoyed. She said, 'Want to hear what else he likes?'

'I think maybe it should have something spilled on it.'

All at once she was furious. She turned around, put her cup down on the edge of the sink and said that before the baby was born she gave Russell excuses for not making love, but that afterwards they'd started to, the way they should have from the beginning, and now they were like any other married couple: they did it all the time; and it was so good with him – yes, honestly – because he was affectionate and made her feel happy.

Carter laughed. He sat down at the table.

She said, 'I'll call you up when we get back from skiing.'

'I'll be reading the obituary columns, looking for Russell.'

'Let's drop it. Please. You're wearing me out.'

'No stamina. You were ready to go through with it.'

'I was never ready to kill anybody. Never. I can't even remember why you told me I had to get married to him. It's always one story on top of another.'

He said, 'If you don't, he'll get you for the insurance money.'

She didn't believe it. She started to pace up and down. She said, 'We're always talking about killing. It's driving me nuts.'

'If you're the one that does it, they won't suspect anything.'

'I don't have to do a thing. No. I can do just nothing and I can have you both. You can tell him what you like. I'll say you're trying to blackmail me. I'll start doing what you do. I don't care. You can go to hell.'

He put his elbows on the table, his hands over his ears, and moaned.

She heard herself panting in the stillness. He looked terrible. He started to whisper to himself, 'They always said it would happen to me. My mother used to warn me: *You'll end up like your father.*'

'What happened to your father?' They were both whispering now.

'One day he just snapped. He killed seven people with an axe.'

Her heartbeat gave a thump and rushed upwards. She came forward slowly. She put her arms around him. 'It's all right,' she said gently.

He lifted his face, took his elbows off the table and suddenly pulled her down into the chair with him. 'You fell for it?' he asked. He picked up his cup and said, 'This is cold.' He poured coffee all over her dress.

They rolled on to the floor, fighting and laughing. He started to tickle her. He got her to unsay everything she'd claimed about her married life, to tell him she couldn't live without him, to say she never stopped thinking about him, and to tell him she wanted more.

'You're so mean to me,' she sighed. 'Honest to God.'

He said, 'I'm not mean. I'm just violent. I thought you liked it.'

*

'We've got everything we want,' she told him. 'We had everything all along – enough money, too. Lots of people in the world don't even get enough to eat every day.'

'The hell with them. They should get up off their knees and start hitting back. They deserve all they get.'

'I should never have married him.'

'Fur coats, diamonds? What's that ring you've got on right now? And that car you told me about?'

'I can get by without any of it. Nothing wrong with buses. I can take the subway. I can walk. All I want is you and Bobby.'

'We wouldn't even be able to afford the bus after a while. I'm leaving my job.'

'Why?'

'Because I'm not going to need it any more.'

'You see? None of it makes sense. If you were really planning to do anything, that would look bad.'

'I can't help it. I can't take it any more.'

'And another thing: they all talk about an accident, but if she just fell, how come you got a suicide note?'

'I've never understood that. All I can think of is that they'd planned to do it a little later in some other way that wasn't going to look so natural. I just don't know.'

He waited in the car outside her hotel and then drove her to the airport. They sat in the parking lot until it was time. 'Remember,' he said. 'Let me know what happens. At the number I gave you.'

'I'll try. I get so mixed up about all the special words.'

'Just keep calm: don't get flustered. I'm going to have to know everything now. I'll be coming with you.'

'I'm not doing it. I told you. And you aren't, either.'

'I'm just going, to try to keep you alive. Even if you start out assuming they didn't do it, why would they want to go back there? Why would innocent people act like that?'

She promised to tell him everything. They kissed goodbye. Then she said, 'You never did tell me about your father, or the rest of your family.'

'Some other time.'

'We've still got a few minutes.'

'Would it surprise you very much to know that Waverley Chase is my father? My real father?'

'Yes, it would. Is he?'

'Maybe.' He kissed her again.

'Carter,' she said, 'I can't put up with any more of this fooling.'

He opened the door, got out, and started to walk around to her side. She was out of the car before he came up to her.

'Is he?' she asked.

'You think about it on the way back.'

'Tell me now, Carter, or I'm going to let that plane go without me.'

'OK, OK. As far as I know, that whiskey-sodden old windbag could only be the father of those three jerks you're living with. Satisfied?'

'Was there something wrong with your father?'

'Why?'

'Because you won't tell me about him.'

'Nothing to tell, about either of them. Just ordinary people.'

'But you aren't ordinary.'

'I was adopted.'

They reached the departure lounge before she turned to him and said, 'Then Julie wasn't your real cousin?'

'She was adopted, too.'

'I don't believe it.'

He laughed.

'Are you adopted?' she hissed at him. 'I'm not getting on the plane until you tell me. Are you?'

'We are boarding at this time,' a stewardess said almost in her ear. She backed towards the exit, still asking, 'Are you?'

He shook his head.

She wanted to sleep on the flight, but couldn't. She kept thinking about heredity and everything she'd read in the books and magazines. Such a sweet baby, always laughing, couldn't have inherited anything bad. But Carter laughed a lot, too. And maybe his father had been laughing when he'd had the axe in his hand; except – there hadn't been any axe. It was made up. She was so confused that each time she thought she'd figured something out, she had to accept a new contradiction. A few days later, she thought: If Carter kept telling her Julie was his favourite cousin, that must mean he had more than one. Who were the other ones?

The only person she could think of asking was her husband. She told him that when she'd been in town seeing her friends backstage, she'd heard about another girl, who was going around with Carter and wasn't very happy.

'What do you know about him?' she asked.

'Not as much as you,' he said. 'You were going out with him. In fact, you were sleeping with him, weren't you?'

His tone was light but nasty. She hadn't expected that he'd give the affair a thought. She said penitently, 'Just at the beginning, yes. It was before I met you. And anyway, I never knew where I was with him. That's why I want to find out. He was always so secretive about himself.'

'I can tell you what he was like in school and college: in on every scheme you could name, even some that were a little risky. And getting away with everything. And a big reputation with the girls, which you know about.'

'He kept talking about his cousin all the time. About Julie. He said she was his favourite cousin. I just wondered – who were the others? His other cousins.'

'Oh. That's us. Didn't he tell you? We're cousins, too. What did he say when he brought you here?'

'That Waverley and Katherine had been his parents' best friends. Why would he lie?'

'Why would he do anything? That's the way he is. None of us liked him. Since we've grown up, we haven't seen much of him. Once a year, maybe, or less.'

'So it was a big surprise when he showed up with me that time?'

'He wanted to talk with Father about his shares in the bank.'

'Carter's shares?'

'That kind of thing. We don't see him for just family feeling. My parents don't mind him. And you thought he was all right.'

'I still think so, but I never got the feeling I really knew him.'

'Sometimes it's hard to tell with people,' he said. 'They put on an act.'

'You mean me?'

'Of course not. With you, I can always tell.'

'Oh?'

'Always,' he said.

*

She'd never been to another country. She didn't like the idea. Katherine, who delighted in travelling and holidays, was considerate to her and patted her arm as they sat in the airport bar. 'You'll love it when we get there,' she said. 'I know you will. Just relax and have a good time.'

Waverley bought her a good stiff drink. He had one himself. She became sentimental and frightened when she thought about leaving Bobby. She whimpered into her drink, 'I don't think it's right for such a little baby to be away from its mother for such a long time.'

'Oh, you can count on Evie,' Katherine told her. 'She's got all the right references. She'll have him in a fixed routine before you know it. When we get back, you'll find him doing everything like clockwork. All our friends say she's a marvel at discipline.'

She couldn't say what she thought. The moment the brisk and self-important Evie had marched across the threshold, Mamie had detested her. There was nothing she could do about it. The choice wasn't hers; perhaps it never would be. She wouldn't have known how to go about hiring someone, or which nurse to pick. She wouldn't have wanted to choose anyone in the first place.

They stepped into the plane, buckled themselves in, took off. They were on a night flight. She hugged the airline pillow to her. She hated the plane, she hated Russell. She hated everything and she couldn't sleep.

*

'Isn't this better?' Katherine asked.

Mamie looked around at the blue sky, the white snowfields, the tiny villages down below. The world was bright and sparkling. 'It's all like toys,' she said.

They were escorted into their hotel. Uniformed bellboys carried their bags, opened the doors. She hadn't imagined the mountains would be equipped with anything so luxurious. She'd had a vague picture in her mind of a lot of people in leather shorts.

Carter was staying in the neighbouring valley. They were to meet the next day. She had the excuse of not knowing how to ski, so she was going to be down at the beginners' practice area, taking lessons while the others were out on the higher slopes or travelling up and down by the chair lifts and the cable-car.

Raymond had spent all the first morning showing her how the different lifts worked. She'd been strapped in to one mechanical device after another. The most difficult had been the slow one, where you hung on by your arms and had to keep your skis from moving apart as you were pulled along over the ground. But the most terrifying had been the one where you retained the heavy skis, sat on the T-bar, and were lifted so high above the ground that you could look down: on the tops of trees that grew in icy gorges miles below. She'd been so afraid that she hadn't dared to call out anything to Raymond, who was sitting in the seat ahead of her. He'd remained untroubled by the height, and kept turning around to talk. The skis had pulled downward. She'd thought she could keep her leg muscles fixed but if her hands and arms began to shake, that would be the end. The fir trees underneath their path were the biggest she had ever seen and their surrounding landscape looked as forbidding as a scene out of prehistoric times. Raymond twisted his head around and smiled. When they were free of the tow she told him, 'I never want to go on that one again. I was afraid I was going to fall out, or maybe even jump out.'

'Do heights make you dizzy?'

'I don't know. I've never been on anything like that before.'

'I was just thinking – when we take the walk over the pass together; I guess Ross can take care of you.'

She wasn't sure she'd be going on any walk. She felt stiff all over. She passed the greater part of that first afternoon picking herself up off the ground and trying to keep the skis from sliding in opposite directions. In the end she gave up and went to sit on the observation porch and drink cocoa while she watched the skaters. And she rehearsed what she was going to say to Carter.

*

Carter's village was unspoiled compared to the complex of big hotels, restaurants, discothèques and casinos higher up the mountainside. It was still a real village, with a church, and local people who didn't speak English. The children slid down the steep main street on sleds, the grown-ups were climbing or leaning from ladders propped against a group of mammoth snow-statues that they were building. The statues portrayed characters and stories from the Bible. The three kings were finished already, while work went on around the ox, the ass, and – the most important – the Virgin holding her child in her arms. The tallest figures stood higher than the housetops nearby; and they seemed to have been shaped according to some principle handed down through the generations, since all had approximately the same look, or style. They reminded Mamie of the faces on playing cards, or of chessmen, or certain kinds of puppet.

'There's a lot less neon down here,' Carter said. 'See all this authentic culture? You don't get that up in the fleshpots.'

'What do you do in the evenings?'

'There's a tavern. And the pensions serve beer and liquor.'

'No dancing?'

'Next village.'

'But I guess it costs a lot anyway. How can you afford to be here at all?'

'I sold some stuff. And I borrowed some.' He pulled her along by the hand, up a set of steps cut into the snow. 'Come look at the church,' he said.

'What for?'

'Listen.'

They stopped outside the doorway and waited while two men moved what looked like part of a wardrobe into the building. Mamie could hear music coming from somewhere ahead of them.

She stepped forward, through the thick curtains and into the church. Carter followed.

He put his arm around her, led her into a pew, and began to whisper in her ear. 'They practise every morning and afternoon. I think it's just the local schoolkids, but maybe they're from the whole area. Pretty good, aren't they?'

She looked around at the carved wood, the painted plaster

lilies and angels, and at the schoolchildren playing their fiddles and flutes. It was the only nice church she'd ever been in. She'd have liked to stay all day.

He took her to a different village in order to talk. They sat in the corner of a dining-room that belonged to a small hotel. For an hour and a half they talked. He drank three beers, she had four cups of coffee. He wanted her to kill Russell. She said, 'Don't be ridiculous.' He threatened to go to the Chase family with lies, or even with the truth; he started to make her laugh. He told her stories.

She could see what he was doing; she'd watched it on the stage so many times when they'd played farce, but she'd always gotten it wrong herself because she couldn't keep the tempo – that was what it depended on: his timing was perfect. He knew how to slow you down and when to accelerate, to make you shape your timing to his. He made you believe from moment to moment that it was all real, that he was telling the truth, that the way he'd put it was right, and that he loved you best.

'No,' she said. 'I'll get a divorce.'

'I know that bastard. He'll keep the kid.'

'They wouldn't allow that.'

'They'd prove you were an unfit mother. An unwholesome moral influence. Under-educated, no money of your own, no background.'

'They can't. The law wouldn't let them.'

'Oh, a few dollars in the right places. I told you, I know how these things work.'

'Don't,' she said.

'It's true.'

'They wouldn't let him. You couldn't blame him for trying, I guess. He'd have a right to try. He really does love Bobby.'

'Rights over my kid? Mine?' He sounded just the way he'd sounded when he talked about all the money that was supposed to be his.

'I liked that church,' she said. 'The last time I was in church was when I had a headache. I just wanted to sit down and rest.'

She told him about the preacher who believed she'd come into his church to commune with God. Carter was highly amused. And, as always, she felt inordinately pleased at having been able to entertain him. But when she thought back, she remembered that sitting in the church that time hadn't been so funny.

He raised his glass of beer. He said, 'That's what I love about you, Rhoda. You make me laugh.'

'I guess not many people go into churches at those in-between times unless it's a kind of emergency.'

'Maybe he thought you were a fallen woman.'

'Especially young people. Church wouldn't be the first place any young person thinks of. It was fun to see all those schoolkids playing their music.'

'Are you thinking of going religious on me all of a sudden?'

'I never told you much about the birth, did I? You aren't interested in things like that. There was one point where I was having a pretty bad time. I was sure I was going to die. I really was. I couldn't kill anybody, Carter.'

'We'll see.'

'No. I couldn't.'

'We'll talk about it tomorrow,' he said.

'I can't keep talking about things. I'm worn out.'

'You look all right. All this healthy air. How do you like this part of the world?'

'Oh, it's very – well, it's nice, of course. But it's so different.'

'It looks beautiful, doesn't it?'

'Yes.'

'So white, so clean. But the cold can be without pity. I remember reading about those mountaineering teams when I was growing up; all the famous ones – Everest, and everything. There was one story I remember, about going up the Eiger: one guy was left out there for a long time, and when they got to him, all he could say was, "Cold, hungry". He'd already eaten up the leather straps on everything he owned and he'd started to eat his lips.'

'Don't tell me. I hate that kind of thing.'

'I love it. Stories like that tell you what people are really like.'

'That's only what they're like when awful things happen.'

'They happen all the time. You can't say people only behave that way in extremity. All life is extremity. What about right at the beginning of that climb – that man's decision to set out in the first place? Was that a crazy idea?'

She thought about the snow outside and said, 'Yes, of course it was.'

'Well, I can see myself doing the same thing.'

'So can I.'

'You'd never get past the ski lift.'

'So can I see you,' she said. 'I can see you doing the same thing. I wouldn't want to.'

They walked out into the cold again. A girl coming towards them smiled knowingly at Carter and said, 'Hi, there.' He said, 'Hi,' and kept going.

'Who's that?' Mamie asked. She was angry for not being able to stop herself saying anything. What would he tell her, anyway? Just the usual.

'Oh,' he said, 'somebody. I don't know. A snow-bunny.'

The girl had been wearing a red fox jacket. A girl like that would have plenty of money. And she hadn't looked too obvious, either. She looked born-rich: she'd have come to the ski resort as a victim, not a predator. With so many women like that around, Carter wouldn't have to kill for money; he really could marry it. He'd reminded her before that he was still free.

She could sense him preparing to frighten her with the possibility. She'd be too tired to rise to it at the moment, but on another occasion, it might work.

When they passed by the church and the snow statues, it was already getting dark. There were lights on in front of the inns and hotels. People called to each other, their voices carrying clearly in the cold, pure air. The giant snow figures glowed with their own whiteness; even in the twilight people were still working on them. He pulled her into an alley between two houses, to kiss her before she went back up the mountain.

She arrived at the hotel in plenty of time to take a shower before dinner. Russell talked to her from the other side of the door. He said, 'Mother doesn't want me in the casino. It's such a bore to be told the same thing over and over.'

'Well, she worries about you,' Mamie answered. 'She doesn't understand why you'd want to keep doing it when you always lose. Like she said: you're throwing it away.'

'Why don't you try to stop me?'

'I'm not your mother,' she said. 'Besides, you wouldn't quit until you wanted to, would you?' She hung up her bathrobe and put on a slip.

He sat on the stool in front of the dressing table until she came over and moved next to him. He got up, crossed to the windows and stood there, fingering the drawn curtains. He said, 'I saw Carter down in one of the villages this morning. Were you with him today?'

She said yes without turning her head. She heard his feet moving. He came into sight in the mirror. He sat down on the bed.

He asked, 'Are you still sleeping with him?'

'No,' she said quickly, 'I told you all about that.'

'Oh, I know what you told me.'

'Well, it's true.'

'That day you took the baby to town,' he said, 'I followed you. That's another good thing about a job like mine. But I took a plane. It was easy. You went to the theatre. Yes. To the department store. And then you met him in the park. That's when I knew: when I saw him playing with the baby. It's his child, isn't it?'

She put her head down in front of the mirror. For months she'd expected him to say something and she'd gone over her answer – lots of different possible answers; and now she could barely get the sound out. She sobbed and said no, Bobby was his child, but Carter wouldn't let her alone and kept threatening to tell lies about her, and in fact that was just what he'd said he was going to do: 'He said he'd even go tell you our baby was actually his, unless I did what he wanted.' She got up from the stool, fell towards the bed and threw herself at him, protesting. She wept noisily, happy to let go. It was making her less afraid. And it dismayed him. Carter was unmoved by tears, but Russell couldn't deal with them.

'Stop, please,' he said. 'Don't cry like that.'

'But you wouldn't believe him, would you?'

'OK, I know all about Carter. We've been through that. He was after Julie's money.'

'He said he loved her.'

'Love? Carter doesn't work that way.'

She sniffed and stopped crying. She said, 'Do you think we ought to get a divorce?'

'Of course not. Why?'

'If you're suspecting things like that, I don't know. You can't love me much.'

He put a finger on the side of her jaw and turned her face towards him, saying, 'You know, in certain lights you look just like her. Like my first wife. You're such different types, but it's there.'

'Do you think about her a lot?'

'No. But here in the mountains, I guess it can't help but be on our minds.'

'It must have been terrible,' she said. 'I've wanted to talk to you about it before, but I thought it would bring back painful memories.'

'Yes, it was,' he said. 'Terrible.' He drew in his breath and added, 'She was a real bitch. Always telling me what to do. Always right about everything. Always knew best.'

*

Late in the night she woke up and felt scared. The room was hot and completely dark. She told herself that the dressing-table was in front, the yellow curtains to the left, the bathroom at the right. She grew more and more afraid.

She thought Carter was lying to her, but she loved him. She

didn't know anything about Russell any longer and suddenly wondered if he liked her at all.

He liked biology. He liked the subject. She wasn't sure how much he liked people. He was polite, which made it harder to tell. His own mother wasn't sure how he felt.

In spite of all the lies Carter told, maybe it really was possible that Russell had pushed his first wife to her death. If there were some way of knowing for certain whether Russell believed that Bobby wasn't his – then, Mamie thought, she'd feel safer.

*

She wanted to see Carter right away, but he was out. She took her skiing lesson on the slope, went back to the hotel for lunch and played cards with Katherine, Waverley and an old woman they'd run into, who was a friend they hadn't seen for many years.

During one hand when she was dummy, Mamie was called to the telephone. It was Carter, saying that he'd found the note she'd left and that they could meet late in the afternoon.

There was to be a hockey game in one of the valleys that night. Randall and Raymond were planning to go to it, but Russell had said he wanted to see the movie the hotel was showing. Mamie told Katherine that she had to pick up a sweater she'd left down at the ski lodge: she'd go get it, have something to eat, and meet the boys later at the hockey game.

'I'd like to get down there early and watch them working on the snow statues while it's still light,' she explained. 'I can get a snack. I'm already eating too much.'

No one questioned her about anything. She'd left her partner, the little old lady, to play out a small slam doubled and redoubled; that was a lot more important than the fact that she was going to spend an evening away from her husband and have dinner alone. No one, except perhaps Russell, would notice her absence. And he probably wouldn't, either. He'd be thinking about going to the casino.

*

People were crowding together in the village. She and Carter were swept along down the streets with the others heading for the game.

They passed an inn where a woman stood with her back to them. Mamie thought for a moment that she looked just like her mother; and then the woman turned around. She still looked like her mother, but younger. And Mamie thought: *That's what she must have been like before I ever saw her*.

'What's wrong?' Carter asked. He had his arm around her. She said she was fine.

It was almost dark. The lights were already on in the houses. As soon as they started on the road up the hill to the stadium, they had the snow and starlight to see by, nothing else. She was puffing by the time they reached the stands of the open arena. The darkening air was deep and freezing.

Carter bought some sausages and beer. They ate and drank as the seats filled up around them. Mamie kept watch for Randall and Raymond. She noticed that she appeared to be the only woman there, although it was hard to tell when everyone was so bundled up. Nobody near her seemed to be speaking English.

'Can you see Randall?' she asked. 'Or Ray?'

'We're fine,' Carter said. 'Now tell me. You're going on the big walk tomorrow, right?'

She said yes, and told him the times and where they planned to start, where they'd end up: at the inn on top of the mountain.

Then she told him what Russell had said about seeing them in the park that day in town.

'Right,' Carter said. 'That's it. There's no sense in going on with any of it now.'

'That's what I think. We go to him together and ask for a divorce.'

'And he keeps the kid and the money, too. Nope. You start off on that walk, and make sure you two are the last ones – which you'll be, anyhow, because he's going to do to you just what he did to her. Oh yes, he is.'

'I'm not doing anything.'

'I'll do it,' he said. 'I should have known I'd have to. You'd just mess it up.'

She felt the same sensation that had come over her on the open ski-lift: of steep, quick falling before the fall should begin.

She reached over and put a hand on his knee. She leaned against him. 'I don't want – ' she said.

'It's all right. We won't talk about it again. Leave it to me.'

She tried to say she didn't want it to happen, she didn't want to be there, in a foreign country, surrounded by strangers, and talking about murder. She only wanted to be with him, and get their baby back, and forget everything else.

She stayed clinging to him as the cold grew excruciating. Her feet froze. She couldn't even get the feeling going by stamping up and down on the wood planks. Despite the low temperature the smell of garlic and red wine was overpowering.

The players came skating out on to the ice; red and black jerseys, faces livid under the lights. Up above, in the open air, you could see the stars.

The game began. It looked rough: the teams seemed to hate each other.

'Who are they?' she asked.

'The local boys against somebody – I think it's Vienna.'

She couldn't follow the action. Men on the ice were shouting at each other and also being yelled at from the stands. A fight broke out. When another commotion started among the spectators down near the ice, she said, 'Do you want to stay till it's over? I'm frozen,' and they left.

She almost fell to her knees on the walk to the cable-car. He whispered, 'Remember tomorrow,' as she got in. She was numb with the cold and too tired to answer.

*

She woke late at night. Someone was knocking at the door. She got up and went to answer it. Her mother stood in the doorway with a baby in her arms: she said, 'Help me.' And she started to tell Mamie that there were people chasing her – she was in danger and needed someplace to hide. But Mamie was afraid and said she couldn't let her in. She closed the door. She woke up.

Later she remembered the baby her mother had been holding. The baby must have been herself. It must have been, because she'd been her mother's only child.

*

'If you come with me,' Katherine said, 'we can set the pace.'

'You set it too slow,' Randall complained.

'You go on ahead with Father,' Russell told Katherine. 'In case he needs you. Let Ray and Randy try to beat each other to the top. I'll keep Rhoda company.'

The sun came out. It was a wonderful day. They didn't have to exert themselves much at all on the earlier part of the climb, but Mamie tried to go slowly anyway.

'Are you sure your father's going to be all right?' she asked.

'He's in better shape than any of us. A walking advertisement for the health-giving properties of bourbon. Mother's OK, too.'

'Oh, I know that. She does all those exercises.'

They came to a bend and saw that far above them two other walking parties were starting out from higher lookout posts. Russell said, 'This is the last point where you can turn around and look up like this. All the other places are set in. You see the second and third, but there are five more after that: the dangerous ones. The view is incredible – you look right down into crevasses. You'll see. It's like something out of the Ice Age.'

'When do you want to eat our sandwiches?'

'We can do that at the next stop. There's a picnic place and a kind of lavatory.'

The next lap was a good deal harder. She kept plodding forward without thinking. She could tell already that she was too tired, and that she was going to be stiff and sore for days afterwards.

The four others were waiting for them, but had started to eat. Waverley scanned the valley through his field-glasses. He broke off to take a swig from a canteen he had with him. 'Want to look?' he said.

Mamie lifted the binoculars to her face. It was like seeing into another planet, like being at the movies. Everyone was unaware of the eyes watching from above.

'But it's even more surprising without them,' she said. 'Everything so little. I can't believe we've gotten this high up, so quickly.'

'There's a lot more, and a lot wilder, beyond this,' Russell told her. 'But you can't see it from here.'

She unpacked her knapsack and started to eat. She was beginning to feel better. Katherine asked assertively whether it wasn't exhilarating up on top of the world. Mamie said yes, definitely.

She wished that she could take the past two years, except for the baby, out of her life and start again. Here, all in brightness, with light bouncing off the blank slopes, she could feel something approaching: it was like the moment before the curtain came down at the theatre. Whatever it was, it might fall over her past and cover it forever; and perhaps her future, too.

'It looks like a long way to the end,' she said.

Russell stretched out his arm across the picnic table and took her hand in a strong grip. He said, 'Rest here a while longer. I'll stay with you.' He smiled. The sun shone on his teeth, his hair, his tinted glasses, through which she could see his eyes. He looked very healthy. He looked as if he were enjoying himself. She nodded and said, 'All right.'

The others left. She divided the coffee from the thermos bottle between her plastic cup and his.

'How was the casino?' she asked.

'Fine. I lost 12,000 dollars. How was the whatever-it-was?'

'Hockey game. There were fights, so I came home early. I couldn't even find Randy and Ray.'

'Next year,' he said, 'I think I'll choose a warmer climate.' He looked at the view, not at her.

She swallowed. She could believe in anything now. She wasn't afraid, as she had been in the darkness of the hotel bedroom, but she knew: it was going to happen. Everything was going to happen.

They set out on the climb once more. Twice they met up with the others and then they fell behind again. She had to stop to catch her breath.

'Three more lookouts,' Russell told her. 'And you'd better hold on to me when you lean over.'

'I'm OK. I don't need to hold on.'

'We're right near the top now. Three-quarters of an hour and we should be at the end.'

'Thank God,' she said.

'Are you coming?'

'I'm pretty tired. I think maybe I'll stay here for a while.'

'At this stage you should keep moving. Here, I'll help you.'

'No,' she yelped.

He smiled. He stepped towards her. They were under the overhang, where no one could see. In front of them the snow came to an end, the whole mountain seemed to tumble away downward and then stop – ending in the air, with nothing else beyond but the tiny villages miles below.

She thought she heard a voice. She said, 'There's somebody walking behind us.'

'There isn't anybody.'

'Yes, there is.' She rushed away from him, slid back down the way they had come, and kept going. He called after her, 'It's only a little way to the top. Come on, Rhoda.'

She skidded sideways around the corner and fell. As she got to her feet, she saw Carter moving up along the path. She opened her arms.

'Did you do it?' he said.

'Of course not.'

'What the hell are you doing? You got everything all wrong. You were supposed – '

'Please,' she said, 'let's go. Let's just go back down, please.'

'We can't. We've got to go up.'

'He's there,' she whispered.

He moved his lips silently, asking, 'Where?'

'Around the corner.' He'd be standing right there, listening. He wouldn't have gone on without her, and he couldn't have seen Carter, because the view was blocked where they were.

'All right,' Carter said. 'I'll get him. You stay here.'

'No,' she wailed. She fell down again and clung to his legs. 'No. We'll get a divorce.'

'I don't want the divorce,' he said. 'I want the money.' He kicked her hard in the ribs.

She let go, staggered to her feet, and tried to steady herself by grabbing his shoulder. He went backwards, his mouth open. He was sliding, falling. He went over the edge. She slithered farther down the path, calling out to him, and landed heavily against a mound of snow.

He was gone. There was nothing. The drop was sheer, the precipice so angled that he would have fallen nearly to the bottom of the mountain. She couldn't believe it. He hadn't made a sound. She kept staring as if he might reappear.

'Perfect,' Russell said. He was standing at the bend in the path. He might even have seen it happen. She looked up and saw that he was grinning.

'Beautiful,' he said. 'So, that's him out of the way.'

'He just slipped.'

'Now there's only you.'

'He kept saying you'd killed your first wife.'

'Sure. She made some joke about being insured and I realized it would work. It was a gamble. The big ones always pay off, remember? Let's go. We'll have to report it.'

She moved carefully towards the outside of the path, near the edge.

'Watch out,' he said. 'That's dangerous.'

'Why should I wait for you to do it some other way?' She was excited and terrified, nearly prepared to throw herself off into the emptiness behind her. She raised one foot, put it down and lifted the other, as if dancing. She said, 'He was always a real bastard to me, but I loved him.'

'Don't,' he told her.

'Why not? If I jumped, you'd be in it up to your neck, wouldn't you? Two wives going over the brink the same way – I don't think the insurance companies would like that.'

'I'd say he did it.'

'They wouldn't believe you, Ross.' She took another step backward, intoxicated by fear. She could feel the open space drawing her away as if a tide were racing out behind her, pulling. It reminded her of the repeating dream he'd told her about; his nightmares had become hers to live out. She was slipping. She could go, any minute. She played with the last few feet, the last inches. It was like being in the spotlight, surrounded by deathly brilliance, watched by the whole world.

'Don't step back,' he shouted. He started to move towards her.

'I loved him,' she said. 'And Jesus was he good in bed – he didn't have to get it out of a book.'

He came at her, his arms held in front of him, the hands set, ready to push her over.

She waited until he was almost touching her, then she feinted to the side, just as Mr Moto had taught her to, and knocked his leg out from under him with a sharp kick.

He flew straight into the air, out across the chasm and down. He howled as he went over. And she scrambled to safety; up the path and around the corner. The rescuers would trample on all the prints, so that was all right, and they'd have to take her word for it that the two men had been quarrelling about the death of the first wife, but she was pretty sure people would believe her.

She took a deep breath, threw back her head and screamed, a long trembling call of horror. If they'd been in the avalanche season, she could have brought down the mountainside with it. It made no difference now, at this time of year: let them hear it back in the villages and up in the resort hotels. It was the one thing she was good at.

She was crying; bereaved, pretty, a young mother: this time she was the star. Everyone would respect her grief. They'd all be

kind to her. When she told her story, saying that Carter and
Russell had been fighting, she'd be standing centre stage where
the brightness of the sky, the white shine from the ice peaks,
would beat upon her like limelight on a heroine; like truth itself;
till she outshone the light-reflecting surfaces of nature: candid,
diamond-dazzling, pure. She screamed and screamed.